P9-DJV-730

THE
KILL
ZONE

DAVID
HAGBERG

TOR®

A TOM DOHERTY ASSOCIATES BOOK
NEW YORK

This is a work of fiction. All the characters and events portrayed in this book are either products of the author's imagination or are used fictitiously.

THE KILL ZONE

Copyright © 2002 by David Hagberg

A Tor Book
Published by Tom Doherty Associates, LLC
175 Fifth Avenue
New York, NY 10010

www.tor.com

Tor® is a registered trademark of Tom Doherty Associates, LLC.

ISBN 0-812-57779-5

First edition: October 2002
First mass market edition: December 2003

Printed in the United States of America

0 9 8 7 6 5 4 3 2 1

NOVELS BY DAVID HAGBERG

Twister
The Capsule
Last Come the Children
Heartland
*Without Honor**
*Countdown**
*Crossfire**
*Critical Mass**
Desert Fire
*High Flight**
*Assassin**
*White House**
*Joshua's Hammer**
Eden's Gate+
*The Kill Zone**
By Dawn's Early Light

WRITING AS SEAN FLANNERY

The Kremlin Conspiracy
Eagles Fly
The Trinity Factor
The Hollow Men
Broken Idols
False Prophets
Gulag
Moscow Crossing
The Zebra Network
Crossed Swords
Counterstrike
Moving Targets
Winner Take All+
Kilo Option+
Achilles' Heel+

*Kirk McGarvey Adventures
+Bill Lane Adventures

This book is for Lorrel
and for our son, Kevin,
whose imagination is second
only to his kindness

ACKNOWLEDGMENT

Special thanks to Dr. Michael Mattice
for his kind and patient help.
The mistakes are all mine.

Soul Mate

We share a single soul . . .
fates soft embrace
a tale many times told
then usually laid to waste.

Looking towards touch
the steadfast mediator
we steep in it much
only to drown in it later.

An age-old rhyme
we all but actually hear
cutting swiftly through time
to covet what is near.

What barbaric thought
propelling one's self
from what is sought
to unequivocal hell.

It is inside the stillness
warmth permeates the being
inside the willingness
one truly begins seeing.

Remember the soul . . .
it knows our name
gives us all we need to know
and how it is *we* became

—Gina Hagberg-Ballinger

PROLOGUE
THE LEGATEES

Those who cannot remember the past
are condemned to repeat it.
—George Santayana

Let us alone. Time driveth onward fast,
And in a little while our lips are dumb.
Let us alone. What is it that will last?
All things are taken from us, and become
Portions and parcels of the dreadful past.
—Alfred, Lord Tennyson

ONE

IT HAD BEEN MADE TO LOOK
AS IF HE HAD SHOT HIMSELF IN THE
TEMPLE WITH THE GUN.

MOSCOW

Dr. Anatoli Nikolayev was an old man, and the summer heat was oppressive to him as he hauled his thin body up the dark narrow stairs. He wasn't sure that he wanted the answers that he had come here to find. Yet with everything that he'd learned so far he couldn't simply turn his back like an old lover who'd found out he'd been betrayed.

His research was almost finished. He had ground his way through a million pages of old records, starting in 1917 with the Soviet Union's first secret intelligence service, the Cheka, until the breakup under Gorbachev and the dismantling of the KGB in 1991; the kidnappings and terrorism and sabotage; poisons, electric guns, honey traps, brainwashings, intimidation of countless thousands of officials and diplomats from nearly every country in the world. And assassination. The ultimate act of the state other than war. Bodies stretching back almost ninety years; piled to the rafters; more bodies than even Hitler had been credited with, making him wonder why the Soviet Union hadn't been as reviled as the Nazis were.

His boney, blue-veined left hand trailed along the cracked plaster wall, and he could smell the terror in the stifling air like last night's cabbage dinner; urine and shit from the over-flowing communal toilets; the accumulated filth of ninety years of negelect.

When the KGB came it was almost always easier to commit suicide the moment the knock came on the door than to endure what would come next. But all of that was finally coming to an end. The money to operate the vast worldwide spy network was drying up.

Sleeper agents in place for years, some of them for thirty years or more, were being cut free from funds. Forgotten about. Their original missions no longer valid. They were the unmentionables. No one at the Kremlin wanted to know about them, let alone speak their names.

That meant trouble was coming. Agents cut off with no way out became desperate men. And desperate men sometimes did horrible things.

He stopped on the third floor landing in the rundown apartment building a few blocks north of the Bolshoi Theater and stared at the small, dirty window at the end of the hall. He waited patiently to catch his breath. His longish white hair was plastered to his neck. His research was almost done and he was afraid to think about what he had uncovered. What might be about to happen. He needed names. A way to stop the madness that he had been a part of a long time ago.

Last of three doors in the corridor. He'd asked at the Pivnoy Bar around the corner on Stoleshinkov pereulok for the exact address. General Gennadi Zhuralev lived alone with his books; no friends, no lovers, no trouble except his lights, which were always on until dawn. No one had thought to ask why.

"Tall man, was he? Broad shoulders, big ears, scar on his forehead?"

"No taller than average, but he always carries a canvas satchel. Heavy. Books maybe, certainly not money."

Dr. Nikolayev tried to dredge up a personal memory of the face from his own days as a psychologist with the KGB. But he could not. Zhuralev worked for General Baranov and the crowd in Department Viktor; assassinations, executive actions, they were called; wet affairs, *mokrie dela*, the spilling of blood; formerly the Thirteenth Department or Line F. It was

Division 17 now though no one outside the SVR's First Chief Directorate was supposed to know it. He would recognize the man's face, though, from the photographs, and his voice, which had sounded gravelly on the phone.

He walked to the last door. The building was not quite silent; a radio or television played softly in one of the apartments, and in the other it sounded as if someone was practicing on a piano, tentatively, unsure of the notes. He hesitated out of old habit to listen for trouble sounds; the snick of a pistol slide being drawn back, sirens down on the street, boots on the stairs. The light filtering through the window was pale yellow, and his eyes were drawn to it like a moth to flame. The ceiling and walls angled inward to him, crushing his breath; he longed to escape to the clean air on the street.

There was someone inside the apartment who didn't belong there. He was hearing hard-soled shoes. At the Pivnoy they laughed and said that the old man always wore his bedroom slippers outside.

Nikolayev turned and went silently to the end of the hall, where he flattened himself in the corner next to the small window in the darker shadows. He hadn't brought a pistol.

The door opened, and two men came out. They were very large, their heads were shaved and they wore shiny leather jackets despite the heat. One of them carried a canvas satchel. Nikolayev's legs felt like straw. They closed the door, turned away and headed to the stairs. He watched the doorway until they were gone and he could no longer hear them on the stairs, wondering what he would have done had they turned around and seen him.

Zhuralev was part of the Baranov crowd. If anyone had the answers it would be him. Someone who had been there, someone who knew if the bridge still existed between then and now. He waited for a long time, thinking that he could walk away. The August heat seemed even more oppressive now.

He let himself into the overstuffed two-room apartment. Books and magazines and newspapers were strewn everywhere, but not as if the place had been searched. This was the way the man lived. The rooms were like a furnace, but filled with the odors of musty books, pipe tobacco and something else. Unpleasant. The hairs on the back of his neck bristled.

He went to the bedroom door. Gennadi Zhuralev, his blood-filled eyes open, lay on his back on the bed. He was fully clothed, carpet slippers on his feet, a silenced pistol in his slack hand. It had been made to look as if he had shot himself in the temple with the gun. But suicides did not usually go to the trouble of using a silenced pistol so that their neighbors would not be disturbed by the noise.

Nikolayev was conscious of his heart arrhythmia, a fluttering in his chest that made him dizzy and empty. With a feeling of deep despair he knew that he was utterly alone. He was an old man, and he valued his peace, but at what cost, he wondered, looking at Zhuralev's body. Lie down with the lions but don't expect to remain safe forever. He couldn't make his wife understand that; she loved the perks that his KGB colonel's rank brought them; food, apartment, dacha on the Istra, a car; until she bled to death on the surgeon's table. A simple gallbladder operation. But nothing was as simple as all that, not even in Moscow.

What was it that they hoped to cover up by killing a retired KGB officer who couldn't sleep nights and who wore carpet slippers? Nikolayev tried to feel some sorrow for the man, but he could not. Zhuralev had been a murderer.

What had died with him up here under the eaves? Nikolayev thought he knew the answer now, and he was frightened. Some important Americans were going to get killed if he was right and unless he did something. He could not turn away. It was far too late for that, no matter how dearly he valued his peace.

He got in his old BMW without windshield wipers, parked around the corner, and headed toward the Lefortovo Prison on Moscow's northeast side. They had gotten to Zhuralev, and he would be next because he had tinkered with the old files. He had to move decisively now—surprise them, give them pause long enough for him to get out. But he needed the proof first; otherwise, no one in the West would believe his fantastic story. What was in the satchel they'd carried out?

He was stuck, caught between a rock and a very hard place with no simple way out. He hadn't meant to uncover the operation. Hadn't meant for that to happen at all. But now it was far too late for him to turn back. Like an insect caught in the spider's web, the more he struggled, the more terrible his situation became.

TWO

. . . TOO LATE TO STOP WHAT COULD WELL TURN OUT TO BE A BLOODBATH . . .

The director of archives, SVR Captain Aleksei Budakov was speaking to three junior grade clerks, all of them pretty young women from the country. He looked up through bottle-thick glass as Nikolayev came in and gave him a nod. Budakov said something to the girls and walked over.

"Finished with the interview so soon?" The KGB's old case files were open to the public like an old whore's thighs, and no one knew why he cared as much as he did, but he was almost always angry, and frightened. At least in the old days a man knew who his enemies were.

Nikolayev shook his head as he took a half-dozen request slips from the wooden tray on the counter. "There was no answer over there." He had been perfectly open about his research to this point.

"Will you try again tomorrow?"

"I'm not going to waste my time," Nikolayev said, filling out the request slips for six specific operational files from the Baranov days. "I still have fifty thousand pages of reading to do, and perhaps five times that many to review." He looked up and smiled tiredly. "I'm not getting any younger." He pushed the slips across.

"None of us are," Budakov replied snappishly. He scooped up the slips without looking. His mood was explosive, but Nikolayev politely pretended not to notice. "This may take a while unless I'm lucky and everything is in its place."

Nikolayev shrugged. "I have the afternoon." He offered a tentative smile. Budakov might know what was going on, but if he did Nikolayev couldn't see it in his eyes. No suspicion there—simple anger and boredom with a stupid job in a stupid place with nowhere for his career to go. This was a dead-end job in any army. But it was Russia, too, where almost every career was a dead end. The girls helped some, he supposed.

The reading room was large, with tall imperial ceilings, sturdy oak tables and broad uncomfortable chairs. Several historians like himself and a couple of well-dressed men who were probably Western journalists were at tables on opposite sides of the room. Nikolayev took his usual table near a side door to the bathrooms. He'd made no secret that he had bladder problems.

Russia was a dark, brooding nation of suspicions. Nikolayev had always felt eyes watching him. Legmen behind him; artists who could shake down a second-story man's apartment with such a light touch he'd never know that he'd been violated; opened mail, wiretaps; KGB psychiatrists so adept at reading facial expressions and body language that they could almost read a man's thoughts. Who better to watch a spy than another spy? So he had made his preparations. Who better to slip past a spy than another spy?

Network Martyrs. General Illen Baranov's final legacy. Delving into the files had been like descending into the dark realms of fantasy and insanity. But he'd been there himself; been a part of it thirty years ago when they experimented with LSD and a dozen other mind-altering drugs. Brainwashing brought to the peak of awful perfection so that the subject continuously teetered on the brink of insanity but could be made to do anything for their control officer. The ultimate kamikaze weapon. Baranov had gone forward with the experimental program even though he'd never formally applied for authorization. Zhuralev had been the chief of operations and he would have known the details then and now.

His death proved that Martyrs was still active.

"Who should care about this old news," Budakov said twenty minutes later, wheeling a pushcart filled with thick files up to the table, a scowl on his chubby, pink baby face.

Nikolayev looked up. "It's a matter of history, Aleksei."

"This lot will take the rest of the day."

"Longer than that." Nikolayev opened his battered leather briefcase and took out paper and pens. He picked the first thick file folder marked with four stars to designate highly sensitive, though not top secret, material and opened it to the promulgation page. It was titled: BUDGET PROPOSALS: UN OPERATIONS: FISCAL 1971–72. He looked up again, but Budakov had gone back to the adjacent computer center, a large glass window separating it from the reading room. He could see the back of the director of archives's head.

Nikolayev selected several other files, which he laid out on the table, before pulling out the folder marked with three diagonal red stripes from the bottom shelf of the cart. NETWORK MARTYRS: MOST SECRET, with a need-to-know list on the inside front cover that included only seven names; among them Baranov, Zhuralev, a couple of KGB generals, two ministers and Brezhnev himself. The file, which was contained in a buff gray accordion folder fifteen or sixteen centimeters thick, was bound with a heavy red ribbon. One of the other files he had pulled was just as thick, and contained in a buff-colored accordion folder, but this one was tied with a green ribbon and marked with only one star, meaning low-grade confidential material. Making sure that he wasn't being observed, Nikolayev switched files. When he was finished he got up, took the one star file now containing NETWORK MARTYRS and stepped out into the corridor to the bathrooms. He propped the door ajar with a chair as he usually did so that he would arouse no suspicions; so he could get back into the locked reading room without going all the way around to the front of the building.

He moved slowly, nonchalantly, as if he didn't have a care in the world, though his heart was racing impossibly fast; the fluttering in his chest was very pronounced, his knees were weak and his stomach was sour. His jaw and left shoulder ached, and he tried to ignore it. The pain would go away, it usually did.

He passed the rest rooms and at the end of the corridor turned right past the guard, who looked up, smiled and waved, then went back to the television program he was watching.

Nikolayev went to his car and tossed the folder on the passenger seat. There was no guard at the front gate. No one to challenge him. In the old days it would not have been so easy. He drove directly to Komsomol Square, with its crowds of beggars and drunks and its three fantastic train stations: the Yaroslavl art noveau monstrosity, which was the start of the Trans-Siberian line; the rather Asian-looking Kazan Station on the south side of the square, from which trains bound for central Asia and western Siberia departed; and the Leningrad Station, Moscow's oldest, with its grand soaring clock tower where trains started for St. Petersberg and beyond to Finland.

Later, on the Finnair flight from Helsinki to Paris, Nikolayev thought that by now his abandoned car would have either been stolen or certainly stripped to the bare chasis. It would make it more difficult for the SVR to pick up his trail when Budakov reported him missing. A lot would depend on how soon they discovered that he'd switched files, but in the meantime he was able to relax for the first time in days with a glass of good white wine, safe for the moment.

There had been no one to notice him parking his car two blocks from the Leningradsky vokzal, packing the file in his overnight bags in the trunk, destroying his old passport and papers after retrieving his new identity from a hollow behind a body panel and going the rest of the way on foot.

Just another old man on a journey; with a serious heart problem and the fear that he might be too late to stop what could well turn out to be a bloodbath from which no one would come out the winner; not the United States and certainly not Russia.

Everything depended on what was in the file—names, operational details, timetables. All that would have to wait until he reached Paris, and safety. But Martyrs had lain dormant for all these years, another day or two would not make a difference.

Hopefully.

ONE

PROMISES

The self-hatred that destroys is
the waste of unfulfilled promise.
—Moss Hart

SUNDAY

ONE

CHEVY CHASE

It was the beginning of one of the coldest, snowiest winters in Washington, D.C.'s history. The house backing on the fifteenth fairway of the Chevy Chase Country Club was long, low; a modern colonial with a swimming pool, covered now, the patio snowbound; but with long lawns and bright flowers in hanging baskets from the broad eaves in the summer. It was at the end of a cul-de-sac of similar houses seven miles north of the capital. A few minutes before noon of a Sunday morning a stereo softly played Vivaldi's *Four Seasons*. Kirk Cullough McGarvey was seated at his desk in his study reading copies of some never-been-published letters of François-Marie Arouet—Voltaire—that an old friend at the Sorbonne in Paris had sent over on loan. Kathleen, his wife, was at church, and he was waiting for her to come home. As had happened several times in the past hour, his concentration was broken, and he looked up, his wide, honest, gray-green eyes narrowing in concentration. Had he heard something? He listened intently, but there was nothing except for normal house sounds; the rush of warm air through the vents, the music. Falling snow blanketed sounds from outside. No one was sneaking up on them from across the golf course as had happened before. There was no reason for it this time.

He got up and went into the kitchen to pour another cup of coffee, his moccasins whisper soft on the tile floor. He looked out across the snow-covered fairway. No one there. No tire tracks or footprints. And nothing from the air; visibility was less than a few hundred feet. He was a tall, well-built man with a rugby player's physique, a thick shock of brown hair starting to go gray at the temples, and an air about him that when he was around everything would be okay. He exuded self-confidence, and the easy, relaxed manner of the consummate professional that he was, even dressed in faded jeans and a worn pullover sweater.

But sooner or later paranoia comes to all intelligence officers, even the pros. It was the old line. Awareness, heightened perceptions, hair trigger reflexes, an automatic processing of information as fast as it arrived to find the out-of-place bits and pieces that if you were not careful could suddenly rise up to kill you.

Sometimes he felt like a besieged king who was trying to make this place a fortress. A lot of Americans felt the same since the terrorist attacks in New York, Washington and Pennsylvania. It had almost become a national obsession.

In the stairhall he looked up at the landing. The Russian clock he'd been given from a Typhoon class submarine kept perfect time except that its red second hand was permanently stuck at four. He'd not gotten around to taking it to a clockmaker.

From some points of view the world was a more dangerous place than it had ever been. Terrorists could strike anywhere. But as terrible as that had become, no country seemed to be on the verge of starting an all-out global thermonuclear war. Not North Korea or Iran, and not Pakistan or India. That's what the Cold War had been all about, he thought, staring at the Russian clock. We won, the bad guys lost.

But something was coming. He could feel and taste the menace on the air like smoke from a not-so-distant forest fire.

At fifty he had been appointed as the youngest director in the history of the Agency; a job that he was uneasily settling into since Roland Murphy had retired two months ago. His Senate confirmation hearings were scheduled to start on Tuesday, and he could not say which he dreaded most, being rejected or being confirmed.

He wanted out. After twenty-five years of service he wanted to go back to teaching Voltaire, even to bored young undergraduates who wouldn't recognize a line worth remembering if it came up and bit them on the ass. Good years, some of them, and very bad some of the others. In his mind's eye he could see the face of every man he'd ever killed in the line of duty. Bad men all of them, but just men for all that. They'd been in pain, surprised that the end had come; the looks haunted him every day of his life. Especially at night when he couldn't sleep; especially at this moment when he couldn't concentrate.

"I've seen things and done things that I'm not proud of," he'd told Katy one late night when he'd awakened in a cold sweat. She'd been holding him in her arms like she would a troubled child. "Things that I can never take back."

It was a sentiment that Minnesota senator Thomas Hammond, Jr., would agree with. Hammond, who was chairman of the Senate Select Committee on Intelligence, was telling anyone who would listen that McGarvey was exactly the wrong sort of person to become DCI. "This is a job for a man of the very highest moral principles. A wild card is exactly the kind of person we do not want providing intelligence summaries to the leadership of this nation. He is a bad apple in an already suspect barrel. The CIA needs to be cleared of the thugs and criminals who have given this country a bad name."

But something or someone was coming again. Goddammit, he knew it.

He went to the corridor and at the head of the stairs glanced toward the bedroom at the other end of the house where their daughter Elizabeth used to stay when she came over. Now she had a husband, and in a few months there would be a baby. After all the sadness in their lives, her pregnancy was an oasis for them all.

There'd been nothing in the directorate summaries over the

past few weeks to indicate that trouble was brewing. Not so much as a hint.

McGarvey sincerely wanted to be happy with his life, optimistic about his future with Katy. But he couldn't be. Not yet. Something, some whisper of trouble nagged at the edge of his consciousness. Once a spy always a spy: Was it as simple as that? Sometimes in the field he would develop an almost preternatural awareness of his surroundings: a van with silvered windows; a car with too many antennae; the glint of binocular lenses on a rooftop; a window shade open when it was usually closed; a stranger in the crowd; something, an accumulation of things. Anomalies. The pieces that no longer seemed to fit the puzzle.

But there was nothing this time. Nothing but the falling snow outside and Vivaldi inside.

He'd been running away for the past fifteen years to protect Katy and Liz, and somehow to escape his own horrible past. Maybe Hammond was right. Maybe he *was* unfit for the job. It was something to be seriously considered, he told himself, and he went down to the kitchen, got his coffee and headed back to his study.

The upcoming hearings had affected Katy, too. She had carefully avoided the subject, but she was upset. Nothing was doing for the rest of the day, and they would have a relaxing afternoon together. They both needed it.

The letters were a series of essays that Voltaire had written in 1777, the year before his death, to Pope Pius VI. They'd never been meant to be actually sent to the Vatican; rather, they were to have been published in a public forum. But Voltaire's argument that a Bishop of Rome, by definition, could never get to heaven, but would have to go straight to hell, was so controversial even for him that they were never published. McGarvey had been on the trail of this material for nearly eight years. The end of a lot of detective work that he had somehow managed to do between assignments. It was right up his alley, finding things. But he could not keep his head on straight.

He looked up. This time he was sure that he heard a car

revving up in the driveway. A diesel. Valves loose, exhaust loud.

Otto.

Annoyed now, he went to the front hall and looked out the window beside the door in time to see a battered old gray Mercedes diesel disappear in the snow toward Connecticut Avenue. He opened the door and stepped outside into the cold. Tire tracks led halfway up the driveway, but they were already beginning to fill in with snow, as was a small patch of black soot from the tailpipe.

Okay, that explained he wasn't going crazy. He *had* heard something earlier. He closed the door and went back to his desk. Something was up. Otto Rencke, his special assistant for research, had been acting strangely the past few weeks. When he was in the middle of some project he became even more squirrely than he usually was, and did odd things: sit cross-legged on top of his desk; eat nothing but Twinkies and drink heavy cream for days on end; not bathe for weeks. Once, security found him wandering around the seventh floor at Langley at 2:00 A.M. completely naked. "Looking for one of Diogenes' honest men," he told them with a stupid smile. He was stoned.

They put up with his eccentricities because he was a genius. He probably knew more about computers and what they were capable of doing than any other person in the world. He had brought the CIA and most of the rest of the U.S. intelligence establishment into the twenty-first century. And he was an unofficial member of the McGarvey family; he had saved Katy's and Liz's lives.

McGarvey tried to reach him on his cell phone, but he wasn't answering or his phone was switched off. He tried through the Agency's automatic locator system without success which meant that no one was at his apartment, and finally he called the OD in Operations who had no luck either.

"Is there a problem, sir?" the OD asked. "Should I alert Security?"

"No. I just wanted to chat."

"Yes, sir. If he checks in, I'll have him call you."

He had probably driven over, forgotten why he was here,

and when he couldn't remember, driven off embarrassed. It was like Otto.

McGarvey went back to his reading, more at ease now that he had found an explanation for his jumpiness, but after a minute he heard the garage door open. Kathleen was home from church.

He touched the words on the page as if he could absorb Voltaire's thoughts through the tips of his fingers like a blind man understanding braille. For just an instant he was back in the late 1700s, where even in France life for most of the people was short, dirty, brutish and dominated by superstitions; fears, black magic and withchcraft, the devil, and the bad vapors to be found in the night air; an all-consuming reliance on religion to show them a way to a much better life.

"I'm home," Kathleen called from the kitchen.

McGarvey looked up, his breath catching in his throat, his hand giving an involuntary start as he came back two hundred plus years.

"In here," he answered. For another moment he sat staring at the letter, feeling how it must have been. Open sewers in the streets; disease and illnesses; dirty drinking water; an uncertain food supply; and in the nights, darkness. A modern man going back would be dead in a week.

"I was going to ask if you missed me. Apparently you did not."

Kathleen still wore her dark brown butter-soft leather coat, but she'd taken off her Hermès scarf and stood in the doorway fluffing her medium-length blond hair where it had been flattened. She looked like royalty—high cheekbones, finely defined eyebrows, oval face, flawless complexion and full lips—but her deep green eyes were almost too bright, as if she had just done something exciting and she couldn't wait to tell him about it.

"I just got back from France," McGarvey said, apologetically. He got up and they embraced. He followed her into the stairhall, where he helped her with her coat and hung it in the closet. She wore a cream white pantsuit and soft half boots. "How was church?"

"Safe." She gave her husband a sudden, shy glance, as if

she had made a poor choice of words and wanted to see if he was going to laugh. "Father Vietski is always good," she said. She chuckled. "Anyway, what's doing this afternoon? Want to go to a movie?"

"Not unless you want to. How're the roads?"

"A little slippery. Not bad."

"Why don't we stay in? We can watch an old movie on TV, say the hell with a big dinner and just snack all day."

Her smile was warm. "I was hoping you would say something like that." She looked into his eyes and touched his face with her right hand as if she was seeing him for the first time in many years. "I love you."

He took her into his arms, and they kissed deeply and for a long time. At fifty her figure had matured, but she was still on the slender side, the price of which she admitted to only a few friends was a very careful diet and a regimen of hard exercise almost as strict as Kirk's. She wasn't chasing after her lost youth, but she was hanging on to every year in any way she knew how.

When they parted she was a little breathless. "We're definitely staying home."

"Bloody Marys?"

"I'll change first."

"Don't be long." McGarvey watched her walk upstairs, admiring the line of her back, especially the back of her neck, and then went into the kitchen to fix their drinks. They were married at the beginning of his career with the CIA. But shortly after Elizabeth's birth she gave him an ultimatum; her or the Company. He chose the Company, and they were divorced. They loved each other, there was never any question about that, but she couldn't stay married to a spy, and he wanted to distance himself from his wife and child in case someone with a grudge came gunning for him. Of course you don't protect the ones you love by abandoning them. It was something that took both of them a very long and painful time to realize. They were remarried a few months ago, and to this point their lives had settled into a wonderful routine; comfortable, warm, fulfilling. It's what he wanted, wasn't it?

He looked up and caught his reflection in the sliding door

to the patio. He was a bit too rugged-looking, too craggy to be considered handsome; but Katy thought that he cleaned up good, and she was in love with his graying hair. "Dress you in a tuxedo, put a glass of Dom Pérignon in your hand and let you speak a little French; there's not a woman I know who wouldn't come running." But he'd ruined almost everyone he'd ever come in contact with; like a moth to a flame. And on Tuesday Senator Hammond was going to point out his faults—all of them, detail by painful detail. Maybe he would save them the trouble and resign. He brought the Bloody Marys into the large, comfortable family room off the kitchen.

Katy was hunched in front of the shelves below the television looking through their videotapes and disks. She was dressed in CIA sweats and fuzzy slippers which made her seem smaller, younger, defenseless. McGarvey stopped and looked at her. She was working very hard to make their marriage work this time against terrible odds. Memories of bad men coming after her and Elizabeth, trying to kill them; memories of her husband living with other women, two of whom had been killed because they had gotten too close to him; memories of what he'd done for the past twenty-five years and what he was still capable of doing. Memories, even, of her own past indiscretions; the haughtiness and aloofness that had isolated her like an ice queen in an unassailable palace. But all that was in the past. They'd finally shown each other their vulnerabilities.

"Find anything good?" he asked, putting the drinks on the coffee table.

She looked up and smiled. "You have your choice. *Platoon* or *The French Lieutenant's Woman*."

"Any other possibilities?"

"No."

"Compromise? Flip a coin?"

She laughed, the sound light and musical. "You should see your face." She held up the disks. "What'll it be?"

"I've always been a sucker for a good love story."

She laughed again. "*Platoon* it is." She loaded the disk into the player. "What'd Otto want?"

"What do you mean?"

"I think I passed him on Connecticut. Wasn't he here?"

"Not this morning," McGarvey said, and for the life of him he didn't know why he had lied to his wife.

She gave him an odd look; one of patient understanding, like she knew that he was lying but she wasn't going to ask him why, then came over and settled next to him on the couch.

"Hmm. Nice," she said.

MONDAY

TWO

AN AIR OF MYSTERY HERE . . . A DARK,
CATHEDRAL HUSH ONCE YOU WERE ADMITTED
TO THE INNER SANCTUM SANCTORUM OF
AMERICA'S INTELLIGENCE ESTABLISHMENT.

The snow stopped sometime in the middle of the night. McGarvey got up twice to go to the bathroom and then take a turn around the house—checking doors, windows, the alarm system. As acting DCI he rated a full-time bodyguard, but he had refused for no other reason than he didn't want the formality that went with a job he wasn't sure that he was going to keep.

Foolish, as were some of his other habits. He stood for a long time looking out the kitchen window across the golf course. It was two in the morning, and he wanted a cigarette for the first time since he had quit several months ago. The stars were ultrabright hard points in the moonless sky; cold and very distant.

This time when McGarvey went back to bed he slept without dreams, as if he had been drugged; hammered into something like a deep coma. When he awoke a minute or two before the six o'clock alarm he felt more refreshed than he had for months, but the same nagging whispers that something was about to go wrong were back in full force.

Kathleen was already up, had the coffee on and was out for

her 5-K run. He splashed some water on his face, then put on a tee shirt, a pair of shorts and gym shoes. He turned the television to CNN and started on the treadmill; slowly at first, with a moderate resistance, the machine automatically building to its maximum within a few minutes. It was a mindless physical routine that felt good. His body was even leaner and harder with more stamina than a few months ago when he still smoked, and he was tromping across the mountains in Afghanistan. But his mind wandered away from the television and he was back in the tunnels beneath the ruins of a sixteenth-century castle in Portugal. No lights, water running because the pumps had failed, explosive charges ready to go off, trapping him in a permanent coffin beneath millions of tons of rock. Somewhere in the blackness Arkady Kurshin was waiting to kill him. I won't die here. Not now, not like this. Panic rising like a secret monster; jaws agape, claws coming to reach. Christ—

He came back to the present, forty minutes later, his shirt plastered to his body, the muscles in his legs beginning to bunch up, his gut hollow.

He switched the treadmill to the cool down mode and looked at the television. Nothing new happening. Still trouble in Afghanistan; an American tourist murdered in Havana; Pakistan reneging on its promises to hunt down al-Quaida terrorists, Iran, Iraq, North Korea.

The treadmill was slowing down. Why had the business with the Russian assassin Arkady Kurshin come to mind now, of all times? He touched the scar on his side, where he had lost a kidney and nearly his life. Kurshin was dead. The era was gone.

He took a long, hot shower and when he had shaved he came back to the bedroom, where Kathleen had laid out a pair of gray slacks, blue blazer, white shirt and club tie. Old-fashioned, but utilitarian; the clothes had become his new uniform.

Downstairs Kathleen was seated at the kitchen counter, the television on *Good Morning America*, reading the morning paper with her coffee. Her cheeks were rosy from outside, and without makeup, her hair undone she looked fresh.

"Good morning, darling," she said, looking up. "Sleep well?"

"Like I was hit over the head." McGarvey poured a cup of coffee and, standing on the opposite side of the counter from his wife, reached over and gave her a kiss. "How about you?"

"Must have been something in the water. I slept like I was dead." She smiled warmly. "But then making love with you always does that to me."

"Maybe I should get a patent."

She chuckled at the back of her throat. "Do you want some breakfast?"

McGarvey glanced at his watch. It was already coming up on eight. He shook his head. "Dick will be here in a couple of minutes, and it's going to be a heavy day." He shrugged. "Mondays. How about you?"

"I have some shopping to do, and Elizabeth and I are having lunch somewhere downtown, if she can get free. She's supposed to call. At two I have a Red Cross executive board meeting, and I'm supposed to call Sally about the Beaux Arts Ball. Oh, and I'm interviewing two housekeepers, and the carpenters are supposed to start on your study this morning."

He'd forgotten about that. Before he'd moved back the room had been a catchall, a place to iron, and sew on a button, a place for the odd cardboard box. With his Voltaire studies, the room had become a serious workplace. Katy had ordered built-in bookcases, recessed lighting, a new desk and computer station, and a cabinet with long shallow drawers to store maps and large manuscripts flat. "How long's that going to take?"

"A few days. They promised they'd be done by Friday at the latest."

"No chintz."

"No chintz," she agreed. "Saturday night we're having the party, so don't forget."

They were having the former DCI Roland Murphy and his wife over for cocktails and a buffet supper. It was supposed to be a surprise party for him. She'd invited some of his old friends from the other law enforcement and intelligence agencies in town, a couple of generals from the Pentagon and a few congressmen from the Hill. Inappropriate because of the upcoming hearings? He'd wondered about it, but she didn't think that it was a problem, and she knew about things like that.

"You worry too much," she said, reading his mind. "Anyway, is there anything you should lock up in your study?"

"Voltaire is in the safe, and there're no Agency files."

"Guns, bombs, missiles?"

He laughed and shook his head. Her sense of humor had come back since they were remarried. She wasn't so desperate to be formal and proper like she used to be.

"Seriously, where's your pistol?"

"One is upstairs under my side of the bed, one's out in the garage—" He opened his coat and turned to reveal the quick draw holster at the small of his back. "And this one."

"Sorry I asked." She was suddenly serious. But it was something that she had to deal with if they were going to be together. They had discussed the situation more than once. It's what I do, he'd told her, and she'd given him the same uncertain look then as she was giving him now. But she was trying.

The doorbell rang. "You okay, Katy?"

"I'm fine. Something light for supper tonight?"

"Sounds good." He kissed her on the cheek, got his topcoat from the closet and went outside.

His driver/bodyguard Dick Yemm was waiting with the armored Cadillac limousine, his eyes constantly scanning the neighborhood. "Mornin', boss." He opened the rear door. He was an ex-SEAL, smart, competent, alert and very tough, hard as bar steel and just as compact.

"Good morning, Dick. Good weekend?"

"Not bad."

McGarvey climbed into the car, and Yemm went around to the driver's side. "I went down to the Farm to do a little shooting with Todd." Yemm chuckled. "Either I'm slipping or your son-in-law has gotten a whole hell of a lot better since he married Liz."

"They're competing with each other."

Yemm pulled out of the driveway and got on the radio. "Hammerhead in route. ETA twenty-five."

"Roger, one."

"Anything interesting in the overnights?" McGarvey asked. He unlocked the slender steel case that Yemm had brought out from Operations and withdrew the leather-bound folder that contained the highlights of what the Agency had taken in and analyzed over the weekend.

"Pretty quiet for now, knock on wood."

"Let's hope it stays that way," McGarvey said absently. He started to read and was back on the job, unaware that Yemm was watching him in the rearview mirror.

Pakistan and India were rattling their nuclear sabers again, no surprise. Tribal wars continued to erupt all over Afghanistan, but there wasn't much we could really do about that situation either, except provide support to our peacekeeping forces there. The international hunt for terrorists went on, amidst sharp protests from Iran and North Korea and bombast from Baghdad. The murdered American in Havana hadn't been a tourist, he was a military intelligence officer from Guantanamo Bay. McGarvey made a mental note to have his acting deputy director Dick Adkins find out what the hell was going on and why this joker had been in Havana in the first place.

Mexico was being besieged by an independent group of wealthy businessmen to destabilize the peso in favor of the American dollar. Tajikistan, Azerbaijan, Russian nuclear stockpiles, the rusting sub fleet in Vladivostok, another attempt on the Pope's life in Rome and riots in Brazil, where a hard-liner faction of military generals were again gaining power. A dozen other trouble spots around the world to absorb his thoughts so that by the time they arrived at CIA headquarters and drove around to the DCI's private entrance, he was up to speed and ready for Monday morning, the nagging worries of the weekend gone now that he was in the middle of the real world.

He had been coming to this place in the woods outside of Washington for a quarter century; he had seen a lot of changes, including the addition of the two annexes behind the main seven-story building of glass and steel. An air of mystery here; of men and women scurrying about with dedicated purpose;

rooftops bristling with antennae and satellite dishes; armed guards, closed-circuit lo-lux television monitors, infrared and motion detectors; metal detectors and watchful serious people on every floor; a dark, cathedral hush once you were admitted to the inner sanctum sanctorum of America's intelligence establishment. He wanted to hate it, hate its necessity, but each time he came back something stirred in his blood. He glanced toward the main parking lot. It was already filling with a steady stream of traffic off the Parkway; by nine, a half hour from now, more than eight thousand people would be at work here. Monday morning. Some of them excited at the prospects for the new week; some hating it, but for most the same weary acceptance of a job that everyone felt.

He and Yemm took the elevator up to the seventh floor, the broad corridor carpeted in soft gray, reasonably good art, including an eclectic mixture of Wyeth, Picasso and Warhol prints on the walls, his suite of offices straight ahead through double glass doors, the offices of the deputy directors of Intelligence and Operations in the corners. The guard at the main elevator down the corridor was on his feet. He'd seen them on the television monitor.

"Good morning, sir," he said.

"Mornin' Charlie."

"Will you be needing me this morning, boss?" Yemm asked.

"I don't think so."

"I'll be in the ready room. We're trying to straighten out the security schedules. You're not making it any easier going it alone at the house, you know."

"I may not be working here next week."

Yemm's eyes narrowed with good humor. "Right, I'll believe that when I see it."

Yemm took the elevator back down, and McGarvey went into his office. His secretary Dahlia Swanfeld, had his safe opened and was laying out classified material on his desk, along with his schedule for the day and the remainder of the week, his telephone appointments, speeches, staff briefings and meetings, awards ceremonies for outstanding officers, visiting dignitaries and the heads of friendly foreign intelligence services, plus the new ambassador to India, who was coming in for his CIA briefing.

A highly competent woman in her early sixties, Ms. Swanfeld had worked for the Agency longer than McGarvey had. Never married, no children, no siblings, no real life that anyone knew about beyond the job, everyone who met her for the first time fell immediately under her spell of good cheer and kindness. Her gray hair in a bun, her suits always proper, she came from another era; even her voice and diction were those of Miss Manners.

"Good morning, Mr. Director," she said. "I trust that you and Mrs. McGarvey spent a pleasant weekend."

"Relaxing. How about you?"

"A very quiet weekend, thank you." It was the same answer she always gave.

She took his coat, and while he flipped through his schedules she went for his coffee. At nine the first meeting of the day with the top officers in the CIA was held in the main conference room. This morning's agenda covered his Senate subcommittee hearings, a request by the NRO for increased funding to upgrade the present Jupiter satellite system that watched over India and Pakistan; a request by the Directorate of Science and Technology for an expansion of its system QK, which monitored every officer in the field from every foreign station on a twenty-four-hour-per-day basis, comparing each individual's work with everyone else's. They would also go over the draft of a brief that McGarvey was scheduled to give the National Security Council on the nuclear situation between Pakistan and India, a half-dozen requests from the *Washington Post, Time, Newsweek* and the television networks for interviews on his appointment as DCI, as well as requests for backgrounders on Pakistan, Afghanistan, Cuba and Chechnya.

At ten he was to meet with the U.S. Intelligence Board, which consisted of the heads of all the U.S. military and civilian intelligence agencies, over the Pakistan issue. There was a possibility that Pakistan and India would soon be going thermonuclear. The President and his National Security Council were going to want a very tight estimate on the situation, and soon.

At noon he was scheduled to award four medals to two of Dave Whittaker's clandestine ops people for work they'd done in Tajikistan uncovering the links between four Russian officers who'd stolen a small nuclear device from a military depot in Dushanbe and Osama bin Laden. Afterward he was having lunch with four postdocs from Harvard who were working on research papers dealing with the economic impact that the CIA's presence in some third world countries was having. His job was to help them as much as possible to find the right answers and point them in directions that would do the least harm to the Company.

At one he would be returning phone calls and working on the draft of his opening statement to the Senate Armed Forces Subcommittee on Intelligence. At two he would be meeting with the CIA's general counsel, Carleton Paterson, about the hearings. At four he had a series of meetings with various department heads in the Directorates of Operations and Intelligence on specific issues and concerns, many of them about personnel, committee appointments, mission emphasis and, as usual, funding.

Sometime after that he had to fit in the new ambassador to India. By six he would do his laps in the CIA's basement swimming pool, and hopefully by seven he could leave for the day.

Floor-to-ceiling windows looked out over the snow-covered woods, and for a moment McGarvey stopped to think how many decisions had been made from this room—some of them good, even brilliant, others incredibly stupid—all of them affecting the lives of someone somewhere in the world. Now it was his turn if he wanted to run the gauntlet in the Senate. Something he still wasn't sure that he wanted to do.

There were a couple of Wyeth prints on the walls, bookcases along one, couch, leather chairs and a coffee table along another; a private bathroom and, directly off his office, a small private dining room that he often used for small conferences. A door connected directly with the office of the Deputy Director of Central Intelligence.

Underlined in red was the meeting with Carleton Paterson. The patrician former New York corporate attorney had a respect for McGarvey that just bordered on the grudging, but he had done his best to pave the way for the hearings. "Hammond will try to embarrass you and the Agency at every possible turn," Paterson kept warning. "His aim is to get you to withdraw of your own accord; short of that he'll want to prejudice public opinion so badly against you that the President will be forced to pull your nomination. It's happened before."

"Maybe Hammond is right," McGarvey told him.

"About you being the wrong man for the job?" Paterson asked. He shook his head, took off his glasses and wiped the lenses with his handkerchief. "The CIA has been run by political animals for too long."

McGarvey started to object, but Paterson held him off.

"In the end the general became your friend, I understand your feelings. But Murphy was primarily a politician. Something you are not." Paterson put his glasses back on. "When someone cuts open my chest I don't want it to be the president of the hospital board. I want it to be the surgeon who's gotten his hands bloody; someone who's done a thousand heart transplants, the last dozen of which he did just last week." He inclined his head. "You, my scholar with a gun, are just that man." He chuckled. "The problem will be getting you confirmed. Hammond's not your worst enemy. You are."

Ms. Swanfeld set his coffee down. "You're free after lunch, the four professors from Harvard canceled, and the pool is yours at six."

"Where's my daughter?"

"She and Mr. Van Buren are still at the Farm. They're scheduled to come back later this morning."

McGarvey took off his jacket and loosened his tie. "Have Carleton up here at two sharp, I think I can give him two hours."

"Yes, sir."

Dick Adkins, the Deputy Director of Central Intelligence came from his adjoining office with a newspaper. "You'll need every bit of those two hours, and then some," he said. He nodded to Miss Swanfeld.

"Will that be all, sir?" she asked.

"Let's do letters after lunch."

"Yes, sir." Miss Swanfeld turned and left the office, softly closing the door behind her.

"She's priceless."

"I'd be lost without her."

"Have you seen the *Post*?"

"Not yet."

Adkins laid the *Washington Post* in front of McGarvey. "Apparently we tried to recruit the good senator right out of college in '69, but he couldn't make it through the confidence course. He ended up getting himself drafted and sent to 'Nam."

The headline read: CIA WANNA-BE GUNNING FOR NATION'S TOP SPOOK.

"Maybe this will quiet him down."

"Not likely. Nobody likes us right now, and Hammond didn't dodge the draft. There's talk about putting him up for President in three years."

McGarvey sat back. "We've survived worse."

"Name one," Adkins shot back. He was a little irascible this morning, his eyes red. He was a short man, a little paunchy and usually diffident; this morning his cheeks were hollow, and he looked like he wanted to bite something.

"Bad weekend?"

"Ruth is sick again." His eyes narrowed. "Every goddammed doctor we've taken her to says the same thing; it's in her head. There's nothing physically wrong with her." His jaw tightened. "But they don't have to hold her shoulders while she's heaving her guts out in the toilet bowl at three in the morning—for the fifth time that night."

"What about a psychologist?"

"She won't see one," he replied bitterly. He had changed over the past months. They had two girls, but they were away at school. It was for the best, but it left Dick alone to handle the tough situation.

"Maybe you should get out of here for a couple of weeks," McGarvey suggested. "Take her someplace warm. Hawaii."

"After the hearings." Adkins cracked a smile. "God only knows what I'd come back to if I left now."

"Seriously, Dick, there's no job in the world worth your

wife. Anytime you want to pull the pin, say the word and you're out of here."

Adkins nodded tiredly. "I appreciate it. But for now she doesn't seem to be getting any worse—same old same old. We'll go after the hearings."

"I was thinking about that over the weekend."

"I know, I talked to Carleton on Friday. He's worried that you're going to tell the President no thanks, and hang on here only until someone else can be confirmed."

"It wouldn't be the end of the world."

"True. But the general picked you for the job, and he's a pretty good judge of character. At least stick it out for a couple of years. This place has never been run so well."

"Did you read the overnights? An idiot could do this job."

"And some have," Adkins said. "Lots of grass fires out there, any one of which could start a forest fire."

"Haynes has other people he can name who'd get past Hammond without a problem."

"Need we say more?" Adkins asked. "This place would go back to being run like a Fortune 500 company, or worse, like a political constituency. I for one don't think that would do the country any good. And I'm not alone in that opinion. But it's your call. Take your own advice; if you want to pull the pin, just say the word. But don't screw around, Mac. Don't bullshit the troops. Either do the job, or get the hell out right now and save us all a lot of trouble."

Adkins was right, of course. Lead, follow or get out of the way. Harry Truman had a sign on his desk that said THE BUCK STOPS HERE. The sign on McGarvey's desk could have read, THE BULLSHIT STOPS HERE. He had a hell of a staff; the right people at the right time; professionals who were willing, like Adkins was this morning, to tell the boss the way it really was without fear of repercussions. The CIA had not been run that way for years, if it ever had.

He looked up. "I want to see the in-depths on the overnights, especially the India-Pakistan situation. I think it's going to heat up even faster than anyone believes, and we'll have to play catch up over there."

"I'll set up an Intelligence Operations briefing this afternoon."

"Let's put it on the nine o'clock agenda. I want something for USIB at ten. But first I want to see a file summary of everything we know."

"Will do."

"Now, what do we have on the situation in Havana? Do you know who the guy was?"

"Navy lieutenant commander Paul Andersen, stationed at the Naval Intelligence unit at Guantanamo Bay. He flew up to Miami on Thursday, picked up a new identity, and Friday flew to Havana with a delegation of travel agents and cruise ship reps. He'd apparently set up a meeting with Hector Sanchez, the second-in-command in Cuban Military Intelligence Internal Affairs. Something is supposedly going on in Castro's private security detail. Sanchez was going to talk to Andersen in trade for asylum and presumably a stack of cash."

"Was it a setup?"

"Naval Intelligence is still working the problem. Havana police found his naked body in the alley behind his hotel. He'd been beaten up and then took a dive, or was thrown, out his tenth-floor window. That was about ten minutes after the prostitute he'd hired left the room."

"What about our people on the ground?"

"They're working on it. But they'll have to burn a couple of assets to get anywhere."

"Do it," McGarvey said.

"All right," Adkins replied. "No one is safe anymore. But that has to change."

"We'll give it a try."

When Adkins was gone, McGarvey called Otto Rencke's extension in the computer center on the third floor. Back like this he was having trouble with people depending on him. Part of the job. But trust gave him an odd feeling between his shoulder blades, as if someone with a high-power rifle was taking a bead on him.

Otto answered on the first ring, his voice sharp, even shrill. "What do you want?"

"Good morning, what's eating your ass?"

"I'm busy. What do you want?"

"I want to know what you were doing at my house yesterday, and why you just sat in the driveway without ringing the bell."

"Somebody else."

"What?"

"Somebody else. I wasn't out there. Louise and I spent the entire weekend painting the apartment. And each other." Otto's tone of voice softened a little; more like his old self. "Maybe you oughta get security out there, ya know. Don't want it purple. That's the color for a shroud. Bad. Bad. Bad dog. Something might be gainin' on you, ya know."

"What are you talking about?"

"Not ready yet," Otto replied distantly, as if his mind had suddenly gone elsewhere. "Difficult, delicate. Still pastels, but I don't know, can't say. Just look up, Mac; we all gotta keep our eyes really open, ya know. All the time, not just in the night."

Rencke broke the connection, something chiming in the background noises of his office, and McGarvey was mystified. When Otto was in the middle of something he tended to go off to his own little world. But this was different. He had never had this harsh an edge before.

THREE

> . . . HE HAD TO WONDER IF WHAT HE HAD
> ACCOMPLISHED HAD REALLY MATTERED AT
> ALL, OR IF HIS CAREER HAD BEEN NOTHING BUT
> A WASTED EFFORT.

The U.S. Intelligence Board meeting ran ten minutes past the lunch hour, but nobody grumbled. There was a sense of accomplishment now that a new DCI was at the helm.

McGarvey presented the distinguished service intelligence medals to Whittaker's people, grabbed a quick sandwich at his desk while dictating letters to Ms. Swanfeld, then returned a few phone calls and did some work on the draft of his opening statement.

He spent a couple of contentious hours with Carleton Paterson, who insisted on playing devil's advocate; acting as he thought Senator Hammond might act, working at every turn to provoke McGarvey into making an angry outburst; say something impolitic. "If it gets too bad, I'll keep my mouth shut," McGarvey promised. "I might throttle the senator, but I won't say a thing."

"Hammond's not a bad man like Joe McCarthy was," Paterson said seriously. "He really believes that what he is doing is for the good of the country."

"I know, and I won't actually choke him to death," McGarvey said, smiling. "Not unless I snap."

Paterson gathered his papers and stuffed them into his attaché case. "I used to wonder if there was anything behind that superefficient, cool, macho exterior of yours. Like maybe a sense of humor." He shook his head. "I guess I just found out. I suggest you don't take your wry wit into the hearing chambers. You won't have a lot of understanding friends there."

"No DCI has."

"True."

After his directorate meetings and his talk with the ambassador to India, he went down to the competition-size pool in the basement gym to do his laps. It was 6:00 P.M. Yemm swam with him, as usual. DCIs were not allowed to drown themselves, even accidentally, especially not on Yemm's watch. And anyway, Yemm needed the exercise, too. The act of swimming was mindless, just like the treadmill in the mornings, freeing McGarvey's mind to drift to Otto Rencke, who, despite his eccentricities, or perhaps because of them, was possibly the most valuable man in the Agency. He was able to see things that no one else could. He'd once explained to McGarvey that he had worked on the problem of describing color to a blind Indian mathematician. "Toughest thing I ever did, ya know. Oh, wow, but it was cool." Using a complicated series of tensor calculus matrices, he was able to first establish neutrality—white. Then he separated the equations into their constituent parts; the way white light separates into a rainbow of colors through a prism. "The eighth-order equations were my prism, and in the end Ravi kissed me, and said, 'I see. Thank you very much.'" The same concept in reverse, representing very difficult mathematics by colors, was Otto's breakthrough. He'd already quantified millions of pieces of seemingly random data and intelligence information into the form of mathematical equations, so now he could reduce the complicated decisions that an intelligence officer had to make into colors. Pastels were at the edge of his understanding; not strong, not clear. But lavender, and especially purple stood for very bad situations—acts of terrorism, assassinations, even wars. To this point Rencke had never been wrong, not once. When a color showed up he could predict what was coming.

They got dressed at seven. On the way down to the car they stopped at the third-floor computer center. This was where Otto usually worked, in the midst of the Agency's mainframe and three interconnected Cray supercomputers. The huge, dimly lit blue room was kept cooler than the rest of the building. It smelled strongly of electronic equipment, and no one ever wanted to speak above a whisper. Mysterious forces beyond human ken were in operation here. The computer was like the tabernacle that held the host on a Catholic Church altar; holy of holies. There were niches and alcoves scattered throughout the room, nestled amidst the equipment, where the human operators worked. They hadn't seen Otto for most of the afternoon, though no one could say exactly when he had left. It was like that down here; he was an elusive figure, like the shadows beneath a shifting pattern of clouds. The niche where he usually worked was a filthy mess of computer printouts, paper cups, milk cartons and McDonald's wrappers strewn on the floor and on a long worktable; wastepaper baskets overflowing, shredder baskets filled, classified satellite downloads lying everywhere. The infrared and visible light images appeared to be mostly of Eastern Europe and Russia. McGarvey recognized the Baltic coastlines of Lithuania, Latvia and Estonia up to Finland, and then the cities of Helsinki, Leningrad and as far east as Moscow. One of the monitors displayed the sword-and-shield logo of the old KGB against a pastel pink background. McGarvey touched enter, and the screen immediately went blank.

"Doesn't look like he wants anyone snooping around," Yemm said.

"Apparently not," McGarvey replied absently. He stared at the blank screen. He was concerned. There was nothing currently on the front burner about the KGB. But Otto was in the middle of something. What?

Time to talk to the Company shrink? He looked at the piles of classified photographs littering the area. He didn't want to lose Otto. Or even worse, he didn't want Otto to run amok; the entire CIA could suffer. The damage could ultimately be worse than what Aldrich Ames had done to them.

He telephoned the computer center night duty supervisor

and asked him to clean up the monitor area that Rencke had been using and secure any classified documents he found.

"He won't be happy, Mr. McGarvey."

"I'll talk to him."

On the way home he stared at the heavy traffic on the Parkway, suddenly depressed. It was dark already, and it was supposed to snow again. He shivered even though it was warm in the car.

"Do you ever think about getting out of the business, Dick?" he asked.

"Every day, boss," Yemm replied. "Every day."

The answer seemed particularly bitter to McGarvey. But then everyone was in a screwed-up mood lately. It had to be the weather. And for him it had to be that he had no real idea why he had accepted the President's appointment.

Time to step down. He'd done his bit. He'd fought the wars, though very often he had to wonder if what he had accomplished had really mattered at all, or if his career had been nothing but a wasted effort. And here he was now at the helm. It was a job he'd never wanted. Yet almost every DCI whom he'd served under had been in his estimation primarily a politician. Not a career intelligence officer, like in Britain.

The CIA was falling apart. Had been for years. The Agency had become nothing more than a glorified extension of the White House; DCIs told the administration nothing more than it wanted to hear, when it wanted to hear it.

Time for the truth. Trouble was that McGarvey didn't know if he was up to the job.

FOUR

SCOUT'S HONOR . . . THE WORDS WERE
COMING BACK TO HAUNT HER.

H e let himself in with his key, and his spirits lifted. It
was good to be home, another Monday behind him.
He entered the alarm code on the touchpad, put his
briefcase on the hall table, hung his coat in the closet and went
back to the kitchen. Kathleen was putting a pan in the oven,
and something on the stove smelled wonderful.

"Hi, Katy, how was your day?"

She gave a sudden start and turned around. She was dressed
in a sweatshirt and blue jeans, and wore a pair of his white
socks. On her the clothes looked like something out of a fashion magazine.

"You startled me." She looked like she had been pulled back
from a millon miles away against her will, and she resented
it. But then she shook her head ruefully. "Sorry, darling. I
guess I was daydreaming."

"I know the feeling." He went around the counter and gave
her a kiss. "Do I get to see what's cooking?"

"Don't push your luck, I don't do this for just anybody."
She gave him a stern look, but she couldn't hold it. She
smiled. "Chili, corn bread and a salad. Down-home."

"Sounds good," McGarvey said. "So, how was your day?"

"Busy. How about you?"

"It was definitely a Monday."

"Go change. I'll make you a drink."

"You've got a deal," he said, suddenly weary. He went upstairs, changed into a flannel shirt, jeans and moccasins. His eyes were bloodshot from the pool water, and his muscles were sore. Each year it seemed to get a little bit tougher to come back from a strong workout. He stopped and looked out the window. The wind had risen, and the snow had a definite slant. Bad night to be out. He shivered, for some reason thinking about bad nights like this one, and some a lot worse, when he'd been out; stalking his prey—someone unexpected, some monster coming out of the blizzard and darkness. What other monsters were lurking out there now, coming toward them? He couldn't shake the feeling of foreboding, of menace that had been hanging over him like a dark cloud for the past several days.

Time to get out, the thought once again flashed across his mind. Go. Run. Run. Run. Find a hole and jump in like he had done before. For the sake of Katy and Liz. Or for self-preservation? He'd never had the guts to ask himself that question. Maybe it was time to start. Self-doubt settled heavy on his shoulders, pushing him down; a nearly impossible burden to bear. He walked out of the bedroom and went downstairs, pushing those thoughts to the back of his mind, grasping for a lightness that he didn't feel because he owed it to his wife to try at least as hard as she was trying.

She had poured him a cognac neat, and she was laying out the place settings at the counter. "I thought we'd eat in here. That okay with you?" She had turned on the gas logs in the French fireplace that separated the kitchen from the family room.

McGarvey nodded. "How was your day, Katy?"

She shrugged. "Okay, I guess. Nothing unusual."

"You look a little frazzled."

She was on the other side of the counter, and she cocked her head as if she was listening for something. "The confirmation hearings start tomorrow, don't they?"

"Is that what's getting to you?"

"I saw the *Post* this morning. They think that you're going to have a bad time of it. Are they going to stop you?"

He was relieved that that's all that was bothering her. They'd not talked very much about the Senate hearings except that their lives, hers included, would be under a microscope for a week or two. It was an inevitable part of the process. Worse than running for elected office because you couldn't campaign. No one was supposed to want this job. If you did, you were automatically suspect. "They might. Would that bother you?"

She thought about it. "What if you are confirmed as DCI, Kirk? How long will you keep the job?"

"I don't know. Maybe I won't take it in the first place. Look, Katy, if—"

"I'm serious. Would you make a career of it like Roland did? Peggy told me that it almost killed him." She was stressed out. "Now that we've come this far I want some time with you."

"I'll call the President in the morning and tell him I'm out."

"No," Kathleen replied sharply.

"It's not worth it, what it's doing to you. I'll stick it out until they get someone else."

She shook her head as he was talking. "That's not what I meant. I simply want to know how long you'll stay."

McGarvey didn't know what to say. He felt that whatever answer he gave her would be the wrong one. "Three or four years," he finally said. "I owe them that much."

Kathleen stared wide-eyed at him for a moment or two, then nodded. "I can deal with that," she said, simply.

"I haven't been confirmed yet."

"You will be," she said, her mood a lot lighter now. She laughed. "They'd be fools to let you go. You're what the Agency needs right now, and everybody knows it."

"Is that the scuttlebutt in town?" McGarvey asked. Katy had always been well connected in Washington. She knew people, heard things, noticed things.

"What an ugly word," she said, amused. "But that's the consensus." She turned and got the plates and bowls from the cabinet. "I'm not going to watch on television. Hammond is a pompous ass, and he'll try to score points off you." She got the silverware and napkins. "But if you push back, he'll quit. He's all bluster."

"That's about what Carleton said," McGarvey replied. "How long before dinner?"

"Twenty minutes."

"Right, I have to make a phone call." McGarvey took his drink, got his briefcase from the hall table and went into his study. The room was a mess. His desk and chair had been moved to the middle and covered with plastic, but the couch and everything else had been moved out somewhere. Sections of two walls had been stripped to the bare studs beneath the drywall, wires dangled loosely from a hole in the center of the ceiling, plaster dust and sawdust covered every surface, and the blinds had been removed from the big window. The carpenters had left their toolboxes and a portable radio in a corner.

He uncovered his desk, found the telephone and called the night duty officer in the Directorate of Operations on the encrypted line. He had thought about this all the way home after seeing the logo on Otto's computer.

"Four-seven-eight-seven, Newby."

"This is McGarvey. How're things shaping up?" It was after midnight, Greenwich Mean Time and the twenty-four-hour summaries were starting to arrive at Langley from the foreign stations and posts.

"Good evening, Mr. McGarvey," Jay Newby said. He was one of the old reliable hands who'd cut his teeth in Eastern Europe during the Cold War years. At one time he had been a hell-raiser. But he was on his third marriage now and he had become a stay-at-home, though he didn't mind night duty. "Nothing significant."

"How about Moscow station?"

"Nothing above a grade three," Newby said. "I'm scanning. Are you looking for anything in particular, Mr. Director?"

"Just fishing."

"The SVR is asking Interpol for some help," Newby said. The SVR was the renamed and slightly reorganized foreign section of the old KGB. "Evidently they lost track of one of their people, and they want him back. Probably cleaned out someone's bank account and skipped the country."

"Do we have a name?"

"Nikolayev. Dr. Anatoli Nikolaevich. Would you like me to send his file over to you tonight?"

"Not right now. But you can include it in the morning report. Anything else?"

"Not from Moscow. The navy is asking for help in Havana, that just came over. And we've got the heads up on a possible operation in Mexico City. We're passing both items to Mr. Whittaker right now." Dave Whittaker was the DDO, and nothing escaped his attention.

"Quiet night."

"Yes, sir."

McGarvey was about to hang up, but another thought struck him. "Have you already pulled Nikolayev's file?"

"Yes, sir."

"Why?"

"Mr. Rencke asked for it yesterday."

"Thanks, Jay. Have a good one." McGarvey hung up and stood there, lost in thought for a few moments. Nikolayev was a name he hadn't heard in a lot of years. If he had to guess he would have thought that the old man was dead, along with just about the entire Baranov crowd. He had been the chief psychologist for Department Viktor. One of the handpicked few. A golden boy.

Now he was missing, and Otto was looking for him.

He went back to the kitchen as Kathleen was about to call him. She had put some soft jazz on the stereo, and they sat together at the counter. She'd always been an elegant woman but something of an indifferent cook. Once they hired a new housekeeper the woman would cover that task. In the meantime Katy's cooking had improved, though he figured that if he told her as much she'd probably quit and they would end up eating out every night or making do with TV dinners. The other problem was that before they hired any house staff the

CIA would first have to do a background check, and that could take time. Her old housekeeper had been a good cook, however, and the chili and corn bread were her recipes.

"Just what the doctor ordered," he said when he was finished. Katy got up to pour them coffee, and he thought that a cigarette would be good right now. A Company shrink had told him once that among other things he was an obsessive/compulsive.

"Do you want anything else?" she asked.

McGarvey looked up at her, and at that moment he thought that he had never been so lucky in all of his life that they had come back to each other. All the wasted, terrible years they had spent apart, mad at each other, could never be regained. But that didn't matter as long as they had here and now.

She gave him a quizzical look. "A penny."

"I was thinking how lucky we are."

She smiled but then looked away. "I'm getting worried about Elizabeth. I think that something might be wrong."

"Physically? Mentally?"

"With her pregnancy. But she won't tell me anything."

"She and Todd probably had a fight."

Kathleen shook her head. "I don't think it's that."

"I'll talk to her in the morning—"

"Tonight, Kirk. Please."

Kathleen refused his help with the cleanup so McGarvey took his coffee into the study to call their son-in-law. Van Buren had been a hand-to-hand and exotic weapons instructor at the CIA's training facility outside Williamsburg when Elizabeth took the course. She was a few years younger than Todd, but every bit as stubborn and willful. They were madly in love with each other, but their relationship was complex and extremely competitive. No rookie field officer, especially not a woman, not even if she was the boss's daughter, was going to tell him how to do his job. And no bullshit testosterone factory was going to hold doors and fight off the gremlins to protect the little woman tending the home fires for her.

She had gotten pregnant last year, but lost the baby in the

third month. The miscarriage devastated both of them until she got pregnant again. But more than that the ordeal had bonded them even closer than before. They were a single unit as flexible as a willow tree and yet as strong as bar titanium. But they still fought like cats and dogs.

They lived down in Falls Church in a carriage house that belonged to the estate his parents owned. He answered after a couple of rings. It was an unsecured line so McGarvey's number showed up on Van Buren's caller ID.

"Hi, Mac, you all set for tomorrow?"

"As ready as I'll ever be, I guess." McGarvey pulled the cover off his chair and sat down. There was classical guitar music in the background, and Todd sounded relaxed, even mellow. "But at least it'll be interesting."

Van Buren chuckled. "That it will be. Did you know that the pool is up to eight hundred bucks?"

"I almost hate to ask: What pool?"

"The exact hour and minute you take a shot at Hammond and he goes down in flames."

"That'd be about three minutes before Carleton Paterson has a heart attack."

"Two for one," Van Burean said. "How's Mrs. M.?"

"She's a little worried about Liz," McGarvey told him. "Is everything okay?"

"If you mean her pregnancy, she's healthy as a horse. She saw the doctor this afternoon and he gave her the thumbs-up. But I think that she's going crazy on me."

"Pickles and ice cream?"

"I wish it was that easy. She's into conspiracies. It's bad enough when a civilian goes looking for monsters under the bed, but it's ten times worse when a CIA field officer does it, especially a pregnant one."

"Are you serious?"

"She's got Otto convinced. They've been working on something for the past week or two. I can't get it out of her, maybe you can."

McGarvey tried to decide how he should be taking this. His daughter was a trained CIA field officer, who, along with her husband, worked special projects for the Directorate of Operations. If she was working on a legitimate operation, there were certain procedures she was required to follow that would eventually come to his attention. He'd seen or heard nothing until now. On the other hand, McGarvey encouraged all of his people to take the initiative. Nobody would get cut off at the knees for following up on a hunch even if it led nowhere.

"Keep an eye on her, Todd. I don't want her going too crazy on us. But don't tell her I said so."

Van Buren chuckled again. "I'm just her husband. What am I supposed to do if her own father is afraid of her? Do you want to talk to her? She's in the shower now, but when she gets out I'll have her call."

"Tell her to call her mother."

"Will do," Van Buren said. "Good luck tomorrow."

"Thanks." McGarvey put the phone down and sat for a long time staring at the bare studs in the wall, but not really seeing them. The same nagging at the back of his consciousness had started again; like someone or something gently scratching at the back door in the middle of the night.

He went back to the kitchen to get more coffee. Kathleen was just finishing up. She gave him an expectant look.

"Liz was in the shower. Todd's going to have her call when she gets out."

"Is everything okay?"

"She saw the doctor this afternoon. Everything's fine."

Kathleen was relieved, yet she looked like a startled deer caught in the flash of headlights, frozen in place but wanting desperately to run.

McGarvey took her in his arms and held her. "It's going to be okay. Not like the last time."

She looked up at him. "Promise?"

He smiled. "Scout's honor."

Kathleen had a strong sense of social order and traditions and proper behavior. For her they were the distinguishing marks of civilization. She'd always felt that way in part because she was her father's daughter. Walter Fairchild, until he killed himself, had been the CEO of a major Richmond investments and mortgage banking company. He'd been a Southern gentleman of the oldest tradition—proud, arrogant, even vain. When his wife took off with another man, Kathleen was left in his care.

She'd been twelve. For a long time she hated her mother and idolized her father. But those emotions had changed with time, and with her father's death, left her with an over-developed sense of right and wrong; truth and lies; responsibility and commitment, fair play.

But then she met Mac at a navy commander's ball in Washington, D.C. He was a spy working for the Central Intelligence Agency. He was ruggedly handsome. He looked dangerous; there was even a hint of cruelty in his green eyes that she found devastatingly attractive, He was the opposite of the men she'd known in Richmond, the boys she'd dated in college and the men she worked for in the Smith Barney Washington office.

In a week they were sleeping together. In a couple of months they were married. And in the first year Elizabeth was born.

It was shortly after that when Mac began disappearing without explanation. Sometimes he was gone overnight; sometimes for days; and a couple of times for several weeks.

He would not give her a straight answer, except that it had something to do with the CIA. He would make vague hints that it wouldn't do for them to develop any close friends. It was nobody's business what he did for a living. To avoid the lies, you avoided people.

She was infuriated. How dare her husband isolate her and keep things from her. It was like her parents' marriage, only in reverse. Her husband was secretive, just like her mother had been. He was frequently gone, just like her mother had been. And she was certain that he would leave one day and never come back, just like her mother had.

She was well enough connected in Washington because of her father and because of her own work at Smith Barney that she began getting discreet answers to discreet questions. Her husband worked for the CIA. He worked in something called Clandestine Operations. And it was possible that he was a black operations officer.

That meant he did things. Spying in Russia and Germany. Sabotage. Blackmail. Maybe even murder.

The Santiago trip had been the last straw, though at the time she had no idea where he had gotten himself off to. When he came home, however, she could tell just by looking at him that he had done something that was over the top even for him.

"That's it," she'd told him. "No more. I want your word on it. Scout's honor."

"I can't," he'd told her.

"Then it's going to be either Elizabeth and me, or the CIA. Your choice."

He'd turned without a word and walked out.

Scout's honor, she thought now. The words were coming back to haunt her.

FIVE

> "WE'RE IN KIND OF A GEOPOLITICAL ROAD RAGE
> THAT'S HARD TO FIGHT AND ALMOST
> IMPOSSIBLE TO PREDICT."

McGarvey took the half-dozen situation reports he'd brought home with him from his briefcase, piled them on the corner of his desk and opened the first one. It was titled: *Afghanistan: Probable Escalation.*

The Directorate of Intelligence produced the reports on a weekly basis for every hot spot. They were classified so they were not supposed to leave the building, but that was a rule that McGarvey and a lot of DCIs before him broke. The workload was simply too great to get it all done at Langley.

This report was bound in a gray cover with orange diagonal stripes, which meant fighting was going on right now. It had only been a year since he had returned from Afghanistan himself. They had been fighting then, and they were still fighting amongst themselves even though the Taliban had been defeated and bin Laden's al-Quaida terrorists were all dead, in captivity or on the run. A stupid waste of lives, he thought. Yet for the Afghanis there really wasn't much in the way of other options. He had seen the apathy in the eyes of the mujahedeen fighters: the hunger, the lack of education, the fear and suspicion of outsiders, especially of the modern world, the West. Even now.

McGarvey took his cup into the kitchen, got some coffee and then looked in on Kathleen at the computer in the next room. She was engrossed with her work on the Beaux Arts Ball, the second most important social event of any Washington season behind the presidential inaugural balls. She had raised millions for the Red Cross and for the Special Olympics. A lot of people, including three presidents, had a lot of respect for her. She was something, he thought.

He went back to the study with his coffee and picked up his reading.

The DDI's Situation Reports, some running to five hundred pages with maps, graphs, photographs, satellite and NSA electronic information as well as on-the-ground eyewitness reports, came out every Monday. They were distributed to the top officials in the U.S. intelligence establishment; the CIA, FBI, National Security Agency, National Reconnaissance Office, the Pentagon and the State Department. The reports were digested, rewritten and updated so that every Thursday a National Intelligence Estimate and Watch Report could be generated. The NIE gave information on everything going on in the world that had a potential to threaten the security of the U.S. The Watch Report was a heads up on situations where fighting was going on or could be about to start. Both reports were sent to the President and his National Security Council, who set policy.

It was up to the Director of Central Intelligence to oversee the process and to be called to account on Fridays. Then, on Mondays, like now, it started all over again. But he was having a hard time keeping on track tonight. Something was whispering in the wind around the eaves; in the sighing of the tree branches on the fifteenth fairway behind the house; in the nasty rumor-filled crackle of the plastic pool cover burdened with snow and ice. The pool water had not frozen. It was a death trap, the thought came to his mind. Fall in by accident, become entangled in the blue waffle cover and drown or suffocate.

He telephoned Jay Newby on the night desk again. For some reason Mondays almost always seemed to be quiet. It was as if the bad guys had stopped after the hectic weekend

to catch their breath. The night duty staff usually played pi-
nochle at a buck a point. It was a ruthless game, and they
hated to be interrupted.

"Four-seven-eight-seven," Newby answered sharply.

"Did the Russians mention when Nikolayev went missing?"
McGarvey asked.

"Ah, Mr. McGarvey, we were just about to call you, but
just a minute and I'll pull up the Moscow station file," he said,
shifting gears.

McGarvey could hear several computer printers in action,
someone talking and music in the background.

"Mid to late August," Newby said. "But they don't say who
reported him missing, or why the urgency to find him. But
they do want him back."

"Okay, now what were you going to call me about?"

"The operation in Mexico City. Tony wants a green light.
We expected to pass this to Mr. Whittaker, but he asked not
to be disturbed for anything below a grade two." Antonio Lan-
zas was the Mexico City COS.

"He's at his daughter's wedding rehearsal dinner."

"Yes, sir. And Mr. Adkins is at Columbia with his wife."

McGarvey had been expecting it. "Any word from the hospital?"

"Nothing yet."

"Keep me posted," McGarvey said.

"Yes, sir. Dick Yemm is coming out with the operational
order for your signature."

"Very well." The CIA hadn't been run with such a tight
rein since the forties and fifties in the days of Allen Dulles
and Wild Bill Donovan, who insisted on knowing everything
that was going on. Such close control was impossible now
because there was far too much information streaming into
Langley twenty-fours hours a day for any one man to handle.
But McGarvey insisted on knowing the details of any action
that had the potential to threaten lives or embarrass the U.S.

The operation called NightStar was the brainstorm of
George Daedo, one of Tony's field officers. Six months ago
he'd gone to a concert by the National Symphony Orchestra
of Mexico, alone for once, although he had the reputation of

being a ladies' man. At the first intermission he went to the smoking courtyard where he stumbled on a terrific argument between Fulvio Martinez, who was a vice counsel in the Mexican Intelligence Service, and his horse-faced wife, Idalia. As far as Daedo was concerned it was a gold seam; an opportunity not to be missed. Over the signature of his COS, Daedo began his careful and very delicate seduction of the intelligence officer's unhappy wife.

The affair had caused some heated discussion in the DO which was headed by a very moral David Whittaker, who thought that such operations were fundamentally wrong. McGarvey agreed with his DDO in principle. But in the real world the righteous way wasn't always the right way. Even though he had been overridden, Whittaker insisted on being included in the loop every step of the way. The entire DO had taken an interest in the case; in fact; it had become like a soap opera. Will she or won't she? What was at stake was nothing less than the inside track to Mexican intelligence. At risk, of course, was the acute embarrassment to the U.S., as well as the final destruction of a troubled marriage, but a marriage for all of that.

The request for the go/no go decision tonight meant that Daedo was asking permission for the final action; that of taking Mrs. Martinez to bed.

McGarvey went into the hall and switched on the outside lights, then went back to the kitchen. Kathleen stood, her hip against the counter, cradling a cup of tea in both hands and staring at the telephone.

"I'm not sneaking up on you, and I'm not scaring you, so don't jump out of your skin this time."

She turned and smiled. "I was just thinking that after the hearings maybe we should take a few days and get away from here. Does that sound good to you?"

"Someplace warm."

"Absolutely," Kathleen said enthusiastically. She nodded toward the study. "Are you getting anything done in that mess?"

"Some reading. Most of it pretty boring. But it'd be easier without the plaster dust."

"Just a few days."

"Dick Yemm is on his way over with something for me to sign."

"Use the family room," she said automatically. "The two of you can't get anything done in the study."

"How're the invitations coming?"

"Pretty good. But the final list is going to depend on whether or not you're confirmed as DCI."

"You don't want to know which list I'd prefer."

She laughed lightly. "I wouldn't even have to guess. But there are obligations that come with the job."

"I know—"

"*Social* obligations, my darling husband," she stressed. "That means a tuxedo and no smart-alecky comments to get a rise out of our guests."

"Throw a stick at a pack of dogs, and the one that yelps is the one that got hit."

She gave him a sharp look.

He spread his hands. "I'll behave myself." He came around the counter, rinsed his cup in the sink and gave her a peck on the cheek. "Really."

"I'm going to hold you to it," she said sternly.

The doorbell rang. "Has Liz called yet?"

Kathleen's lips compressed. She shook her head. "I'm going to have to call her since she's obviously too busy to pick up a telephone and call me."

"She's a little shit," McGarvey said, trying to keep it light. "It runs in the family."

"I'm going upstairs. Say hi to Dick," Katy said, and she took her cup and the guest list and left the kitchen as McGarvey went to answer the door.

The fact that Kathleen was having her own tough time because of the hearings right in the middle of their daughter's pregnancy made it difficult all around. But this, too, will pass, he thought. And the sooner the better.

Dick Yemm, a leather dispatch case in hand, his coat collar hunched up against the cold, his dark hair speckled with snow, was grinning crookedly. "No rest for the wicked," he said.

"Don't you ever sleep?" McGarvey asked, letting him in.

"About as much as anyone else in the business, boss." He

followed McGarvey down the hall into the family room, where McGarvey motioned him to a bar stool.

"Want a beer?"

Yemm hesitated.

"How about a cognac?"

"That sounds good," Yemm said. He unlocked the dispatch case and withdrew the thin file folder with the mission authorization form.

McGarvey gave him his drink and took the folder.

"Used to be in the old days that everybody was screwing everybody else, and no one took any notice," Yemm said gloomily. "Now it's different, and I don't know if we're better off for it."

"These days we think twice before we do something. That's a change for the better."

"She was at the wrong place at the wrong time."

"Yeah," McGarvey said. He took a pen from Yemm, signed the form and handed them back. "Sometimes we're not very honorable men. Expediency without integrity."

"At least we're fighting on the right side," Yemm conceded.

"Sometimes I wonder."

Yemm gave him a critical look. "Problems, boss?"

McGarvey took a drink. "I wasn't kidding when I asked you this afternoon if you ever thought about getting out of the business."

"I wasn't kidding when I said every day." Yemm took a pull at his drink. "But it's too late for us."

"What do you mean?"

"What else could we do?" Yemm answered morosely. "What else are we trained for except opening other people's mail, eavesdropping and shooting people who don't agree with us?"

McGarvey shrugged. "We do the best we can," he said. He swirled the liquor around in the snifter and took another drink as if he needed it to buck himself up. "When the Soviet Union packed it in we lost the bad guys. The evil empire. An idea that we could rally around the flag against. They were worse than the Nazis and five times as deadly, because they had the bomb."

"You almost sound nostalgic—"

"They had the bomb, everyone was afraid that they might actually use it. Remember the nuclear countdown clock? Missiles over the pole; Vladivostok to Washington, D.C.; Moscow to Seattle, equidistant. Or, tactical nukes across the Polish plains into Germany. Or missiles in Cuba."

"They held our attention there for a while," Yemm said.

"That they did. But since 9-11 all bets are off. The bad guys are everywhere."

"Like I said, boss, time to get out."

McGarvey shook his head. "Not yet, Dick. I'm going to need you for the next two or three years."

"You're taking the job then?"

"If I can get past the hearings. There's a lot of truth to what Hammond's saying."

"Bullshit," Yemm said.

"I'll try," McGarvey promised, his eyes straying to the fireplace. "It's like road rage; people jumping out of their cars and shooting each other because someone pissed them off by doing something stupid. Minor shit. Only now everybody's been infected, even entire governments. We're in a kind of a geopolitical road rage that's hard to fight, and almost impossible to predict." He looked back at Yemm. "That's our job now. Figuring out who's going to go crazy next."

"That include us?" Yemm asked softly.

McGarvey nodded. "Yes." How to get that across to Senator Hammond and the others tomorrow, he wondered. He was guilty of a mild form of treason. He had a feeling that he'd always been guilty of that crime. He'd always seen both sides of every issue.

Yemm pocketed his pen and put the authorization form back into his dispatch case. He finished his drink. "Sorry, boss," he said.

"For what?"

"I came over to cheer you up for tomorrow. Guess I didn't do such a hot job of it."

"It's the weather. It's got everybody down."

At the door Yemm buttoned his coat. "I used to like the snow when I was a kid. Now I hate it."

"Yeah, me too," McGarvey said.

"You need a security detail out here around the clock."

"I'll think about it," McGarvey said.

Yemm nodded glumly. "See you in the morning, then," he said. He went down to the driveway, got in his Explorer and drove off.

McGarvey stood at the open door for a bit, feeling the bite of the cold wind and smelling the snow and the smoke whipping around from a half-dozen fireplace chimneys in the neighborhood. When it snowed, city kids went out to play, but ranchers' sons, like he had been, went out to work. Snow meant feeding and watering animals. Blizzards meant staying out until lost cattle were rounded up before they froze to death.

When he went back inside he locked the door and reset the alarm. He glanced up to the head of the stairs. Kathleen stood there hugging her arms to her chest. Tears streamed down her cheeks.

His stomach did a flop, and he hurried upstairs to her. "What's wrong?"

"Elizabeth told me to mind my own business."

McGarvey took her into his arms, She was shivering and crying, and she clutched the material of his shirt as if she were trying to rip it off his body.

"You can't press her. Remember how she was the last time?"

"But I'm her mother, I just want to help."

"I know, but she wants to do this herself. She's trying to prove that she's all grown-up now, and not as worried about everything like she was last year."

Kathleen looked into his eyes to make sure that he wasn't patronizing her.

"When she gets herself figured out she'll come back to you for help. Especially when she realizes that Todd and I are hopeless."

Kathleen smiled hesitantly. "It's just me," she said. "I think that I'm more frightened for the baby than she is."

"So am I," McGarvey admitted. "But it's their turn, their baby. All we can do is stand by if they need us."

She lowered her eyes. "It hurts."

"It shouldn't."

"But it does," she said.

McGarvey held her close again. "I'll talk to her," he promised.

After a moment Kathleen shook her head. "You're right, Kirk," she said. "Elizabeth needs her space. Let her be for the moment."

"You sure?"

"Yeah," Kathleen said, and she started to cry again, but this time without any urgency or tension—merely a safety valve for her emotions.

"Are you okay?" he asked after a bit.

"Just a little tired. It was a tough day. Maybe I'll take a bath."

"I'm done for the night, too. How about a cup of tea or a glass of wine?"

"Some wine." She brushed her fingers across his lips. "I do so love you."

McGarvey smiled. "I'm glad."

She turned and went down the hall to their bedroom, McGarvey went downstairs, rechecked the alarm setting and the front door, then shut off the lights in his study after locking up the DI reports.

He stood in the dark for a few minutes listening again, as he had been doing for the past several days, for something—the sounds of the house, the sounds of the wind, the sounds of his own heart, the sounds that the gavel would make tomorrow.

"Fuck it," he said. He went back to the kitchen, where he checked the patio doors. He opened a bottle of pinot grigio from the cooler, got a couple of glasses and went upstairs.

The big tub on a raised step was only one-third full and the water was still running, but Kathleen had already disrobed and gotten in. She was lying back, her eyes closed, a look of contentment on her finely defined oval face.

McGarvey sat down on the toilet lid, careful not to clink the glasses or make any noise to disturb her, but she opened her eyes and smiled at him.

"If you only knew how good this feels," she murmured luxuriously.

He poured her a glass of wine and set it on the broad, flat edge of the tub. "I'm going to take a shower," he said, starting to get up.

"Don't go."

"Don't you want some peace and quiet?"

"I had twenty years of that; now I want you." She ran a hand across the top of her chest, letting droplets of water run down between her breasts. "Even if we were in the same room for the next twenty, it wouldn't make up for what we lost." She shook her head thinking back. "Such a stupid waste, actually. My fault."

"*Our* fault," McGarvey corrected. "I had a habit of running away, remember?"

"At least you had a reason," she flared mildly. "I was just . . . arrogant. Young, dumb, ambitious. I wanted to be a perfect mother, I really did. I loved Elizabeth with everything in my soul, but I wanted my freedom, too." She absently touched the base of her neck, her collarbones and shoulders. "I tried Valium, because I felt guilty, but it didn't work for me. Made me sick at my stomach." She laughed. "The doctor said that I was tense."

"It wasn't much better for anyone else. It's time to stop beating yourself up. You were hiding out in the open, and I was hiding underground. You had the tougher assignment."

"Everybody hated the CIA. My friends used to tell me that kicking you out was the best decision that I'd ever made. But they were jerks. The kind of people you and I always hated. I would look at our daughter and wonder why they weren't seeing what I was seeing; a perfect little girl who was half you." She closed her eyes and laid the cool wineglass against her forehead. "I wanted to tell them, but I didn't."

"We spent a lot of time being mad at each other," McGarvey said sadly. "We both made some dumb decisions."

"When you came back to Washington out of the clear blue sky I thought that you'd come for me. When I found out that the CIA had hired you to dig out Darby and his crowd, I was mad at you all over again." She was looking inward, regret all over her face. "I threatened to sue you for money, I flaunted myself all over Washington and New York, and I even got word to you that I was thinking about getting married, but nothing worked. Then the CIA comes to see you in Switzerland to offer you a job, and you come running. It wasn't fair."

McGarvey didn't know what to say. It was a time for going back, and the memories were just as painful for him as they were for her. But maybe necessary, he thought.

She opened her eyes wide to look at him. "Do you know the worst part?" she asked. "When I saw you walking down the street it was like someone had driven a stake into my heart. I made a mistake, pushing you away, and here you were back in Georgetown even more inaccessible to me than ever. I had become the kind of person we hated; I had become one of my friends, a pretentious bore."

"But here we are, Katy," he said softly.

She smiled, some of the trouble melting from her face. "It's going to be okay, isn't it, Kirk?"

"Guaranteed."

TUESDAY

SIX

IF KIRK MCGARVEY WERE CONFIRMED AS
DIRECTOR OF CENTRAL INTELLIGENCE HE
WOULD BE ASSASSINATED.

MONTOIRE-SUR-LE-LOIR, FRANCE

Nikolayev walked along the country road into town
as the sun reached over the distant line of poplars
marking the edge of the wheatfield. He encountered
no one this morning. Loneliness, he decided, was a subject on
which he could write a very long book. Now there wasn't even
a routine to look forward to as he grew older. He could not
return to Moscow, nor would he be able to remain here much
longer.

Sunday's edition of the *New York Times, Washington Post*
and *Le Monde*, carried the same story. Each newspaper had
given the facts its own spin: the liberal press was against
McGarvey's appointment; the conservative was for it; and the
French press was confused but angry. It was always anger that
seemed to fuel the public debate; especially the international
dialogue.

Nikolayev could have refused to read the newspapers. Not
listen to the radio, or watch television, especially not CNN.
But the facts would have been there all the same, and he would
know it. Like the feral cat crouched in front of the rabbit; the
predator did not need to read a book to smell the fear. The

ability to sense the real world was built in, and perfected by years of experience.

Nikolayev heard the church bell tolling the hour in town.

Turn away. Now, before it's too late.

In the night he felt them at his back. Coming for him. There would be no arrest for him, though; no cell at Lefortovo, no torture, no drugs, no sewing his eyelids open, rubber hoses up his anus, glass rods shattered inside his penis. They were coming with Russian insurance—his nine ounces—a nine-millimeter bullet to the base of his skull.

"Comrade Nikolayev?"

He stopped and turned, but no one was there. Only the farm fields, the trees, the white clouds in the blue sky, the empty road and the church bell. The voice had been Baranov's. He recognized it. But the general was long dead. Killed by Kirk McGarvey outside East Berlin.

He walked the rest of the way into town where he stopped first at the *boulangerie* for his baguette and his morning raisin buns, then around the corner in the square to the little shop selling tobacco, chewing gum, stamps, magazines and newspapers. The old woman had his three newspapers waiting for him.

"*Bonjour, monsieur,*" she said pleasantly. "*Ça va?*"

"*Bonjour, madame. Ça va, et vous?*" Nikolayev responded with a genuine smile.

"*Je vais bien,*" she said brightly, inclining her head coquettishly. It took him a second to realize that the old woman was flirting with him. He paid her, accepted his change, got his newspapers and fled the dark shop into the bright morning sun. He thought he could hear her laughing as he hurried down the street.

He folded the newspapers under his arm, refusing the temptation to look at the headlines, and after twenty minutes he was back at the small farmhouse he'd rented at the agency in Paris. It had become a familiar haven for him. He put on the water for his tea, put the baguette away and brought the newspapers and buns to the table at the edge of his small vegetable garden in back. From here he could look across the wheatfield, stubble now, to the intersection of the farm road and the main highway D917 across the narrow Loir River. It was the only way here from the outside. The tiny window in his bedroom under the eaves also faced the river and the highway. Basic tradecraft. *Habit is Heaven's own redress*, Alexander Pushkin had written in *Eugene Onegin. It takes the place of happiness*.

There was the occasional car and a few trucks on the highway. The bus from Le Mans passed a few minutes after nine in the morning, and returned from Orleans in the afternoon around two. Six weeks ago a police car passed by, its blue lights flashing, its siren shrieking. Nikolayev had leaped up from the table and had nearly headed off across the fields in a dead run until he realized that they were not coming for him. If Moscow was searching for him, they were not looking here.

When his tea was ready he took the pot and a cup out to the table, put on his reading glasses and settled down with the newspapers. He started with *Le Monde* to see if the French were reporting anything new and because it was today's newspaper. The *Times* and the *Post* were Monday's and probably contained only rewritten versions of Sunday's accounts.

McGarvey's Senate committee hearings were scheduled to begin today. The Paris newspaper wondered if the senators would consider the French government's position that McGarvey was no longer welcome here. A highly placed source inside the DGSE (the French secret intelligence service) had agreed to answer questions provided his anonymity could be protected. On the surface of it, Nikolayev thought that the request was stupid. By definition spies were supposed to be anonymous figures; once they opened their mouths they forfeited that right. It was a plant. But he read the article anyway.

"Despite M. McGarvey's background in the CIA, he was generously given a resident alien visa as early as 1992. Of course he had to agree never to conduct an operation on French soil or against a citizen of France. We sent people to watch him, to make certain that he complied with those conditions. This of course cost the French people a certain amount of money. But in the past M. McGarvey had provided us with a valuable service, so we were willing, even happy, to allow him a pleasant retirement, providing he remained retired."

Q: "Did he stay retired?"

R: "*Non.*"

Q: "What happened?"

R: "We are getting into an area now in which I cannot delve too deeply. Let's just say that there were some unpleasant circumstances which ultimately resulted in a death."

Q: "Of a French citizen?"

R: "*Oui.*"

Q: "Are you able to give us a name?"

R: "*Non.*"

Her name was Jaqueline Belleau. Nikolayev had gleaned most of the details from his computer searches here. What the gentleman from the DGSE did not tell the journalist was that Mademoiselle Belleau was a French spy sent to McGarvey's bed in order to keep a close eye on him. When he returned to the States she followed him, instead of remaining in Paris where she belonged. The mistake had killed her, though it was not McGarvey's fault. She had been caught in the middle of a terrorist bombing of a Georgetown restaurant.

Unlike the American newspapers, *Le Monde* drew no conclusions, leaving the story with vague references to perhaps as many as a half-dozen illegal operations that McGarvey had been involved with on French soil. Neither the anonymous man from the DGSE nor the journalist from the newspaper raised any questions about why McGarvey was not currently serving hard time in a French penitentiary, or, if he were to be appointed DCI, would the French secret service be willing to work with him.

McGarvey's wasn't the only name in the Network Martyrs file. Just the first to come into the media spotlight.

Baranov had known what was going to happen. He'd tried several times to destroy McGarvey's career, even planting false evidence in CIA archives that his parents had been spies for the Soviet Union. Mightn't it pass down to the son?

He'd tried to have McGarvey killed without success. Tried to drive him to ground. If Baranov couldn't kill him, perhaps he could render the man ineffectual.

None of that had happened.

Now it had come to Baranov's endgame. Martyrs.

Nikolayev drank his tea and ate his raisin buns, appreciating what he had here, all the more so because he knew that he would be leaving France soon.

If Kirk McGarvey were confirmed as Director of Central Intelligence, he would be assassinated. In fact the assassin was almost certainly already making his opening moves; preparing for the strike.

The Martyrs file had listed the targets, among them President Jimmy Carter, several admirals and army generals, a half-dozen U.S. senators and congressmen, none of whose names Nikolayev recognized. And McGarvey.

But the names of the assassins had been left out, either because they had not been selected when the original documents had been drafted, or because Baranov wanted the extra layer of security.

When he was finished with his breakfast, he took his things back into the kitchen and went upstairs to pack a bag for Paris. He needed more information than he could get here, and he needed a safe city from which to mail his letter.

The assassin would be making the opening moves now. It was time for Nikolayev to make his next move.

The jackals were snapping at his heels. He had only three choices. Go back and be shot to death for what he had uncovered. Try to disappear and hide for the remainder of his life. Or go forward and try to put a stop to Martyrs.

Some old men got religion, while others filled the endgame by trying to make amends for a lifetime of sin. Martyrs had been his sin just as much as it had been Baranov's.

No choice, really, he told himself. No choice at all.

SEVEN

THE IMAGE THAT REMAINED . . . WAS OF A HELL
IN WHICH DOZENS OF PEOPLE WERE FALLING
BACK IN SLOW MOTION; BLOOD SPLASHING IN
EVERY DIRECTION . . .

CHEVY CHASE

McGarvey slept very hard and dreamless; nevertheless, when the telephone rang at 4:00 A.M. he answered it on the first ring as if he had been lying
there waiting for the call.

"Yes." He glanced at the clock.

"Mr. McGarvey, this is Ken Marks on the night desk. One
of our personnel has been involved in an automobile accident
that could have compromised security."

"Hang on a minute," McGarvey said. Kathleen stirred as he
got out of bed.

"What is it, Kirk?"

"One of our people was in an accident."

She sat bolt upright. "Was it Elizabeth?" she demanded.

"I don't think so," McGarvey said. He was going to take
the phone into the bathroom so he wouldn't wake her, but it
was too late. "Who was it?" he asked the OD.

"Mr. Rencke, sir. His emergency locator was activated at
one-seventeen on the Parkway a couple of miles this side of
Arlington. We tried to call him, but there was no response,

and by the time Security got down there the Virginia Highway Patrol had already responded."

McGarvey put his hand over the phone's mouthpiece. "It was Otto," he told his wife. "Where did they take him?"

"Bethesda. He's listed in good but guarded condition. Mr. Yemm is on his way to you right now."

"Right. I'm going to the hospital. Have a unit sent out here to keep a watch on Mrs. McGarvey."

"Mr. Yemm is bringing someone with him."

Kathleen got up, threw on a robe and started picking out clothes for Mac to wear, a pinched expression on her face. This was the old days all over again. Nothing had changed.

"What about the security problem?"

"Mr. Rencke was carrying his laptop along with a number of classified CDs."

"Who gave you the heads-up?"

"No one, sir. I know Mr. Rencke personally. He never leaves his shop without a bagful of work. Anyway, Security arrived on scene the same time the EMTs got there, and they tidied up."

"But there was a gap between the accident and the time our people got there?"

"Yes, sir. An inventory is being taken right now, but it'll be slow; he's probably got everything bugged."

"You can bet on it. How'd the accident happen, do we know?"

"Apparently he lost control, left the roadway and flipped over. There were no other vehicles involved, according to the VHP. Stand by one, sir—"

Kathleen was looking at him.

"He'll be okay," McGarvey told her. "He worked late and was on his way home when it looks like he fell asleep at the wheel and crashed."

"He never wears a seat belt."

"He got lucky."

Marks was back. "Sir, are we authorizing visitors?"

"Only Agency people."

"How about Major Horn?"

"Her too," McGarvey said. Otto and Louise Horn lived together. She worked for the NRO.

"Mr. Yemm is pulling into your driveway now, sir."

"Tell him I'll be out in a couple of minutes."

"Yes, sir."

Since he was probably going directly from the hospital to his office, and from there to the Senate subcommittee hearing chambers, Kathleen laid out a dark blue suit, white shirt, and tie.

"Why do you want bodyguards out here?" she asked.

"Standard procedures," McGarvey said, getting dressed.

"It might not have been an accident, is that what you're saying?"

He nodded. "We don't know yet, and until we do we're taking no chances."

She turned away but then looked back. "Give Otto my best. Tell him that I'll come up to see him later today if it's allowed."

"I'll tell him." McGarvey gave his wife a peck on the cheek, went downstairs, got his coat and went out to the waiting limo. A dark gray van was parked across the street. It was still snowing heavily, and it was very cold and blustery.

Yemm had the door open. McGarvey nodded to him. "Did you get any sleep?"

"A couple of hours."

McGarvey got in, and Yemm headed out, his driving precise in the difficult conditions.

"Hammerhead en route Star Seven. ETA twenty," Yemm radioed.

"Copy."

"What do we have?" McGarvey demanded.

"The wheel bearing on the front right wheel fell apart, somehow pulled the cotter pin out and sheared the king nut so that the wheel fell off."

"Doesn't sound like a simple mechanical failure."

"We're checking to see if he had any brake work, or anything like that done in the past few days or weeks. But if it was an accident, whoever did the work was a piss poor mechanic."

"It's been known to happen."

With all the snow and ice on the roads, the emergency room at the hospital was busy. McGarvey and Yemm went up to the seventh floor, where a pair of CIA Office of Security people were stationed at Otto's door. The police had already left, and the ward was quiet for the night, though breakfast would be served in a couple of hours.

McGarvey went inside the darkened room alone. Otto was propped up in bed, asleep, his head swathed in bandages, his left arm in a sling that held it against his chest. Louise Horn, tall, skinny, her angular features making her look more gaunt than usual, sat in the chair next to the bed. She held Otto's right hand in both of hers. Her cheeks glistened with tears.

She looked up. "He finally got to sleep, please don't wake him."

McGarvey squeezed her shoulder. "I won't. How is he?"

"Couple of broken ribs. He'll be okay. His left shoulder was dislocated, that's why they immobilized his arm. And he banged up his left knee on the bottom of the steering wheel or something."

McGarvey touched his own head. "What about the bandages?"

Louise Horn looked back at Otto. "The side of his face got cut up with flying glass. Looks worse than it is. But he was lucky. He was wearing his seat belt. Saved his life." She looked up again, more tears welling from her eyes. "He really could have been killed out there."

"When did he start wearing a seat belt?"

Louise Horn had a blank expression on her face. She shook her head. "I don't know."

McGarvey smiled. "He sure picked a good time to start," he said. "Give me a call as soon as he's awake, I want to talk to him. And tell him that Mrs. McGarvey will be up later today to see him."

"Thanks. That'll mean a lot to him."

"Try to get some sleep yourself." McGarvey gave Otto a last look, then started to go. He stopped at the door. "He's been pretty intense lately."

She nodded. "Tell me about it."

"He's been pulling some long hours. Working on something that's bothering him. Has he said anything to you?"

"Nothing," she said. "And I don't pry." She gave McGarvey a faint smile. "We have that rule in our house."

McGarvey nodded. "Good rule." he said, and he left.

LANGLEY

Before they went back to the Agency, they had a word with Otto's doctor. Heshi Daishong, a slight, dark, high-strung man.

"We're waiting to see signs of concussion. For now he looks okay. His biggest problems are a slight malnutrition and exhaustion."

"He's been working hard."

The doctor pushed his glasses up. "We all do. But for Pete's sake, tell the man to slow down." He looked very tired himself. "If all is well, I'll release him at noon."

Back at his office McGarvey had the executive kitchen send up coffee and a basket of muffins. He hadn't had time for breakfast, and he was hungry. He managed to get in a couple of hours of uninterrupted reading before his secretary showed up. She was followed a few minutes later by a strung-out Dick Adkins.

"Well, Ruth was right and the rest of us were wrong," Adkins said. "They found lumps in both of her breasts. How they missed them for so long is anybody's guess. But no one's talking."

"Is she still at the hospital?" McGarvey asked, concerned.

"Yeah. They want to do a bunch of tests, and then, depending on what they find, they'll want to talk to us about our options."

"I'll ask Katy to stop over. In the meantime I want you to get out of here and get some sleep."

Adkins shook his head. "If I go home I'll just sit around and worry myself into drinking. If I go back to the hospital there's nothing I can do until the tests are done. They won't let me in the room with her, and they all but kicked me out of the hospital." He looked like he was floundering, but he was determined not to cave in. "The hearings are going to keep you busy for at least the rest of the week. In the meantime we have the NIE and Watch Report to get out."

"Get out of here anytime you have to, I mean it, Dick."

Adkins nodded. "Thanks."

Elizabeth called a couple of minutes after nine from the Farm outside Williamsburg. "Hi, Daddy, how's Otto?"

"Good morning, sweetheart. He was banged up pretty good, but the doctor says he'll be okay. Should be out of the hospital sometime today. What are you doing back at the farm?"

"We have a class of husband and wife recruits, and Stu has made Todd and me stars of the show. There's lots to go over." Stewart Walker was the new commandant of the training facility. A former Green Beret full colonel, he'd been McGarvey's first choice for the spot, and he was doing a very good job.

"How long are you going to stay there?"

"We'll be home for the weekend. Todd doesn't want to drive back until the snow lets up. Unless you want us to chopper back. Otto is going to be okay, isn't he?"

"He'll be fine. How about you?"

"Aside from the fact I'm grumpy all the time, and I'm fat, I feel great." She hesitated. "Tell mom that I'll call her tonight."

"I will."

"Good luck with the hearings. Are you sure you don't want me to come back?"

"Stay there and do your job."

"We'll definitely be back for the weekend. Give 'em hell, Dad."

WASHINGTON

The Senate hearing room was filled to capacity, mostly with media. When McGarvey and Paterson came in and made their way to the witness table the noise level rose, flash cameras went off and television lights came on. Under normal circumstances presidential appointees came to their confirmation hearings with a cadre of attorneys and advisers. But McGarvey had vetoed the plan because, he explained to a reluctant Paterson, no one knew his background except himself. And if there was to be any fallout, he wanted all of it on his shoulders.

McGarvey recognized many of the people in the audience; friends from the other U.S. intelligence services, the military, the FBI and from at least a half-dozen embassies around town. Dmitri Runkov, the chief of the SVR's Washington operation was missing, however, which was bothersome to McGarvey. Connections within connections, or the lack thereof. He put the Russian's absence at the back of his mind.

Paterson took a number of file folders out of his briefcase, extracted a four-page document and laid it on the table in front of McGarvey as the clerk of the hearings came to the front.

"Hear ye, hear ye. All those having business before the United States Senate Armed Force Subcommitttee on Intelligence rise for the honorable members: Senators Thomas Hammond, Junior, Minnesota, chairman; John Clawson, Montana, vice chairman; Brian Jackman, Mississippi; Brenda Madden, California; Gerald Pilcher, New York; and Arthur Wright, Utah."

Everyone stood as the senators filed in from a door at the side and took their places behind a long oak desk on a raised platform at the head of the chamber. Hammond was a stern-looking man with thick white hair and bushy Dirksen eyebrows. He looked like a Moses without a robe and tablets. He glared down at McGarvey and Paterson as he removed a number of fat file folders from his briefcase.

Of the others, according to Paterson, his second worst enemy was Brenda Madden, a raging knee-jerk liberal who'd been one of the original bra burners at Berkeley. Hers was the same goal as Hammond's. They wanted to punish the CIA for failing to warn the nation about the attacks of September 11. According to them, the Agency was riddled with incompetent, self-serving fools. The U.S. intelligence community needed revamping and streamlining from the top to the bottom. They were happy just now to start at the top with McGarvey.

Mississippi's Jackman and Montana's Clawson were for keeping a strong CIA, though they were asking for more efficiency for the same dollars. New York's Pilcher and Utah's Wright, both junior senators, and both fairly new on the committee, were still on the fence.

Hammond brought the meeting to order, then swore in McGarvey. C-SPAN's television cameras continued to roll.

"Mr. McGarvey, I see by your witness list that you've brought only the CIA's general counsel Carleton Paterson with you this morning."

"Good morning, Senator. Yes, that's correct."

"Will you be bringing other advisers or witnesses in the coming days? I ask because if you are, their names will first have to be presented to the committee."

"Mr. Paterson will be sufficient to keep me out of serious trouble, Senator," McGarvey said.

There were a few chuckles around the room, and a slight smile played at the edges of Hammond's mouth. He had been waiting for just this sort of opportunity ever since Lawrence Haynes had become president when the former President had resigned because of health problems. Haynes and Hammond had been rivals and then bitter enemies in the House and in the Senate, their careers nearly paralleling each other's. Haynes was a tough-talking, no-nonsense conservative Republican, while Hammond was what the *New York Times* called a "touchy-feely New Democract with teeth." Haynes wanted a strong military and a national missile defense shield. Hammond wanted billions diverted from defense and plowed into social welfare and health care reform programs. Haynes promised to take back the fear of terrorism on American soil and against Americans anywhere in the world. Hammond wanted to close ninety percent of our overseas military installations and start bringing Americans home, where they belonged. Haynes was a president *of* the people. Hammond was a ranking senator *for* the people.

McGarvey was the president's fair-haired boy at the moment because of an incident last year in San Francisco when diplomacy would have worked much better than guns blazing. Showing the American people, and especially his fellow senators what sort of a monster McGarvey was, and why he should not be allowed to run the CIA, would be striking a blow at the President. One that would not go unnoticed by his party. Hammond wanted to be president. But for the moment Haynes's numbers were too high.

"Very well," Hammond said. He fiddled with some notes. "We'll have a light session today. I'll make a brief opening statement, and I would ask that Mr. McGarvey or his counsel do the same. Afterward I will allow the general, nonclassified questions concerning Mr. McGarvey's background." He looked at his calendar. "If we can cover enough ground today to everyone's satisfaction, the next few days will be in camera."

Most of the operations that McGarvey had been involved with during his twenty-five years with the CIA were still classified. When the committee began delving into those areas the hearings would have to be held in executive session, closed to anyone without the proper security clearances and the need-to-know.

"I wouldn't give so much as a confidential security clearance to any of them," McGarvey had told Paterson. "If they could get a political boost, they'd leak anything that they could get their hands on. The Bureau's helpless to stop them."

"Their privilege," Paterson replied laconically.

"They could get people killed."

"That's the fine line you'll need to walk," Paterson warned. "You have to make them think that they're getting what they want while protecting our current assets. In the process you'll take the heat."

McGarvey watched Hammond posturing for the TV cameras. It came down to the question of how much he really wanted the job, and why he wanted it. They were questions he'd been asking himself every day since the President had asked him to serve. Questions for which he still didn't know if he had all the answers.

A little over three months ago he and Roland Murphy, then the DCI, had been called over to the White House. They met the President, his chief of staff and adviser on national security affairs in the Oval Office.

The meeting was Murphy's call. He'd announced that he

was retiring as DCI because of his health, and that he wanted McGarvey to succeed him.

Murphy's retirement had been hinted at in the media, and just about everybody at Langley knew it was coming, and yet it came as something of a surprise to McGarvey that morning. Probably because he'd been too involved in running the Directorate of Operations to see the larger picture.

"I'd like you to take the job," President Haynes had said. "Or at least give it some serious consideration."

"I'm not the right man," McGarvey replied, shaking his head. "I'm just a field officer—"

"You're a hell of a lot more than that, and you know it," Murphy interjected. He turned to the President. "Everybody in the Company would be shocked if Mac *wasn't* appointed. Right now the DO is functioning with a greater efficiency than it ever has, because of him. He's a born leader. His people practically fall over themselves to do what he wants, because they know that if they didn't or couldn't do the job, he'd step in and do it for them."

"I'd probably be impeached if I didn't hire you," the President said.

McGarvey had to chuckle. "You'll probably be impeached if you do, if Hammond has anything to say about it."

"You'll have to face him and his crowd, but you leave handling him to me," the President said sternly. "The CIA has been run by politicians, or by military men who've turned politician, entirely too long," He glanced at Murphy. "No offense, Roland."

"None taken, Mr. President."

"I need a career intelligence officer at the helm. A man who knows the Agency, what it can and can't do from the ground floor up."

"I was a shooter," McGarvey said, no apology in his voice.

"Did you ever shoot at anybody in your military career?" the President asked Murphy.

"Yes, as a tank commander."

"With the intent to kill?"

"Yes."

"We're in trouble right now and you know it." The President turned back to McGarvey. "Besides fighting terrorists, Pakistan has gone back to its old tricks. They're on the verge of developing a thermonuclear device that could be strapped atop one of their missiles. The PRC is on the verge of a Pearl Harbor attack on Taiwan. Russia is falling apart faster than we thought would happen. All of Lebanon is on fire again. And half of the African continent is slaughtering the other half. I need information. I need it fast. And I need it unvarnished. You're the only man I know who can do the job the way I want it done, because you're not afraid to tell the truth no matter how much it hurts." The President sat back. He'd taken his shot. "I need you to run the CIA. Will you do it?"

"I'll think about it," McGarvey said.

"Fair enough. When Roland steps down you'll take over as interim director until you're confirmed or until you step down."

Once an intelligence officer, always an intelligence officer. God help him, but the past couple of months had been interesting.

"The matter before us today is whether this committee should recommend to the full Senate that it consent to or reject the President's nomination of Kirk Cullough McGarvey as Director of Central Intelligence."

McGarvey took a look at his opening statement, which Paterson had completely rewritten this morning, as Hammond droned on about the procedures for the witnesses, the questions and evidence that could be presented, and the documents that the CIA might be required to turn over. Paterson's theme was that since the attacks on the World Trade Center in New York and on the Pentagon, it was more important than ever for the United States to be well informed about what was going on in the world. There would almost certainly be more attacks on our military installations and ships, and on civilian targets. It proved that we needed a strong intelligence agency. In order to maintain superiority we needed an experienced man at the helm of the CIA. Not the CEO of a major corporation, but a person well versed in the business. Someone who had worked at every level; from field officer in Germany, France, Russia, Hong Kong, Japan and France to deputy director of

Operations at headquarters. A loyal American. A man who obviously and repeatedly had placed his own safety and that of his family second to the security of his country. A man young enough to understand the new millennium with all of its technical means to lead the Agency to the next level of excellence.

Hammond had started on his opening statement, but McGarvey wasn't really listening. He laid Paterson's document back on the table. This was not going to be so polite, so neat and tidy as the Agency's general counsel wanted it to be. The hearings would mirror the real world; they would be down and dirty, contentious, and filled with bullshit because Hammond would tell a version of the truth as he saw it, and McGarvey would tell the committee a sanitized version of the way things really were. It would be like two women at an expensive cocktail party telling each other how good they looked while actually despising one another.

The other senators on the committee paid no attention to Hammond. They shuffled through their files and notes. The opening hours of these kinds of hearings were usually mild and polite. The real fireworks wouldn't start until later, perhaps in the second or third day, when the pressure would build. These were seasoned politicians who well understood that public perception and reality were often two separate things.

One of the C-SPAN cameras was trained on McGarvey, looking for his reaction to what Hammond was saying. He kept his face neutral. Every DCI before him had gone through this process. He suspected that none of them had enjoyed the experience any more than he did. And if he was confirmed, he would be back up here on the Hill testifying before Congress several times a year.

Paterson held a hand over the microphone and leaned toward McGarvey. "He's being too polite. He knows something, so you're going to have to stick with the script, at least today."

"It won't matter what I say. They're going to hear what they want to hear and nothing more." McGarvey glanced over his shoulder toward the back of the room.

"Who are you looking for?"

"Nobody important," McGarvey said.

Senator Hammond wound up his remarks and looked up from his notes. "Mr. McGarvey, do you wish to make an opening statement at this time?"

McGarvey glanced at the script that Paterson had prepared for him. He'd read it on the way over from Langley, and he more or less agreed with everything the CIA's general counsel had written. More than ever before, the United States needed the presence of a strong and capable spy agency to protect her interests in a world gone mad. The CIA needed a strong director; someone with experience and decisiveness; someone who not only understood America's enemies, but who perfectly understood the exact nature of the country.

That had been McGarvey's personal philosophy from the beginning of his career; you could not protect a flag that you didn't understand.

He'd always thought that he understood what it was to be an American. But suddenly he wasn't so sure any longer. Perhaps people like Hammond and Madden were correct after all; perhaps he was unfit for the job.

That was a question that had plagued him ever since the President asked him to take the job. Maybe he didn't have the moral or philosophical equipment.

He was, or at least he had been, an assassin. Such acts were against the law. Yet the law had never stopped him.

A few years ago someone had asked him who the hell he thought he was. "What gives you the right to be judge, jury and executioner?"

And now someone or something was coming after him; stalking him and his family; some dark, malevolent beast out of his past. Something. It was something whispering at his shoulder. He couldn't shake the growing feeling of dread.

He looked again over his shoulder for the Russian SVR *rezident*, but the man wasn't there. His absence meant something.

"Mr. McGarvey," Senator Hammond prompted.

"I'll reserve my opening remarks until later, Senator Hammond. But I'd like a written version to be entered into the record at this time."

"Very well," Hammond said.

A clerk came over, and Paterson handed him a copy of McGarvey's opening statement, a puzzled but resigned expression on his face.

Senator Madden sat forward, an almost radiant expression on her round face. "Excuse me, Senator Hammond, I would like to ask Mr. McGarvey a question before we proceed."

Hammond motioned for her to go ahead.

"It has come to my attention that you might not even want this job," she said. "Is that true?"

"Frankly no, I never wanted the job," McGarvey replied before Paterson could stop him.

"Well then—"

"I have a great deal of respect for President Haynes. He asked me if I would take the job. I couldn't say no. If I'm confirmed, it's my intention to remake the Agency completely."

Madden smiled warmly. "Maybe you and I are in agreement after all. I've been campaigning for quite a while to revamp the CIA. It's long overdue."

"I agree," McGarvey said. "But probably not along the same lines you've been talking about. I firmly believe that there remains a very strong need for the CIA. But for an agency that's leaner, meaner, better funded and equipped, and without three-quarters of the bureaucracy that has hamstrung almost every operation before it ever got off the ground."

"There's a great deal of inertia in an organization as vast as the CIA, wouldn't you say?"

"Too much."

"So it would take a very capable administrator to accomplish such a reorganization as you envision. Isn't that correct?"

"I might say yes, Senator, if we were talking about almost any other organization than the CIA."

"I expect so," Senator Madden responded smugly. "But isn't it a fact you have admitted that you are no administrator?"

"An officer in the field, whose life may very well be jeopardized by the kinds of policies being put in place at headquarters, respects professional competence over administrative expertise."

"Spies managing spies?"

"Yes, Senator. Just like the old days, when spies like Dulles and Donovan grew the Agency from nothing."

"But they were gentlemen."

Paterson reached for the microphone, but McGarvey responded to Madden's thinly veiled insult.

"Yes, they were, Senator. They came from the old school, when people believed in building institutions to help make this country strong, not tear them apart with no clear idea what should replace them."

The *Washington Post* had quoted Madden on more than one occasion calling for the dismantling of the CIA. The Agency, in her estimation, had cost the United States far more money and far more embarrassment than it was ever worth even on its best day. "A den of thugs," she had said.

She caught his insult, but if it bothered her, she didn't let it show. "You are going to tell us how you mean to bring the CIA back to the good old days?"

"If that's what you want to call it, yes, I will." McGarvey returned her smile. "I think it's time that we stop apologizing to the rest of the world for who and what we are." He looked at the other senators. "I'm here this morning to answer your questions, but not to make excuses."

"That's all well and good," Senator Hammond said. "But today has been reserved for opening statements. Are we to understand that you are passing on that opportunity?"

"That's correct."

"Why?"

"As I said, Senator, I'm here to answer your questions, not to make any kind of a political statement that would in any event be misunderstood."

Hammond laughed, and glanced at the others on the committee. "Very well, we'll leave it at that for today."

On the drive back to Langley Paterson was in an odd, buoyant mood, as if he was happy the way things had gone.

"They're either going to hire me, or they're not, Carleton. But I'm not going to screw around. I'll tell it like it is."

"When haven't you?" Paterson asked. "I'm surprised that the President hasn't phoned already to tell you to cooperate."

"We had the discussion two weeks ago. He told me to call them as I saw them." McGarvey had to smile. "He did ask me to promise not to shoot any of them."

Paterson laughed. "There's at least that."

It was around four when McGarvey got back to his office. His desk was stacked with memos, letters and files. In the couple of hours before he left for home he fended off a dozen phone calls congratulating him on his performance at the hearing. The calls were mostly from old friends, but not from the President.

One of the files on his desk was the Nikolayev dossier. There wasn't much to it, only one grainy black-and-white photograph showing him in a group at the Frunze Military Academy, and a few pages of dry facts. He had been an experimental psychologist in Baranov's old Department Viktor, though there was almost nothing on what his duties were. He was an old man now; his wife dead, no children or any other relatives alive. It was a wonder the SVR was still interested in him. McGarvey couldn't fathom why Otto was also interested.

Adkins had the NIE and Watch Report in good shape for Thursday's meeting of the U.S. Intelligence Board. By throwing himself into work Adkins was in much better shape than he had been this morning. He was going back to the hospital around six, and he asked McGarvey to thank Kathleen for stopping by.

"It cheered her up having another woman to talk to."

"How'd she know that Ruth was in the hospital?" McGarvey asked.

"I assumed that you told her."

McGarvey shook his head. "I didn't have a chance. But she knows more people in this town than I do. Somebody must have told her. Anyway, I'm glad she got up there."

Kathleen's ability to find out things apparently without working at it, was another trait he found attractive. She was bright, intuitive and seemed to know when and where someone needed her. She would have made a great spy. Like the good ones she was able to see connections between seemingly unrelated bits and pieces. And it was just this sort of activity, helping other people, that would bring her out of the blue funk she'd gotten herself into.

He got word from Security that their Bethesda detail would have to be extended through the night because Rencke had not yet been released. Louise Horn was still not back at the NRO, nor was there any answer at the apartment. She was staying at Otto's bedside around the clock. She was like a lioness with her cub; no one would get near him without answering to her.

It took several minutes for Dr. Daishong to answer his page at the hospital. He sounded cheerful but all out of breath as if he had just run up a flight of stairs. He'd been on duty a straight twenty-four hours, and he was finally on his way home, he explained.

"I'm keeping him until tomorrow afternoon."

"Why? What's wrong with him?" McGarvey asked.

"His injuries from the accident are superficial. Not serious. But the poor man is tired, anemic and quite possibly on the verge of a nervous breakdown. Good heavens, I'm told that he possibly eats nothing but junk food."

"He's been under a lot of pressure."

"He's sleeping now, and we're filling him with vitamins to build up his system. I suggest that you go easy on him."

"Yes, thank you, I'll try."

"I have told your security people that he is to have no further visitors."

"Who has come to see him?"

"In addition to his friend who will stay the night, only Mrs. McGarvey."

"Take care of him, Doctor. We need him back here."

"Better that you take care of him so that he doesn't come back to me."

On the way home, traffic snarled because of the heavy snow, McGarvey had time to put everything that had been happening into some sort of perspective. Troubles came in threes. There were weird weeks in which everything seemed to go wrong at once. The trick was to take it a step at a time. All things would pass, even the bad times.

"Has Liz called yet?" he asked Kathleen. "They're back down at the Farm for the next couple of days. But she promised that she would call you."

"Not yet, but she will," Kathleen said brightly. Her dark mood of last night and this morning seemed to have dissipated.

They kissed, and he sat down at the counter as she stirred a pot on the stove. "Smells good whatever it is."

"Spaghetti. Is that okay?"

"More than okay, I'm starved."

She gave him a smile. "What'll it be, a double or a triple?"

"How about a beer?"

She laughed as she got him his beer. "Tom Hammond must be slipping."

"Did you watch any of it?"

She shook her head. "Between that arrogant prick, and that tight-assed Madden broad I didn't dare. I might have been tempted to storm down there and rip out their tongues."

McGarvey was shocked. He'd never heard his wife talk like that.

"Close your mouth, dear," she said sweetly. "There are times when only a certain kind of language seems appropriate."

"It's a good thing that you didn't watch."

"That bad?"

He nodded. "Yeah. But from their standpoint they're right."

"Oh, for goodness sake, think about what you're saying."

"When we get into the closed sessions there'll be a lot of . . . incidents out of my past laid on the table." He looked inward for the flash of an instant. The image that remained in his mind's eye, like a sunspot on his retina, was of a hell in which dozens of people were falling back in slow motion; blood splashing in every direction; rivers of blood; people screaming in terror, their hands out in supplication. He flinched.

Kathleen poured a glass of wine. She put it down and came around the counter to him, a look of deep concern on her face. "What's the matter, Kirk?"

For a moment longer McGarvey couldn't speak. He shook his head and looked up into her eyes. "I've done the right things, haven't I?"

She took him in her arms. "Not always, my darling. None of us ever do, didn't you know that?" She looked down at him and offered a small reassuring smile. "But on balance you've always been headed in the right direction. That's a lot more than most people can say."

"They were bad."

"Yes, they were. And if you didn't have a conscience, if you didn't feel remorse almost all the time, you would be no different than they were. Nothing more than mindless, immoral thugs."

WEDNESDAY

WEDNESDAY

EIGHT

MAYBE IT WAS HIS PAST
CATCHING UP WITH HIM.

WASHINGTON

McGarvey arrived at the Hart Senate Office Building a few minutes before 10:00 A.M. wearing a dark blue suit with side vents, a pale blue shirt and plain matching tie. Kathleen had laid out the clothes for him, as she did most mornings. If Hammond and the others were going to shoot him down, at least he'd crash in style.

Two dozen newspaper and television reporters were waiting in front of the Capitol as McGarvey's limousine pulled up.

Yemm headed a phalanx of four bodyguards, who escorted McGarvey and Paterson across the sidewalk and up the broad marble stairs, keeping the media at arm's length. The extra muscle was the Office of Security's idea, and though McGarvey initially objected Paterson convinced him to go along with it. "Hell, if nothing else a little extra show of force right now might put a burr under Hammond's saddle."

McGarvey had to smile. He was being manipulated. But it was for his own good, though it was still another thing he was having trouble getting used to. "Well then, I guess it's the least we can do."

McGarvey's name had never been exactly a household

word, but after yesterday's televised hearing and the front-page stories in the *Washington Post* and *New York Times*, in which he was characterized as having drawn the battle line in the sand, he was becoming fair game for the crazies.

Before they left Langley Yemm insisted that McGarvey wear body armor under his shirt. "You're a tempting target now, boss," Yemm said, trying to keep it light. But he was deadly serious.

"If they know what they're doing, they'll go for a head-shot."

"Nothing we can do about that, but even guys like Begin would have come out alive if they'd been wearing."

The vest was light, and not noticeable, but it was hot. McGarvey figured that it was going to be a bitch of a day on more than one account. But at least the process had begun. There would be no more waiting for the other shoe to fall, no more wondering if he should take the job or even if he was going to be confirmed.

Like yesterday the hearing chamber was packed. Capitol security officers at the tall double doors were turning people away. As McGarvey and Paterson worked their way to the witness table, McGarvey scanned the crowd for any sign of Dmitri Runkov, the SVR *resident*. But he didn't spot the Russian, who would have been sitting with the other foreign service officers.

"Can we get a list of who was here yesterday and today?" McGarvey asked Paterson as they took their seats.

"Sure," Paterson said. "Do you have a reason?"

"I'll tell you about it later."

Almost immediately the clerk of the hearings came in and announced the committee members. Opening the sessions this way was Hammond's idea. He'd been a circuit court judge in St. Paul before being elected to the Senate. He thought that the clerk added dignity to the proceedings.

The senators filed in, and when they'd taken their places and the audience was settled, Hammond reminded McGarvey that he was still under oath.

"I had hoped to be further along then we are," Senator Hammond said. "But it seems as if there is even more material to cover than I first supposed." He gave Paterson a stern look. "I would hope that we can keep today's session on a more businesslike basis in the interest of saving time."

"If that is your hope, Senator, it's our hope as well," Paterson said with a straight face. "Mr. McGarvey has a very full schedule at Langley, as you can well imagine."

"Mr. McGarvey is not the Agency's director yet," Brenda Madden interjected.

"He is working as interim director, Madam Senator," Paterson said. "And has been for some time now."

"Surely the intelligence professionals at the CIA are used to the comings and goings of political appointees and are capable of doing their jobs unsupervised by a titular director for the time being."

"On the contrary, Senator Madden, as you well know, Mr. McGarvey is a twenty-five-year veteran with the Central Intelligence Agency. He has earned the respect and loyalty of everyone out there."

"Including you, sir?" she gibed. It was well-known that Paterson had only reluctantly left his New York law practice to help straighen out the sometimes sticky legal positions that the CIA found itself in. Because it was a challenge, and because the previous president had asked him to do it, he had agreed. He had no love for the world of the spy, like his predecessor Howard Ryan had, but he was doing a good job.

"Yes, including me," he said.

Madden's expression darkened. It wasn't the answer she'd wanted.

Hammond glanced over and gave her a questioning look. She shrugged and sat back. Hammond turned to the first of the fat files piled in front of him.

"I think we can dispense with the usual examination of Mr. McGarvey's personal data. Let it be noted in the record that Kirk Cullough McGarvey was born October 9, 1950 in Garden City, Kansas. Parents were Herbert Cullough and Claire Elizabeth, both deceased. Attended Garden City elementary, middle and high schools, graduating cum laude in 1966. He attended Kansas State University, graduating in 1970, also cum laude. Two bachelors of science, one in mathematics the other in political science." Hammond looked up. "That is an unusual combination."

"Is that a question, Senator?" McGarvey asked. Kathleen said to push back, and he was already starting to feel irascible. His desk *was* piled with work.

"No," Hammond said after a beat. "I won't belabor the point, but looking over your high school and college records I see that you were not involved in any extracurricular activities. No sports, no clubs, not the debating team, or the trap and skeet squad. Can you tell us why?"

McGarvey leaned over to Paterson. "Is this necessary, Carleton? What the hell is he looking for?"

"Leadership qualities, and they can ask anything they want to ask."

McGarvey turned back and shook his head. "None of that interested me, Senator."

"What did you do with your spare time? Scouting, fishing, hunting, camping?"

"I wasn't in the Scouts, but I did fish and hunt with my father. I helped around the ranch, and when I was fifteen I learned how to fly-fish."

"You were a loner even then," Hammond said, and before McGarvey could say anything, Madden sat forward, a file open in front of her.

"Were you large for your age, Mr. McGarvey," she asked. "I mean in school, were you bigger than the other kids in your class?"

"I don't understand the question."

"Oh, it's simple. I'd like to know if you were the big kid on the block. You know, the class bully."

McGarvey smiled and shook his head. "I was big, but I wasn't the bully. My father drummed into my head from the start that fighting never solved anything. We had one rule in our house, and that was: no hitting. My father never even spanked me."

"What if you did something wrong? Did he send you to bed without supper?" Brenda Madden asked with a smirk.

"He would explain to me what I did wrong and tell me that

he was disappointed in me. That's all. That was worse than a beating."

"That's a curious view for a man who, along with his wife, worked on nuclear weapons at Los Alamos. Wouldn't you think?"

"No."

"No hitting," Brenda Madden mused, as if she found the notion quaint. "And no involvement in the glee club, no homecoming king, or football team—excuse me, I forgot, no hitting. But you didn't even join the cheerleading squad. Or was it because you were barred from those activities?"

Paterson's hand shot out and clamped over the microphone. "What's she getting at?"

"I'd almost forgotten," McGarvey answered.

"Mr. McGarvey?" Brenda Madden prompted.

Paterson hesitated a moment, then removed his hand.

"No, I was not barred from after-school activities. It was a mutual agreement between my parents and the school board. It was a small town, and I was a good student."

"But you agreed not to play sports. Why?"

"I was involved in an after-school fight. It was a long time ago."

Brenda Madden held up a Finney County Department of Juvenile Justice file. "There were four of them. Football players. It was strongly suspected that you had used some sort of a weapon. They believe that it might have been a baseball bat. All four of those boys ended up in the hospital, two of them in critical condition."

Senator Hammond was beaming. Some of the other senators, however, looked either uncomfortable or puzzled.

"One of them is still confined to a wheelchair," Brenda Madden hammered. She looked directly at the television cameras. "But I find it terribly odd that nothing happened as a result except to bar Mr. McGarvey from after-school activities. The families of the four boys didn't even sue. Certainly your parents had enough money. They owned a rather substantial ranch. In fact they were wealthy by the standards of those days. Yet no lawsuits. Unless payments were made under the table." She smiled viciously. "Which was it, Mr. McGarvey?

Payments under the table, or were the families simply terrified of retribution from a loner. Maybe by today's standards a Columbine High School odd duck."

"Objection," Paterson broke in. "I assume that those are sealed juvenile court records, Madam Senator."

"That's of no consequence—"

"There was no weapon," McGarvey said.

"You don't have to answer to such an obvious smear tactic," Paterson warned. He was angry. Madden and Hammond were loving it.

"You were saying, Mr. McGarvey?" Madden prompted again.

"I didn't use a weapon."

"You hurt those boys with your bare fists?"

"Yes."

Madden looked to Hammond, but he shrugged. This was her ball, he would let her run with it. "Over what? Were you arguing over something they said to you. Did they call you a name?"

"They were gang-raping an eleven-year-old girl in the woods behind the school. I stopped them."

Brenda Madden's mouth opened, but nothing came out.

"We'll check that," Hammond said. He shuffled some files. "Now, moving—"

"If Senator Madden had done her homework, she would have discovered that the four boys were sent to juvenile detention until they were twenty-one. One of them died in a knife fight in prison, one of them committed suicide shortly after he got out, and the other two, so far as I know, are still alive. I never followed up."

Except for a few sniggers in the audience, the chamber was silent.

"It's not something I'm proud of, Senator Madden," he said. "But I don't like bullies. Never have."

"What sort of chores, Mr. McGarvey?" the committee's vice chairman Senator John Clawson, asked. He was the senior Republican from Montana, a Westerner, tall, outdoorsy, who felt more comfortable in jeans than in a business suit. He was a rancher.

"On the ranch?" McGarvey asked.

Hammond broke in. "I think that we have spent sufficient time on Mr. McGarvey's youth."

"Indulge me, Tom," Clawson said easily.

McGarvey shrugged. "Mostly feeding cattle."

"While they were out on the range. Probably during the winter when the grass was scarce for them. You rode in the back of a truck or hay wagon, and tossed hay bales to them."

"Something like that."

"That's not an easy job," Clawson said to Brenda Madden. "I did it myself as a kid. Builds up your muscles, gives you a huge appetite. Puts on pounds real early." He smiled. "No mystery there."

"I wouldn't know," she replied.

"At least you have one friend," Paterson said in an aside to McGarvey.

"I would like to move on, if possible," Hammond said. "There are a few areas of concern that I'd like to touch on today. If we can get to them we'll meet in camera tomorrow."

There were no objections.

"You joined the air force directly out of college, finished OCS and were commissioned a second lieutenant in October. Subsequently you attended the Air Force Intelligence Officers schools at Lackland Air Force Base and Kelly Field in San Antonio, Texas, and then were assigned to embassy duty in Saigon." Hammond looked up from the file he was reading from. "Is all of that correct?"

"Yes."

"What was your job in Saigon?"

"Senator, I don't know if that material is still classified. I'll have to check on it for you."

"It's not classified," Hammond said. He passed a document to one of the Senate pages, who brought it to the witness table. It was a release of documents form under the Freedom of Information Act.

Paterson looked it over and gave it to McGarvey. The release contained a list of twenty-one separate operations for a period between the summer of 1970 and the winter of 1972.

McGarvey had been there for most of that time. "Recognize any of these?"

McGarvey glanced through the list, and he knew immediately which operation Hammond would home in on and why. "Most of them."

"Operation Phoenix-II," Hammond said. "Were you involved with it?"

"Yes, I was," McGarvey said. Hammond had not disappointed him.

"Could you tell us about it?"

"It was a South Vietnamese military operation. Captured VC and North Vietnamese regular army prisoners, especially officers and noncoms, were brought in from the field to a divisional headquarters in Saigon, where they were extensively debriefed. The results were collated and the information was shared with special U.S. and South Vietnamese field units."

"What kind of information?" Hammond asked. "What were they looking for, specifically?"

"They were trying to find out the names, ranks and locations of high-ranking North Vietnamese officers."

"For what reason?"

"They were targeted for assassination."

"Were you personally involved in any of these hit squads?" Hammond asked. "Did you assassinate any of the targeted officers?"

McGarvey glanced again at the list. "Phoenix-II was the fact-finding mission. The field operations themselves are still classified."

"But you were involved, weren't you," Brenda Madden said, unable to contain herself. "You were right up to your elbows in blood over there. It must have been a grand time."

McGarvey counted to five, maintaining as close to a neutral expression on his face as he could. But Senator Madden must have seen something, because she flinched. "Fifty thousand American men and women were killed in Vietnam, Senator. I can't believe that it was a grand time, as you put it, for anyone over there." He shook his head. "Senator Hammond spent a tour in Vietnam. Maybe you should ask him."

"There were torture squads conducting Phoenix," Hammond

continued without missing a beat. "What was your part?"

"I was an observer."

"Did you participate in the torture of any North Vietnamese prisoners of war?"

"No, Senator, I did not."

"But you didn't stop it."

"No."

"You spent two tours of duty in Vietnam," Brenda Madden said. "You must have, at the very least, found the place interesting."

"There was a job to be done, and I thought that I could help make a difference."

Brenda Madden could hardly contain herself. She nearly laughed out loud. "Come now—"

"The CIA recruited you right out of the air force," Senator Clawson broke in. "You spent a third tour in Saigon as a civilian. Do you believe that you made a difference?"

McGarvey had asked himself that same question many times. It was one of the questions on his recurring list. He shook his head. "I don't think that any of us made a difference in Vietnam, Senator. We should not have been there in the first place. But since we were, we should have been allowed to fight the war to win it."

"Then why did you keep going back?" Brenda Madden demanded.

"Because I love my country," McGarvey said. His tone of voice and posture were a direct challenge to her. She had been skirting around the issue of his loyalty as well as his abilities to run the CIA, during the hearings and in the media.

Television cameras were split between focusing on Brenda Madden's face and on McGarvey, who sat unmoving, looking at her as if he might be looking at an interesting new species of animal in a zoo. Almost no one missed his expression, least of all Senator Madden.

Paterson sat forward. "Mr. McGarvey has demonstrated his loyalty to his country time and again over a long and distinguished career," he said. "I might respectfully remind the senators that Mr. McGarvey took the same oath of office that every CIA officer takes—"

"The same oath that Aldrich Ames swore to?" Brenda Madden blurted. She immediately recognized her mistake. She tore her eyes away from McGarvey and looked over at Hammond, who had his gavel in hand.

"Excuse me, Mr. Chairman," she said. She turned back to McGarvey. "I did not mean to imply in any way a comparsion between you and Mr. Ames."

McGarvey nodded. "I didn't think you had, Senator."

"Thank you, Mr. McGarvey," she said. "There will be other areas that I'll want to explore with you."

"But not today." Senator Hammond jumped into the breach. "These proceedings are adjourned. We will reconvene tomorrow at ten o'clock in the morning." He banged his gavel once, and started gathering his files.

An even bigger mob of reporters was waiting for them in the corridor and outside on the Capitol steps.

Yemm and his security detail kept them at arm's length, and Paterson thought it best that McGarvey answer no questions on the way out.

Riding away, McGarvey thought about all the other DCIs who had been called to the Hill and raked over the coals. Now it was his turn, and he was feeling something dark riding over his left shoulder. Maybe it was his past catching up with him. Tomorrow the questions would begin in earnest: in the meantime he had the India-Pakistan problem to deal with.

NINE

EVERY MAN BELONGED TO HIS OWN AGE.

LANGLEY

Otto Rencke stopped at the security gate leading to the CIA, trying to quell the voices inside his head that threatened to drive him nuts. He'd been going crazy all of his life. But this time it was serious. He was frightened. He rolled down the window of Louise Horn's RAV4 and handed out his security pass to the civilian guard. He recognized the man. But he thought that he recognized everybody. He couldn't get the pictures out of his head.

"How're you feeling, Mr. Rencke?" the guard asked. He was a younger man, very short hair, stand up bearing, probably a former marine. He was smiling pleasantly.

"Well, ya know, I've had better days," Rencke said. He spread out his arms and let his head droop. "Hell of a way to spend Easter." The guard didn't get it, and Rencke saw it at once. He grinned. "Sorry. Bad, bad joke. I feel like I've been in a car accident. My head hurts, my shoulder hurts, even my butt hurts."

"You'll be black-and-blue. But from what I heard, you were lucky." The guard handed Rencke's ID back. "Anyway, welcome back."

"Yeah, thanks."

The road had been plowed, but it was icy in spots. Rencke drove very carefully though he wasn't paying attention to what he was doing. Sometimes he was superattuned to his surroundings. At other times, like now, the world around him was an out-of-focus blur.

Early in his study of mathematics, when he was seven or eight, he had learned to compartmentalize his brain. Much like a computer works on a complicated problem by breaking it down into its constituent parts and then chewing on each of the parts simultaneously, Rencke had learned to divide his thinking.

He'd explained to a mathematician at the University of Wisconsin's Van Vleck Hall that he was like a juggler keeping a half-dozen balls in the air while balancing on one foot, singing and watching television. He was able to work on a number of different problems at the same time. There were perhaps as many as a half-dozen compartments running as many problems at any given time in his head. When he had the bit in his teeth, like now, the number rose to a dozen or more. He'd never been able to count them all without breaking his concentration. He thought of his abilities like a Heisenberg Uncertainty Principle. If you stopped to count the operations, the operations themselves fell apart.

But the problem he'd always faced, especially now, was that each compartment in his brain was separated from all the others by a gigantic wall. Sometimes when he wanted to find the doors between the walls he couldn't. It was like being lost inside a constantly moving kaleidoscope. The images were beautiful, and complex, and very often useful, but he wasn't able to see the real world because of his fragmented thinking.

Usually, if he tried very hard, he could find a ladder and climb over the top of the wall and look out over the entire field. But this time he couldn't even find the ladder. Which is why he thought that he was going seriously crazy.

The driveway through the woods branched off into the various parking lots. It was a few minutes after noon and all but the visitors' lot were full. Rencke was a high-ranking officer, so he had an assigned spot in the underground garage.

This place had become home to him. Everyone else came here to work. He came to live.

The nurses had given him a sponge bath at the hospital, and Louise had brought his fresh jeans, a bulky knit sweater, clean socks and new Nike running shoes, and she'd had his MIT jacket cleaned. His long frizzy red hair was covered by the bandage, over which he wore a watch cap. When he came through the doors the guards did a double take. They'd never seen him cleaned up.

Upstairs in the computer center he went directly back to the area he'd been using for the past few weeks. He stopped in his tracks. The dozen monitors were still up and running, but the desk and long worktable he'd used were clean of everything except nonclassified materials. The wastepaper baskets and shredder bins were empty, the photos and charts he'd taped to the wall dividers had been taken down, and the litter on the floor had been picked up.

"Sorry, Otto," Karl Zimmerman, chief of computer services, said.

Rencke spun around so fast he almost lost his balance. He was light-headed from the accident. Louise wanted him to stay at home, but he'd left as soon as she'd lain down on the couch and fallen asleep.

"Hey, take it easy," Zimmerman said, reaching for him, but Rencke pulled away.

"Where are my things?"

"It was Mr. McGarvey's call. We put everything in the safe room. Are you okay?"

"What about the stuff in my car?"

"We've got that, too," Zimmerman said. "Would you mind telling me what you've been working on? We burned a couple of your disks trying to find out."

Rencke glanced at his monitors.

"We didn't dare touch them," Zimmerman said. "The whole place would probably blow up." The chief of computer services was a slightly built man with thinning gray hair and a pencil-thin mustache. He was very bright, although his real strength was administration: "If you can direct the geeks, you can run the system," he said, not unkindly.

"It's too early," Rencke mumbled. "Lavender, you know. Bad. Getting badder." There was light spilling over some of the walls in his head, like the sun on the horizon, or like the blue glow from the core of a swimming pool reactor. That in itself was a thought: a chain reaction building like a chain letter. What if there were impurities in the core? What if just the right impurities were added, would the results tell what was going on inside. Like an alloy. "Bring my things back," he said, absently.

He took off his jacket, tossed it toward a chair, which it missed, then started bringing his search engines back on-line one at a time.

Even now when his head was fragmenting he could appreciate the simple beauty of his programs. His machines had no opinions except for an appreciation of a deft touch on the keyboard. They didn't care about his background, about how he looked, his clothes, his hair, his mannerisms, which he knew were sometimes odd, out of the ordinary. They did things for him without question or judgment.

When he looked up it was a few minutes after six and he was surprised to see that someone had brought back all of his files. The table was piled, the floor was littered and several satellite shots of downtown Moscow were pinned to the divider.

Zimmerman was gone and McGarvey stood in the doorway in his place. He seemed tired to Rencke, maybe even a little battered and bruised, as if he, too, had been in a car accident. He looked sad, the thought popped into Rencke's head.

"Oh, wow, Mac," Rencke said. "What are you doing here?"

"Trying to find out what the hell is happening to a friend of mine. His name is Otto Rencke. You haven't seen him, have you?"

Rencke turned back to face his monitor. He was inside the SVR's Washington embassy computer center. He touched the escape key and the monitor went blank.

His narrow shoulders were hunched forward. He was aware of the aches and pains from his accident; he wasn't taking the pills the doctor had given him. He wanted his head screwed on as straight as possible under the circumstances.

For the first time ever he didn't know what to say to Mac. Something terrible was about to happen, and he had no idea how to explain it to anyone. Even his own thoughts were so compartmentalized that his brain was a jumble; a jagged mish-mash of garishly colored shards of glass. He remembered when Mac had come to him the first time here in Washington, in Georgetown, at the Holy Rood house. The CIA had dumped them both. Mac had gone to ground in Switzerland, and Otto had hidden out in the open at home. Neither one of them had been doing much of any significance.

But then Mac had come calling with a little problem that had wound up with the deaths of Baranov and the Company's DDO, John Lyman Trotter, Jr. But more than that, Mac's coming back had legitimized Otto. Given him a fresh purpose for his life. It was a gift that he could never repay. Not in a thousand years, not in ten thousand million years of trying.

He could see McGarvey's reflection in the blank screen of his monitor. "I'm busy, what do you want?"

"I want to know what's going on?"

"What do you mean?"

"Louise called. She's worried. You should be at home."

Rencke shrugged. "How about that." He spoke to the computer screen. "My girlfriend calls, and the DCI comes running. What are you *really* doing down here?"

"The Russians have been looking for one of their people from the old days. They've asked Interpol and the DGSE for help. He disappeared in August, and you requested his file not too long after that. You've got Liz involved now, and Karl is worried that you're going to fry his entire system. Put all of us out of work."

Rencke had been holding a pent-up breath. He blew it out all at once as if he was trying to fog up his monitor. His fingers flew over the keyboard, burying the program he'd been working with to a place where it could not be retrieved by anyone but himself.

"It's lavender, didn't I tell you?" He glanced at the extremely high-altitude Moscow photos on the wall, then turned to McGarvey. "I'm down here in my lair doing my job, just like you hired me to do, ya know," he grumbled. "But I can't do it like this. People coming and going, screwing with me."

Some of the files on the table lay open, some of them displayed the old KGB's sword-and-shield logo. Post-it notes were stuck to some of the pages.

"The hospital was boring," he said, looking away again. "Nothing to do. The nurses were as bad as Louise. She's trying, ya know, but trying too hard. Sometimes it drives you crazy, ya know?" He grinned and shook his head. It was the best he could do, but he was bleeding inside. Hemorrhaging. "She should be at work. We should all be at work. Twenty-four, seven."

McGarvey cleared a spot on the table and perched on the edge. Otto kept trying to avoid eye contact, but McGarvey was patient. As if he had all the time in the world.

"Sometimes it's easier to see than other times. Then Zimmerman comes in here and wipes out everything I was trying to do. Tossed some of it, cause I can't find a whole bunch of stuff. Shelved the rest. I lost good time here." His left hand rested on the keyboard, as if he were making reassuring contact with an old, troubled friend.

"His name is Nikolayev," McGarvey said. "The Russians haven't been able to find him, and neither has Interpol. He was one of Baranov's Department Viktor experts. I think maybe you've found him."

Rencke shook his head. "I don't know what you're talking about."

"You requested his file."

"No."

"Jay Newby said you did," McGarvey said, suddenly angry. His patience was wearing thin. "What the hell are you playing at, Otto?"

Rencke's eyes were wide. "If I pulled his file, it had to be something routine. Probably the Interpol request. But I don't remember, Mac. Honest injun." He waved his arms. "Circle the wagons, but I'm on the inside, kimo sabe, not on the outside."

"You're lying—"

"No!" Rencke cried. "Liz is just looking down your track

to write the history. She wants to be her father's biographer. But it's hard on her, too, ya know?"

"What are you talking about?"

Rencke was frightened. His eyes were filling. He couldn't control his hands. "It was the pictures of your folks. The accident. She saw the file. I tried to stop her."

McGarvey's parents had been engineers at Los Alamos toward the end of the Manhattan Project. For a few years they were suspected of being spies for the Russians. The taint had carried over to their only son. But it wasn't true, of course. The whole thing had been a complicated Baranov plot to discredit McGarvey before he rose to become a power in the CIA. They had been killed in an automobile accident that had probably been engineered by the Russians. The Kansas Highway Patrol accident scene photographs had been explicitly grisly.

Elizabeth had a chip on her shoulder. Maybe she was angry at her father for not sharing the details about her grandparents' deaths. Seeing those pictures now had to have been a terrible shock.

"What are you doing rummaging around inside the old KGB files?"

"It's for Liz."

"She can run a computer," McGarvey said. "You were supposed to be working up the NIE in-depths on Pakistan's and India's technical capabilities."

"I transferred the file to your machine two days ago," Rencke said. He was defensive, like a cornered animal.

McGarvey glanced at the Moscow photos. They were date- and time-stamped for sometime in August. "You're lying to me, Otto. You're into something down here that you're not telling anybody. Lavender, you said. What's lavender?"

"Maybe it's you who are lying," Rencke shot back. There was a cold, distant edge in his voice. "Maybe you don't want to be DCI after all."

The remark took McGarvey's breath away. It was so unlike Rencke. He was practically family. It was as if a favored son had turned on his father for no reason.

"You're right, it is lavender, and it's getting worse," Rencke said. "Two weeks, maybe less, then I'll tell you."

"Now—"

Rencke shook his head. "You can't be boss of everything. You lost that right the first time you pulled a trigger." Rencke suddenly clasped his hands in his lap, and his jaw tightened. He was on the verge of something terrible.

McGarvey nodded. "Get out of here, Otto. Go home and get some rest."

"Are you firing me?"

"Go home and get some sleep. We'll talk later." McGarvey walked out without looking back.

Rencke closed his eyes and saw bright flashes of color: spikes of blue, circles of orange, shards of red; violets, purples, lavender.

The dark beast was coming, and he didn't know how to stop it. He was sure that he was finally going crazy.

McGarvey went downstairs to the indoor pistol range in the basement more than a little confused. Otto was an odd duck, but he was a friend. He'd never thrown a tantrum like this before. Something was eating at him; something serious enough to change him. He'd had a maniacal look in his eyes that McGarvey had never seen. He was on the verge of fragmenting into a billion pieces. McGarvey was afraid that if Otto fell apart, there'd be no one strong enough or bright enough to put him back together.

And the CIA needed Otto.

McGarvey had always used the compact Walther PPK autoloader in its 7.65mm version. But recently he'd been convinced to upgrade to the 9mm version, and he was still having a little trouble with the placement of his second and third shots. The more powerful ammunition tended to raise his pattern. But he was quickly getting a handle on the problem.

Yemm went with him, and they each fired two hundred rounds. Afterward McGarvey went back to his office. He had to get some help for Otto before it was too late.

Dr. Norman Stenzel, chief of the CIA's Office of Medical Services Psychology Clinic, came right up. Ms. Swanfeld was gone for the day, and Yemm waited in the outer office, the door to McGarvey's office open.

It was snowing again. McGarvey watched how it blew around the lights, and he shivered. Every man belonged to his own age. It was a snatch of something he'd picked up somewhere. Voltaire would not have liked the twenty-first century. Nobody these days cared about the primacy of the Catholic Church. Religion was not such a big part of most people's lives as it had been in the eighteenth century, though Voltaire would have perfectly understood the current struggle between Islam, Christianity and Judaism.

McGarvey turned when he heard the Company psychologist come in. Dr. Stenzel looked like an academic, as did a lot of the people in the CIA. Beard, longish hair, tweed jacket with leather elbow patches, even corduroy trousers and a serious, studious demeanor; all of it was right out of the sixties. He reminded McGarvey of the actor Robin Williams, with his boyish, off-center smile.

"Have a seat, Doc," McGarvey said. "It's not me who needs you, I'm asking for a friend."

Dr. Stenzel's grin widened. "That's what they all say."

"It's Otto Rencke."

Stenzel had started to sit down, but he stopped, his good cheer instantly evaporating. "I see." He sat down. "What's the problem."

"He's under a lot of strain. I think that he might be on the verge of a nervous breakdown."

"I'm not surprised, Mr. Director. In fact I've expected it for a long time." Stenzel tried to regain his smile, but it was uncertain. "People like him are always on the edge. Classic."

"I'd like you to talk to him."

Stenzel thought about it for a few moments. "I'll try, if you can get him to come to my office. We'll have to do this on my turf. God only knows any shrink would love to get his hands on someone like Otto Rencke. The man is fascinating. But I don't know if I'll be able to do anything for him."

"But you'll try."

"Sure. It's guys like him who design the tests I'm going to use. If he doesn't want to open up, it'll be me who comes out looking like a basket case." Stenzel shrugged. "What's he done that made you call me?"

"He's irritable, forgetful, off in another world. More than normal. Maybe even dangerous. It's like he's ready to explode. The person I used to know as Otto Rencke isn't the same person working for me now. It's like somebody's impersonating him."

"That's not possible, is it? A double?"

"No," McGarvey said. "He's coming apart, Doc. I think he needs help."

"I'll do what I can. How about tomorrow morning. Ten?"

"He'll be there."

Dr. Stenzel eyed McGarvey with some curiosity. "What about yourself, Mr. Director? You look as if you could use some R and R."

"It's the season."

Stenzel waited.

McGarvey got up and came around the desk. "We're putting in a lot of hours because of my confirmation hearings and because in the meantime the real work still has to get done around here."

The meeting was obviously over, but Stenzel didn't get up. "My job description is real simple. I'm supposed to look after the mental health of everyone in this building. A lot of bad stuff can happen if someone goes nuts around here. Including you, Mr. McGarvey. Maybe especially you."

"No, I didn't hate my mother."

"That's nice," Stenzel said, grinning like he was getting a joke.

"It's overwork. We're all tired."

"I understand that you and your ex-wife got remarried. Congratulations. How is she handling what they're trying to do to you on the Hill?"

Yemm had come to the door. McGarvey glanced over at him, and Yemm shrugged. Stenzel was doing his job.

"It's depressing her," McGarvey said. "She's tired, like the rest of us. Distant sometimes, forgetful. She and our daughter are going round and round."

"Speed bumps," Stenzel said. He got up. "We all get them

from time to time. Tells us to slow down and smell the roses."

"That simple?"

"Yup. You need a vacation."

"Tell me about it," McGarvey said. Stenzel made to leave, but McGarvey stopped him at the door. "How can you be so sure about my wife without first talking to her?"

"When you were put up for DCI, another background check was automatically put into motion. That includes the backgrounds of your wife and daughter, as well as your friends. I'm a part of the process."

Speed bumps, McGarvey thought. They all were going a little crazy because of the hearings, because of the workload and, in Liz's case, because she was pregnant.

His daughter hadn't been herself for several months. Part of it was the pregnancy; she was a little frightened about losing the baby again, and a little angry because her physical abilities were diminishing. But that was only a part of it. According to Otto she had set herself up as her father's biographer. Looking down his track would affect her. But he didn't know if he could help her come to terms with what she was discovering, because he himself hadn't fully come to terms with his own past.

Rencke was already gone, so McGarvey phoned the apartment and got a worried Louise Horn.

"I made an appointment for Otto to see Dr. Stenzel in Medical Services tomorrow at ten. Make sure he's there, would you?"

"I'm worried about him, Mr. Director."

"Yeah, so am I."

After he hung up he stared out the windows for a long time. The entire world around him was going crazy. But thinking like that was in itself crazy.

What price? he asked himself. What price?

THURSDAY

TEN

THEY WERE COMING FOR HIM NOW. BACK FROM
THE GRAVE. FROM A PAST THAT HE COULD NOT
CHANGE.

WASHINGTON

They arrived at the committee hearing room a couple
of minutes before 10:00 A.M. McGarvey hadn't slept
well last night, and he looked forward to being here
with a sense of despair, of uselessness, of wasted effort.

The same media crowd waited on the steps and in the broad
marble corridor, but civilian guards at the chamber doors
barred their entry. Only those with the proper passes were
allowed inside. This morning's session was to be held in camera. Dark secrets were to be revealed, senators exercising their
oversight duties. All patriotic and necessary.

But it was a horrible joke as far as McGarvey was concerned. DCIs had been testifying before Congress in secret
sessions since before Colby, and reading their exact words the
very next morning in the *Washington Post* or *New York Times*.

There were more people in attendance than McGarvey had
expected. He didn't know most of them, but the senators had
the right to invite anybody they chose.

A Senate page brought over a manila envelope to Carleton
Paterson. "Senator Clawson sends this to you with his com-
pliments, sir," the young girl said.

The envelope contained lists of everyone who'd attended the hearings on Tuesday and Wednesday, as well as a list of those expected to be here this morning.

Dmitri Runkov, the Russian intelligence service Washington *rezident's* name wasn't on either of the first two days' lists. Neither were any Russian embassy representatives. Their absence struck McGarvey as ominous.

Something was happening. Something just beyond his grasp. Otto knew about it and was lying. The Russians not being here meant something.

"Problem?" Paterson asked.

"I don't know. Maybe. But it's nothing urgent."

"Wouldn't do me any good to press you, I suppose," Paterson said. He handed another list to McGarvey. This one contained a couple of lines on each of ten supersensitive Track III operations that McGarvey had been involved with during his twenty-five-plus-year career with the CIA. Track I operations were intelligence-gathering missions. Track II, which were more sensitive, involved some type of covert action. Track III actions, the most secret and most sensitive, involved the use of deadly force. In each of the cases on McGarvey's list there had been a death. In some cases many deaths.

The list brought back a lot of very bad memories for Mac. Too late to erase them now, he thought. Too late to go back and undo what had already been done. We can only hope to change the future, and even that hope is a slim possibility.

"Those are the problem areas we discussed," Paterson explained. "Whatever you do, don't volunteer information. But if Hammond or Madden has this same list, or even a part of it, we're in a fair bit of trouble."

Former CIA director Bill Colby called such operations the CIA's family jewels. They had to be protected at all costs.

McGarvey pulled himself out of his funk, and smiled. "Not too late to pull out, Counselor."

Paterson shook his head. "I wouldn't miss this brouhaha for all the world, Mr. Director."

The clerk came in, called the chamber to order and the senators, led by Hammond, filed in and took their places.

"I remind Mr. McGarvey that he is still under oath as far

as concerns these proceedings," Senator Hammond said. He looked as if he hadn't slept well last night either. It was well-known that the senator was a big drinker. Yesterday's contentious session could not have done much for his stress level.

"Yes, Senator, I understand," McGarvey said, thinking suddenly about Katy. At least she would be spared most of the ugly details today.

Paterson sat forward. "Do we have this committee's assurances that the members of the audience have the proper clearances and have been briefed on the necessary security procedures?"

"That goes without saying," Senator Hammond sputtered.

"Excuse me, Senator, but I'd like to ask a question before we get started this morning," New York senator Gerald Pilcher said.

Hammond motioned for him to go ahead.

"Mr. McGarvey, on Tuesday you were asked if you wanted this appointment, and you told us no, that you did not. But that you would accept the job because President Haynes asked you to."

"That's correct, Senator."

"Then let me ask you a related question. Why did you join the CIA in the first place: What was it, twenty-six, twenty-seven years ago? And two follow-up questions: Who recruited you and how was it done?"

McGarvey went back. He'd been young, cocky, brash, certainly arrogant. He was doing something that counted, something that his father and mother could be proud of. He caught Brenda Madden's eye. She was sitting back in her tall leather chair, fingers to her lips, a scowl on her face, her eyes narrowed. She looked like an animal ready to pounce.

"The CIA recruiters were on campus in my senior year. I talked to them. But Vietnam was chewing up our people, and I thought that I could do some good in the military rather than dodging the draft. By the time I finished OCS and Intelligence Officers School it was the spring of 1972, and I was sent to Saigon. I did my two tours, came back to the States and resigned my commission in June of 1974."

"Our troops were being brought home by then," Senator Pilcher said.

"That's correct, Senator. The drawdown began in 1973." McGarvey was back in full force; all of his memories intact and vivid. "I'd been given a telephone number by the CIA recruiters, so I called it, and the next morning I met with Lawrence Danielle who was the deputy director of Operations. He knew my parents, or knew of them, and he told me that I could do just as important a job, maybe even more important than I had in the air force or than my parents were doing down at Los Alamos. I thought about it and agreed."

"How long did you think about it?" Brenda Madden mumbled. But everyone heard her.

"About five seconds, Senator. I believed in my country just as strongly then as I do now."

"What happened next?" Pilcher asked.

"I went through the CIA's training program and worked on the Vietnam desk at headquarters until late 1975, when I was assigned back in-country."

Pilcher was startled. "Saigon had already fallen by then, hadn't it?"

"Yes, it had. But besides our POWs who were being repatriated, there were Vietnamese nationals who had worked for us who were marked for arrest and execution. I was sent in to help find them and then get them into Laos and eventually to Thailand."

"Who were those people?" Brenda Madden asked.

"The program was called CORDS. Civilian Operations Revolutionary Development Staff. They were part of what was being called the Hamlet Pacification Program to identify Viet Cong infiltrators at the village level."

"And mark them for assassination?"

"No. The VC were being offered amnesty. If they didn't want to switch allegiance to the south, they were treated as POWs for the duration."

"None of them were killed?"

"Some of them were killed, yes, Senator."

"Then the real reason that you joined the CIA and went back to Vietnam was exactly as I suggested yesterday. Because you wanted to involve yourself in the action by rescuing fellow assassins."

"By saving the lives of men and women who gave loyal service to the United States," McGarvey countered.

"If we could move along now," Senator Hammond prompted. "We have a lot of material to get through—"

"Were your rescue efforts effective, Mr. McGarvey?" Brenda Madden pressed.

"Not very."

She glanced at her fellow committee members. "Don't be modest. How many of the CORDS people, as you call them, did you actually rescue? I mean get across Laos to freedom in Thailand and then here to the United States. One hundred? Two dozen? Five or ten?"

"No."

"One?" Brenda Madden demanded. "Isn't it true that not a single one of those people was brought here?"

"There were some, I think," McGarvey said. "But not by me."

"Why?"

All the frustration came back to him. He shook his head. "They were not issued visas for one reason or another."

"You have no idea why not?"

"It was political. The war was unpopular, and it was over. We lost. Nobody wanted to deal with it anymore."

"Which made you angry," Brenda Madden said. She didn't wait for his answer. "That was simply the first step in Mr. McGarvey's disillusionment with his country, with the CIA, with power in general. With following orders." She glanced at the other senators while gesturing toward McGarvey. "It was the same in Berlin and Hong Kong and France. Every assignment ended up a disaster for one reason or another. But always it was Kirk McGarvey in the middle of it. Not following orders. Working outside of his charter. Taking matters into his own hands. Charging in, guns blazing."

McGarvey sat back in his chair to let her rant. She was right in more than one way. The CORDS rescue operation had been a total disaster. Not as a field exercise, but in the political arena at home. And she wasn't far off the mark when she accused that the aftermath of the Vietnam War had started him on the path of disillusionment. But then she hadn't brought up the sorry episode of James Jesus Angleton, who looked so hard for moles inside the CIA that he all but brought the Agency down. And she wasn't aware of John Lyman Trotter, Jr., McGarvey's friend since the CORDS days, who turned out to be the mole that Angleton had sought.

But that was much later, after McGarvey had been fired.

Brenda Madden stopped to take a breath, and McGarvey stepped into the breach. "Was there a question in there, Senator?"

Even Hammond seemed to be fascinated by the California senator's hatred for McGarvey. But he was content for the moment to allow her to continue. His agenda in the hearings was a purely political one. He wanted to be president, and he wanted to cut President Haynes down to size at every possible opportunity.

But Madden, who'd moved to San Francisco as a young woman, had shaped her political career as an activist. She was anti–nuclear power plants, anti–free world trade, and virulently anti-Republican and the party's fiscal conservatism. In her estimation the only reason the social welfare programs of the last half century had failed was because not enough money had been spent on them. Instead of squandering our taxes on the B-2 bomber and stealth fighters, or nuclear submarines and fabulously expensive aircraft carriers, the money could have been much better spent on educating young, black, single mothers.

President Haynes and the Central Intelligence Agency were prime examples of the people and Beltway "old boys" clubs that she most despised. And McGarvey, who'd once inadvertently wondered out loud at a Washington cocktail party why Madden had never married, epitomized both. He was a friend of Haynes, and he was running the CIA.

"Let's cut to the chase," she said. "Actually you weren't in the CIA for very long. At least not as a card-carrying employee with a desk, a regular paycheck and benefits. Saigon, Berlin, Hong Kong, and Paris with stints at Langley, and then you were fired. Everything that you did afterward for the CIA was freelance. Isn't that so?"

"That's correct, Senator."

"Good. Let's talk about Santiago, Chile. Operation Title Card." She smiled. "You people at Langley come up with the most interesting code names."

"A machine picks them," McGarvey said.

"Yes, I know," she said. "It's too bad that the entire Agency couldn't be run with such imagination."

Title Card was not on Paterson's list. It was a Track III ops, but tame by comparison with some of the other operations McGarvey had been involved with. But she would milk it for all it was worth. Sensationalizing a dismal mission that had satisfied no one. Hopefully she was so blinded by her own agenda that she would miss the connection between Santiago and two other operations that sprung out of it. One involved a director of the CIA and a former U.S. senator. The other involved a president of the United States.

"What would you like to know?" McGarvey asked.

"Tell us about the operation, in your own words," Brenda Madden said.

"I was sent to assassinate Army general August Piñar, who had been indicted by a U.S. court for ordering the deaths of more than two thousand civilians, most of them dissident students, some of them the wives and mothers of the opposition party, and several of them Americans."

No one stirred. This was the first time in history that such a high-ranking officer of the CIA had made such an open admission.

"Actually I didn't catch up with him until three days after I got to Santiago and checked in with the chief of station. The general suspected that he was being targeted by us and barricaded himself with his wife and three children in their compound in San Antonio, about sixty miles outside the capital on the coast.

"I had seen the documentation, the pictures of the bodies lined up inside the Estadio Chile, audio recordings of torture sessions, and three film clips of three groups of women and some children lined up on their knees in front of a long trench.

Officers walked down the line firing their pistols into the backs of the prisoners' heads. The bodies fell or were pushed into mass graves. Some of them were still alive, raising their arms for mercy.

"General Piñar was in all three of the film clips. He personally shot at least a dozen women, and when it was over he refused to order his soldiers to fire the coups de grâce into those still alive. Instead he ordered the bulldozers to bury them alive."

The picture had been so vivid in McGarvey's mind that when he arrived in Santiago he was sure that he could smell the stench of the rotting corpses. He shuddered.

All eyes were on him. Even Brenda Madden had nothing to say for the moment. Paterson looked at him with an expression of sorrow mixed with a horrified fascination.

"I am what I am," Mac had once admitted to Larry Danielle. "An assassin." The acting DCI had been an old man then, with his own memories starting as a senior member of the OSS during the war, and participating in the formation of the CIA. The motto in the early days at the Agency had been Bigger than State by '48. They'd gotten their wish and then some. "What you are is a product of this business, dear boy," Danielle told him in his fatherly way. "Get out while you still can."

Turn away now and run, run, run. Don't look back. Get out while there's still time to save Katy and Liz and the baby. Hide. Jump out of the light, and pull the shadows back in around you.

"I got to him by subduing one of his guards, dressing in the man's uniform and entering the compound. He was in bed asleep with his wife. I shot him once in the head with a silenced pistol, and then got out of there, back to Santiago. The next morning I flew home."

"Did you harm his wife or children?" Senator Clawson asked.

"No."

Brenda Madden roused herself. But for the moment even she was subdued. "His wife had to have been damaged psychologically."

"I'm sure that she was," McGarvey admitted. What he hadn't told the committee, or anyone else for that matter, was that the general was not asleep. He and his wife had been in the act of lovemaking. His wife spotted McGarvey and was about to cry out, alerting the guards just outside, so McGarvey had killed her.

"Who issued the orders?" Clawson asked.

"Mr. Danielle. He was acting DCI at the time."

"That's very convenient. He is now deceased," Brenda Madden said. "But your orders were changed. A Senate intelligence oversight committee voted to reject the assassination, and you were ordered not to go through with it. Yet you ignored those orders and went ahead on your own. Isn't that so?"

"I wasn't informed of the new orders until after I had returned to Washington."

"According to you."

"Yes, Senator, according to my sworn testimony, then and now."

"But you were sacked anyway, weren't you?" she continued to hammer.

"Yes."

Senator Clawson interrupted. "Knowing what you know now, would you have gone ahead with the assassination?"

McGarvey had agonized over that question for a very long time. He could never forget the horrifed look on the woman's face, knowing that she was about to die. It wasn't until years later that he had learned that Christina Piñar had styled herself as a female Mengele. She had tortured many of the prisoners, and had even ordered the harvesting of their hair and gold fillings, the money going directly to her. Knowing that she was a monster just like her husband did not erase his memories, however. Nor did they ease his pain. He had murdered two defenseless people.

He nodded. "Yes. General Piñar was a bad man. He would almost certainly have continued killing innocent people. The CIA thought that there was a real possiblity that he would take over the military government."

"Why were you fired?" Clawson asked.

"Political expediency," McGarvey answered without hesitation. "The CIA is an executive branch agency. The Senate was trying take control, as it has on several occasions since."

"Oversight—" Hammond blustered.

"Yes, Senator, I agree that the CIA needs oversight. But *responsible* oversight." He looked directly at Brenda Madden. "I have no doubt that I'll read about my testimony in tomorrow's *Washington Post*."

There was an angry stir from the senators as well as from the audience. Hammond banged his gavel for order.

"You're not doing yourself much good here," Senator Clawson said, not unkindly.

"You'll either recommend to confirm me or you won't. But for the sake of the men and women working for me I want you to understand that you're putting their lives at risk by criminally sloppy security measures. If you want answers, then understand that the information you're looking for could cause the United States a great deal of damage if it becomes public."

"Like everything you've ever been involved with, the outcomes have always been the same," Brenda Madden interjected. "Bodies stacked like cordwood. Yet you have the gall to sit there and point a finger at us?"

Hammond was again banging his gavel for order.

"I have just one further question for Mr. McGarvey," Brenda Madden said.

Hammond stopped his gavel in midswing, and Brenda Madden turned back to McGarvey. Her voice was calm now, soft, even reasonable.

"Do you know how many men, and probably some women, whom *you* have murdered in your career, Mr. McGarvey?" she asked. "Do you even care?"

"I know the number," McGarvey replied softly. It was etched on his soul. "And yes, I do care."

They were coming for him now. Back from the grave. From a past that he could not change.

This time he could not stand up and face them because he didn't know who they were, or from what direction they were coming.

ELEVEN

"YOU'RE THE DCI. SOMEBODY'S ALWAYS AFTER
THE DCI. IT'S WHY YOU HAVE BODYGUARDS AND
RIDE AROUND IN AN ARMORED LIMO."

LANGLEY

Early in the afternoon McGarvey and Paterson rode back
to CIA headquarters. The hearing had dragged on for
nearly five hours without letup and Mac was bone
weary.

"Reading the records and hearing about those kinds of
things in person are two wholly different experiences," Paterson said.

"Living through them is even worse," McGarvey replied.
He managed a tired smile. "Still with me, Counselor? Still
think that I'd make a good DCI?"

Paterson nodded. "My friends call me Pat. If anything I
know for sure now that you'll make a damned fine DCI." His
lips compressed. "People like Senator Madden have their circles of friends. But they're usually very isolated and they
know it. Makes them bitter. Most Americans are reasonable
people. That includes politicians."

McGarvey had to laugh. "You're becoming more convinced, and I'm becoming less convinced."

"Come on, Mac, you can't believe that the direction they've
taken will hold up in the full Senate. It's primarily Hammond

and Madden who want to dump you. The others are, at worst, neutral."

McGarvey pulled himself out of his downward slide. "You're right, Pat." He glanced out the window at the snow piled along the road up to the headquarters building. Already it was dirty; mixed with salt, oil, dust. The next snowfall would cover it, but a day later it would be grungy again. He turned back to Paterson. "Postpone tomorrow's hearing until Monday. I need a couple of days off. Can you do that without creating a firestorm?"

"Sure. I don't blame you; we all could use a break."

"I'm taking Katy out of town for a long weekend." He caught Yemm's eye in the rearview mirror.

"Good. Don't even think about this place while you're gone," Paterson said.

They went through security together at the executive entrance. Paterson headed off to his office, leaving McGarvey to ride up with Yemm.

"Do you want me to have travel section work out something?" Yemm asked.

"Yeah. Let's go down to Jeff Hamil's place." Hamil had been the deputy director of Operations during planning stages for the Bay of Pigs. He had set up a CIA-owned compound on St. John in the U.S. Virgin Islands to train some of the top Cuban officers. In addition to the old sugar plantation great house with its long verandas, there were a half-dozen outbuildings, some of them barracks, that the National Park Service sometimes used for ranger training. Most of the island was national park land. McGarvey had been down there a couple of times with Roland Murphy, but Katy had never been. He expected that she would fall in love with the place, as he had. It was an idyllic tropical paradise.

"When do we leave?"

"I have to take care of a few things in the morning. Let's say we leave at noon, and come back Sunday afternoon."

"Just you and Mrs. M.?" Yemm asked.

"I'll ask the kids if they want to tag along."

"Safety in numbers," Yemm murmured.

McGarvey turned. Yemm had an odd, hooded look on his

face, as if he was hiding something. "What are you talking about?"

"In case somebody wants to take a potshot at you, boss. The more people that are around you, the tougher it becomes for an assassin to get close."

"I didn't know that anyone was after me."

Yemm shrugged. "You're the DCI. Somebody's always after the DCI. It's why you have bodyguards and ride around in an armored limo."

Dick Adkins agreed to take care of the President's Friday briefing. Mac would come in for a couple of hours to help put it together. There was nothing urgently pressing on the horizon. Even the Watch Report, which covered hot spots where fighting was taking place or was about to erupt, was mostly clear.

"How'd it go on the Hill today?" he asked.

"About how you'd suspect," McGarvey said.

Adkins shook his head. "I don't know why the hell you put up with it. If it was me, I'd tell them to take the job and shove it where the light never shines." He was bitter. "Murphy finally did, but at least he had a few friends up on the Hill. You don't have anybody. They all want to see you dead."

"Is that the consensus around here?" McGarvey shot back. He was getting irascible. His confrontation with Otto yesterday afternoon still weighed on his mind. Last night Katy had been in one of her dark moods because Liz hadn't called her. Senator Madden had gotten under his skin. Even Yemm had sounded a bleak note of discord. And now, Adkins.

"You know what I mean, Mac," Adkins said, not backing down. He looked like he wanted to hit something.

"No, I don't."

Adkins finally turned away. "Ah, hell. What's the use anyway?"

"What's the matter? Is it Ruth?"

"She's made up her mind to go the radiation and chemo route, rather than a mastectomy. She'll be sick as hell for months, but she wants to stay . . . intact for as long as possible, even though it might kill her."

"I'm sorry, Dick."

"Yeah."

"Do you want me to stick around for the weekend? Katy and I can go later."

Adkins shook his head. "You need the break worse than I do. I gotta keep busy, and you need to recharge your batteries for the big fight coming up."

"Do you think that the Senate is going to bounce me?"

"Of course not. I meant keeping you alive once you're sworn in. There're a lot of people out there who could come gunning for you and feel like they were doing the world a big favor."

Sitting alone at his desk, McGarvey asked himself the same question that Adkins had posed: Why the hell was he putting up with the pressure? He had an inkling of what a newly sworn in president felt on his first day in the White House. Despite all the Secret Service protection he was given, he was still vulnerable to some nut with voices in his head.

But if someone decided to come after the Director of Central Intelligence, it would most likely be a professional. The kind of man McGarvey had been. Still was.

He turned and looked out the windows at the snowy countryside. If someone was coming, it would be a person out of his past. Someone with a grudge, he wondered. Or someone with a darker purpose?

It would have to be someone who knew about his habits, about his comings and goings. Somebody who even now was watching him. Waiting for him to make a mistake. Waiting for him to slip up; one lapse of caution; the one time he left the house without his bodyguard, or without a weapon.

He shook his head. Or most likely no one was coming. Paranoia was not just a field officer's malady.

In the meantime the CIA needed help. A top-to-bottom reorganization that several directors before him had tried to do but failed. He was just egotistical enough to think that he could do it.

The President called on the direct line. "I think I'm going to recommend some remedial reading for you. Political science. You need it."

"I'm not going to give them the answers they want, Mr.

President," McGarvey said. "And without that I'll never get confirmed."

The President chuckled. "You let me worry about that part. The budget bill is coming up, which gives me some wiggle room. So long as you stick to the facts, you'll come out okay. But when you try to play their game, they'll eat you alive."

"I'm not a politician—"

"Nobody expects you are. But as DCI you're going to have to deal with the bastards whether you like it or not. So you might as well start practicing right now."

"You're right."

"Of course I am," the President said. "You can start by getting back on track with Hammond and especially with Madden. And before you jump up and down, hear me out. Those two are going to be on your back for as long as you're the DCI. That's a fact of political life. But Hammond wants to be president, so that's something I can use against him. And Brenda Madden has a deep dark secret that causes her to be afraid of me and be pissed off at the same time. She's dangerous, but she can be reasoned with, as long as you don't try to score points off her. Go along with whatever she says. Answer her questions with direct answers. Eventually she'll stick her foot in her mouth enough times so that Hammond will be forced to put a lid on her."

"Are you going to share the secret with me, Mr. President?"

"Nope. Just take it a step at a time, and we'll get through this."

"I'll do my best."

"If I didn't need you, if the Agency and your country didn't need you, again, I wouldn't have asked you to take the job. The CIA is in a mess. Fix it, Mac, or we're going to find ourselves dead in the water as a nation."

"Does that mean I can't shoot her?" McGarvey asked.

The President laughed. "Anything but."

McGarvey had his secretary telephone his son-in-law. She got him on his cell phone. He and Elizabeth were on their way back from the Farm in Williamsburg.

"How are the roads?"

"Slippery," Van Buren replied. "But we're just a couple of

miles from 495." They lived in Falls Church, so they were less than ten miles from home.

"If it doesn't get any worse, how about coming over for dinner tonight?"

"Good idea," Van Buren agreed immediately. "Liz wants to talk to her mother, and she wants to get her skis. We're going out to Vail for a long weekend unless you need us in town."

"What's the doc say?" McGarvey asked, alarmed.

"He told her to take it easy, that's all."

"We'll see you in a few hours then."

"Right," Van Buren said.

McGarvey phoned Yemm to tell him that Todd and Elizabeth were skiing at Vail this weekend, so it would be just the two of them going down to St. John.

Next he tried to reach Otto, but Ms. Swanfeld found out that he was still in conference with Dr. Stenzel. McGarvey went downstairs and used his security card to gain access to the observation room. They no longer used one-way mirrors; they were too obvious. Instead, they employed hidden cameras. Rencke's image was projected on the high-definition large-screen closed-circuit television monitor on the wall.

Two of Dr. Stenzel's assistants were monitoring the interview and taking notes. They started to get up, but McGarvey waved them back.

"I just came in for a quick look. I thought the interview was supposed to start at ten."

"It did," one of the assistant psychiatrists answered. "They've been at it ever since." He shrugged. "For all the good it's doing us."

"Isn't he cooperating?"

"Oh, he's cooperating all right, Mr. Director. Trouble is we can't make any sense out of what he's telling us."

Dr. Stenzel sat back and lit a cigarette. His jacket was off, his tie loose, his shirtsleeves rolled to the elbows. He and Otto sat across from each other in easy chairs, a large coffee table strewn with files, computer printouts and coffee cups between them. They were in Stenzel's office, a large book-lined room with a big window.

Otto was sitting back, his legs crossed, his Nikes untied, a dark, but mildly condescending expression on his face. McGarvey had a momentary doubt that the man with Stenzel was Otto Rencke. Yet it was Otto. He knew it was Otto.

"So, you've been fucking with me all day," Stenzel said. "What else did I expect?" He didn't seem bitter, just resigned.

Rencke shrugged.

"There are a lot of people in this building who are worried about you. Mr. McGarvey asked me to find out what's going on in your head. But it looks as if that's not going to be possible. Leastways not today."

"Do you want me to take another test?" Rencke's voice was flat, with only the vaguest hint of contempt.

"You've taken them all." Stenzel glanced at the papers on the coffee table. "I suppose that I could certify that you're unfit for service. But hell, you're probably just as sane, or insane, as the rest of us here."

"We all have our crosses to bear, Stenzel. Even me. Only I have a lot of work to do."

"So do I," Stenzel said. "But if you go off the deep end on us, you could do a lot of damage."

Rencke laughed. "If you mean to the Company's computers, you're right. But I wouldn't have to be here in the building to do it."

"The one thing that's clear in the mess that you've created for me is that you're depressed. Whether it's clinical depression or just the garden-variety blues, I can't tell. But I'll give you a piece of advice, the only advice I intend giving you. Keep up whatever it is that you're doing and you *will* have a nervous breakdown. Guaranteed."

Stenzel got up, rolled down his sleeves, snugged up his tie and put on his jacket.

Rencke got languidly to his feet. "What are you going to tell Mac?"

"The same thing I told you. That, and the fact I don't like being toyed with. You're a very bright man, but from where I sit I don't see anyone who is very nice. In fact, you're an asshole." Stenzel smiled and shook his head. "Now get out of here, please."

Rencke stared at the doctor for a long beat; hesitating as if he wanted to say something. But then he turned and left.

McGarvey knocked once and went into Stenzel's office. The psychiatrist glanced over McGarvey's shoulder to the open door into the observation room.

"How long were you watching?"

"Long enough to wonder who the hell you were talking to. That wasn't Otto Rencke. Or at least not the Otto Rencke I know. I thought I was watching a complete stranger."

"Unless he faked his eye prints he was the real McCoy," Stenzel said. "And not very nice. But I suppose nobody likes a company shrink poking into his head. Their jobs are usually on the line. You'd be amazed at some of the stories I've heard."

One of his assistants came to the door. "Do you want an inventory made up?"

"Don't bother," Dr. Stenzel said.

"We'll append our notes to the file."

Stenzel motioned McGarvey to have a seat, and he went around behind his desk and looked out the window. "I administered every test that I knew. MMPI, Rorschach, TAT, Edwards Personal Preference, Cattell, the works." He shook his head. "They were loaded with all the control keys. No way that he could have defeated them." Stenzel turned to face McGarvey. "And in the end I couldn't have told you for sure that Rencke wasn't, in fact, a ten-year-old black girl with schizophrenia, or a sexless alien from Antares."

"You said that he was depressed."

"That came out loud and clear, especially in the TAT."

McGarvey raised an eyebrow.

"Thematic Apperception Test. It's a series of twenty pictures showing ambiguous scenes. Like a man coming into what might be an old-fashioned sitting room or living room, with an odd look on his face. We ask the subject to tell us what he sees. Like what led up to the event in the picture. Or, what's happening, and how does the man feel, and what's going to happen in the end.

"Picking out Rencke's depression from his answers was fairly straightforward. But the test is usually invalid if the subject has no respect for the test or the person administering it."

"He had a tough childhood," McGarvey said.

"I'll bet he did," Dr. Stenzel replied. "I tried to work out a Maslow Hierarchy to see where he was going wrong, but even that didn't work out."

"What's that?"

"About fifty years ago a shrink named Maslow figured out that people have five basic needs, starting with the physical stuff, like food and clothing and shelter. Without those nothing else is possible.

"Next up the chart is security, which is our safety margin. We do whatever it takes to make sure that next week, next month or next year we'll have everything we need to maintain our physical needs. So we buy food and put it in the fridge; we save money; we try not to piss off someone who'll someday come back at us with a gun.

"After that is love, then respect, and finally what we call self-actualization. We want to be the best we can, self-improvement. Going to bed at night and being able to think that we're okay, that we're not doing so badly."

"What about Otto?"

"Well, for one he has some serious security issues. It's the same with DO people out in the field. They don't know when they'll be burned. Maybe they'll get shot, maybe they'll be imprisoned. Tortured. It's why they have a problem with divorce; love is next up on the scale."

"Should I force him to take a leave?" McGarvey asked. "We need him here, but if he's on the verge of exploding, it wouldn't do anybody any good to keep him. The man you talked to today was not the real Otto Rencke."

"Yeah, I know. I think he has another even bigger problem he's trying to deal with," Stenzel said. "He's hiding something, maybe even from himself."

"What is it?"

Stenzel spread his hands. "I don't know. But whatever it is could be tearing him apart worse than his depression. It's certainly feeding into his mood swings." Stenzel shook his head.

"He's in denial, I caught that from the test, too. But beyond that it's anybody's guess. Leave him in place, and he might do fine. On the other hand, if you pull him away from his job, you'll be interfering with his esteem needs. Self-respect."

"Damned if I do, damned if I don't."

"Sorry, Mr. Director, but it's the best I can do without his cooperation," Stenzel said. "The ball's back in your court."

TWELVE

. . . SOMETHING WAS COMING. GAINING ON THEM. SKULKING IN THE NIGHT. WAITING TO POUNCE.

CHEVY CHASE

McGarvey got home a few minutes after seven. Something that he had forgotten to do; something that had nagged at him all afternoon, even during his swim with Yemm and laps around the gym, came to him the instant he opened the door and smelled something good from the kitchen. He had forgotten to let Katy know that Liz and Todd were coming over for dinner.

The workmen were almost finished with his study already. Only some trim pieces had to be installed, along with the track lighting and carpeting. He put his briefcase on his desk, hung up his coat in the hall closet and went into the kitchen. She had a brandy waiting for him. The dining room table was set for four.

"Liz must have called," McGarvey said, giving his wife a kiss.

"Good thing she did; otherwise, you and Todd would have been taking us out to dinner." Kathleen gave him a warm smile. "How did it go today?"

"They didn't quite shoot at me, but it was close."

"Posturing peacocks," she said. "Hammond and Madden,

preening for each other. I wonder if they're sleeping together?"

McGarvey had to laugh. "Good thing you weren't up there with me. There probably would have been gunfire."

"You have just enough time to shower and change clothes before the children arrive. I told them to come early because of the weather."

"Did Elizabeth tell you that they were going skiing in Vail this weekend?"

Kathleen gave him a sharp look. "No," she said tightly. "Go change."

McGarvey took his drink, but stopped at the hall door. "We'll have to cancel the party this weekend."

"It's already been taken care of. And I'll finish packing in the morning." She gave him another warm smile. "Close your mouth, sweetheart. Your secretary called me."

"I thought we needed to get away."

"I know. But what about Otto? Is he back at work?"

"I sent him home for a couple of days. I think he might fall apart if we push him."

"I know."

"What do you mean?"

"Oh, I talked to Louise this morning. She was worried about getting Otto to see Dr. Stenzel. I had her put him on and explained to him that this was for his own good. He should grow up and get on with life." Kathleen pursed her lips. "He's needed someone like Louise for a long time. I'm glad he finally has her."

McGarvey studied his wife for several beats. She was an amazing woman. And she had changed again from earlier this week, and from last night. She was calmer, even serene; more like the old Kathleen; self-assured, happy, content. He didn't know if her anxiety had simply worn away of its own accord, or if it was because they were getting away for the weekend. Either way he was happy for her, and more than a little relieved.

"What?" she asked self-consciously.

"You're beautiful."

This time she smiled with her eyes. "Thank you."

McGarvey left the kitchen and went upstairs.

He finished his brandy, then took a shower and changed into a pair of khakis and a comfortable old flannel shirt. It was snowing lightly. Since Sunday the Washington-Baltimore area had received more than thirteen inches; probably a record, McGarvey figured. Some schools in the outlying districts had been closed yesterday, although downtown and all the way out to the Beltway, plows were keeping up with the snowfall for now. Playing in the snow while on vacation was entirely different from having to go to work in it every day. He was ready for the Caribbean.

When he got downstairs Katy and Liz were going into his study. His daughter stopped to give her father a peck on the cheek.

"Hi, Daddy," she greeted him brightly. At twenty-five she looked just like her mother had at that age: she was slender, with a pretty, oval face, high, round cheekbones, sparkling green eyes and medium blond hair that always looked a little tousled. Ordinarily her figure was boyish, but she had blossomed with her pregnancy. Her figure was fuller now, though unless you knew her well it would be difficult to tell that she was four months along.

McGarvey thought that she'd never looked more beautiful. In fact, in his estimation, all pregnant women were stunning. "Hi, sweetheart. How are you feeling?"

"Fat, grouchy and mean," she replied. She nodded toward the kitchen. "Go in and have a beer with Todd, would you? Convince him that I don't hate him. Mom and I have to talk."

Kathleen gave him a look that nothing was wrong. Girl talk. Men need not be present.

He smiled. "Will he believe me?"

"He'd better, or I'll pop him."

"Dinner's in a half hour," Kathleen told him, and she and Elizabeth went into the study and closed the door.

Todd had a beer. He was perched on the fireplace hearth in the family room, a glum expression on his broad, pleasant face. McGarvey got a beer and joined him.

"She told me to tell you that she doesn't really hate you."

Todd looked up and shook his head ruefully. "One minute

she's as sweet as Mother Teresa, and the next she's as mean as a junkyard dog." He was broad-shouldered and solidly built, like an athlete. When he got older he would probably be chunky, but for now he was formidable. His eyes were as bright a blue as Liz's were green. McGarvey couldn't wait to see what color the baby's eyes would be.

"Besides being mean, what's her latest project?"

"Just before we came over here tonight, she tried to move the refrigerator because she was convinced that there were bugs and mice nesting in the dirt behind it."

"If it's any consolation, her mother did the same thing," he assured his son-in-law. "Has she said anything else about the conspiracy theory that she and Otto were working on?"

"That was before the accident. She's into her superclean and superfit mode now. By the time we leave for Vail tomorrow, the apartment will be spotless, and she'll be itching to ski me into the ground."

"Her doctor said that's okay?"

"I talked to him myself. He wants her to stay off the black diamond runs. No booze and lots of rest. But he told her that this would be her last fling. Starting Monday she can't even go back to the Farm."

"Take it a little easy on her, Todd. And I'm not saying that just because she's my daughter," McGarvey advised. "Right now she feels fat, ugly and useless."

"Tell me about it."

"You need to assure her that in your eyes she's beautiful, that you still love her, and that you won't abandon her."

"She knows better—" Todd protested, but McGarvey held him off.

"Doesn't matter what you think she knows. It's what she wants to hear. What every woman going to have a baby wants to hear. That her partner is going to be there for her, no matter what."

"She's so goddammed stubborn."

"And you aren't?"

Todd flared, but then grinned ruefully. "If she could just relax once in a while."

"Is the honeymoon over?"

"I don't know if it ever began."

McGarvey knew that they argued, but this sounded like trouble. They were practically clones of each other, but they couldn't see it.

"Maybe you should get a divorce," McGarvey suggested.

Todd's grip tightened on the beer bottle. "That's not an option," he answered.

"Then do something about the situation."

"What?"

"Either roll over and play dead, or finesse her."

Todd shook his head. "She'd hate me either way."

McGarvey almost hated maneuvering his son-in-law so blatantly. But not quite. "Do you love her?"

"What?" Todd sputtered. "Of course I do."

"Then you have the magic bullet. Whenever she gives you some shit, tell her that you love her. It'll stop her in her tracks every time, provided she can see that you mean it."

"Oh, yeah?"

McGarvey nodded. "But it won't work unless you ease up on her, too."

Todd looked away. "I'll try anything."

"That's good," McGarvey said.

He turned around as Elizabeth and her mother came in. Katy had a glass of white wine, and Liz was drinking what looked like a plain soda water on the rocks with a twist.

"Just in time. We're starving," he said.

"If Todd missed a meal now and then, it wouldn't hurt him," Liz said crossly.

Todd pursed his lips and nodded. "You're right. You're beautiful, Liz. I love you."

Elizabeth started to make a sharp retort, but something in his eyes got to her. She softened and grinned at her father. "If you're his chief adviser, keep it up." She looked at her husband. "Flattery will get you anything you want."

He brightened. "Anything?"

Elizabeth glanced at her parents. "Well, you might have to wait until later for *some* things."

The moment remained in tableau, Todd and Elizabeth grinning at each other, until Kathleen motioned for Kirk to go out to the kitchen with her. She had him take the roast out of the oven and put it on the carving board.

"Ten minutes and you can start cutting it," she told him. She glanced toward the family room. "Something's wrong with her. She's hiding something."

McGarvey nodded. "I think it has something to do with work."

"This is starting to get ridiculous, Kirk," she said sharply. "She's pregnant. She has no business working in the field. She's your daughter, fire her."

"Do you think she'd stand still for it if I tried?"

"It would put her nose out of joint, but I'd rather see that than have something happen to her or the baby." Kathleen gripped McGarvey's arm. "Dave Whittaker can do it. You can make him understand."

"I can pull her from Williamsburg and put her on the Russian desk, but I'd have to give her and her section heads a good reason."

"She's pregnant, for God's sake."

"She's not in the field, she's not running the Course at the Farm, no combat sims, nothing but lectures and paperwork."

Kathleen gave her husband a critical look. "There's even more. You're hiding something, too. I can see it in your eyes."

McGarvey nodded. "She and Otto are working on something. All he tells me is that Liz is looking through some of my old files, maybe to do an in-house biography. She may have seen the file on my parents, including the accident pictures."

She closed her eyes for a moment. "Do you see what I mean?"

McGarvey was confused. "No, I don't."

"Otto and Elizabeth are working on something together. And now you're sending Otto home because he's falling apart." She spread her hands. "Do you think that it's a coincidence that our daughter is lying to us?"

"There's not much we can do for her if she doesn't want us to get involved with her pregnancy. At least not for now. And the other thing, with her and Otto, will be resolved in the next couple of days. I'll make sure of it."

Kathleen nodded after a moment, then busied herself with the rest of the dinner while McGarvey carved the roast. They all had wine except for Elizabeth, who stuck with Perrier. She and Todd seemed relaxed with each other, but there was an underlying tension around the table.

"I've relieved Otto from duty for a couple of days," McGarvey said when they were finished.

Elizabeth's eyes narrowed slightly. "That's probably a good idea. He came back too soon after the accident. But if he wants to keep working, he can do it from his apartment."

"What are you two working on that's got him so heated up, and you climbing down everyone's throats?" McGarvey asked his daughter.

"Otto and I aren't working on anything."

"Come on, Liz. You're putting together my bio, everybody knows that. Otto's got you digging through some of the old records at Fort Hill. But he's been working on something else, too. He won't tell me what it is yet, but it's got something to do with KGB files and with an old Department Viktor psychologist by the name of Nikolayev. Does any of that ring a bell?"

"No."

Elizabeth said it with a straight face, but this time McGarvey knew damned well that she was lying to him. "Maybe I should relieve you of duty, too."

"Come on, Dad. I have a job to do. But if I'm going to be treated like the director's daughter, I won't be able to get anything done. I'll never know if people are telling me the truth or just something that they *think* I want to hear. Let me get on with it."

"On with what?"

Something flashed across her face. "My job."

"You're four months pregnant, Elizabeth," her mother said.

"In the old days women went to bed for the entire nine months, Mother. This is the twenty-first century. Not only am I going to keep working, but Todd and I are going skiing this weekend. *With* my doctor's permission."

"Okay, sweetheart, if you want to be treated like an ordinary intelligence officer, so be it," McGarvey said.

"That's exactly what I want," Liz responded defiantly.

"You and Todd are relieved from duty at the Farm as of right now. I'll talk to Dave Whittaker and Tommy Doyle about your transfers. Starting Monday you'll be assigned to the Russian desk, and Todd will work for Jay Newby in the Operations Center."

"Dad—"

"Since you're going away for the weekend, I'll cut you some slack. But no later than Tuesday noon I want a full report on what you've been doing for the past ninety days. That includes *all* your day sheets and contact logs."

"What if I don't?" Elizabeth flared.

"Then I'll fire you."

Elizabeth started to protest, but Todd put a hand over hers. "Shut up, Liz," he told her. "The transfer is just until after the baby is born, right?" he asked McGarvey.

"We'll see. Once the baby comes your job specs will have to be reevaluated anyway."

Todd nodded after an awkward silence. "Liz's day sheet will be on your desk Tuesday morning."

"What time are you leaving for Colorado?" Kathleen asked. She was brittle.

Elizabeth turned to her mother. Sensing trouble, her lips tightened. "Eight in the morning." She glanced up at the clock. It was coming up on 9:00. "In fact we should get going now. We still have to get our ski stuff together, and I need to get some sleep. It's been a long week."

"Did your doctor consider the risk you're taking, going out to Colorado, considering what happened . . . last time," Kathleen asked.

"It's still snowing, Mrs. M.," Todd said. "The Beltway is going to be a mess. We have to go."

"I asked a question."

Elizabeth held herself tightly. "Yes *my* doctor considered the risk to *me* and *my* baby, and he gave me permission to go skiing if I was careful."

Kathleen turned to her husband. "What do you think, Kirk?"

"If they don't get going right now they'll have to stay the

night and they'll miss their flight. The roads won't be any better by morning."

Kathleen clenched her hands. "Be careful, Elizabeth. Would you do at least that much for me?" she said. "I'll worry all weekend about you and the baby. I'm sorry, I can't help it."

Elizabeth softened. "It'll be okay, mother. I want you and daddy to have some fun too. Soak up some sun. Washington will be here when we all get back."

"I'll get your skis out of the garage," Todd told Elizabeth. "Great dinner, Mrs. M." He got up and McGarvey went with him.

Elizabeth's skis, in their hardshell traveling case, had already been taken down from the rack on the back wall. Todd carried them out to his Land Cruiser SUV and attached them to the roof rack with bungee cords.

McGarvey glanced back at the house. He could see through the hall window that Kathleen was helping Elizabeth with her jacket.

"Watch yourself out there," McGarvey told his son-in-law.

"I'll make her take it easy."

"I don't mean just that," McGarvey said. "You and Elizabeth are field officers and I'm the acting DCI. We're targets. All of us, all the time."

A flat, professional look came into Van Buren's eyes. He nodded. "There isn't a day goes by that I don't think about it. Especially now with the baby coming."

McGarvey clapped him on the shoulder. "You know what to do. Both of you do. Watch your backs."

McGarvey helped his wife clean up, and afterward they went up to bed. He made sure that the house was locked up and the security system was up and running first. At the head of the stairs he stopped and looked down at the front door in the gloom of the front hall.

The scratching was coming again. It was like an animal in trouble trying to gain entry to the house. A rough beast, or merely a stray, he couldn't tell. But something was coming. Gaining on them. Skulking in the night. Waiting to pounce.

"Paradise is where I am," Voltaire wrote in *Le Mondain*. Life was what you made of it. Either a paradise or a hell. McGarvey wasn't sure which life he had created for himself and his family, though he was certain that he wanted paradise, or at least a little peace.

By the time he got undressed, washed up and climbed into bed, Kathleen was already half-asleep.

"Good night, Katy," he said.

"I wonder what we'll come back to," she mumbled. She rolled over, and within a minute her breathing deepened. She was asleep.

McGarvey turned off the lights, and for a long time he listened to the winter wind whipping around the eaves; the scratching, nagging feeling rising again at the edges of his consciousness.

In the old days he would have run first and looked back later. But he couldn't do that now.

Not now, he thought as he drifted off to sleep.

FRIDAY

THIRTEEN

MCGARVEY COULD FEEL THE PISTOL IN HIS
HANDS. FEEL THE RECOIL AS HE FIRED THREE
SHOTS AT THE TRAITOR. KILLING HIM.

CHEVY CHASE

McGarvey got home a few minutes before noon.
Three leather bags were packed and lined up in
the front hall. But Kathleen wasn't home. She'd
left a note on the hall table promising that she would be back
by noon; she had a couple of errands to run before they left
for Andrews Air Force Base.

Yemm came in, glanced at the bags and cocked an ear to
listen. "Mrs. McGarvey's not home?"

"She had a couple of errands to run," McGarvey told him.
"Put the bags in the trunk, would you, Dick? I'm going upstairs to change."

True to form, Kathleen had laid out his clothes; boat shoes,
white slacks and a colorful Hawaiian print shirt. She'd also
laid out a jacket for the trip to the airport.

He felt faintly foolish putting on summer clothes while
snow was falling, but when he was dressed his mood was
lighter than it had been all week. He found that he was looking
forward to the weekend for his own sake.

He transferred his Walther to an ankle holster strapped to
his right leg under his slacks. When he put his foot down and

turned around, Kathleen, snow still clinging to her Hermès scarf, was at the door, looking at him, an intense expression on her face.

"Is that necessary?" she asked. She sounded winded, as if she had just finished jogging a couple of miles.

"Considering what I am, yes, it is, Katy."

"Kathleen," she corrected. But then she smiled and shook her head. "There I go again." She came to him and they embraced. "Sorry, darling," she said.

"It's all right. Old habits die hard. For both of us."

She shivered.

"Come on, Katy," McGarvey said. "We're going to have a great weekend."

She looked up and squared her shoulders. "You're right," she said. "Give me ten minutes, and I'll be ready."

"I'll check to make sure that we're locked up."

"Does Dick have to come with us?"

"It'd be tough trying to get rid of him," McGarvey told her. "Having a bodyguard is part of the job."

"I suppose," she said.

McGarvey stopped at the door. "Did you get your errands done?"

"I went to church," Katy muttered.

"What?"

"I didn't think that I'd be so late. Father Vietski heard my confession. No big deal."

McGarvey came back to her. "Are you afraid to fly? We don't have to go to St. John. We can take the train to Florida and have just as relaxed a time."

"No, it's all right. I've never been to the islands."

"Are you sure?" he asked.

She nodded. "One hundred percent," she said. She gave him a reassuring smile. "Now, get out of here so I can change."

VC-12

The moment they lifted off from Andrews Air Force Base and broke out into the bright sunlight on top of the low deck of snow clouds, Kathleen's mood took a dramatic swing. She became bright and animated, as if she were onstage even though she was playing to a very small audience.

The Gulfstream VIP jet, one of several that the CIA used, was a navy aircraft, maintained and operated by naval personnel. Their captain was Lt. Cmdr. Frank White, a veteran of the Gulf War and the Bosnian peacekeeping operation. He was only forty-seven but looked much older because his hair was perfectly white. He smiled with his eyes and handled the airplane as if it were a toy in his capable hands.

His copilot, Lt. Rody Johnson, was a short-timer. He was going to work for Delta Airlines in the spring.

Their flight attendant was Ens. Judy Dietrich, a blond German from Milwaukee, who looked fifteen but was in fact in her thirties, married and the mother of three boys.

As soon as they were at cruising altitude and heading southeast out over the Atlantic, Ensign Dietrich offered them drinks. Yemm stuck with Pepsi, but Kathleen asked for Dom Pérignon.

"We're on vacation, and the government is paying for it, so why not live a little," she said. The remark was uncharacteristic. McGarvey could see a sharp edge of tension at the corners of her eyes and mouth.

"Maybe you should wait until we get on the ground," he suggested.

She waved him off airily. "Nonsense. It's going to be a lovely weekend. You said so yourself."

"Are you a little nervous about flying, Mrs. McGarvey?" Ensign Dietrich asked under her breath as she poured the champagne.

"Absolutely petrified."

"Would you like something—"

"The champagne is fine, thank you," Kathleen said. "But tell the captain to get us there posthaste if he would."

McGarvey took a glass of champagne and sat back. "We'll be in the islands in time for dinner."

"Let's eat out. I feel like I've been in jail for the past month."

McGarvey glanced at Yemm, who shrugged. "There's a

nice place in Frenchtown on St. Thomas. We can have dinner there before we take the ferry over."

"Do we have to dress?"

"Not in the islands," McGarvey told his wife. "That's the whole point."

"Because if we have to dress, we're in trouble," Kathleen said as if she hadn't heard him. "I didn't bring any good clothes. Just shorts and swimming suits and summer clothes." She sounded almost manic.

"That's fine, Katy," McGarvey said.

"I thought that if the restaurant in Frenchtown is nice, we might feel out of place dressed like this." She wore a soft yellow maillot over which she had put on a linen skirt, sandals and a scarf around her neck. She looked like a model in a Club Med commercial.

"You look great, Mrs. M.," Yemm said.

Kathleen dismissed him with a gesture. "You know that we have to be careful. Because of the hearings. Everybody in Washington is watching us."

"Not where we're going," McGarvey said. "And even if they are, it doesn't matter."

Kathleen shook her head. "It might not matter to you, Kirk. But appearances matter to just about everyone else in Washington." She smiled at Ensign Dietrich, who stood in the galley separating the main cabin from the cockpit. "Women know more about these things than men do." She was verging on the edge of hysteria. "Bill Clinton and his two-hundred-dollar haircut." She laughed. "Jimmy Carter and the killer rabbit, or his ridiculous *Playboy* interview. Lust in his heart, indeed." She laughed again and turned to her husband. "Do you remember Darby Yarnell, darling?"

It was a name out of the clear blue sky, and there was a clutch at his heart. He nodded. "That was the old days."

Yarnell, who had worked for the CIA in the fifties and sixties, had been a two-term senator from New York. He had been one of the people responsible for getting McGarvey burned after Santiago. He had been brought down during the Donald Powers investigation, and had been shot to death in front of the DCI's residence a million years ago.

McGarvey could feel the pistol in his hands. Feel the recoil as he fired three shots at the man he thought was a traitor. Killing him. He closed his eyes for a moment, and he could see the image in the surveillance camera trained on Yarnell's Georgetown house. The third-story bedroom window. Kathleen was there in Yarnell's arms. It was an image that was etched in his brain.

Of course the final blow came when they realized that Yarnell wasn't a traitor after all. But the man had caused a lot of damage. Ruined a lot of people because of his arrogance, his cocksure attitude that his was the only vision.

"It was before you came back from Switzerland the first time," she said. "Darby was part of the in crowd, and I was trying to storm the gates, as my father would say."

"He hurt a lot of people," McGarvey said.

"That's my point," Kathleen countered, and McGarvey had no earthly idea where she was going with the story, or why she had brought Yarnell's name up.

"I don't understand."

"He was the one man at the time in Washington for whom appearances meant everything. And yet he was the only man I ever met who apparently didn't need to care. Everything he did was perfect. His house was perfectly decorated. The clothes he wore were perfect; his shoes were always shined, his cologne wasn't overpowering and his parties were the best in the city. He spoke a half-dozen languages, he could quote Shakespeare, and there wasn't a restaurant or private collection in Washington that had a better wine cellar than his."

"I still don't understand."

"Why, appearances mean everything," she said, as if she were telling him a universal truth that everyone instinctively knew. "He was a spy, after all. And a bastard. Yet everyone in Washington, including me, thought that he was perfect. We were drawn to him like moths to a flame." She gave her husband a wistful smile. "That's what's important in Washington, don't you see, my darling? It doesn't matter if you're the best DCI ever to sit on the seventh floor if Washington doesn't accept your appearance. It doesn't matter if you're good; the only thing that matters is if you *look* like you're right for the job."

McGarvey forced a smile. "I don't really care—"

"You should." Kathleen held out her glass for more champagne. "Hammond and his bunch do." She was brittle.

"It doesn't matter if they confirm me or not. They'll get somebody else."

"Don't be silly, Kirk. You're the best DCI there ever was. It's only the idiots who don't know it yet." A dark cloud passed over her. "But once you're there, even your friends will try to cut you down." Then she smiled. "Isn't that so, Dick?"

"It's part of the job, Mrs. M.," Yemm answered. He was glum.

"Do you think someone will shoot him?" Kathleen asked. The question startled everyone. Ensign Dietrich almost dropped the champagne bottle, and the pilot looked over his shoulder through the open cockpit door.

"Come on, Katy, we're supposed to be on vacation." McGarvey tried to stop her, but she held up a hand.

"No, wait. Let him answer my question. I have a right to know if someone out there wants to make me a widow."

"There's a lot of them want it," Yemm said. He glanced at McGarvey, who shrugged.

"But will they go for it?"

After a moment Yemm nodded. "I think so."

"Well," Kathleen said. She looked at the others. "Isn't that peachy."

U.S. VIRGIN ISLANDS

They landed on St. Thomas when the sun was low on the horizon. By six it would be dark and after the stress of Washington, Kathleen admitted that she was too tired to eat out. She wanted to get directly over to the house on St. John, sit on a veranda with a cup of tea and look at the tropical stars.

Captain White taxied over to the private aviation terminal. When the engines spooled down, Ensign Dietrich opened the hatch. A pleasant, soft-spoken immigration official in short sleeves came aboard and checked their papers and aircraft registration. Even though these islands were a U.S. Territory, the formalities were still observed. When the man found out who he was dealing with he practically fell all over himself with hospitality. Drug trafficking throughout the Caribbean was a big problem; that, along with money laundering and gunrunning, had corrupted officials all the way up to the USVI's governor's office. It made the people here very nervous. Yemm took the man aside. They would be here only for the weekend. They did not want to read about the director's visit in the newspaper or hear about it on the radio. There would be no meetings with territorial officials. The CIA would take it unkindly if the news were to leak.

"Do you think that he'll tell anybody?" McGarvey asked. Kathleen was in the Gulfstream's head, touching up her makeup.

"The first man he sees," Yemm said. "But he'll pass along my warning, too. We'll be okay."

The crew would stay at a nearby hotel for the weekend. They were busy securing the aircraft's systems. Even here at the airport, security was a problem.

Yemm made a brief call with his cell phone. "Island Tours is sending over a helicopter," he told McGarvey when he was done. "It'll be faster than the boat."

"Good idea," McGarvey said. He, too, was tired after the busy week.

The Island Tours Bell Ranger helicopter came over and settled down on the tarmac twenty yards from the Gulfstream. McGarvey glanced out the door. It was just the pilot in the blue-and-white machine. He wondered how fast news traveled in the islands, if the pilot knew who his passengers were.

He and Yemm gathered up their bags, and when Kathleen was finished in the head they walked across to the chopper. He wondered if two days was going to be anywhere near enough time for them to come down.

McGarvey and Kathleen rode in the back while Yemm rode

shotgun next to the pilot. They headed immediately over Lindbergh Bay, then Water Island, skirting the south coast of St. Thomas. The sun had just dropped below the horizon, but already it was dark, and the hills rising up behind the city of Charlotte Amalie were studded with lights.

Three cruise ships, lit up like store windows at Christmas, were getting under way from the main docks east of downtown. The entire harbor was filled with more than one hundred boats of every size and description; most of them cruising sailboats escaping the northern winter. Traffic along the waterfront and commercial docks in town was heavy. This was a weekend at the height of the season; everyone in the islands played.

Pillsbury Sound, which separated St. Thomas from St. John, was only three miles wide. As they rounded Long Point, the smaller island came into view, as did the British Virgin Islands of Tortola and Jost Van Dyke to the north. All of the islands, including dozens of smaller ones, many of them uninhabited, rose out of the sea like something out of a James Michener South Seas adventure.

McGarvey had been here before, but he never got tired of the scenery. He could feel his tension beginning to subside.

Kathleen was looking out the window, her shoulders hunched forward as if she were carrying a huge weight on her back. She was strangely silent.

McGarvey touched her arm. "Are you okay, Katy?"

"They don't have a clue," she said. "Most of them. This is where they come when they want to climb off the real world. Tune out." She sounded tired and bitter.

He studied her profile. An unaccountable sadness rose up inside of him for all the years that they had lost together. But it was getting better, and he would make sure that they stayed on track. His premonitions of disaster were nothing more than the result of a guilty conscience. For years he had gone to sleep every night dreaming about the people he'd killed in the line of duty. Those dreams were coming back to haunt his waking hours now.

Yemm motioned for McGarvey to put on a headset. "The

pilot wants to know if you'd like to do a little sight-seeing tonight."

"No. We want to get settled in."

"There's no staff, so we're on our own for dinner."

"Just what the doctor ordered, so long as the kitchen is stocked."

"It is."

"How about tomorrow, sir?" the pilot came on. "Would you be needing our services? Perhaps an air tour of the islands. The Baths are a little crowded, but still nice. Or perhaps a picnic on Hans Lollick. No one lives over there, and I can guarantee you a deserted beach."

"The picnic sounds good," McGarvey replied. "Let's make it for lunch. Eleven o'clock."

"Very good, sir. And we will even provide the picnic lunch."

McGarvey heated a can of tomato soup and made BLTs. He brought their supper along with a pot of tea for Kathleen and a beer for himself on a tray out to the long veranda, which stretched the length of the main house. Kathleen sat in a tall wicker chair, her bare feet up on the rail, her eyes half-closed.

"Penny," McGarvey said, setting the tray on the low wicker table next to her.

"I never want to go back," she replied dreamily.

"It's a thought. But I think we'd get tired of the isolation after a while."

"Do you want to bet?" She sat up and looked at the tray, her eyes bright. "He can run the CIA *and* cook."

"The bacon is burned on one side and raw on the other. But if you don't mind, I don't mind."

She poured a cup of tea, and McGarvey opened the can of Bud. The house was perched on top of a steep hill that looked southeast across Coral Bay toward the open sea. The sky was filled with stars, but the horizon where the sky met the sea was impossible to make out. The trade wind breeze had died to a whisper, bringing with it smells of the lush jungles on the islands. The air was as soft as lotion, in the mid to high seventies. The television and phones in the house were shut off. They would remain that way. Yemm had retired discreetly to his wing of the house. Liz and Todd had arrived safely at Vail. And Washington and Langley were an entire universe away.

McGarvey had changed into a pair of swimming trunks and nothing else. He sat back, put his feet up on the railing and sighed.

"That's a pleasant sound," Kathleen said.

Several small boats were anchored in the bay. Their tiny masthead lights were white pinpoints on the water, swaying slowly in the gentle swells.

"Presidents run the country from Camp David," she observed. "Why couldn't you run the Agency from here?"

"I'd miss the traffic."

She looked at him and grinned. "Yeah, right."

"I'd never get anything done," he said after a while.

She shrugged.

McGarvey could feel himself drifting. A rooster crowed somewhere in the distance. Here they crowed all hours of the day and night, not just at dawn. It was *island time*, Murphy had explained it to him the first time he came here. Inappropriate and yet appropriate.

Something about that thought percolated at the back of his head, but he couldn't put his finger on what it might mean.

"Soup's getting cold," Kathleen said languidly.

"Yeah," McGarvey agreed. He put down his beer, got up and held out his hand. "Let's go to bed, Katy."

She smiled up at him. "Best offer I've had all day."

SATURDAY

FOURTEEN

"IT'S LIKE BEING STRANDED ON A DESERT
ISLAND . . . ALMOST OVERWHELMING, IF YOU
THINK ABOUT IT."

VIRGIN ISLANDS

They were up with the rising sun a few minutes after
6:00 A.M. Yemm had already started breakfast. While
Kathleen was taking a shower, McGarvey got a cup
of coffee and went out to the swimming pool. The morning
was gorgeous. The pool, held against the side of the hill by a
concrete retaining wall, was filled to the brim. Swimming in
it seemed as if you were flying over the hills and the sea
below.

"What would you and Mrs. M. like to do this morning?"
Yemm asked from the open patio doors.

"Let's see if we can round up some horses. I'd like to go
riding on the beach."

"No problem. The chopper won't be here until eleven."

"In the meantime, I'm coming in for a swim," Kathleen said
from the open bedroom doors at the other end of the house.

McGarvey looked up. She stood, one knee cocked, one hand
on the doorjamb, completely naked, a big grin on her pretty
face.

"I think that it's a good time to get back to the kitchen, I smell something burning," Yemm said, and he disappeared back into the house.

Kathleen came around to the deep end of the pool, walking on the balls of her feet, her narrow back arched, her movements like those of a runway model's.

She gave her husband a lascivious look, then dived cleanly into the water, surfacing a few seconds later right in front of him. "Last night was nice," she said in his ear as she pressed her body against his. "How about an encore before breakfast?"

"If you're going to act this way when we're on vacation, we're going to leave town a lot more often," McGarvey said.

"Making up for lost time," she murmured.

Their ride took them almost as far as East End, about six miles from the compound. Their horses were dove gray Arabians, gentle and very well trained, with a good turn of speed if they were left to it. Yemm had never sat on a horse in his life, but within fifteen minutes he could at least keep up with McGarvey, though not with Kathleen, who'd competed in equestrian events as a young girl and well into her college years at Vassar.

She was a superb horsewoman, and McGarvey was content to let her run circles around him without rising to the challenge. She was a pleasure to watch. He admired competence above almost everything else.

With the sun on his bare shoulders, his face shaded by a straw hat, the powder white sand, the aqua blue sea framed by the dense, intensely green jungle growth that rose into the hills, this was paradise.

McGarvey pulled up to let Kathleen ride on ahead. She was in her own world, just then, oblivious to the fact he had stopped.

"Mrs. M. knows how to ride," Yemm said at his side.

"Yes, she does. But I don't think she's been on a horse for twenty years."

"Some things you don't forget how to do," Yemm commented.

"How are we doing on time?" McGarvey asked. He refused to wear a watch today.

Yemm glanced at his. "We should start back."

"What about the horses?"

"I'll call the stable to come pick them up."

Kathleen looked around, realizing that she was alone, and pulled up short, wheeling her horse around.

McGarvey gave her a wave, turned his horse sharply back the way they had come, and jammed his heels into the animal's flanks. He took off down the beach as if he'd been shot from a cannon. He'd been raised on a ranch, and learned to ride about the same time he'd learned to walk. The horse was an extension of his own body; instead of two legs, he had four.

He leaned forward, giving the horse its head, and he flew along the hard-packed sand at the water's edge. It had been a long time since he had ridden like this, but Yemm was right; there were some skills that you never forgot.

Yemm shouted something from down the beach. McGarvey looked over his shoulder as Kathleen came up next to him.

He was leaned forward, riding flat-out, but Kathleen sat very high, her back straight, one hand on the reins as if she were on a leisurely trail ride.

She smiled sweetly, blew him a kiss with her free hand, and barely nudged her horse's flanks with her bare knees. The animal took off as if it had switched gears. The sound of her laughter drifted back to Mac, and he shook his head.

He reined his horse back to a slow canter, allowing Yemm to catch up with him. Kathleen looked back, then slowed her horse to a walk.

"Nice race, boss," Yemm said.

The Island Tours Bell Ranger helicopter touched down in the compound precisely at eleven. It was the same pilot as last night. His name was Thomas Afraans, and he was a native West Indian of Dutch ancestry. His English was British of the last century; but he seemed very knowledgeable and competent about flying.

The picnic lunch was caviar with toast points and lemon wedges, a good champagne, fried chicken and cold lobster, potato salad, French baguettes, an assortment of sliced cheeses and pickles, and, for dessert, strong black coffee in a large thermos, Napoleon brandy and petits fours.

They flew northwest across the jungle interior of St. John, coming out at Cinnamon Bay, where they crossed the Windward Passage between the islands.

Afraans kept up a running commentary about the fantastic scenery passing beneath them. There were dozens of islands between the north coasts of St. John and St. Thomas. Almost all of them were uninhabited. Lovango and Congo Cays, Mingo and Grass Cays, then Middle Passage across to Thatch Cay.

All of the islands were within sight of each other, many of them seemingly within swimming distance. Boats of all sizes and descriptions were everywhere; everything from tiny outboard motor boats to husky interisland cargo ships.

"The U.S. Navy comes here, too," Afraans told them. "To St. Croix. Mostly nuclear submarines. Now, my Lord, that is a sight to behold."

Hans Lollick Island, less than three miles off the north coast of St. Thomas, was the largest of the smaller unihabited islands. There were only a couple of places to land along its oblong shoreline. For the most part the island quickly rose from the water in a series of cliffs and densely overgrown hills to the interior summit almost seven hundred feet above sea level. But the beach that Afraans touched down on was broad and white, and was protected by headlands northeast and southwest that formed a perfect cove about eight hundred yards across.

Yemm jumped out first and helped Kathleen down. She immediately walked down to the water's edge. There was almost no wave action, and the water was so perfectly clear that they could see fish swimming and their shadows on the white sand bottom.

They unloaded the picnic baskets and coolers and took them up to the edge of the wide beach in the shade of the trees.

"I will be back at two o'clock to pick you up, if that is agreeable, sir," Afraans told McGarvey.

"Two is fine," McGarvey said.

"If there is trouble, you may simply call our dispatcher. Your cell phone will easily reach from here." Afraan's smile widened. "But, please, sirs. You will experience a most enjoyable time today. Guaranteed."

Yemm went to set up their picnic after the helicopter left. McGarvey went to Kathleen and took her hand. She seemed a little subdued, almost withdrawn. Her moods were volatile.

"You okay?" he asked.

"It's like being stranded on a desert island," she replied dreamily. "Almost overwhelming, if you think about it." The helicopter was rapidly disappearing in the distance. "There's no noise here."

"Would you like to go back?"

She looked up at him and shook her head. Then she smiled, coming out of her mood. "This is fine here, so long as I'm with you."

"Go for a walk?"

"Sure," she said.

They headed northeast along the beach, up to their ankles in the warm water. Kathleen was right, he decided. There were no sounds except for the splashing of their feet in the water. No people talking or laughing, no steel drum bands, no jet aircraft for the moment, no birds. The weather, the scenery and now the silence; it was a total contrast to Washington.

"You rode really well, this morning," McGarvey told her.

"Thanks," she said softly.

"Impressed the hell out of Dick. There's no way we could have kept up with you."

"I picked the best horse."

McGarvey had to laugh. "That's clever. But I think that you would have beat us if you'd ridden a donkey." He put an arm around her narrow shoulders, and they walked for a time in silence.

There was a jumble of large black boulders blocking the end of the beach. Beyond them, the sea came to the edge of a sheer cliff that rose a hundred feet or more into the jungle. They had to turn back.

She stopped. "I don't know what's wrong with me, Kirk."

He gave her a critical look. Except for her long face she seemed perfectly fine. Her old self, with a little color already from the sun this morning.

"What do you mean?" he asked.

"One minute I'm so happy I could burst. But then I get so sad I want to cry. Half the time I'm frightened out of my mind for you, for us, for Elizabeth and the baby."

"Stress. Overwork. You've been running off in all directions lately, trying to make everybody happy all the time. That's one of the reasons we're here this weekend. Maybe take the edge off the pressure for both of us."

"I hope so," she said. She didn't sound very sure.

"Combine that with worrying about the Senate hearings, my job, and some of the bad things that have happened to us in the last few years, it's a wonder we're not both in a loony bin somewhere."

She clutched at his arm. "It's like somebody's sneaking up on us again. In the night I think I can hear them."

McGarvey felt instant goose bumps on the back of his neck. "Nobody is coming after us, Katy," he told her with more conviction than he felt.

She looked back to where Yemm had finished setting up their picnic. "I want to get off this island, Kirk," she said. "Right now. I mean it."

"Katy, there's nothing wrong—"

"Goddammit, I want to get out of here!" she shrieked. Suddenly she was at the edge of hysteria; her eyes were wild, her face screwed up in fear.

"It's okay, sweetheart. We'll call for the helicopter. We can have our picnic back at the house by the pool. Nothing's going to happen."

Yemm had heard the scream and he headed up the beach at a dead run, his pistol in hand.

"I don't know," she said. "It's like I'm going crazy. I'm hearing voices inside my head. Warning me. Telling me someone's coming." She gave her husband a plaintive look; as if she were drowning and she wanted him to hurry up and rescue her. "I don't like it here. I'm afraid."

It was possible that someone could be watching them from up in the hills. But McGarvey doubted it. If they made a hit here, the assassins would have trouble getting away. Boats were slow, there were very few airstrips, and everyone on the islands knew everyone else. This was a very closed community, despite the tourists.

"What's going on?" Yemm demanded when he reached them. His eyes flitted from the dense jungles above the cliffs, the rocks at the end of the beach, and the few boats in the distance.

"Nothing," McGarvey said. "But we're getting out of here. Call the helicopter. The picnic was a bad idea."

They headed down the beach toward the picnic area. Yemm put away his gun and used his cell phone to call the Island Tours dispatcher. He kept his eyes in constant motion, scanning the beach, the ocean and the hills.

"They'll be here in under ten minutes," Yemm informed them.

By the time they reached the spot where Yemm had set up their lunch on blankets, Kathleen was shivering and starting to cry. She tried to hold it back. "I'm sorry I'm such a pain," she apologized.

"You're not alone, Mrs. M., it's been a tough week for everyone," Yemm tried to console her. "The Washington grind gets to all of us sooner or later."

He set about packing up the picnic things, and McGarvey helped him.

"Even you?" Kathleen asked. She stood in the shade, hugging herself as if she were cold.

"Especially me, sometimes," Yemm told her. "My solution is to go down to the pistol range and shoot off a box of ammunition. All the noise does the trick. Usually."

She managed a tentative smile. "How about your wife?"

Yemm shook his head. "She died about ten years ago. Car accident. A drunk broadsided her over in Alexandria."

"I'm sorry," Kathleen said, and her eyes started to fill again.

"Easy," McGarvey said softly.

"It's okay, Mrs. M.," Yemm told her. "It really is. Taking care of your husband and you is a good job for me."

They heard the helicopter in the distance. McGarvey looked up and waited until he could see the registration number on the fuselage. It was the same chopper that had brought them out here. He allowed himself to relax a little. But Kathleen seemed to be getting worse. Her complexion had turned pale.

They waited until the helicopter touched down and the fury of blowing sand dispersed before they carried the picnic things down the beach.

Mr. Afraans, a puzzled, unhappy look on his face, reached across and popped open the passenger door. "Has something gone terribly wrong?" he shouted. He looked at Kathleen and a genuine expression of sympathy came over him. "My heavens, Mrs., it's nothing to worry about. Nobody has stolen your bag. I still have it."

Kathleen shook her head. "What bag?" she asked.

"Why, the one you left in my machine."

"No," Kathleen said. She held up a brightly colored canvas bag. "This one is mine."

"But Mrs.—"

"No," Kathleen shrieked. She shoved her husband aside. "Something's wrong."

"What's going on?" McGarvey demanded. Kathleen was out of her head with terror.

The pilot reached in the back for a canvas bag, the twin to the one Kathleen was holding.

Yemm was the first to react. "She's right," he shouted. He shouldered McGarvey away from the open passenger door.

Mr. Afraans was trying to lift the bag, but it was caught on something.

Sudden understanding dawned on McGarvey, too. "Get out of here!" he shouted. "Go! Go! Go!" He turned away from the helicopter, grabbed Kathleen by the arm and headed down the beach.

They got twenty yards before the helicopter exploded with an impressive flash and bang; the pressure wave knocked the three of them off their feet.

Metal, plastic and burning pieces of something fell all

around them, as a giant fireball rose two hundred feet into the sky, followed by a thick plume of black smoke.

Yemm had scrambled over to them and had shielded their bodies with his. When the debris stopped falling he rolled off, and they all sat up.

There was nothing left of the helicopter except for a pile of burning wreckage. The heat made their eyes water, and the smell of burned fuel, and burning rubber and plastic, was very strong.

Kathleen's face was coated with sand. She sat looking at the fire, shaking her head. "No," she said softly. "Oh, God, no. No. Oh, God, no."

TWO

SUSPICIONS

Jealousy feeds upon suspicion, and it turns it into
fury . . .
—François de La Rochefoucauld

Suspicion is the companion of mean souls . . .
—Thomas Paine

ONE

"A TRIGGER WAS TRIPPED SOMEWHERE . . . A
THRESHOLD REACHED. IT WAS DESIGNED TO
BEGIN AUTOMATICALLY."

PARIS

t took a week for Nikolayev to find the man he was looking for in the crowded Montmartre, what the locals called
the Butte.

Nikolayev was an old man, but he had not forgotten his
tradecraft—fallbacks, switched cabs, boarding the metro train
and leaving it at the last second as if he had changed his mind.
Window stops to catch the reflections of the pedestrians coming up behind him. Crossing a street in a crowd with the light,
then turning around and darting back the way he had come as
the light changed. Turning down narrow side streets that were
completely devoid of traffic to see who followed.

He was a man not frightened of physical harm at those
times. His primary objective was to find Vladimir Ivanovich
Trofimov without leading another pair of shaved-headed,
leather-jacketed thugs to him.

Trofimov apparently lived quite in the open in a small apartment building off the rue des Trois Frères near the Place Émile
Goudeau. But when Nikolayev arrived and spoke with the old
lady concierge it was only to find that the place was simply

an accommodation address. M. Trofimov lived somewhere else.

"*Peut-être dans les quartiers.* Perhaps elsewhere, monsieur."

After one hundred francs exchanged hands, the woman suddenly became Nikolayev's sly confidante; batting her eyelashes and coquettishly lowering her eyes. What was it about him that suddenly attracted old Frenchwomen?

"On Saturdays M. Trofimov is to be found at the Louvre. In the Cour Carrée. The department of Egyptian Antiquities. I tell him that Sundays have free admission, but he insists on Saturdays. I have seen the *carnets des billets*, and the special notices he receives."

More misdirection? Nikolayev wondered on the way back down into the city. But for all spies there was a level ground—home plate, the Americans called it. A place where the spy's own truths were known, where he was safe, in order to preserve his sanity.

Spies often met their end not because they were betrayed at the field level, or because their tradecraft was faulty. They very often failed because their home plates were insecure. They had no place to run to.

The bad ones invented a series of truths that sometimes they could not unravel themselves. Those were the ones who ended up putting a pistol to their own heads and pulling the trigger.

If the concierge and the accommodation address were not Trofimov's home plate, the man would nevertheless be watching the Louvre for whoever might be coming behind him.

Since General Zhuralev's death in Moscow, Trofimov would be taking care with his tradecraft. He would have to think that he might be next.

The cabbie dropped Nikolayev across from the Place de Valois, and he went the last few blocks on foot to the Place du Louvre. He entered the museum through the Porte St-Germain l'Auxerrois, turning immediately to the left into the ground-floor ancient Egyptian exhibits. A stairway led to the crypt of Osiris, and, at the end of the long hall, stairs led up to the galleries where Egyptian history was traced forward to Roman times.

He stopped just within the gallery at the head of the Osiris stairs. The museum was not as crowded as it can get, but there were enough people coming and going that he had trouble keeping track of them all. School groups on field trips. A tour guide and his flock of elderly people, possibly Americans. A half-dozen Catholic nuns in black habits. A few young artists, sitting cross-legged on the marble floor, sketching exhibits.

Trofimov had been a small man, with a narrow face and rapid, birdlike motions. He was a few years younger than Nikolayev, but still an old man by now. Possibly stoop-shouldered; certainly wearing glasses; white hair, pale complexion. He had worked in Department Viktor as General Baranov's chief of staff in the sixties and right up to the early seventies. He would have been privy to everything, or nearly everything that went on in the department.

Nikolayev had been certain that he would be able to convince General Zhuralev to cooperate. It was still Moscow, and there were a lot of long memories there. Memories that were easily accessible so that an old man might be frightened by them. In addition, Zhuralev had lived in near poverty. His meager military pension could have been discontinued at any moment.

It was different with Trofimov. This was Paris, and from what Nikolayev had been able to gather from his researches, the man had left Moscow, if not wealthy, at least comfortable, even by Western standards. There'd be no interrupting his pension.

Nikolayev started through the main gallery. It was arranged to look like an Egyptian temple, lined with statues, columns and carved doorways. The hall was impressive. Some of it reminded Nikolayev of the Hermitage in St. Petersburg. That museum had the tsars to thank; this exhibit had Napoleon's army to thank.

"I suppose that I should be flattered that someone has come all the way from Moscow to seek me out," someone said in Russian at Nikolayev's shoulder.

Without breaking his stride, Nikolayev glanced at the skinny old man beside him. "Vladimir Ivanovich—"

"*Da*," Trofimov replied. "What do you want?" His tie was

crooked, and it did not match his brown houndstooth jacket or dark blue dress slacks. He almost certainly lived alone. His hair was dyed black, and he wore dark glasses. He looked like a spy from a fifties movie.

"Do you know who I am?"

"I know you. Otherwise, I would never have allowed you to see me. What do you want?"

"Operation Martyrs. I think it has started."

Trofimov stopped. He looked like a deer caught in head-lights. "Do you think that's why Gennadi Zhuralev was mur-dered? The old fool."

"I wanted to talk to him."

"So did a lot of people. But it's over now, or very nearly so. Just a few more months. Maybe six or seven."

"What are you talking about?"

"The bank accounts, of course. The money. That's what it's about now." Trofimov gave Nikolayev a curious look. "What's your part in Martyrs? You were a Baranov man, weren't you?"

"I want to put a stop to it."

"Why?"

"The old days are gone. They're starving in the streets of Moscow. We need the West's help. I don't want to die eating rats for my dinner."

"They're always starving in Moscow. But they always have enough vodka." Trofimov shrugged. "Anyway, it's going to stop of its own accord once the money is gone." He shook his head, then gave Nikolayev another appraising look. "What does this have to do with me? Why did you come here? What do you want?"

"I need the names of the assassins and their targets. Martyrs has been buried all these years. Why all of a sudden has it gone active? Why all of a sudden is somebody closing the funding accounts?"

"A trigger was tripped somewhere," said Trofimov. "A threshold reached. It probably happened by accident. Some bright young officer found the money trail and went after it. Then when the agents in place found out that their paydays were about to end, they went into action."

"The men who came after Gennadi took something away

with them. Something that the SVR was afraid of."

Trofimov wanted to be amused. He took Nikolayev's arm and led him across the hall to one of the stone benches. "You don't understand something," he said.

"I understand that people are going to start dying unless we can stop it. The SVR isn't interested in doing anything except covering it up. If Martyrs follows the procedures we used to use, there'll be a big payday at the end. Providing the operation has been accomplished. That's quite a motivation."

"People die every day, but there's only ever been one Valentin Baranov." Trofimov looked inward. "He was a genius, of course. No one could keep up with him. He worked with a Cuban defector living in Miami. A little nobody by the name of Basulto. We didn't know what the general was up to. But when it was ended, maybe six months after it had begun, two extremely important men in Washington were dead. One of them was the director of the CIA, and the other was his friend, one of the most influential lobbyists in America." Trofimov smiled with admiration. "The general scarcely lifted a finger. The work was done for him. All he did was talk to a few people. 'It's the talking cure,' he told us. Baranov was the Sigmund Freud of Department Viktor. His friends called him Sigi for a few months afterward. Until the next operation."

"Who set up Martyrs?"

Trofimov looked at Nikolayev. "Why, you, of course. Isn't that why you really came to see me? To salve your conscience?"

"I don't know what you're talking about," Nikolayev said. But he supposed that Trofimov was right. The man's next words nailed it.

"You asked who the assassins were? Your research with LSD and brainwashing helped make the program possible. The assassins were people who became killers because they were led to it. They were conditioned to become assassins." Trofimov smiled and spread his hands as if the conclusion was so simple it needed no explanation.

"Each of the killers has a target and a control officer?" Nikolayev asked.

Trofimov nodded. "I suspect that's what the SVR took from

Zhuralev. A list of the control officers and their Johns."

"What was he doing with such a list? He must have known that someone would come after him once it was known what he had."

"You made the appointment with him. You were the one conducting the researches." Trofimov held up a tiny hand that looked like a bird claw. "That's all I know."

"You must know the triggers," Nikolayev insisted.

"That kind of information was only in Baranov's head. He told me that the supreme irony would be that he'd be credited with more operations *after* his death than while he was still alive."

"Meaningless—"

"Maybe not. You already have the name of one of the targets, or you would not be so concerned about Martyrs that you came to see me. If you know that name, then you must look for the people who have access to him and the control officer who will always be at their side. The assassin must get constant reassurance, constant pressure, constant brainwashing in order to remain active."

"That could be anybody," Nikolayev said in despair.

Trofimov nodded. "Indeed. General Baranov sowed suspicion like wheat seeds in the wind. The method was his trademark, and the soil was, and still is, fertile."

"That's not enough."

Trofimov got to his feet. "Don't come looking for me again, because the next time I see you, I'll kill you."

He turned and headed back to the Porte St-Germain l'Auxerrois and the street outside.

Nikolayev watched in frustration. There was more. Trofimov had to know the names of at least some of the control officers. One of them. It would help him understand who they were and the nature of their connections between what they were doing now, and what they had been doing more than twenty years ago that engendered such loyalty to a dead KGB general.

He got up and hurried down the gallery as Trofimov disappeared around the corner. His heart fluttered in his chest, and his jaw on the left side ached as if he'd been struck there.

Trofimov had reached the street and was hailing a cab when Nikolayev got outside to the stone bridge that once crossed over a moat. A dark Peugeot sedan pulled up. Its passenger-side doors opened, and two men jumped out. They rushed to Trofimov's side and grabbed him by the arms.

Nikolayev stepped back into the shadows beneath the tall archway. There was nothing he could do to help. If they spotted him, they would take him, too.

Trofimov managed to struggle free. He turned but got only a few steps before one of the men pulled out a pistol and fired three shots. At least one hit Trofimov in the back, sending him sprawling forward. Another hit the back of his skull, the side of his head erupting in a spray of blood and bone.

A woman began screaming as Trofimov hit the sidewalk. The two men scrambled back into the Peugeot, and the car was gone in seconds.

Nikolayev walked back through the museum, emerging a few minutes later from the Porte Marengo. He hailed a cab back to his hotel, and, three hours later, his business finished, he was boarding a train for Orleáns.

Someone would be coming for him. He would make sure that it was the right person. He did not want to end up like Zhuralev and Trofimov.

TWO

"WE DO NOT BELIEVE THAT THE EXPLOSION WAS
AN ACCIDENT. WE THINK THAT THE INCIDENT
WAS AN ASSASSINATION ATTEMPT ON THE LIFE
OF MR. McGARVEY."

WASHINGTON

Otto Rencke took the call at four in the afternoon, when Louise Horn was at the grocery store.

The McGarveys were picnicking on a deserted island. The helicopter that was supposed to take them back to St. John exploded on the ground. Mr. McGarvey, his wife and their bodyguard, Dick Yemm, were unharmed. The civilian pilot was dead.

"Bad dog. Bad bad dog—"

He held the phone to his ear, and he began to hear that the OD was still talking.

"They're all right, Mr. Rencke," the OD said. "They were airlifted to the navy hospital in San Juan. They'll be flown back sometime tomorrow."

Rencke started to panic. "What are you talking about?" he demanded. "You said they weren't hurt. Why are they at the hospital?"

"Nobody's hurt, sir. It's Mrs. McGarvey. She's under sedation. The doctors don't want to move her. She was very frightened."

It was starting. He could feel it in his bones. The walls were closing in on them, and before long they would be so tightly boxed in that none of them would be able to move.

"Mr. Adkins is calling the senior staff for a briefing at five-thirty in the main auditorium. Do you require an escort, sir?"

"No. No. I'll be there." Otto put the phone down. The air in the apartment was suddenly very thin, as if it were perched atop Mt. Everest.

He went through the motions of putting on a jacket without thinking about what he was doing. He left a note for Louise on the kitchen counter so that she wouldn't worry about him. He couldn't stand knowing that Mrs. M. was in a hospital, or that she *needed* to be in the hospital. Besides Mac, Mrs. M. was his Rock of Gibraltar. His ideal of a strong woman.

He called for a cab and on the way out to the CIA he sat hunched in a corner of the back seat. He felt guilty. He should have known that something like this would happen. He should have guessed that an attack would be made on Mac before the hearings were over. He had treated his researches as an academic project. But Mac had serious enemies who did not want to see him make DCI. Even after all this time— Vietnam over with, the Cold War run its course, the bad guys either dead or in retirement. Ineffectual. Old. Without mandate. Without purpose. No reason now.

Other than revenge.

He'd been renting a small stone house that had been used for the caretakers at Holy Rood Cemetery in Georgetown when Mac came out of retirement for him. Otto had been doing some computer consulting on the side, but in those days computers were so new that the few people who had them mostly knew what they were doing. Or they knew so little that they didn't know enough to understand that they needed help. The caretakers' house was cheap: Who wanted to live in a cemetery? But it had fitted his funereal mood.

He had his computers and his cats, and he didn't know the depth of his loneliness and discontent.

But then Mac had come to put him to work hacking the CIA's computers for information on the East German secret police, Stasi. That was the beginning for him. The Agency kept coming back to Mac for help, and Mac kept coming back to Otto.

Mac had legitimized his life.

He got to the CIA before many of the other senior staffers, and he went directly up to his office in the computer center. He checked a couple of his ongoing search programs, which were looking for references to Dr. Nikolayev in Moscow communications, especially SVR telephone intercepts that NSA was providing him. There was nothing yet. But, then, the computers had to sift through tens of thousands of telephone calls that involved tens of millions of words and combinations of words.

A couple of minutes before five-thirty he took the elevator down to the first-floor main auditorium. More than fifty people had gathered in the front rows. In addition to Adkins and the deputy directors of the CIA's four directorates, a lot of section heads and desk supervisors had also been called in.

The mood was subdued. Mac had had his share of scrapes and close calls, but a lot of the people here today only vaguely knew the full extent of what their new director had gone through. But they all knew about this, and they were mad. One of their own had been a target.

Adkins came in and went directly to the podium. He held up his hand, and an immediate hush fell over the room.

"About three hours ago a civilian helicopter which was to have picked up Mr. McGarvey, his wife and their bodyguard, Dick Yemm, exploded, killing the pilot. The incident occurred on the uninhabited island of Hans Lollick in the Virgin Islands, where Mr. and Mrs. McGarvey were having a picnic lunch." Adkins looked up from his notes. "We do not believe that the explosion was an accident. We think that the incident was an assassination attempt on the life of Mr. McGarvey."

An angry murmur passed through the audience. Though it was what most of them suspected, hearing the deputy DCI say it out loud made it official.

"The director and his wife were airlifted by the U.S. Coast Guard to the American navy hospital at San Juan, Puerto Rico, where they will remain under observation until sometime tomorrow, when they will be flown back to Washington. A detail was dispatched from Andrews to provide security at the hospital. It's my understanding that they'll be arriving within the hour."

Rencke sat on the edge of his seat, holding tightly to the back of the seat ahead of him. He was three rows from anyone because he was afraid that someone would see the guilt on his face.

"An investigative unit is being put together that will work with an FBI crime scene and forensics team and experts from the NTSB. They expect to be on-site first thing in the morning. In the meantime, a U.S. Navy SEAL team, which was dispatched from Guantanamo Bay, has arrived on Hans Lollick to secure the remains of the helicopter."

Adkins paused again to gaze out over the audience. He looked as if he'd aged ten years since yesterday. He was having his own problems at home, and now this.

Rencke did not feel any pity for him, however. They all were in the same boat. If anything, besides guilt, he felt fear. He should have known. He'd seen the developing lavender; he should have realized that something like this would happen.

"The media is not on the story yet, and we're going to try to keep it that way for as long as possible," Adkins told them. "The explosion was witnessed from St. Thomas, and the Associated Press did pick up the story, of course, but they don't know who was involved."

"Come on, Dick, they're going to put it together," said Deputy Director of Operations David Whittaker. "They'll see the SEALs, and they'll find out soon enough that the Bureau and the NTSB are investigating the crash."

"All air crashes are investigated," Adkins said. "This one will be no different as far as the media are concerned. We'll keep this a secret for as long as possible, and that's a direct order from Mr. McGarvey. I spoke with him by phone two-and-a-half hours ago. It's his intention to show up for work Monday morning as if nothing happened."

"How do we justify this meeting?" Tommy Doyle, the deputy director of Intelligence asked. There were almost always media watchdogs outside all major government agencies. The CIA was no exception.

"Pakistan will announce its intention to test a thermonuclear weapon. We got the heads-up from State this morning."

"That's been on the burner for two weeks," Doyle argued.

"Yes, but it becomes official on Monday. We're here today to outline the Agency's intelligence strategy."

"Who had access to the helicopter?" Whittaker asked.

"That's one of the items our team will be looking for," Adkins said. "We suspect that there will be a fair number of possibilities."

"How do we know that it wasn't an accident after all?" Whittaker pressed. "Maybe there was an electrical short in the fuel tank. Not unheard of."

"We don't have that answer either, David. But Mac and Yemm agree that from where they were standing it appeared as if the explosion originated in the cabin of the aircraft."

Rencke closed his eyes. He could almost feel the heat of the explosion on his face. A determined assassin, willing to give up his life in the attempt, was almost impossible to stop. The key was to get to him *before* the attempt was made.

He opened his eyes. Maybe it was the helicopter pilot.

"This was a close one," Adkins said. "Any operation that is below a Track Three will be put on hold for the duration. I want every man and woman, every asset, domestic and foreign, focused on finding out who wants to kill Mr. Mc-Garvey, and bring them to justice." Adkins closed his file folder. "Soon," he said.

Rencke jumped to his feet. "Mr. Adkins," he shouted.

"Yes, Mr. Rencke."

"How about Todd Van Buren and Elizabeth?"

"They're skiing at Vail. We have a security team on the way out there, and the FBI has sent two agents up from Denver. We're keeping this low-key, Otto. Mac wants it that way. They'll be okay."

"Oh, wow, okay," Rencke said. He stood for a time, then left the auditorium.

Everyone had been looking at him. He felt their eyes all the way down the long corridor. Freak, queer boy. Nerd. Geek. He'd endured it all as a kid. The memories never went away.

And now the only family he'd ever known was in danger, and he couldn't do a thing to help keep them safe.

Stupid, stupid man. Bad, bad dog.

He was too tired to wait for a cab, so he had a driver from the Office of Security take him home. They rode in silence. The snow had finally stopped falling, but there were still slippery spots on the highway. When they passed the place where he'd had his accident he couldn't see any sign that it had happened. It was another world, another lifetime ago.

"Thanks," Otto mumbled in front of his Arlington apartment building.

"Have a good one," the driver said, and took off.

Otto hunched up his coat collar and watched the taillights disappear around the corner. He was cold and felt more alone than he had in years. For a little while he felt as if he didn't belong to anyone, as if he didn't fit in anywhere. Stuff and nonsense, he told himself, looking up at the second-story windows of his apartment. But he felt it just the same.

Louise Horn met him at the door, a deeply concerned, motherly expression on her long, narrow face. She was an air force major and worked at the National Reconnaissance Office as an image interpretation supervisor. She was almost as bright as Otto, and nearly as odd. Until Otto she'd never had any real friends or family; her parents were both dead, and there were no siblings. She and Otto had been living together for less than a year, but he was her entire world. There was no mountain too tall for her to climb for his sake, no task too difficult. His pain was her pain. She felt every bit of his hurt now, and her reaction was written all over her sad face.

"What's happened?" she asked, taking his coat and tossing it aside.

Now that he was home and safe, his fear bubbled to the surface, and he began to sob. Louise Horn's wide, brown eyes instantly filled, and she took him in her arms. She was six inches taller than he, so she had to hunch over, but she didn't mind. For Otto she couldn't possibly mind. He was the most brilliant man she'd ever known, and he was in love with her. She would have gladly cut off her legs at the knees to accommodate him.

For a second he was embarrassed.

"They tried to kill Mac and Mrs. M.," he blurted. His stepfather would call him a big baby if Otto cried when he was being sexually abused. It was a sign of weakness that he hated in himself. When he was on his own, before Mac and before the CIA, he counted every day that he didn't cry a victory. He'd wanted to cry at the briefing in the auditorium and in the car on the way home. But he didn't.

"Are they okay?" Louise Horn asked.

"I think so, but they're in the hospital until tomorrow." Otto looked into Louise Horn's eyes. "I should have known. I could have prevented it from happening. I could have helped. But I didn't. I'm stupid, stupid. Baddest dog—"

"No," Louise Horn said sharply. "You're not stupid. You're anything but."

"I'm going crazy, I'm losing it. Oh, wow, I'm not smart enough now. It's going—"

She took his hands. "Listen to me, my darling. You are not losing your mind, and you definitely aren't losing your smarts."

"It's lavender, but I can't see anything else."

"The problem that you're facing is a tough one, that's all. You've been there before, and you'll be in that stadium again. So break it down. Analyze the pieces. Understand it. Make it yours. Absorb it."

She wasn't ashamed of him. She wasn't laughing at him or calling him names. There was nothing in her eyes except genuine concern.

"One step at a time," she said.

"Thank you," Otto told her.

She studied his face for a few moments, then smiled. "I'll make dinner for us. Now tell me everything that you can. What are they doing in Puerto Rico, and what about Todd and Liz?"

THREE

SOMEBODY HAD TRIED TO KILL HER. IT WAS
IMPORTANT THAT HE AND LIZ DROP OUT OF
PUBLIC VIEW RIGHT NOW.

VAIL

It was nearly 6:00 P.M. and off piste it was already getting
dark. Elizabeth was about twenty yards ahead and to the
left of her husband, moving fast through the trees along
the side of the last bowl before they came out over the ridge
behind the groomed and lit slopes.

It had snowed heavily last night and most of this morning.
Most of the territory they'd covered today had been unmarked
by anyone else's skis. The feeling was exhilarating.

Liz had laid off the wine, as her doctor had told her, and
she had skied well. Better, Todd had to admit, than he had.
And she was four months pregnant.

But he was getting worried about her. He'd wanted to quit
two hours ago and return to the chalet. She was pushing too
hard, as usual, and she wouldn't listen to him.

"This is my last shot before I get as big as a house, and
everybody starts worrying about me again," she argued.

He'd not been able to resist her big green eyes, the promise
in her face, in the way she held herself. He saw a lot of his
mother in her—spoiled, willful, but almost painfully desperate
to be needed. For somebody to depend on her.

His father had made a killing on Wall Street before he was born, so Todd never knew what it was like to live an ordinary life. He'd grown up rich, so he never thought about money. At least not consciously. If you wanted something, you simply acquired it. He was nearly thirteen before he understood the meaning of the word need, or the concept of dependency.

He was allowed to pick from a litter of prize-winning English sheepdogs. He wanted to tie a paisley bandana around the dog's neck and teach it to catch Frisbees on the fly.

Flyer was his dog. He made his parents, and especially the house staff, understand in no uncertain terms that no one else was to go near the dog. No one was allowed to feed, water, or train the animal, which slept at the foot of Todd's bed in the west wing of their Greenwich mansion, except for Todd.

All went well for the first six months, until summer, when Todd and his parents left for their annual eight-week tour of Europe. Since nothing was mentioned to the staff, they thought the Van Burens had taken Flyer with them, and Todd's parents had assumed that their son had given the staff instructions. Flyer was Todd's responsiblity.

Flyer was eight days dead by the time one of the servants noticed the smell and opened young Master Van Buren's room. Flyer had died of thirst and starvation, but not before the poor animal had tried to claw and chew its way out of the room.

Forever after Todd maintained an extremely acute sense of duty, of responsibility and of need. Not a day went by that he didn't think about what had happened. He still had occasional nightmares about Flyer's desperate attempts to escape.

Elizabeth cut sharply left off the narrow track to pick up a series of moguls; on the side of a very steep and heavily wooded slope.

"Goddammit," Van Buren shouted. He turned after her, carving a sharp furrow in the powder, sending a rooster tail of snow downslope.

She disappeared in the darker shadows amongst the trees, leaving him with no other option than to follow her tracks.

"Liz! Goddammit, slow down!"

He caught a glimpse of her bright yellow ski jacket farther

to the left, and much farther down the slope than he thought she'd be, and she disappeared in the trees again. He saw that he could bear right and cut her off near the bottom, where she would have to traverse toward him along the lower part of the ridgeline. They were less than three hundred yards from Earl's Express Lift. He could make out the top of the lead tower but not the chairs. The lights were on. It meant that the lower slopes were in darkness, and there was less than a half-hour of daylight up here.

He spotted her yellow jacket again, then lost it, and found it again. She had made a sharp turn to the right and was just unweighting her skis, coming partially out of the powder, when there seemed to be a flash at her feet.

She planted her left ski pole as if she was setting for a sharp turn to the left, but her body continued in a straight line.

It was all happening in slow motion. Van Buren was above her and less than twenty yards away when she struck the bole of an eight-foot pine straight on. He heard the crash and snapping of the branches, then the watermelon thump as her helmet hit. She crumpled to the snow.

Van Buren panicked. It was his wife and child down there. But then his training kicked in, and he skied down to her. He activated his emergency avalanche transponder that most off-piste skiers carried with them. The ski patrol would pick up the emergency signal and home in on the transponder's exact location within minutes.

There was blood on the side of Elizabeth's head. It had run down under her helmet to the collar and right shoulder of her yellow ski jacket.

Van Buren released his ski bindings, got rid of his poles, raised his goggles and tore off his gloves. He shook so badly inside that he had trouble keeping his balance as he ducked under the tree branches and knelt in the snow beside Elizabeth.

Her eyes were fluttering, and her breathing came in long, irregular gasps. Blood trickled from her nose and mouth. Her complexion was shockingly white, and the way she was slumped forward against the tree made him sure that her neck and maybe her back were broken.

He was afraid to touch her for fear that he would cause

further damage. "Liz," he said to her. "Sweetheart, it's me. Can you hear me?"

She didn't respond.

He eased the ski glove off her right hand and held her fingers.

"Liz, squeeze my hand if you can hear me." He looked down at her unmoving fingers. Tiny, narrow, delicate, lifeless. "Oh, God, Liz, please," Todd said close to her ear. "Just a little squeeze. I'll feel it."

She was on her knees, almost as if she were praying. Her ski goggles were askew on her face, the right lens shattered and covered with blood. He wanted to take them off, but he didn't dare.

He looked back the way she had come, then up toward the chairlift tower at the top of the ridge. He could make out two figures starting down the slope into the bowl. Even from this distance he could see that they were pulling a stretcher sled and were clad in the orange jackets of the ski patrol.

"Help is on the way, Liz," he told his wife. "Hang on, sweetheart, they're coming." He shifted so that he could look up into her face. There was a lot of blood from a big gash low on her forehead, but it wasn't arterial, and because of the cold air the bleeding was already slowing down.

There was blood in the snow between her legs. At first he thought that it was from her head wounds, but then he realized that the front of her ski suit was soaked with blood.

He fell back, a moan involuntarily escaping from his throat. The baby. Not again. Please, dear God, not again.

The ski patrol was moving fast down the slope. Todd looked up and desperately waved to them. They waved back.

"Just a couple of minutes now, Liz," he said to her. "I swear to God." He didn't know how he could face Mac and Mrs. M. This was all his fault. He should have been an asshole and canceled the ski trip. He'd known better. The doctor, who'd been somewhat skeptical, would have sided with him.

If he had been strong enough. Responsible.

He glanced at the ski patrol rescuers, who were getting closer, then turned the other way, hardly able to contain himself. He felt helpless.

His eyes lit on one of Elizabeth's skis. It had gotten tangled in the lower branches of a couple of small pines a few feet away.

Elizabeth's condition didn't seem to be getting any worse. She was starting to breathe a little easier, and there was nothing he could do for her.

He wanted to scream. To lash out at someone, at anyone.

He crawled over to the lone ski and pulled it out of the branches. He brushed the snow from what was left of the bindings. The rear mechanism had shattered. Nothing remained attached to the base of the ski except for some jagged pieces of metal.

He stared at the mechanism. It hadn't broken apart. The metal hadn't simply failed because of work fatigue. The binding had shattered.

As if it had been blown apart, from the inside out.

He bent forward and sniffed the binding, then reared back. He knew the smell. He should. He'd smelled it often enough during training at the Farm.

It was Semtex. A Polish-made plastic explosive. Very stable, very powerful, very easy to get on the open market.

The ski patrol was a little more than one hundred yards out now. Van Buren buried the ski, then scrambled back to Elizabeth. She was still unconscious, and although she was pale, he couldn't see anything catastrophic.

He unzipped her belt pouch and took out her wallet. He removed her CIA identification card, driver's license, and two credit cards under her real name and pocketed them. The ski patrol was coming on quickly, but they were still too far away to make out what he was doing.

He took a small, plastic-wrapped package from a back compartment in Elizabeth's wallet and extracted a Minnesota driver's license, social security card, bank debit card, and University of Minnesota student ID and medical insurance card all in the name of Doris Sampson, and distributed them in her wallet.

Somebody had tried to kill her. It was important that he and Liz drop out of public view right now until he could call for help. His cell phone was at the hotel.

Van Buren replaced Elizabeth's wallet in her pouch. "It's going to be okay, sweetheart. I promise, nobody's going to hurt you again."

Van Buren stood up, glanced at the ski patrol rescuers, then scanned the ridgelines. Either the plastique had been set on a fuse, possibly by someone back at the chalet, or it had been remotely detonated by someone up here. Someone who was watching them, someone who had followed them.

But there was no one around. The bowl was empty.

The ski patrol arrived, secured the sled and stepped out of their skis.

"What happened, sir?" one of them asked. His name tag read LARSEN.

"She hit a tree," Todd said. It was difficult to keep on track. He wanted to fight back.

The second ski patrol volunteer whose name tag read WIL-LET, brought a big first-aid kit over to Elizabeth, took off his gloves and knelt beside her to start his preliminary examination. "What's her name?"

"Doris," Todd told him.

"Okay, Doris, how are we doing this afternoon?" Willet said, taking her pulse at the side of her neck.

Larsen pulled out a neck brace and backboard, which he brought over to where Elizabeth was crumpled.

"Breathing is labored, but breath sounds are equal and symmetrical. Her heartbeat is fast, but strong," Willet said. "Some trauma to the forehead and right temple, some bleeding but not heavy."

They'd worked as a team before. Their moves were quick and professional. They knew what they were doing; they'd been here many times before.

Larsen took out a wireless comms unit a little larger than an average cell phone. "Base, this is Ranger Three in Pete's Bowl beneath Earl's Express."

"Stand by, Ranger Three."

"Are you the husband, sir?" he asked Todd.

"No. I'm her brother. She's four months pregnant."

Larsen's lips compressed, and he nodded. "How old is she?"

"Twenty-five."

"General health?"

"Very good—"

"Ranger Three, go ahead."

"We have a white female, twenty-five, with blunt trauma to the head, chest and abdomen. Some blood loss, but she's wearing a helmet."

"Okay, pulse is one fifteen; regular and strong." Willet called out. "BP one hundred over fifty. Patient is unresponsive, but her pupils are equal and reactive to light."

Larsen relayed the information to the clinic at the base of the slopes down in Vail Village. "The patient's brother is with her. He says that she is four months pregnant. There is evidence of some bleeding around the perineum of her ski suit."

"Stand by," the on-call doctor ordered.

"Is she going to make it?" Van Buren asked. He had to keep it together, but it was hard.

Larsen nodded. "She was wearing a helmet. Probably saved her life." He glanced over at Elizabeth. Willet was taking off her helmet, careful not to move her head. "Where's her husband?"

"She's a widow," Todd said. "That's why she wanted me to come skiing with her."

"Tough luck. She's a good-looking girl."

"She is," Todd said, his nerves jumping.

"Ranger Three, give her 500 ccs of normal saline and start her on O$_2$. The medevac chopper is en route. We'll transport her to Denver General when you have her ready to move."

"Hang in there, Doris," Larsen said. He and Willet attached the neck brace, their movements very gentle, very precise.

Todd could only stand by and watch. But already he was working out the steps he would have to take in the next twenty-four hours to protect his wife and child. They were priority one; everything else was secondary.

SUNDAY

FOUR

IF THE CIA HAD DEFINED (McGARVEY'S) CAREER,
THEN KGB GENERAL VALENTIN ILLEN BARANOV
HAD DEFINED (HIS) LIFE WITHIN THE COMPANY.

CIA HEADQUARTERS

f it hadn't been for Elizabeth's hero worship of her father,
Rencke would not have begun his quest, as he thought of
it.

He stood on one leg just inside his office in the computer
center, staring at his monitors. The lavender displayed as wallpaper on the screens had darkened since the last time he'd
checked. His programs were chewing on data, and what they
were finding was being evaluated as ominous.

The swing shift operators knew that he was here, but no
one had stopped by to say hello. He had no friends here. Only
the McGarveys.

*"A friend of mine. His name is Otto Rencke. You haven't
seen him, have you?"*

Mac had said that to him, and Otto could feel his presence.
He wished that Mac were here now. He wished that he could
talk to Mac, tell him what was so bothersome. But Otto didn't
know what the problem was himself, except that the walls
seemed to be closing in on all of them. It was lavender, and
the color was getting stronger.

He took off his jacket and sat down at one of his monitors.

Louise hadn't wanted him to leave. But she understood the necessity for him.

One step at a time.

Ten months ago Elizabeth had begun a biography of her father. It was obvious even then that he would be named DCI. She and Otto both thought that an accouting was important. She decided to begin with his career in the CIA because it was the definition of his life. She would go back later and find out about his life in Kansas, and about her grandparents, whom she'd never known, and about her aunt and nephews in Utah, whom she hadn't seen since she was a little girl.

If the CIA had defined her father's career, then KGB general Valentin Illen Baranov had defined her father's life within the Company.

It was at Otto's suggestion that she had begun there. He had showed her how to enter the CIA's computerized archives, and then how to get into the underground caverns at Fort A.P. Hill, south of Washington in the Virginia countryside, where the old paper records were stored.

He showed her how to read between the lines by paying special attention to the promulgation pages and budget lines in each classified file. The first was a list of everybody who had a need-to-know in the operation, and the second was a detailed summary of where the money to pay for it came.

He who holds the purse strings *as well as* the operational strings is the actual power to be reckoned with.

He showed her how to cross-reference personnel files with operational files to look for the anomalies. John Lyman Trotter, Jr., for instance. He'd become DDO and a friend to Mac. But he turned out to be a traitor, lured into General Baranov's circle. In hindsight the signs had been there. Trotter had spent more money than he'd earned. His name was on more promulgation pages than his early positions should have allowed for. As an operations officer—this was before he'd become DDO—he had personally signed off on too many budgetary requests.

But the old KGB general had been a master of the game. Starting in the days after Korea and through the Bay of Pigs and Cuban Missile Crises, he had developed and run CESTA and Banco del Sur, the most fabulously successful intelligence networks anywhere at anytime in history. They'd been administered from the Soviet Union's embassy in Mexico City, which was cover for the largest KGB operational unit in the world outside of Moscow. Through a vast network of field agents and governmental connections, General Baranov knew just about everything that went on in the entire western hemisphere during those years. From Buenos Aires to Toronto, and from Santiago to Washington, he had his ear to the most important doors.

Insiders like Trotter were the frosting on the very rich cake. By feeding Trotter accurate information that sometimes was actually damaging to the Soviet Union, in exchange for even more important details about the inner workings of America's intelligence establishment, Baranov made his prize mole a hero on the Beltway. By making sure that key operations Trotter had backed succeeded as if they were planned by angels, his mole's stock rose to astronomical levels.

All that could have been seen, should have been seen, from the almost reckless abandon with which Trotter flitted from one desk to the next; from one supersuccess to another. Never mind the occasional star agent who was burned while a dozen not-so-hot field officers succeeded. Never mind that Trotter's rise through the ranks was at the expense of some very capable, even brilliant men and women. If they became disenchanted with a system that seemed to reward ass kissing and apparent legerdemain over good, solid and imaginative intelligence work, then all the better for Baranov's plans.

The general was a great success, until in the end Kirk McGarvey had dismantled the entire house of cards. When it was over, Baranov lay shot to death in a KGB safe house outside of East Berlin, and Trotter lay dead in a CIA safe house in West Berlin.

Both assassinations were carried out by McGarvey. And that was the end of the story. A lesson to be learned. The field officer who developed a peripheral awareness, a skill necessary in order to preserve his life, should not lose the skill once he was recalled to a desk assignment.

No place was safe. Hadn't they learned that lesson before?

Rencke focused on the monitor in front of him. Streams of data crossed the screen so fast it was impossible to focus on any one item. They were telephone intercepts that the National Security Agency was supplying him from the Moscow exchange over the past six months.

So far his program had come up with a few bits and pieces, each item deepening the lavender.

In August Dr. Anatoli Nikolayev disappeared from Moscow after stealing sensitive, though unnamed, files from the KGB's paper archives at Lefortovo. Nikolayev had worked in the KGB's Department Viktor during the Baranov years.

Around that same time, retired general Gennadi Zhuralev had been found a suicide in his Moscow apartment. Zhuralev had worked as deputy operations officer for General Baranov.

By October the SVR, with help from Interpol, thought it had found Nikolayev in Paris. But then the leads dried up. Nikolayev knew the city very well. He'd spent a lot of time there working for Baranov.

The fact that one old man could not be found by the combined efforts of the Russian SVR, Interpol and presumably the French intelligence service, or at the very least, the French police, meant that Nikolayev had not simply wandered off. The old spy had gone to ground, using his tradecraft skills.

Rencke had become a skeptic under McGarvey's tutelage. He did not believe in coincidences.

McGarvey was hired as interim DCI until his Senate confirmation hearings. His daughter went looking down his history to write his biography, focusing her energies on General Baranov. And things suddenly began to happen.

An old Baranov man goes walkabout after snatching some files that make the SVR nervous. Another old Baranov man turns up dead. Now the Senate hearings were dredging up ancient history, opening old wounds, exposing old cesspools, revealing desperate Cold War battles that were best left undisturbed.

Rencke had started to look over his shoulder as soon as his programs began to shift to lavender. A dead man was seeking revenge. It was spooky.

The accident with his car had been no accident. He'd done

no work on his front wheels, as he told Security. Someone had tried to kill him, and he wanted to give them room to try again.

Neither had the helicopter explosion in the VI been an accident.

Rencke drew a triangle on a sheet of paper. McGarvey's name was at one of the points, Baranov's at the second and Nikolayev's at the third.

Mac was on his way back from the Virgin Islands with Mrs. M. and Dick Yemm.

Baranov was long dead.

Which left Nikolayev.

Rencke felt a sudden stab of fear. He dialed up the CIA's Office of Security's locator service and found out where Todd and Liz were staying at in Vail. He got an outside line and called the number. It was a little after five o'clock there.

"The Lodge at Vail, how may I direct your call?"

"I want to talk to one of your guests. Todd Van Buren."

"One moment, please," the operator said. She was back a minute later. "I'm sorry, sir, Mr. Van Buren does not answer."

"This is an emergency."

"I'm sorry, sir. Would you care to leave a message on his voice mail?"

Rencke broke the connection. He was starting to sweat.

He composed himself, then called the OD in Operations. This evening it was Chris Walker. Rencke vaguely knew the young man; his impression was that Walker was earnest.

"Operations."

"This is Rencke in the DCI's office. I want to talk to Todd Van Buren."

"We have a team en route, sir. Have you tried their hotel? They're staying at the Lodge at Vail."

"I tried their room, but the hotel operator said there was no answer." Flashes were going off inside Rencke's head. It was like the Fourth of July, only more intense. "Call hotel security, I want someone to check their room right now. And where the hell is our team, and where's the FBI?"

Walker hesitated. "Is there a problem, sir?"

"I don't know," Rencke said, calming himself. Nothing happened to them. They were still on the slopes or in the ski lodge having a drink. "Have them paged if they're not in their room. Then call me back."

"Yes, sir."

Otto stared at his computer monitor. Nikolayev was the key, of course. It was possible that he had murdered General Zhuralev in Moscow, then disappeared. It was also possible that Nikolayev had arranged for the assassination attempt on Mac.

But why, after all these years? General Baranov was long dead. Surely there weren't any vendettas after all this time. Something like that would be beyond all reason. It would be . . . insane.

It was equally obvious that someone did not want Mac to become the DCI and was out to stop him. But could a dead man be behind it?

Chris Walker called back ten minutes later. "They're not there, Mr. Rencke. It looks like they weren't there all day. And they don't answer their page."

Rencke's fear solidified as if his heart had been flash-frozen. "I want them found within the hour. Whatever it takes, find them."

"Yes, sir," the OD responded. "We're on it."

FIVE

PEOPLE REMEMBERED LIES MUCH LONGER
THAN THEY REMEMBERED THE TRUTH.

WASHINGTON

As soon as the Gulfstream jet stopped in the Andrews VIP hangar it was surrounded by a dozen Air Force Special Forces troops armed and dressed in BDUs. Watching from a window, McGarvey spotted Dick Adkins climbing out of a CIA car. He was flanked by a couple of bulky men in civilian clothes. Everyone looked grim, expectant. It was the middle of the night.

Kathleen had refused anything to eat or drink during the four-hour flight from San Juan, and McGarvey was worried about her. She held his hand in a death grip, her knuckles turning white when she saw the armed guards.

"It's okay, Katy," he assured her. "We're home safe now."

"What about Elizabeth and the baby?" Her voice was strident, her mood brittle despite the sedatives the doctors in San Juan had given her.

"Somebody is with them."

Yemm went to the hatch and popped it open. He gave a nod to his people standing next to Adkins, assuring himself that the situation in the hangar was under control. He turned back. "Mr. Director."

McGarvey helped Kathleen out of her seat, and with Yemm's help got her out of the airplane.

Adkins came over, a look of deep concern on his face when he saw what kind of condition Kathleen was in. "Welcome home," he said. "Do you want an ambulance?"

"No, we're going straight home," McGarvey said. "Are Todd and my daughter on the way back?"

"Security is with them. They haven't been told anything yet."

Kathleen clutched his arm. "They're okay, Dick?"

"They'll be okay," Adkins promised her.

There was a wildness in her eyes that was disturbing, as if she were seeing things that were invisible to the rest of them.

"We'll have them back by noon," Adkins said.

She suddenly became aware of her surroundings. She straightened up and brushed a strand of hair away from her eyes. "We weren't expecting this sort of a reception," she said. "None of this has been in the news, has it?"

The question caught Adkins by surprise. "No, we have it contained so far. But it won't hold forever."

She patted his arm maternally. "Nothing ever does, didn't you know?" She managed a weak smile. "How's Ruth?"

"She's back from the hospital. We're going to work it out."

"Good," Kathleen said. "Good for you." She turned to her husband. "It's time to go home now. I'm sleepy."

"Housekeeping has the Cropley safe house ready—"

"We're going home, Dick," McGarvey said.

Adkins seemed embarrassed. "Who do you want to handle the debriefing?"

"I'll come in around noon. We'll decide then," McGarvey said. He helped Kathleen into the back of the limo, then turned back to Adkins. "Ask Dr. Stenzel if he would come out to the house this morning. The earlier the better."

"Will do," Adkins said. "I'm glad that you're back in one piece."

Kathleen said nothing on the way home, leaning back in her seat and looking out the window. The snow had finally stopped, the weather had cleared and the temperature had plunged into the single digits, unusual for Washington.

Yemm, riding shotgun in the front seat, issued a steady stream of orders and instructions on the encrypted radio link with headquarters to make sure that there were no holes in the security arrangements. He'd spent a good deal of time on the radio aboard the Gulfstream setting up their arrival.

Washington seemed like a strange, alien place to McGarvey now. He felt like a boxer who was backed against the ropes. He had the necessary skills to defend himself, but he didn't have the room, not with Kathleen and Elizabeth and the baby to worry about. But he had turned some kind of a corner. He no longer wanted to run. He wanted to stay and meet the enemy head-on; in fact, he looked forward to it. Yet there was the same nagging, scratchy feeling at the back of his head, warning him that this time the situation was different. This was something that he'd never faced before.

The downstairs lights were on when they pulled into the driveway. Security had gone over the house and grounds, including all eighteen holes of the golf course, with infrared and electronics emissions equipment. Motion detectors had been installed, and rapid response monitors had been placed in every room of the house. If anything, no matter how slight, seemed to be out of the ordinary, night or day, a rapid response team would be on-site within minutes. Noises, power surges, unexplained heat or electronic sources, even airborne chemical odors of explosives would trigger the devices.

Yemm got out first and spoke with the watch commander parked in a van at the end of the driveway, then went up to the house. The front door opened as he reached the porch, and a young woman in blue jeans and a GO NAVY sweatshirt was standing there. Yemm said something to her, then came back to the limo.

"We've arranged for you to have a couple of houseguests," he told McGarvey. "They'll act as internal security, and they'll help with the cooking and housework until we get through this."

Kathleen was an intensely private person, and McGarvey didn't know how she was going to react. But it would be useless to argue because Yemm was right. This was part and parcel of being DCI. He didn't think that a lot of DCIs before him much cared for the lack of privacy either. But the help would be welcome. There was no possible way that a house-keeper was going to be vetted before the situation was re-solved. And Kathleen was not up to keeping the house running. Not now.

She was indifferent toward the two Office of Security agents, both women about Elizabeth's age. They introduced themselves as Peggy Vaccaro and Janis Westlake. Vaccaro was short, voluptuous and homely, but she had an incandes-cent smile. Westlake was tall, thin and boyishly attractive. They seemed competent and sympathetic.

They gave McGarvey a reassuring smile and took Kathleen in hand, clucking and cooing over her as they led her upstairs for a nice soak, a cup of tea and fresh sheets on the bed.

Yemm had an earpiece comms unit that picked up his voice from the vibrations in his jawbone. He was speaking softly as he followed McGarvey into the study.

"Security would like to know if you'll make your scheduled appearance on the Hill tomorrow morning."

McGarvey shook his head. "Not tomorrow. Maybe Tuesday. They can put out the word that we're handling the India-Pakistan problem."

Yemm relayed the instructions as McGarvey poured a cou-ple of brandies. The workmen had finished over the weekend, and the soft woods of the desk, bookcases and manuscript cabinet gleamed in the soft light from the front hall. McGarvey handed one of the brandies to Yemm. They drank in silence; watching each other for the effects of what they'd gone through on the island.

"That one was close, Dick," McGarvey said after a long moment.

Yemm nodded. "Mrs. M. saved our lives." He looked at his drink.

"They're not going to give up."

"No, sir, not even if you withdraw your nomination," Yemm agreed. "Somebody wants you."

"Somebody on the inside," McGarvey said, fully aware of where such an idea would take him. When you start suspecting your own people, you might as well give up the fight from the git-go. Jim Angleton had finally figured that out; after practically emasculating the CIA with his paranoia. "Somebody who knew about the VI trip."

This time around the list was way too short for comfort. And giving up wasn't an option, if it had ever been.

McGarvey got a couple hours of troubled sleep on the couch in the den, while Yemm, a pistol in his lap, dozed in a chair across the room. They couldn't settle down. The andrenaline from the near miss was still pumping.

McGarvey opened his eyes when Peggy Vaccaro touched his shoulder. Somebody had thrown a blanket over him. Light streamed in the windows; the morning sky was a brilliant blue.

"Mr. Director, it's eight o'clock, and Dr. Stenzel is here."

He shoved the blanket aside and sat up. Peggy Vaccaro handed him a cup of coffee. "Is my wife awake yet?"

"Yes, sir. The doctor would like to have a word with you before he goes up to see her."

"Where is he?"

"In your study."

"Where's Dick?"

"He couldn't sleep. He's in the kitchen making breakfast. Oh, and we've laid out some clothes and your shower things in the spare bedroom upstairs. Actually it was Mrs. M.'s idea. She's worried about you."

"I'll go up and see her—"

"No, sir. Mrs. M. asked if we would take care of you until she's seen the doctor."

McGarvey mustered a smile and nodded. "It's been a long time since I've had several women fussing over me at the same time."

Peggy Vaccaro lit up like a sunrise. "Our pleasure, Mr. Director."

McGarvey took his coffee across to his study, where Dr. Stenzel, dressed in corduroys, a battered bulky knit sweater and a scarf around his neck, was studying the spines of the books on the shelves.

"Thanks for coming out on a Sunday," McGarvey said. "Coffee?"

Stenzel turned and gave McGarvey a critical once-over. He shook his head. "No. Is someone making a run on the Agency?"

"Otto was an accident, I'm the target," he told the psychiatrist. "But my wife isn't holding up very well."

"I know. I talked to the navy doctors in San Juan this morning. They faxed me their preliminaries, and frankly I'm just as surprised as they are that your wife didn't suffer a total nervous breakdown. She must be a remarkably strong woman."

"That she is."

Stenzel held his silence for a few moments. "I may have to hospitalize her."

McGarvey was afraid of this. But he was resigned. "Whatever it takes. But give us a little lead time, would you. We have some security considerations."

Stenzel nodded. "I understand."

"She's had some difficult times because of my job."

"I'll bet she has," the Company psychiatrist said. "Does she want you to quit?"

McGarvey shook his head. "No. At least I don't think she does."

Stenzel smiled reassuringly. "I'll go up and talk to her now. We'll decide what to do afterward."

One of the girls took the doctor up to see Kathleen. McGarvey checked with Yemm in the kitchen, refilled his coffee cup and went up to the spare bedroom, where he showered, shaved and dressed in the slacks, sweater and tweed sport coat laid out for him.

The assassins had made a big mistake by trying but missing. If there was a next time, and he suspected there would be, he would nail them. He looked at his reflection in the mirror. He'd been down this path before, a lot of times in his twenty-five-year career. He knew the moves and countermoves; the feelings, the impatience, the anxiousness and sometimes the fear. And his family had been involved before too. This time he was sticking it out. He would make his stand here on his home ground. He wasn't going to run in an attempt to lead them away.

But now that he had what he really wanted, now that he was exactly where he wanted to be, doing what he wanted to be doing, and loving and being loved by the woman he'd always admired, he was truly afraid of losing it all.

The muscles in his jaw tightened. One last fight. One last confrontation. One last time.

God help the bastards when he caught up with them.

Stenzel was already finished when McGarvey went downstairs. He was in the kitchen with Yemm.

"How is she?" McGarvey asked.

"Better," Stenzel said. He seemed perplexed. "But she's at her limit, I can tell you that much. If something else happens, I think she'll break."

McGarvey glanced at Yemm, who pursed his lips. The fight was just starting.

Stenzel caught the exchange. "Either send her away or keep her isolated. I'm telling you that her brain is working overtime right now. Probably has been for a while. And from what I can gather, reading all the reports from San Juan and talking to her just now, the helicopter explosion was a damned close thing."

"She saved our lives," McGarvey said. He explained what had happened on the island.

"She probably noticed something, maybe even smelled something wrong," Stenzel said. He shook his head. "We used to call it women's intuition. But that's nothing more than a heightened sense of awareness. Her mind, as I said, is working superfast."

"She won't leave," McGarvey said. "And trying to keep her isolated might be impossible." He was trying to work out the logistics of keeping Katy safe. But sending her away would not work. It'd be nothing more than another form of his own running away.

"Nevertheless, it'll have to be done," Stenzel insisted. "She'll disintegrate unless she's removed from the source of her stress; removed either physically or through drugs."

"We'll do the best we can," McGarvey said. It seemed whatever direction he turned there were emotional roadblocks. "Are you going to hospitalize her?"

"Not now. Are you going to continue the confirmation hearings?"

"I don't have any choice."

"Then keep the details from your wife."

"She hasn't paid any real attention—"

"She knows all about them. Especially the attacks on you by Senator Madden."

McGarvey winced.

Stenzel glanced again at Yemm. "Is she in any physical danger?"

"Possibly," Yemm replied.

"Is she aware of it?"

"She is now." McGarvey said.

"I've instructed your security people to call me if there's any change in her behavior. I've left some Librium; we'll see if that takes the edge off her anxiety. In the meantime she needs to get some rest. If she was in the hospital, I could take care of it, but keep her off the telephone and away from the radio, television, computer, newspapers, whatever."

McGarvey showed Stenzel to the front door, then went upstairs to the master bedroom. Kathleen was up and dressed in jeans and one of his old flannel shirts. She'd just finished with her makeup when he came in. She managed a timid smile for him.

"Good morning, sweetheart," McGarvey said, going to her. They embraced. "How are you feeling?"

"A little tired. A little keyed up. But much better." She brushed a speck of lint off his jacket lapel. "I thought that you might be going into the office this morning, so I had the girls put this out for you." She looked up at him. "They're going to be a big help for a few days."

"The doctor says that you need to get some rest."

"I'll take a nap this afternoon. I've got work to do on the Beaux Arts invitations. And if I'm not going anywhere for the next few days, I'll have some phone calls to make. Will this be resolved by then?"

"I don't know."

"That's not very comforting."

"Katy, this isn't going to be that easy—"

"C'mon, darling, we have a life to get on with. We're right in the middle of season. The baby is due in five months. And you have to wind up your Senate battle." She shook her head. "We can't go on like this, with something like this hanging over our heads."

McGarvey was at a loss for words. It wasn't Kathleen talking to him. It was someone else; someone who wasn't dealing with reality. "We'll do the best we can."

"I know," Kathleen replied. She gave him a pat. "Now get out of here. I have work to do, including soothing our neighbors, who have to be wondering what's going on over here."

"Dr. Stenzel doesn't want you using the phone."

"Piffle," she said with a dimissive gesture.

"Are you going to be okay, Katy?"

"I've been better. Just get it done, would you?"

"I'll be home early," McGarvey said.

He gave her another kiss, then went downstairs. Yemm was waiting in the stairhall, his coat on. He had McGarvey's coat in hand. He looked grim.

"What now, Dick?"

"We have to get to work, boss. Elizabeth was hurt on the slopes. They took her to Denver General."

CIA HEADQUARTERS

The security people inside and outside of the house were informed, but the news was kept from Kathleen. As soon as Yemm pulled out of the driveway and radioed headquarters with the "Hammerhead en route" message, a pair of Maryland Highway Patrol unmarked cruisers moved in front and back as escorts.

McGarvey was beside himself, angry, frustrated, fearful, made all the more worse because he was completely helpless to do anything for them. What could be done was being done by the Office of Security. He had to trust his own people for now.

Adkins was keeping the recall as low-key as possible under the difficult circumstances, but it was impossible to hide the fact that something out of the ordinary was happening. Too many people were showing up at headquarters at odd hours.

By four the telephones had begun to ring, and by 9:00 A.M., when McGarvey walked into his office, the landslide was at full speed. Every newspaper, wire service, television and radio network in the country, it seemed, wanted to know what was going on.

The rumor was that the DCI and his wife were in the USVI for the weekend. The fact was that a helicopter exploded on the beach of a deserted island down there, and within hours the CIA had issued a heads-up to all of its people worldwide.

Yemm went down to Security to pitch in, and Adkins walked in from his office with a stack of file folders, e-mails and faxes from their field people and law enforcement agencies between Washington and the islands.

Ms. Swanfeld had also come in. She brought McGarvey his coffee as he took off his jacket and pushed up his sleeves. "No calls, unless it's someone I have to talk to," he told her.

"Yes, sir," she said. "How is Mrs. McGarvey?"

"She'll be okay. Thanks for asking."

"Of course she will be," Ms. Swanfeld replied as if any other idea were unthinkable. She went out to her desk.

"We couldn't reach either of them because they left their cell phones in the hotel room," Adkins said. He laid the files and messages on McGarvey's desk.

"What happened? How is she?"

"She's going to be fine," Adkins said. "I spoke with the emergency room doctor who said that she was lucky she was wearing a helmet." Adkins looked terrible. He was taking this personally. "They were skiing off piste, and she ran into a tree. The fact she was wearing her helmet, and that she's young, probably saved her life. That, and Todd was carrying an avalanche locator, which he keyed as soon as the accident happened. The ski patrol got to them in minutes. They stabilized her and choppered her down to Denver."

McGarvey reached for the phone, but Adkins stopped him. "It's not such a good idea if you call them just yet, Mac."

"What else?" McGarvey demanded.

"We have people out there with them. They'll be okay. The problem is that they haven't been told about what happened to you. I don't think they need that kind of news right now."

"Is my daughter going to be all right, Dick. No bullshit now."

Adkins nodded. "The docs say she'll come out of this just fine. But she lost some blood, and there was the truama to her head, even though she was wearing a helmet."

McGarvey forced himself to calm down, take this latest round of trouble one step at a time. He nodded for Adkins to continue.

"Jared called about ten minutes ago," Adkins said. Jared Kraus was the director of the CIA's Technical Services Division. "He's on the ground at Hans Lollick. He said the explosion was definitely Semtex. No doubt whatsoever. And a lot of it, by the looks of the damage."

"Someone's after me," McGarvey said, distracted.

"Yeah," Adkins agreed. "But who?"

Ms. Swanfeld came to the door. "Mr. McGarvey, the President is on Secure One for you."

"I want a staff meeting in my conference room at ten o'clock," McGarvey said, reaching for the phone.

"We'll know more about Colorado by then—"

"A *full* staff meeting, Dick. Somebody with an old grudge is gunning for me, but we still have an intelligence agency to run."

Adkins did a double take. "How about first things first?"

"We don't have the luxury."

"Then go out to Cropley and let us handle the situation without having to duck every time someone comes near you," Adkins blurted angrily.

"Staff meeting at ten, Dick," McGarvey said. He picked up the phone and turned away. "Good morning, Mr. President. You know what happened to us in the VI?"

"Your security people sent us the heads-up last night. How are you doing?"

"It was a close call, but no one got hurt except for the civilian helicopter pilot. We're working to see if he was in on the plot."

"It wasn't an accident then?"

"No. It was an attempted hit."

The President was silent for a moment. "Any idea who it might be?"

"We're working on it. We'll get them."

"Will they try again?"

"Probably."

Again the President was silent for a beat. "Do you want to withdraw your name, Mac? Get out of there? No one would blame you if you did. You've given your share."

McGarvey took his time before he answered. The morning sun was very bright. It looked cold outside. The air was superclear. "A few days ago I might have considered it, Mr. President. But not now. I won't leave like this because someone is gunning for me."

"I know the feeling," President Haynes said. Last year McGarvey had broken up an assassination attempt on the President and his family. It had been a very close thing. "The media is starting to make noises. How do you want to play it?"

"As a nonevent for now. I don't think it would do my chances in the Senate much good if they thought that I was a lightning rod for the crazies."

"Okay, if there's anything you need, let me know. And say hello to your wife and daughter for me. They're all right, aren't they?"

"So far."

"Well, good luck then."

"Thank you, Mr. President."

He didn't like to leave it at that, with lies. Once you started down that path there was almost never a redemption. People remembered lies much longer than they remembered the truth. But he wasn't sure of anything, or anyone, now.

Whoever pushed the button in the VI was no stranger, because if they were, it meant there was a mole somewhere here, within earshot of the director's office. Neither possibility was comforting.

Adkins came to the door. "Staff is set for ten. All but Otto."

"Why?"

"No one knows where he is. He's not here, but Louise swears that so far as she knows he's at his desk."

McGarvey closed his eyes for a moment. "Is she lying?"

"I think so. Whenever Otto wanders off she gets hyper. She sounded okay this time."

"Have Security find him."

"Why bother?" Adkins asked with a trace of bitterness. Looking for Otto had become an almost full-time job.

"Because he probably has the key to finding out who's gunning for me," McGarvey explained. "And because he's one of us. And because I said so."

Ms. Swanfeld walked into his office ten minutes later. She looked pale.

"Mr. Director, it's your son-in-law on three. He's calling from Denver General Hospital."

McGarvey had been trying without much luck to concentrate on the India-Pakistan NIE updates that Otto had prepared two days ago. He looked up, a vise around his heart. "Thank you."

He picked up the telephone after Ms. Swanfeld withdrew. "What happened, Todd?"

"Elizabeth has been hurt. She'll be okay, but it wasn't an accident, that's why we're using our work names."

"Someone is with you?"

"We're secure," Todd said. He sounded shook-up, but steady.

"Okay. From the top. What happened out there?" McGarvey asked.

"We were skiing off piste when Liz's bindings came apart and she hit a tree head-on. But they were set to blow. Somebody packed them with Semtex. She never had a chance."

The whispering was loud now, like a waterfall just around a bend in the path.

"But I don't know about the detonator. Probably an acid fuse, anything else would have been too big. Technical Services can retrieve her skis and check it out."

"That means somebody out there at Vail must have set them."

"That's what I figured."

"Let me talk to her," McGarvey said.

"She's in the recovery room," said Todd, his voice deflated. "She'll be out of it for a while."

"You said that she'll be okay—"

"Yeah. But we lost the baby." Todd choked up. "She never had a chance, the doctor said. They tried to save her. But they couldn't." Again Todd was overcome, and he had to stop.

All the air had left McGarvey's office. He looked up. Adkins was there listening in on the extension. He was slowly shaking his head.

"It was our daughter, and they killed her," Todd said. "There was no reason for it, Mac. They could have come after me, one-on-one. I would have fought them any time, anyplace under any conditions they wanted. Christ."

"Stick with her, Todd," McGarvey said. He had to force the words out of his throat, force his lips to move.

"I'm sorry, Dad. God help me, I should have made her stay home. I should have been more responsible."

SIX

THE SCRATCHING, NAGGING WAS BACK. THE
WATERFALL HURLING ITSELF DOWN A MILLION
FEET TO CRASH MADLY ON THE JAGGED ROCKS
DROWNED OUT RATIONAL THOUGHT.

CIA HEADQUARTERS

No one was safe now, McGarvey thought.

Word about the attack on the director's daughter spread through the building like wildfire. Or at least McGarvey supposed it had. Bad news always traveled faster than good.

It had been a girl. An innocent baby, lost for no reason. Who would be next? he had to ask himself as he sat at his desk once again trying without much success to concentrate on the NIE and Watch Report.

How he was going to break the news about the baby to Kathleen he couldn't even guess. But he had a fair idea what it would do to her when she found out.

No one was safe, he thought, staring at the open folder on his desk. But that wasn't quite true. The run wasn't on the Company; it was on him and his family. Otto was almost like a son to them. There weren't many people who knew that fact, but it wasn't unknown in some circles.

And now Otto had gone missing again. McGarvey had to hope he was safe. Security had its hands full, but they were looking for him, just as they were in Denver protecting Todd and Elizabeth, and just as they were working the puzzle on Hans Lollick Island. But McGarvey wasn't sure of himself, of how he fit here, what kind of a job he was supposed to be doing, or even what kind of a job he was capable of.

The closer people got to him, the more they depended on his good judgment and his strength. That was their common mistake, because the fact was he wasn't any stronger than anybody else. He didn't have all the answers. When it came right down to it, he'd abandoned his wife and daughter when they were young and needed him the most. He'd had his pride; no one was going to tell him how he would conduct his life. So he had run, and no one near him had ever been safe again.

In the end now he had come full circle.

Was it one last go-around? he asked himself. Or was this just another operation in a string of operations that stretched forever into the future?

Ms. Swanfeld came to the door. "Your staff is in the conference room," she told him. She looked tired and frightened. It was the first time he'd ever seen the combination of expressions on her face. She held a crumpled handkerchief in her left hand. McGarvey recognized that like the others she was looking for reassurance that everything would turn out fine.

"They'll be okay," McGarvey told her. He was in charge. His blanket of protection covered them all.

"What's happening to us, Mr. Director?"

"I don't know, but I have a feeling that we'll find out pretty soon and put a stop to it." He gathered his notes and the NIE and Watch Report and went across to the conference room.

Adkins, along with the deputy directors of Operations, Dave Whittaker, and Intelligence, Tommy Doyle, and a few of their key staff were gathered. Missing were Jared Kraus, who was heading up the investigation in the USVI, and the deputy director of Management and Services, whose departments, except for Security, had little to do with these kinds of operations. Dick Yemm sat in for Security and Bob Johnson for Technical Services.

Also still missing was Otto Rencke.

"No word yet on Otto?" McGarvey asked, taking his seat

at the head of the long table. The conference room was windowless. It was mechanically and electronically isolated from the rest of the building, and from the outside. Anything said or done here would leave the room only in the minds and the notes of the people present.

"He's not on the grounds, and he's not at his apartment," Yemm said. "Major Horn isn't screaming for help, so I don't think that he's in any trouble. But I do have people out looking for him although we're starting to get spread out pretty thin, Mr. Director."

"Keep on it," McGarvey ordered. He opened his NIE briefing book, which outlined all the problems worldwide that the CIA was tasked to gather intelligence on. But before he began he looked at his people. Old friends, some of them. They had histories in the CIA. Just like Aldrich Ames, he supposed. But he wouldn't become another witch-hunter. The CIA could not withstand another full-scale mole hunt.

"We have to assume that there's a purpose to these attacks," he said. "Some sort of an ultimate goal, other than my death."

"We can't know that," Adkins replied, as if he had expected McGarvey to say something like that.

"The first attack was against Otto—"

"He admitted working on the brakes himself, Mr. Director," Johnson reminded.

"Yes, but I want his car checked again. Front to back, including fingerprints and any material containing DNA that you can find."

"I'll send a forensics unit over first thing Monday morning."

"Today," McGarvey countered. "This morning, please."

"Yes, sir," Johnson said.

"The second attack was against me, my wife and Dick. We can't assume that the bomb was meant solely for me. The Semtex had probably been placed inside a beach bag that was the exact twin of the one my wife was carrying. Maybe she was the target."

"I'm sorry, boss, but if it was anyone except for Mrs. M., she would be the prime suspect," Yemm said. He didn't turn away from McGarvey's sudden flare of anger.

"What are you suggesting, Dick?" McGarvey asked coolly.

"We have to keep an open mind. Just because the bomb was in a look-alike beach bag doesn't mean you *weren't* the target."

"What about my daughter? Where does she fit into the pattern? Her ski bindings were packed with Semtex. No mistaking who they were after."

"Let's take the opposite argument then," Adkins said. "Otto was a target. Your wife and now your daughter were targets." Adkins shook his head. "What's the objective? Get you to quit?" He glanced at the others around the table. "It wouldn't make me want to give up. Just the opposite. I'd be a hundred times more motivated to nail the bastards."

"I agree," Yemm said. "You were the target on Hans Lollick. Nothing else makes much sense. And Otto, if that was an attempted hit, was misdirection to make us look elsewhere. Same with your daughter."

"Hell, they could be thumbing their noses at you," Adkins said. "But I'll tell you one thing. It's someone very close to you. Someone who knows your schedules, your habits, your tradecraft. Someone you've crossed paths with before. Someone who's made a complete study of you. Like a stalker would."

Another word, other than stalker, came unbidden to McGarvey, but he pushed it aside.

"And that includes most of us," Yemm said. "Maybe Otto, too. And Todd Van Buren."

A silence descended over them because of the enormity of what Adkins and Yemm were suggesting. Was it better to risk saving a guilty person than to condemn an innocent one, McGarvey wondered, as Voltaire had. Or was he required now to trust no one?

He had retired from field operations because he was sick and tired of constantly looking over his shoulder; forever wondering from which direction the bullet would come; forever looking for hidden meanings in what everyone said or did. He wanted a normal life. One in which he was finally free to love and be loved. Yet he'd wanted to make a difference. To prove himself worthy of his friends, his family, his sister in Utah, with whom he had not spoken in years.

Ever since Santiago, however, he'd had trouble trusting his own judgment, his own worth. Now he was being asked to mistrust everybody else. Everybody.

Get out. Run, run, while you still can. The monster was coming. Even now it was gaining on him, and he was afraid to look over his shoulder for fear of what he might see.

"That's one possibility, Dick," he said, trying to sound reasonable. "But not the only one. We need to reexamine Otto's car, and we need to cross-match the Semtex in Hans Lollick with what they used in Vail. Maybe we'll get lucky." No one responded. They were waiting for him to make a point. Even now they wanted his protection. "We need a motive," he finished lamely.

"Someone doesn't want you confirmed as DCI," Adkins said. "That's simple."

"Beyond that," McGarvey said. "I can't buy someone thumbing his nose at me, as you suggest. It would be a stupid risk for him to take if he wanted me out or dead." He shook his head. "Something else is going on that we don't know about."

"Relieve yourself of duty, Mac," Adkins suggested earnestly. "Postpone the Senate hearings. Take your wife and daughter to Cropley. Let us work it out."

McGarvey wanted to be angry, but he couldn't be. Not with Adkins or the others. Elizabeth and the baby weighed too heavily on his mind. He looked down at the open NIE briefing book.

The telephone at his elbow chimed softly. He picked it up. "Yes."

"I'm sorry to interrupt, Mr. Director," Ms. Swanfeld said. "But there is trouble at your home."

It was another hammerblow to his system. "What is it?" he asked mechanically.

"Security didn't say, except that Dr. Stenzel is en route, and that they would like you to come home immediately."

"Tell them that I'm on my way," McGarvey said. "But my wife is not to be moved from the house until I get there."

"I understand."

Yemm was already at the door.

McGarvey got to his feet. It was hard to keep his head on straight. "You might be right about Cropley after all," he told Adkins. "In the meantime, I want you to call Fred Rudolph over at the Bureau. I'd like a twenty-four/seven surveillance operation placed on the Russian embassy, specifically on their known or suspected SVR people."

"Do you think the Russians are behind this?" Adkins asked. He seemed startled.

"I don't know. But we need to get some answers. Something that makes sense."

McGarvey was always glad to get home. But this morning the house did not seem warm or inviting. The windows were dark and somehow forbidding, as if they contained horrible secrets within.

A neighbor, whom he didn't know, was in his driveway across the cul-de-sac. He wore a bright plaid robe. He'd come out to get the Sunday paper. He raised his hand and waved. McGarvey waved back.

"Brian Conners," Yemm said at his shoulder. "His wife is Janet. They check out."

McGarvey could only guess what the Connerses thought about the goings-on over here. If they knew the extent of the trouble, there would probably be a moving truck in their driveway right now.

The two officers in the van at the foot of the driveway had the windows down. They looked cold but very alert. Yemm gave them a curt nod, then hustled McGarvey up the walk to the house.

Peggy Vaccaro let them in. She wasn't smiling. She looked determined and a little frightened. A bruise was forming on the side of her face. The house was quiet. "Mrs. M. has finally settled down."

"Where is she?" McGarvey asked.

"Upstairs in her bedroom. Janis is with her." She helped McGarvey off with his coat.

"Dr. Stenzel hasn't been here yet?"

"Not yet," the security officer said. She seemed to be on the verge of collapse. She looked exhausted.

McGarvey glanced toward the head of the stairs. The Russian Typhoon clock had stopped. He supposed he hadn't wound it, but he couldn't remember.

"What happened?" he asked.

Yemm had cocked his head to listen to something, and he stared at the alarm system keypad on the wall next to the closet door. The lights were out.

"She started making phone calls as soon as you left," Peggy Vaccaro said. "She was working on some fund-raising event, because she told us that the best time to catch them with their checkbooks open was on Sunday mornings, when they were still home in their pajamas."

"Did she come downstairs?"

Peggy shook her head. "She never left the bedroom. We brought her some coffee, and Janis and I took turns out in the hall by her door until she lost it."

Janis Westlake came to the head of the stairs. She looked distraught. "She's okay now, Mr. Director," she called down softly.

"It just happened? Out of the blue?" McGarvey asked. His gut was jumping all over the place. He didn't know where to land. "One minute she was raising money and the next she was hanging from the rafters?"

"She got one phone call—"

"From who?"

"I don't know," Peggy said.

"Check it out," McGarvey told Yemm. "Then what?" he asked the girl.

Peggy looked down, girding herself. "She made another call. It must have been Denver General, because she asked for room five-seventeen." Peggy looked up. "She was too fast for us."

McGarvey's heart was ripped in two. He resisted the urge to shove Peggy aside and race up the stairs. He needed more.

Peggy touched his sleeve, her face twisted in an expression of anguish and pity. "She lost it. She started throwing things around. Breaking stuff. By the time both of us got in there, she was trying to bust out one of the Lexan windows with a chair. The big chair in the bedroom. The chaise longue. She was using it like a battering ram." Peggy shook her head in amazement. "Janis and I had a hard enough time getting it away from her and putting it down, it was so heavy. But she was swinging it around like a toy." She glanced at Yemm, who had stepped aside and was speaking softly over his headset. "Then she started screaming at us. Swearing. Calling us all sorts of names."

"Like what?" McGarvey asked.

Peggy was embarrassed. "Motherfucking lesbian dykes. Nonsense like that." She passed a hand across her eyes. "It stopped as fast as it started. One minute she was wigging out, and the next minute she was sitting on the floor crying her eyes out. That's when we called your office."

"And then you called Dr. Stenzel?"

Peggy shook her head. "No. He called us and said that he was on his way."

"The phone call originated here in the Washington area," Yemm said. "But it was a block-trace. Possibly a cell phone."

"No way of pinning it down closer than that?"

Yemm shook his head. "It could have been from anyone. And anywhere, if they used a remailer."

"The Russian embassy?"

"It's possible," Yemm said.

Peggy paid close attention to the exchange. "Is there something going on here that we should know about, Mr. Director?"

"I don't know," McGarvey said. "Maybe. But my wife will probably be hospitalized this afternoon, so your operation will move to Bethesda. And afterward probably to Cropley."

"Yes, sir."

McGarvey went upstairs, gave Janis a pat on the shoulder, then went back to the master bedroom overlooking the fifteenth fairway.

Kathleen stood at the window, her arms clasped across her chest as if she were cold. The room was a shambles. The night lamps were broken into pieces, the lampshades battered out of shape. The bedcovers and sheets had been pulled off and tossed aside. Drawers were lying amidst piles of clothing. Her closet mirror was smashed, some of her clothes and shoes pulled out and scattered. Pictures had been snatched from the walls and destroyed. The curtains had been pulled from the windows. And the heavy chaise lounge was shoved up against the bed.

McGarvey couldn't assimilate what he was seeing. He had stepped into an alien world, a place that bore no relationship to his wife and their home. This wasn't Kathleen's doing. Not this.

The scratching, nagging was back. The waterfall hurling itself down a million feet to crash madly on the jagged rocks drowned out rational thought.

"Katy," he said softly.

Her back was to him. She didn't turn around, but her shoulders stiffened a little. "That's it," she said in a perfectly normal voice. "They've finally beat us."

McGarvey went to her, and she looked up into his face.

"Elizabeth won't want to have children now. Not after this," she said. She shrugged. "So, they win."

McGarvey felt as if he was looking into the eyes of a total stranger. "Who are they?"

"I don't know, Kirk. But you'll have to stop them, you know. They'll never give up until we're all dead. Elizabeth, Todd, Otto, you, me." She spoke in a conversational tone of voice; very matter-of-fact, as if she were discussing the weather or what's for supper. The effect was chilling.

It wasn't that he was looking into the eyes of a stranger, he suddenly thought. He was seeing nothing there. No one was at home. Katy's emotions were gone, disappeared, or whatever. Burned out.

"We have to stop them for good this time," she said. "Because I don't think that I can stand much more."

"We will," McGarvey said, holding her. She was shivering. There was a little blood on the side of her neck, where she had cut herself with flying glass or something. Her hair was mussed up, and her makeup was smeared. "How did you know about the accident?"

"Oh, Otto called. He didn't want me to worry."

It was another blow. McGarvey wasn't surprised that Otto

knew, only that he had called to break the news to Kathleen. It was callous. Thoughtless, even for Otto. More than that, it was cruel.

Someone came in downstairs. McGarvey heard the front door, then the murmur of conversation in the stairhall. He supposed that it was Dr. Stenzel. The future that had seemed so bright just a few weeks ago, was now dark and empty. Perhaps even meaningless.

Dr. Stenzel knocked softly on the doorframe. Kathleen stiffened in McGarvey's arms. She straightened up and stepped back.

"What are you doing here?" she asked. Her left eyebrow arched.

"I'm going to give you a sedative, then take you to the hospital," Stenzel told her as if it was the most natural thing in the world for him to say.

"There's nothing wrong with me."

Stenzel surveyed the damage in the room. "Who did all of this?"

Kathleen refused to look. "I received some bad news," she said.

"I know. But it's not your fault."

"It's someone's fault."

"Yes, but not yours," Stenzel said. He motioned for McGarvey to leave.

"No," Kathleen blurted, clutching her husband's arm.

"It'll be just a couple of days, Katy," McGarvey assured her. "You're overloaded. You're burning out. You can't keep going like this. You have to get some rest."

"That's stupid," she said. "I'm not a fucking invalid, or something." She shot Stenzel a vicious look. "Strap me in some goddamn bed, shoot me full of shit. I can't go through that, Kirk. Not that." She was losing it again.

McGarvey gathered her in his arms and held her tight. Stenzel opened an alcohol towelette and swabbed a spot on her bare arm above the elbow. He took a hypodermic syringe from a small case in his pocket.

"Jesus Christ, don't let them do this to me, Kirk!" she

shouted. She tried to struggle away from him, but Stenzel quickly gave her the shot.

"Goddammit," she said.

She continued to struggle for several seconds, but then she started to sag. She looked up into her husband's face, her anger gone. "Fuck it," she said. "Just fuck it."

MONDAY

SEVEN

WAS IT A MONSTER COMING AFTER THEM? IN
THEIR MIDST? COMING TO SCRATCH AT KATY'S
SANITY? COMING TO KILL THEM ALL?

BETHESDA

McGarvey spent a tense night with Kathleen at the
hospital. Even through she was sedated, she had a
troubled sleep. He went home long enough to grab
a quick shower and change clothes, then got back to the hospital a few minutes after eight.

Katy was still asleep. Peggy Vaccaro and Janis Westlake
were on station in the hall along with a couple of men Yemm
had brought over from Security. Dr. Stenzel was just coming
out of her room.

"How is she?" McGarvey asked.

"She's still sleeping, and I want to keep her groggy all day,"
Stenzel said. He took McGarvey down the hall to the doctors'
lounge, where he got them coffee. The hospital was busy this
morning.

What's wrong with her?" McGarvey asked.

"Well, she's exhausted, for one, but that's just the tip of the
iceberg," Stenzel said. He was careful with his words. "She
could have had a nervous breakdown. Her mind simply shut
down. But I rather doubt that."

"Did they tell you what she did?"

Stenzel nodded. "I've called Bob Love, a neurologist friend of mind, to look at her. The Company has used him from time to time. He's about the best in the business. He said that he'd stop by around nine this morning. I expect he'll order some pictures, probably a CAT scan, an MRI, an EEG, then some blood work and possibly a lumbar tap."

"What are you looking for?"

"Physical causes first," Stenzel said. "Maybe a lesion in her brain. Maybe imbalanced sugar in her spinal fluid, something going haywire with her blood chemistry." He shook his head. "Maybe even temporal-lobe epilepsy. We're not ruling anything out."

"Did they tell you *everything* she said and did?"

Stenzel nodded. "Are there any drugs in the house?"

"If you mean marijuana or speed and shit like that, no. We're both pretty conservative people."

"Right," Stenzel replied dryly. "Did you ever see the movie *The Exorcist*?"

"What, do you think she's possessed?" McGarvey asked. He wasn't amused.

"No. But I think your wife's problem is in her head, not in her physical brain or in her blood. But we have to eliminate all the obvious things first, which Bob Love is going to do for us."

"Assuming it is in her head, then what?"

Stenzel shrugged. "Then I give her some tests."

"Like the ones you gave Otto?"

"More or less. We'll try to find out what's bothering her in a general way, then narrow it down step-by-step until we get to the specific problem or problems. Sorta like a jigsaw puzzle. We're looking for the one piece that makes some kind of sense out of the rest."

"What's your gut reaction?" McGarvey asked. "You talked to the doctors in San Juan, and you talked to her when we got back. Now this."

Stenzel frowned. "I don't know. I mean someone is trying to kill her husband and now her daughter. Any woman would pitch a fit under the same circumstances," he told McGarvey. "But it'd be *just* that. She'd raise holy hell and demand that the people she loved were pulled off the firing line right now. Nothing would stand in her way. You know, like the mama bear and her cubs. Threaten her babies and watch out."

"But that's not what she's done," McGarvey said. He was tired, mentally as well as physically.

"No. Which leads me to suspect that something else is going on." He shook his head. "I'm sorry about your daughter. But from what I'm told she'll mend."

"Physically," McGarvey replied. Another stab of pain tore at his heart. Liz's baby had been a girl.

"This will pass, Mr. Director," Stenzel said with sympathy. "Bob Love will check out your wife, and by this time tomorrow we'll have a much better idea what we're dealing with and we can go on from there."

McGarvey rose to go. "I can't walk away from the CIA with this hanging over our heads."

Stenzel shook his head. "It wouldn't do your wife any good if you did. Right now she needs stability. Change, any sort of change, would be bad for her." He gave McGarvey a critical look. "Any idea who's gunning for you and your family? Or why?"

"A couple," McGarvey said. "We're working on it."

"Then go do your job and let me do mine. You can't help your wife by staying here. She wouldn't have any idea that you were in the room even if you were holding her hand."

McGarvey knew better. "Take care of her, Doctor."

"Count on it."

CIA HEADQUARTERS

The full Monday work shift had already arrived when McGarvey got back to the CIA. Thankfully the media hadn't gotten onto the incident with his daughter in Vail. The CIA's press officer, Ron Hazelwood, was giving his weekly briefing in the ground-floor conference room. At least to this moment he hadn't sent up the red flag for an instant read on some issue he was being pressed on. It was something he would have done had Vail come up.

Yemm had recruited someone from Security to do the driving this morning. All the way out, riding shotgun, he spoke in low tones on the encrypted phone. McGarvey didn't pay much attention; his thoughts were on his beleaguered family. Counting Otto, attempts had been made on all their lives, and it made no more sense to McGarvey now than it had in the beginning.

What the hell were they after? Every scenario he came up with to bring reason to the facts was filled with holes large enough to drive a truck through.

Yemm rode with him on the elevator as far as the glass doors to his office suite. He was preoccupied.

"I'd like a couple minutes of your time sometime today," he said. "I want to run something by you."

"How about right now?" McGarvey asked.

"I've got a couple of things to check out first."

McGarvey looked a little closer at Yemm. "Anything urgent I need to know about?"

"I'm not sure, boss."

"Okay," McGarvey said. "When you're ready." He went in, and Ms. Swanfeld jumped up and followed him through to his office.

"Good morning, Mr. Director," she said. "How is Mrs. McGarvey?"

"They're going to do some tests this morning, so we won't know anything until she gets through with that."

McGarvey handed his coat to her and went to his desk as she hung it up in the closet.

"She'll be fine, we're all certain of it," Ms. Swanfeld said. She poured McGarvey a cup of coffee as he flipped through the stack of phone messages and memos that had already piled up this morning.

"Has Dick arrived yet?"

"Yes, sir. He wants to see you first off."

McGarvey looked up. Dahlia Swanfeld was tough. She'd been through her share of crises in her thirty-plus years with the Company. But she was taking this one more personally than most. The CIA was her family.

"This will pass," he told her, using Stenzel's words because he couldn't think of his own.

"Yes, sir," she said. She wanted to ask something else. But she hesitated.

"What is it?" McGarvey prompted.

"It's about your daughter and the poor baby," Ms Swanfeld said. "I was wondering if sending her a little something would be appropriate under the circumstances? Flowers? A sympathy card? A stuffed animal? Something." She was distraught.

McGarvey's heart softened. He smiled. "I think she'd like that very much."

"Yes, sir. I'll tell Mr. Adkins that you're ready for him. And, Mr. Paterson would like to have a word with you this morning *before* ten. He said that it was extremely urgent."

"I'll call him—"

"He would like to see you in person."

"Okay, ask him to come up now," McGarvey said. "Then get my son-in-law on the phone. And sometime before lunch Dick Yemm wants to see me. Fit him in please."

"Yes, sir. You might want to look through your agenda as soon as possible. I'll need to know what to cancel."

"We're canceling nothing, Dahlia," McGarvey said sternly. "Business will continue as usual. For everyone. Do I make myself clear?"

"We'll do our best, Mr. Director," she said, and she left to get started.

McGarvey sat down and sifted through the stack of memos again, but he couldn't keep his mind off Liz and the baby. Knowing that she had lost the child was terrible enough for him. But the knowledge that it was a baby girl was something far worse. It wasn't a shapeless blob growing inside her body. It was a human being who would have grown up to be another Elizabeth, another Kathleen.

His secretary buzzed him. "Mr. Rudolph from the Bureau is on one. Do you want to take it?"

"Yes," McGarvey said. He hit the button for one. "Good morning, Fred. Do you have something for me already?"

"Not yet. But I need a couple of answers from you. For starters, who are we supposed to be watching at the Russian embassy other than the crowd we normally watch?" Fred Rudolph was the director of the FBI's Special Investigative Division. He and McGarvey had worked on a couple of sticky situations over the past year or two. They had a mutual respect.

"Dmitri Runkov, for one," McGarvey said.

"The *rezident* is a tricky man. He's out in the open most of the time, but he does his little disappearing act every now and then," Rudolph said. "Drives everyone nuts. Do you think that his shop might have had something to do with your brush in the islands?"

"It's a possibility that I don't want to ignore," McGarvey told him. Adkins walked in, and McGarvey waved him to a seat. "None of his people came over to watch me do battle with Hammond and Madden."

"C-SPAN. No need for them to be there in person," Rudolph said. "But it might help if you would level with me up front rather than later. Hans Lollick wasn't an accident. Somebody's after you. Why do you think it might be the Russians? To settle an old debt?"

"It might be as simple as that," McGarvey said. "Dick Adkins is in my office now. I'll have him send over a package on a Russian who used to work in the KGB's Department Viktor years ago. His name is Nikolayev. He's missing, and the Russians think that he might be somewhere in France."

"And you think that there might be a connection?" Rudolph asked. He was a lawyer by training. All problems had solutions if you started at A and worked your way directly toward Z.

"We'd like to talk to him."

"I'll look at your stuff and see what we can do. We have a couple of good people in Paris. In the meantime, we'll see if Runkov has made any calls to France lately."

"Thanks, Fred. Let me know."

"Will do, Mac. But keep your head down, would you. You can't imagine the strain it would place on my people if someone bagged a DCI."

The nagging, whispering again. It wasn't as simple as revenge. But exactly what it was McGarvey had no real idea. Nikolayev was nothing more than a starting point.

"I'll make sure that the file gets over to the Bureau this morning," Adkins said. "In the meantime, Jared's people have come up with something. But I'm damned if I know where it gets us."

"It's Monday morning, what do you expect?" McGarvey said in a poor attempt at humor.

"How's Kathleen?"

"They're doing some tests this morning. We should know something by this time tomorrow. Could be nothing more than nervous exhaustion. They're not sure."

Adkins nodded sympathetically. His own plate was full because of his wife's illness, but he seemed to genuinely care about Kathleen.

"They found Elizabeth's skis and took them to a forensics lab that the Bureau uses at Lowry Air Force Base. Todd was right, it was Semtex. Not only that, it came from the same batch as the Semtex they used in Hans Lollick. Same chemical tags. Jared will have the full report later today, but whoever staged both attacks was playing from the same sheet of music."

It didn't surprise McGarvey. "What about the fuse in the skis?"

"It was an acid fuse, they know that much. But they won't be able to figure out when it was set until they get the skis back here. All Jared could tell me was that the delay could have been as long as ninety-six hours."

"Four days," McGarvey said in wonder. "Starting at Dulles, anybody who had access to the skis could have rigged them."

"Or it could have been anyone who had access to your garage," Adkins said softly.

Dick Yemm and Otto Rencke were the first two names that came to McGarvey's mind. He shook his head. He refused to go there. Dulles and Denver were the best bets. But even if the skis had been rigged at the house, someone could have waited until he and Katy were gone, defeated the alarm system and done their thing. A professional could have been in and out in a matter of minutes.

"Let's develop a list of every person and every opportunity to rig the skis, starting right here in Washington and working forward all the way to Vail. Then develop a separate list for Hans Lollick, and subtract one from the other."

Adkins nodded. Either list would be large, but the combined list would be very small. Frighteningly small.

Ms. Swanfeld buzzed. Carleton Paterson had arrived. "Send him in," McGarvey said, as Adkins got up to go. "Staff meeting at ten," McGarvey told him.

"I'll get on it," Adkins said, and he walked out as the Company's general counsel came in. Paterson looked angry.

"Good morning, Mr. Director," Paterson said. "Although for you I shouldn't think it's very good at all."

"There've been worse," McGarvey replied.

"How is Mrs. McGarvey? I understand that she was hospitalized over the weekend. She wasn't injured on Hans Lollick, was she?"

"Nervous exhaustion. They thought that a couple days' bed rest might do her some good."

"Do us all some good," Paterson agreed. "How is your daughter doing?"

McGarvey's jaw tightened. "She's safe, and she'll mend," he said. He shook his head. "Beyond that I don't know yet."

Paterson nodded as if it was the news he had expected. "Well, you're certainly not out of the woods. Hammond telephoned me at seven this morning. He wants you before the committee this afternoon. Something came up, he told me."

"Not today, Carleton. You have to stall them."

"Not this time, Mr. Director. Either you show up to answer whatever latest questions they have for you—and I expect they'll have something to do with the attempt on your life—or the committee will recommend to veto your appointment. Hammond's words."

McGarvey closed his eyes. "What time?"

"Two."

Ms. Swanfeld called. McGarvey picked up the phone. "Yes?"

"Your son-in-law is on three."

"Thank you," he said. He gave Paterson a nod. "Two o'clock it is. But see if you can find out what's on the agenda."

"I'll try," Paterson said, and he left.

McGarvey hit the button for three. "Good morning, Todd. How are you doing?" He tried to keep his tone reasonably upbeat.

"Better," Todd answered. "At least Liz finally got some real sleep last night. Doctor Hanover says he'll let us get out of here tomorrow morning."

"We'll send the Gulfstream for you," McGarvey said. "It's early out there, but is she awake yet? Can she talk?"

"The doctor came in a couple of hours ago. He's with her right now. I'm out in the hall. I'll see how long it'll be—"

"Wait," McGarvey stopped him. "How are *you* doing, son?"

Todd took a few moments to answer. "I can't get the sound out of my head. When she hit the tree." He was shaky now. "I thought she was dead. But when I saw the blood I knew that we'd lost the baby. Again."

"There'll be another one." McGarvey's heart was breaking for his son-in-law. But there wasn't a thing he could do for him.

"I don't know if we can go through that again."

"Don't give up on each other," McGarvey flared. "Goddammit, Todd. You're young. You're both tough."

"Yeah."

"Have you talked to your folks?"

"My dad called. They wanted to come out here, but I told them that we'd be back sometime tomorrow."

"Do they know what really happened?"

"No. It was just a stupid skiing accident."

"It's better to keep them out of it."

"I know," Todd said. "How is Mrs. M.?"

"We put her in the hospital yesterday afternoon. She's taking this very hard, so they have her on some pretty serious sedatives. And they're running some tests this morning."

Todd fell silent again for a few seconds. "I didn't recognize her voice when she called here. It was like she was a complete stranger. Anyway, how did she find out so soon?"

"Apparently Otto told her. Did he call you?"

"No," Todd said. "But that was stupid of him."

"Yeah. We're still working on the why. But he's disappeared."

"Christ, don't tell me that they got to him."

"We don't think so. At least Louise doesn't think so. We'll find out when he turns up."

"Okay, here comes the doctor," Todd said. "Hang on a minute."

Ms. Swanfeld came to the door. "Mr. Yemm is here. Can you see him now?"

McGarvey looked up and nodded. "Send him in."

Yemm came in, and McGarvey motioned him to have a seat. Todd came back on the line.

"She's fine. Unless something develops today, or sometime overnight, she can get out of here first thing in the morning."

"Good. I'll get Security on getting you back here. Does she know what happened to her?"

"If you mean about the bindings being rigged, no. I haven't told her yet."

"That's okay for now. But she'll have to be debriefed when you get back. She might have heard or seen something."

"I'll bring the phone to her," Todd said.

Yemm was grim-lipped, as if he was the bearer of more bad news. There didn't seem to be any end to it.

Elizabeth came on the line. She sounded sleepy, distant; she was drifting. "Hello, Daddy. I want to come home now."

If McGarvey could have reached through the telephone to cradle his baby in his arms and pull her back to him he would have done it. "You're coming home in the morning, sweetheart. How do you feel?"

"Achy," she said. "And tired," she added after a longish pause.

"Get some rest, Liz. Do what the doctor tells you to do, and you'll be home in the morning."

The line was dead for a moment or two. "Daddy?" Elizabeth said in a tiny voice. "Oh, God, I'm so sorry—"

"It's all right, sweetheart," McGarvey soothed. "Everything will be okay, I promise you. Your mother and I love you very much. Don't forget that."

"That's enough," Todd came back on the line. He sounded matter-of-fact, not angry.

"Take care of her, Todd," McGarvey said. "And yourself. We'll see you in the morning."

"We're going to find out who did this."

"Count on it—"

"There'll be no trial, Dad," Todd said, his voice harsh. "No trial." He broke the connection, and McGarvey hung up.

"How are they doing, boss?" Yemm asked.

It took a moment for him to come back. "They'll be coming home in the morning. Send a Gulfstream."

"We'll get it out there this afternoon so it'll be standing by when they're ready," Yemm said. "I found Otto. Or at least I found out where he got himself off to. He went to France. Commandeered an Aurora and took off from Andrews yesterday afternoon. Late. He logged the flight to what he called Special Operation Spotlight. I checked. There is no such operation."

The Aurora was the air force's new spy plane, replacing the SR71 Blackbird. It flew to the edge of space at Mach 7. Based in New Mexico, it had been a very black project. Damned few people knew that it existed or that it was operational.

"Where'd it land?"

"Pontoise. The French air force base outside of Paris," Yemm said. "We're still trying to unravel how he got the clearances not only from the French, but from our own air force."

"Is he still there?"

"The airplane is," Yemm said. "The French don't know what to make of it, and I didn't think that it was such a good idea to make a fuss. It's better to go along with him for now."

"I'll have Dave Whittaker call the Paris station to be on the lookout for him. Any idea what he's doing over there? Specifically?"

"Nikolayev's name comes to mind," Yemm replied. He was having a hard time of it. Something was bothering him. "Otto got the Colorado search up and running. Chris Walker in the Ops Center logged Otto's heads-up last night. It looks like Otto initiated his own ExComms, under both Elizabeth's and Todd's work names. And he found them before Ops did. Then he phoned Mrs. M."

McGarvey fought down his fear. It wasn't Otto who called the house. Nor had it been Otto in the computer center or in Dr. Stenzel's office. A different personality had taken up residence in Otto's body, and the implications that followed were nothing short of staggering.

"We've pulled his files," Yemm was saying. "Leastways the ones he hasn't blocked out." He averted his eyes. He was embarrassed. It was something new. "We've also looked at Stenzel's report. The *whole* file on Otto, which goes back about twenty years."

"He's done a lot of good things for the CIA."

"Yes, sir. But we think that he might be losing it. Stenzel agrees." Yemm chose his words with care. "If that's the case, then he could be a danger. At the very least he's got the DO's mainframe screwed up pretty good. And he's running some kind of a maverick operation on his own."

"The old KGB. Nikolayev and Department Viktor."

"Yeah," Yemm said. "The assassination squads."

The whispering was there again. The nagging little voices at the back of McGarvey's consciousness. There was nothing he could put his finger on. Nothing concrete; all the more disturbing because of the vagueness. Was it a monster coming after them? In their midst? Coming to scratch at Katy's sanity. Coming to kill them all?

"Otto was wearing his seat belt," Yemm said, before McGarvey could give voice to that one objection. "He never used it before, by his own admission."

"He was worried—"

"I'm sorry, boss, but we gotta keep going on this one. Unless you order me to stop."

McGarvey turned away and looked out the windows. Otto and Louise had been the only guests at the wedding except for Todd and Elizabeth. Kathleen had taken him aside and straightened his bow tie, then given him a kiss on a freshly scrubbed cheek. "He cleans up good," Louise said. She was proud of him.

"Indeed he does," Kathleen had replied. There was just a moment there, an instant when everything had been absolute perfection.

"Do it," he told Yemm. He turned around. "But walk lightly, Dick. If he's done nothing wrong, I don't want him banged up. He's having a hard enough time as it is. And if he's guilty, he'll be watching for someone to come after him. He's capable of doing a lot of damage to the Agency. A *lot* of damage."

Yemm shook his head. "I think it stinks, too, boss. Big-time."

EIGHT

HE KNEW WHAT HE WAS FIGHTING NOW. AND
FOR WHOM. IT WAS AS IF A VEIL HAD BEEN
LIFTED FROM HIS EYES.

WASHINGTON

The limousine that carried McGarvey into the city from
fortress CIA in the woods was a soft gray leather and
smoked glass cocoon. As one crossed the river on the
Roosevelt Bridge the Lincoln Memorial was off to the right,
and the massive granite pile of the State Department was to
the left. One hundred fifty years ago Lincoln dealt with a divided nation. Today State dealt with a divided world, and the
director of Central Intelligence was supposed to be the one
with all the answers.

Since a week ago Sunday his world had been turned upside
down. They were under a siege mentality. Nothing was getting
done. They were merely reacting to whatever came their way.
And he was just as bad as everyone else.

In the old days he had picked up his tent and run.

In the past week he had surrounded his tent with what he
hoped was an impregnable wall and hunkered down.

It was time to fight back.

McGarvey straightened up as they worked their way
through traffic on Constitution Avenue, and he glanced over
at Paterson, who was reading something. Murphy had set great

stock by the Agency's new general counsel, and to this point McGarvey had not been disappointed with the man. But Paterson was an outsider, and that's how he wanted to keep it. At one point he'd explained to Murphy that defense attorneys work with killers, but didn't live their lives. "I'll help keep the CIA in compliance with the law, but I'll never be a spy."

It struck McGarvey all at once that with Kathleen hospitalized he had no one to confide in. Larry Danielle, who'd worked his way all the way up from a job as a field officer with the OSS during World War II, to head the Directorate of Operations, and finally ended his long career as Deputy Director of Central Intelligence, had been McGarvey's rudder, a steady hand, an intelligent, sympathetic ear. Almost a father figure since McGarvey's parents were dead. He'd never once told McGarvey what to do, or even how to do it. But he'd always been there, waiting in the corridor, or getting in his car in the parking lot, or getting a sandwich in the Agency's cafeteria, to give a word of encouragement or advice.

Danielle's favorite lines were: Be careful what you wish for, you might get it. Slow down before and after an operation, but when you find yourself in the middle of the fray, my boy, then go hell-bent for leather. Very often it'll be the only way you can preserve your life. Develop the ability to surround yourself with friends and lovers, but trust no one. If you can't juggle that lot without driving yourself insane, then get out of the business. Better men than you have failed. And lesser men than you have succeeded brilliantly. It's often not a matter of intelligence, rather it's the peculiar mind-set of the spy.

Danielle had been a slow-moving, soft-spoken man for whom appearances belied the truth. In fact he was a man of rare intelligence and consummate good grace and old world manners. The last of the gentlemen spies, Murphy had said at Danielle's funeral.

McGarvey missed him. Missed the old generation that had created the CIA. And somehow that was amusing just now. He smiled.

"What in heaven's name are you thinking about, Mr. Director?" Paterson asked in amazement.

"I'm becoming old-fashioned," McGarvey replied. Danielle would have called it something different.

"From where I sit you're the only one making any sense," Paterson said. "And you'll need to be pragmatic today, because Hammond sounded positively delighted on the phone. Whatever he's going to spring on us will be good. So good, in fact, I wasn't able to get so much as a hint from any of his people."

"One of my old operations."

"Maybe." Paterson shrugged.

"If they're looking for more blood, they'll find it. There's not much we can do to sugarcoat the truth."

They passed the National Gallery of Art and approached the Capitol itself, which was surrounded by the House and Senate office buildings, the Supreme Court and Library of Congress, and the Madison and Adams Buildings.

The stuff of government was done here by men and women—some of them average, some of them dedicated and brilliant; a few others saints or crooks, and still others so dim that they weren't qualified to write a grocery list let alone a law. Average Americans. But the system worked, McGarvey thought.

The crowd of journalists in front of the Hart Senate Office Building was larger than Thursday. Yemm had stayed behind to help direct the investigation into Rencke's background. The replacement driver and bodyguard hustled McGarvey and Paterson up the stairs through the mob.

"Mr. McGarvey, is it true that you're withdrawing your nomination?" one of the reporters shouted.

McGarvey didn't look up at that or any of the other similar questions thrown at him until they were safely inside the building. "That was Hammond's doing."

Paterson nodded. "You're learning. Whatever he has, he thinks it's good."

"Do you think that he and Madden are sleeping together?"

Paterson was startled. "I seriously doubt it, but I wouldn't be surprised." He looked closer at McGarvey. "Have you heard something?"

McGarvey shook his head. "No. Just wondering."

There were only a handful of onlookers in the hearing room, mostly assistants to the committee members, when McGarvey and Paterson came in and took their places. When the doors were closed, the clerk called the hearings to order and the six senators filed in. Hammond and Madden were beaming. The others seemed only mildly interested. Clawson gave McGarvey a sympathetic look, as if to say: Hear you're having some trouble, sorry about dragging you here today.

Hammond reminded McGarvey that he was still under oath.

"Yes, I understand, Senator," McGarvey replied.

"Good. Then let's proceed." He opened a file folder, read for a moment, then looked up. "A number of disturbing items were brought to my attention over the weekend. When we go over this new material I think that we'll all agree that Mr. McGarvey should withdraw his nomination."

"I was asked that question by the media on the way in," McGarvey said. "Evidently everyone knows what's going on except for me."

A few people in the room sniggered.

"Is it true, Mr. McGarvey, that one of your top aides"— Hammond consulted his file—"a man by the name of Otto Rencke, has been missing for the past thirty-six hours and possibly longer?"

"Where did you get that information, Senator?" It had to be someone inside the Agency. Either that, or Louise Horn had told them, though for the life of him he couldn't imagine her having any contact with Hammond.

"This committee's sources are not the issue," Hammond shot back. "Is it true that Otto Rencke is missing?"

"No, it's not true," McGarvey responded.

Hammond glanced at Madden. "You are under oath, Mr. McGarvey."

"Mr. Rencke is in France at the moment on a matter of some importance to the CIA. I can't say anything more than that because it concerns an ongoing operation that's important to national security."

Hammond didn't miss a beat. "But isn't it true that you placed Mr. Rencke on administrative leave after he underwent a psychological evaluation by an in-house psychologist?"

Paterson sat forward. "Senators, that is information from the personnel files of a CIA officer. It has nothing to do with the purpose of these proceedings, which are meant *solely* to determine Mr. McGarvey's qualifications to continue leading the Agency as its director."

Hammond smiled faintly. "I'm glad that we agree on at least that much," he said. "I brought up Mr. Rencke's name because he is a close personal friend of Mr. McGarvey's, and he was involved in a near-fatal automobile accident recently." Hammond looked directly at McGarvey. "If it *was* an accident."

"The accident is under investigation by us and by the Virginia Highway Patrol."

"But in light of subsequent developments the current thinking at the CIA is that the incident with Mr. Rencke was probably not an accident. It fits with the assassination attempt against yourself, your wife and your bodyguard in the Virgin Islands over the weekend, and the nearly fatal attack on your daughter and her husband at Vail, Colorado. Isn't that so, Mr. McGarvey?"

Paterson put a hand over the microphone and leaned toward McGarvey. "Where is he getting his information?"

"I don't know," McGarvey said. "A few people in the building know the whole story. Fred Rudolph knows most of it."

"How about the White House?"

"Not all of it," McGarvey said.

"Mr. McGarvey?" Hammond prompted. He'd gotten the attention of the rest of the committee.

"What was the question?"

"Was an attempt made on your life over the weekend?"

"We're still investigating the incident. But, yes, it appears that someone tried to kill me."

"What about your daughter and her husband?"

"We're also investigating that incident. But it appears that someone tried to kill my daughter."

One of the Senate aides got up and started for the doors.

"Stop right there, Mark, and sit down," Senator Clawson ordered. The aide looked at Hammond, but then sat down. "No one is leaving these chambers until we get some rules straight."

"You're out of order," Hammond said. He was enjoying himself.

"We're talking here about the safety of a very loyal and dedicated American, as well as the safety of his family," Clawson shot back. "I don't know who your sources are, and I doubt if you'd tell me if I asked, but you're overstepping your bounds. Not to mention common decency—"

"Oh no you don't," Hammond responded sharply. "If you'll hear me out I was about to make a valid and important point."

"Everyone will have his or her say, John," Brenda Madden broke in.

Clawson was frustrated. None of the other committee members were offering their support. Most of them owed political favors to Hammond and Madden, or were too junior to protest. "I intend bringing up the conduct of this hearing to the full Senate."

"That certainly is your prerogative," Hammond said benignly. He turned back to McGarvey. "I understand that your ordeal over the weekend, along with the news of the attack on your daughter, caused such a strain for your wife that she was—"

McGarvey raised his hand and pointed a finger at Hammond. "That's enough, you sonofabitch!"

Brenda Madden said something as an aside, Paterson put a restraining hand on McGarvey's arm, and Hammond sat back smiling.

"You *will* leave my wife out of this," McGarvey said, barely in control of himself.

"Or what, Mr. McGarvey?"

"Or I *will* withdraw my nomination, which would make me a private citizen," McGarvey said, steadying down somewhat. "That's something you don't want, Senator. Not that way."

"See here—" Brenda Madden shouted, but Hammond held up a hand for her to be silent.

"Is it a fact, Mr. McGarvey, that at a recent staff meeting the Deputy Director of the Central Intelligence Agency, a career intelligence officer who has time and again demonstrated a *steady* hand on the helm while you were off shooting up the countryside—his name is Richard Adkins—suggested that you step down as director? Not only that, but take your family to a safe place until the real professionals at the CIA and the FBI find out who is trying to harm you, your family and your friends? Is that true?"

"Yes, that is true," McGarvey said, settling down. He knew what he was fighting now. And for whom. It was as if a veil had been lifted from his eyes. "At that highly classified staff meeting we also decided that running away would do us no good. I'm needed to help find out what's going on. If I go into hiding, then the person or persons who are after me will simply hunker down and wait for me to come out of hiding."

McGarvey pushed the microphone away and got to his feet.

"We're not finished here," Hammond blustered.

"We'll find out who your source is inside the Agency," McGarvey promised. "When we do, he or she will be prosecuted under the National Secrets Act, which carries with it a sentence of life imprisonment."

"You *will* sit down, McGarvey," Hammond shouted.

"Sorry, Senators, but I have work to do," McGarvey told them. He turned, and with Paterson right behind him, left the hearing chamber. Hammond was banging his gavel, and Madden was shouting something in her nasal voice.

NINE

LIVING THE LIE FOR JUST ONE DAY MEANT
HE COULD NEVER GO BACK.

SPRINGFIELD, VIRGINIA

Dick Yemm had felt terrible all month. The weekend's events, and his meeting with McGarvey this morning had done nothing to dispel his gloomy mood. Sitting in his personal car, a pearl white Mercedes SUV, in the Springfield Mall, watching the shoppers and traffic on this busy Monday afternoon, his mood deepened. Most people only had to worry about keeping the kids out of trouble, paying the mortgage and kissing enough booty during the workweek to remain employed.

They didn't have to deal with murder, treason or insanity. And all of that against a backdrop of an increasingly hostile world. India-Pakistan, Iran, Iraq, Afghanistan, North Africa, Greece, Mexico, Brazil; on and on, seemingly ad infinitum. Piss on one fire, and a dozen others sprang up around you. Finger one terrorist cell, and two dozen others came into existence as if from thin air. Unravel one alliance, and three dozen others emerged to threaten another 9–11.

Yemm was just the DCI's driver/bodyguard, and number two in the Office of Security. But he saw things, he heard things that he sometimes had trouble dealing with. Troubles

that his wife used to be able to help him with. But she was
dead. On some days he was reconciled to her absence. The
accident had happened ten years ago. But on other days, like
now, he felt a deep ache that he could not salve. She was
gone, and he missed her because she would listen and then
she would give her advice. "The way I see it, Dick . . ." she
would invariably begin. And invariably she was right.

He made a cell phone call to Annandale, just off the Beltway five miles north.

"Hello," a recorded woman's voice answered. "Thank you
for calling Aldebaran Projects. If you know the extension for
the person you wish to reach, you may enter it now . . ."

He entered 562. The call was transferred to the direct line
of Janos Kurĉek the founder and president of the computer
systems design company.

"This is Kurĉek." Janos was a former Polish intelligence
officer under the old regime. It had been fifteen years since
he'd gotten out, but his accent was still strong.

"Janos, I want to talk to you," Yemm said. "Bring a laptop,
I have a secure phone."

In the aftermath and confusion of the Soviet Union's
breakup, a lot of men in Kurĉek's position did not survive the
witch-hunts. Even though he'd worked as a double, selling
information to the U.S., he was a marked man by the new
democrats, who mistrusted men like him because they had no
loyalties to Poland, and by the old hard-line communists, who
hated him for his betrayals.

It was in the spring, April, if Yemm remembered correctly,
though some of his recollections of the operation were a little
fuzzy. He was assigned to the U.S. consulate in West Berlin,
where he made forays into the east zone at least once a month
to organize escapes over the wall. Otto Rencke, who was the
whiz kid reorganizing the CIA's computer system, came over
to Berlin in person and took Yemm out to dinner and drinks
at a sleazy nightblub on the Ku'damm. He had a friend stuck
in Gdánsk who needed help getting out. Name was Janos Kurĉek, and there was an arrest warrant out for him already, so
there was no time to mount a proper operation. Besides, Otto
had worked with Kurĉek for the past couple of years on some

back channel exchanges of information. It was technical means that got Otto access to the old regime's computer systems. He and Kurĉek had developed a secret pipeline all the way back to KGB headquarters in Moscow. But the only way the arrangement would continue to work was for it to be kept an absolute secret. The more people who knew about the pipeline, the less likely that became.

"I'm putting our lives in your hands," Otto said earnestly. "If the KGB finds out, Janos will be a dead man, and they'll come after me." He shook his head. "But, oh, wow, I read your file. Green Beret. 'Nam. Man, you been there, done that. Cool. And you know Mac. He thinks you're good people."

"He's a good man," Yemm said. He had worked briefly with McGarvey in Saigon, and he'd been impressed. McGarvey was steady.

"The very best, ya know," Otto said solemnly. "You gonna help?"

"I'm taking all the risks. What do I get out of it?" Yemm asked. "If I get caught I'm going to jail, at the very least."

"Favors," Otto said. "Beaucoup favors, kimo sabe. You want something, Otto and Janos will come running." Otto looked a little sheepish. "Anyway, if you want to stay in this business, favors are a good thing to have in the bank, ya know."

The operation was set up for three days at midweek, starting on a Tuesday. Yemm was to make his regular run across the border, but instead of making his rendezvous in East Berlin he was to change identities with papers that Otto provided and take the train directly to the Polish shipbuilding capital. Later Yemm could claim that he had got the rendezvous place mixed up, and could make the run to East Berlin again the following week. Things like that happened from time to time.

In Gdánsk he was to meet with Kurĉek at a fish restaurant called Kashubska. There were three times: noon for lunch, four-fifteen for cocktails, and eight for dinner, with a fallback at a park one block away. Kurĉek would be wearing a lime green sports coat and would have a bandage on his left cheek where he'd cut himself shaving.

From there, Yemm who would be traveling as an American

tourist driving a rental car from the train station, would take Kurĉek to the Baltic coast town of Swinourjście right on the German border where Kurĉek would take the ferry to Copenhagen using the papers that Yemm was bringing him.

From there Yemm was to return to East Berlin and make his way back to the west zone as usual.

It had worked exactly as planned until the very end. Kurĉek was in the park at four-fifteen and they drove like crazy, making the 8:30 P.M. ferry. During the four hours they were together Kurĉek poured out his entire life story to Yemm, and by the time he was boarding the boat for Copenhagen and safety they were best of friends. "I will never forget you, Richard," Kurĉek said. "You have saved my life here."

The next morning, back in East Berlin at Checkpoint Charlie, Yemm was arrested by the Stasi and held for ten days. Nothing was asked about his trip to Poland; evidently the Stasi knew nothing about it. They were only interested in his activities in East Berlin over the past year and a half.

Eventually he was released, not too much the worse for wear, except that some of the interrogation methods they'd used on him at the Horst Wessel Center left his head a little fuzzy. He never had all the dates and times straight in his head afterward except that he'd been released on a prisoner exchange. He'd evidently been grabbed solely for that reason.

He was immediately flown to the air force hospital at Ramstein for a checkup, and from there back to Langley, where his debriefing lasted the better part of two weeks.

After that he was given a thirty-day leave, and then reported back to duty, this time in Madrid.

The CIA never asked him about his trip to Poland. They, too, were evidently unaware of his extracurricular activities, and he never volunteered the information. By then he had been in the business long enough to understand that oftentimes the best and most useful alliances were the ones kept closest to the vest. Living the lie for just one day meant that he could never go back, but neither could Janos, who within the year was in Washington, where he'd created a highly successful Beltway computer company.

Otto was out of the CIA again. But true to his word, he and

Janos did lend Yemm a helping hand from time to time, mostly in the form of information.

"Right now?" Janos asked. "Right this minute, Richard?"

"At the fallback," Yemm said. "It has to do with Otto."

Kurĉek arrived ten minutes later, as flashy as usual, driving his bright red Mercedes E430. He was dressed in an Armani suit and hand-sewn Brazilian loafers. His shoes got soaked in the slush when he left his car and came over to Yemm's. He'd brought a laptop computer that looked like a musical instrument in his long, delicate, well-manicured hands. He had the appearance of a magazine fashion model; whip-thin, stylish blond hair combed straight back and brilliant blue eyes.

"How is our friend?" Kurĉek asked. "He must be staying out of trouble now that Kirk is becoming director."

"He's working on something that has us scratching our heads," Yemm said. "Frankly, we don't know what to make of it."

Kurĉek laughed. His voice was baritone, like an opera singer's. "Since I've known Otto he's been working on things to make heads spin. But I'll advise you now. Ask him about it. He trusts you."

"He went to France yesterday, but no one knows for sure why, or even when he'll be back," Yemm continued. "But we think that his trip has something to do with an old Department Viktor psychologist. Anatoli Nikolayev. He disappeared from Moscow, and the Russians asked Interpol and the French police to help find him."

"How long ago?"

"August."

"Otto has gone after him, you think?"

"It's possible." Yemm hesitated. "There are some other things going on here, Janos, that make it important that we find out what Otto's up to."

Kurĉek held up a bony hand. He wore a two-carat diamond ring in a platinum setting on his pinky finger. "I don't want to hear about it."

Yemm took a floppy disk out of his jacket pocket. "I need your help."

Kurĉek refused to take the disk or even look at it. "This is getting into an area that we must not go."

"Come on, Janos," Yemm said. "I'm asking you as a friend."

Kurĉek's shoulders sagged. He opened his laptop and booted it up. He took the disk. "What's on this?"

"It's today's access codes to the CIA's mainframe, and a half-dozen of Otto's most recent encryption busters."

Kurĉek studied Yemm's face. "You want that I should go naked into the lion's den? He's set booby traps, fail-safes, probably viruses."

"That's why I asked you to bring a laptop. If you're compromised, you'll burn one hard disk, nothing more."

"If he suspects it was me, do you know the kind of trouble he could make?" Kurĉek practically shouted.

"Goddammit, this is important. Lives are at stake."

"Yeah, mine." Kurĉek said. He inserted the floppy disk, brought up the screen, then linked with Yemm's encrypted cell phone.

As soon as the call went through, the CIA's logo came up. Using prompts provided by the data on the floppy disk, Kurĉek got into the Agency's mainframe, and then into the Special Operations territory that Rencke had staked out as his own.

Zimmerman had prepared the disk for Yemm, and when he'd handed it over, he shook his head. "I don't even want to know why you want this," he said. "As a matter of fact, I'll deny having anything to do with it."

"Fair enough," Yemm said.

A skull and crossbones appeared on the screen against a lavender backdrop. The skull grinned and began to laugh.

"You have ten seconds to get through the first barrier," Yemm said,

Kurĉek brought up the first series of encryption busters, his fingers flying over the keys as he tried one after the other. Lines of data flashed across the screen.

The skull's grin broadened, but suddenly fragmented and flew off the edges of the screen. As the Directorate of Operations, Special Operations, screen came up, a faint voice in the background whispered: "Ah, shit."

"We're in," Yemm said.

"Not for sure, Richard. This could be a trap. I know Otto."

"We're looking for an operation called Spotlight."

Kurĉek brought up a menu window, and under operations, entered: SPOTLIGHT.

Nothing happened.

Kurĉek tried to back out of the window, but none of his keys worked. However, the cursor was still flashing after the last T in SPOTLIGHT. He backtracked, and the letters began to disappear one at a time.

His keyboard hung up again at the letter I. Nothing he tried worked.

He said something in Polish that Yemm didn't understand, and reached to break the phone link to the computer.

Otto Rencke's image came up on the screen first. "Bad dog," he said, waving his finger. "Bad, bad dog." He glanced at something off camera and smiled. "But I know who you—" The screen went blank, and Rencke's voice cut off.

Kurĉek sat back.

"Were you too late?"

Kurĉek shook his head. "I won't know until he gets back." His eyes narrowed. "You better talk to him, Richard."

"I'll do that," Yemm said. He held out his hand for the floppy disk, which Kurĉek retrieved from the computer.

"You can throw it away," he said. "I think that you will find it's been completely erased."

As Yemm pulled out of the parking lot he got an urgent call from his office. The Aurora was inbound to Andrews Air Force Base and would touch down within the half hour. It was unknown if Rencke was aboard, but it was the same plane he'd commandeered to take him to France.

He had to fight traffic four blocks over to the I-95 ramp, and then from there to the Beltway East, where he was able to make good time.

Otto knew that someone would come snooping into in computer files, and he had been ready for it. Maybe McGarvey would finally see what a few people on the seventh floor—most notably Dick Adkins and the deputy director of Intelligence Tommy Doyle—had been trying to tell him all along. Otto was a wild card, impossible to control. With the simple flick of his fingers across his keyboard he could crash the CIA's entire computer system. He had designed it that way. He had even bragged about it. But nobody took him seriously, or nobody cared, because the system worked. And, Otto was a personal friend of the boss's.

Now the situation was totally out of hand. Kurĉek would be insulated because the call to the computer mainframe would be traced to Yemm's cell phone. But what Otto was going to do when he found out that someone from *inside* the Company was messing with his computers was anyone's guess.

Which left the larger, more urgent problem that Yemm couldn't get a handle on. It seemed as if there was something just at the back of his head that he should understand; some bit of information, a name or a place; something that would make the situation clear.

Someone was trying to kill Kirk McGarvey, and Yemm felt as if he was running through glue in his effort to find the assassin or assassins.

The only thing he knew for certain was that the killer was someone on the inside. Someone close to McGarvey. Very close.

Yemm showed his identification at the main gate. He drove directly over to the 457th Air Wing, where military equipment and personnel used for special missions by the CIA, NSA, FBI, DIA and other government security agencies were staged.

The sleek, all-black supersonic airplane was just taxiing over from the active runway, its canopy coming open when Yemm parked behind a line of start trucks and other maintenance vehicles in the lee of a hangar.

The Aurora looked like a hybrid of the B2 bomber and the Concorde SST, with a drooped nose, canard wings and anechoic radar-absorbing skin.

As soon as it pulled to a stop, ground crewmen checked the wheels, while others brought up the boarding ladder.

Otto, wearing a dark blue flight suit, was first out. He scrambled down the ladder, peeled off the flight suit and got his small bag from a crewman, who'd retrieved it from a locker forward of the swept-back port wing. He no longer wore the sling on his arm.

He gave the pilot a wave, then walked across the tarmac to a line of parked cars. He got into the passenger side of a light gray RAV4 SUV, which immediately backed out and headed to the main gate.

Yemm caught a glimpse of Louise Horn in her air force uniform behind the wheel. She'd lied to them. She'd known where Otto had gone and when he would be returning. It's why she hadn't sounded all that shook-up about his disappearance.

There was no real reason to follow them. Louise would either drive back to their apartment in Arlington first, or she would take Otto directly to Langley. Either way he'd show up out there sometime today.

Yemm headed back to his office, even more depressed and confused than he had been earlier. Otto was a friend who might finally have gone around the bend. A lot of geniuses did.

The problem Yemm was having the most trouble with was Louise Horn's involvement. A woman would do anything for her man. But treason and murder?

$$\nabla^2 \varnothing = 0$$

CIA HEADQUARTERS

When Otto Rencke entered his office, Louise was immediately placed in a safe corner of his head. Sometimes during the day, when he was troubled, he would take her out, look at her beauty, think about how much he loved her, replay a favorite conversation they'd had, then put her back safe and sound. She had become his escape mechanism, a safety valve. He was back, and she had helped him with that much. He didn't want to place her in any further danger.

He laid the case with his laptop computer on the cluttered conference table and let his eyes roam around the room. Everything was as he had left it. No one had screwed with his things this time.

It was a Baranov operation. Otto was sure of at least that much. First General Gennadi Zhuralev, who had been Department Viktor chief of operations in the seventies, had been killed in Moscow.

Then Vladimir Trofimov was shot to death in public in front of the Louvre just days ago. He had been Department Viktor chief of staff and Baranov's personal assistant after Zhuralev had departed.

And Dr. Anatoli Nikolayev, who had worked as a Department Viktor psychologist, left Moscow on the very day General Zhuralev was murdered, and was in France on the day Trofimov was gunned down.

It made Nikolayev the key.

But no one knew where he was, even though he'd left his calling cards in plain sight for anyone to see.

Each spy had his or her particular style of tradecraft; how he ran, his preferred means of conveyance, his weapons, his methods for hiding money trails, his phone calls, letter drops, secret codes. All of his methods taken as a whole marked him as an amateur or a professional, and identified him as surely as his fingerprints or DNA record.

Every good spy had two ways in which he or she disappeared. The first was the most complete. One moment he was there, on a downtown street in front of an office complex in Moscow, and in the next moment he was gone. One day he maintained a household: telephone and credit card accounts, banks, book clubs, favorite restaurants and clubs, e-mails, favorite websites. The next day he disappeared right under everybody's noses.

The second method, more subtle in many ways, was when the spy *wanted* to be found, but found by the correct people. This disappearing act was like the magician's lady and the tiger in a locked steamer trunk. The tiger went in, the curtain was raised, and when it was dropped seconds later the lady came out. Now you see it, now you don't. Except if you had really been on the ball all the clues were there to see.

It wasn't magic, it was nothing more than legerdemain.

Otto brought his monitors up. The screens showed the deepest shades of lavender so far. He started pulling up his primary search engines.

Spies, like magicians, left clues. Calling cards. In Nikolayev's case he'd all but taken an ad in a Paris newspaper that he was there. Trofimov's residence was listed on police reports. His landlady, who was distrustful of cops but fond of money, described the older, white-haired gentleman asking about Trofimov. It cost Otto one hundred francs. She told him about the same book of Louvre tickets she'd told Nikolayev about on the very day that Trofimov had been shot to death in front of the museum.

Nikolayev, using four different aliases, but fitting the same description, had reserved cars at four separate car hire firms, but never showed up.

He'd bought tickets at Orly for a flight to Washington, and at Charles de Gaulle for New York. But no passenger manifest showed his name.

He'd purchased train tickets to four destinations all over France, from the Gares du Nord, d l'Est, de Lyon and d'Austerlitz. But he'd been in a hurry by then. Instead of spreading out around the city as he might have done to muddy his trail, he'd picked pairs of stations that were within walking distance of each other. Four trips in the time of two.

Nikolayev was in France, and he wanted to be found by the right people for some reason. People who by now had figured out that he was on the run from Moscow, but not from the West. But why?

At each of the car rental offices, airline ticket counters and lost and founds in the train stations, Otto left the same message: *Found the novel by B. that you are looking for.* He included a secure telephone number. If the Russians or someone else picked up the message and made the call they would learn nothing except that someone else was interested in Nikolayev's whereabouts.

Each of Otto's special search and analysis programs had its own wallpaper. When the programs were running, but not open for view, the background took on the color of the search, in this case lavender, with a pattern. For Operation Spotlight, his overall analytical program working the Nikolayev problem, the pattern was tombstones that moved in a counterclockwise helical figure.

But the pattern was different now. Every fourth tombstone was flipped forty-five degrees out of alignment with the others.

Someone had tried to get in.

Otto brought up his capture program with shaking hands. Whoever had tried to get into the system had today's CIA passwords, which allowed them to go from the opening menu all the way into the Directorate of Operations. Then they'd tried to enter SPOTLIGHT.

Otto stared at the screen for a long time, trying to envision who knew about that specific operation. It had to be someone on the inside. Right here in the computer center.

He glanced at the door. Someone in one of the research cells. But who were they working for?

When the intruder had entered the Spotlight directory his search engine was frozen by Otto's capture program. But they'd been smart enough to not only back out, but to break the link. The intrusion had been made from off-site, from a cell phone calling from outside the building. The in-house telltale was not tipped over. The prefix and first two numbers came up before the connection had been terminated.

Otto brought up the one hundred possible numbers, which not surprisingly all belonged to the CIA. Currently, seventy-eight of them were assigned, the bulk of which were used by the Directorate of Science and Technology, which included Computer Services. The others were spread throughout the Agency's other three directorates.

Somebody in-house was checking on him. Like he couldn't be trusted. Like he was a criminal. Like he was a suspect.

"Oh boy, oh boy." Otto jumped up and snapped his fingers as he paced the room. He was close. But he was frightened. And he thought that he might be going seriously crazy after all. Some of Stenzel's tests had been terrifying. They'd been so close to cracking open something inside of him that his skin crawled thinking about it.

He stopped at the end of the table and stared at the door. "Oh boy." He suddenly stopped snapping his fingers and looked down at his hands.

He saw blood. Gallons of blood. He stepped back and tried to wipe his hands on his shirt, but still the blood flowed like a river. Over his feet. Above his knees, his waist, his chest. He was drowning in his own blood.

Otto charged out of his office, raced down the aisle between machines and burst into the Office of Computer Security Research. The permanent study / research group had been his idea, but it was independent of him now. A half-dozen men and two women were lounging around the large dayroom. They were arguing about a series of complex equations that filled several white marker boards attached to the walls.

The room was a mess. They were the Company's eggheads, who, like Otto, lived in their own worlds. Conventions such as regular mealtimes, cleaned and pressed clothing, haircuts and the like were meaningless distractions. For them the chase for the most perfect encryption program was life.

Even Otto's encryption programs could be broken sooner or later. He'd formed the group to come up with ever increasingly complex arrangments. All we can do is stay one step ahead of the bad guys until we come up with something really nifty, he'd told them.

Now they had turned on him. They had become spies.

"Who's been fucking with my computers?" he demanded from the doorway.   The windowless dayroom was furnished with a couple of long tables, a broken-down leather couch, several raggedy easy chairs, a coffee machine and a couple of soft-drink-vending machines. One of them had been filled with beer.

The team looked up in mild amusement. Just lately Otto had been throwing a lot of tantrums. His outbursts were becoming routine.

"What are you talking about?" Ann McKenna asked, grinning. She was dressed in jeans, a loose sweater and sneakers. Her long hair was up in a bun, strands flying out everywhere. She looked twenty years older than she was.

"Somebody messed with one of my personal programs. Who was it?"

"Did they get very far?" John Trembly asked, curious. He was the head mathematician in the group.

"Far enough," Otto mumbled. It wasn't anyone here. He could see that now. These kind of people just didn't know how to dissemble. But it was somebody like them. Somebody smart.

"Interesting proposition," Ann McKenna said. "Maybe we could backtrack. Set a trap. Even now."

Otto's attention strayed to the equations on the blackboard. He stood looking at them, following the logic. But something was wrong. It was sloppy.

"We're trying something new," Trembly said.

"Keep it simple, that's the game," the other woman, Sarah Loeffler, said. She'd got her Ph.D. in chaos mathematics from Harvard two years ago when she was nineteen. She still had pimples on her round, chubby baby face.

"Stupid, stupid," Otto said. He went to the first board, picked up a marker and before anyone could stop him, began checking off the correct expressions in the equations, and crossing out and fixing the wrong ones.

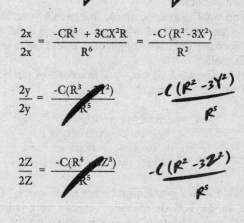

$$\checkmark \qquad \checkmark$$

$$\frac{2x}{2x} = \frac{-CR^3 + 3CX^2R}{R^6} = \frac{-C(R^2 - 3X^2)}{R^2}$$

$$\frac{2y}{2y} = \frac{-C(R^3 - 3Y^2)}{R^5} \qquad \frac{-C(R^2 - 3Y^2)}{R^5}$$

$$\frac{2Z}{2Z} = \frac{-C(R^4 - 3Z^3)}{R^5} \qquad \frac{-C(R^2 - 3Z^2)}{R^5}$$

$$\therefore$$

$$\frac{2x}{2x} = \frac{2Y}{2Y} + \frac{2Z}{2Z} = 0$$

$$\therefore$$

$$\frac{20}{2x^2} = \frac{20}{2y^2} + \frac{20}{2z^2} = 0$$

0 is a function such that

$$X = \frac{2\theta}{2x'} \qquad Y = \frac{2\theta}{2y'} \qquad Z = \frac{2\theta}{2z'}$$

Otto glanced over his shoulder, then wrote:

$$\nabla 2^2 \theta = 0$$

"Does anybody recognize this?" he asked.

"The Laplace equations," Trembly said irritated. "That's what we're working on here. We're looking for an approach to the three-body problem. Gravitational potential. Might be an avenue to explore as an encryption model. Three-body, then four, then N bodies?"

"If you want to keep it simple then watch your stupid mistakes," Otto said. "And why fuck with the field equations you're deriving from Newtonian mechanics? Go to the source, man. Einstein."

He turned, erased all the work from one of the boards and started writing very fast.

$$\sigma x' = \sigma x \cos wt - \sigma \sin wt - $$
$$w(\sin wt + y \cos wt)\, \sigma\, t$$
$$\sigma y' = \sigma \sin wt + \sigma \cos wt + $$
$$w(x \cos wt - y \sin wt)\, \sigma\, t$$

"That's for two events in a homogenous space," Otto said. "Come on, guys, basic physics. You can work it from there. But it'll come to Einstein's tensor equations for the separation of two bodies. You should be able to use the same mechanism for three bodies or more, if that's where you want to go with it."

He turned back to the board:

$$g11\sigma x^2 + g22\sigma y^2 + g22\, \sigma z^2 + $$
$$g44\, \sigma t^2 + 2g\sigma x \sigma y + 2g13\sigma x \sigma z + $$
$$2g\sigma x \sigma t + 2g23\sigma y \sigma z + 2g24\sigma y \sigma t + $$
$$2g34\sigma z \sigma t$$

"Each of the little g's, eleven through forty-four are ten terms in four-dimensional space." Otto put down the marker and turned around again. "You want to keep it simple, there it is." He glanced at his work. "Tedious, maybe. But, oh boy it's pretty."

Nobody said a thing. The approach wasn't particularly novel, and they probably would have gotten around to it sooner or later. But this was sooner. Rencke had pushed the fast-forward button for them.

"Oh boy," Otto said darkly. He lowered his head and stalked back to his own office. He'd made a fool of himself again. The back of his neck was hot, and he could feel people looking at him. He could almost hear their whispers. Their laughter.

Somebody was waiting for him in his office. Coming around the corner, he spotted the pair of dark brown walking shoes and tan gabardines in front of one of his monitors.

"What do you think you're doing?" Otto demanded, his anger suddenly flaring. They wouldn't leave him alone.

Dick Yemm had been staring at the lavender tombstone display. He turned around, a Dutch uncle smile on his face. "Waiting for you. Where have you been?" He was here with bad news or more advice. Otto wanted neither.

"Next door. They were having a problem."

Yemm nodded patiently, as if he knew that there was more, and he was willing to wait for it. He was like a cobra, swaying hypnotically, on the verge of striking at any second.

Otto never knew what to do with his hands when Yemm was around: stick them in his pockets, fold them over his chest, clasp them behind his back. Of all the people in the Company, Yemm was the most invulnerable now. He was tough, he was aloof and he had the ear of the boss. He was almost always right there at Mac's shoulder, watching everybody and everything, almost daring something to happen.

"It was an encryption problem. None of your business," Otto said defensively.

Yemm shrugged. "You're probably right," he said, in the same patient manner. "But that's not what I meant."

"Then what? Oh boy, what the fuck do ya want with me?"

"Let's go for a walk. We can go downstairs to the gym. Nobody will disturb us."

Otto looked at the monitor behind Yemm. The screen showed the lavender tombstone pattern. Yemm hadn't touched anything.

"It's about what's going on around here," Yemm said. "I need a favor."

"Okay," Otto reluctantly agreed.

They took the elevator to the gym, where they sat on the raised platform leading to the showers and the pool. No one was here this afternoon; the Agency was on emergency footing, and everybody was too busy to come down.

"We've put together a special flying unit to find out who's after the boss," Yemm said. Otto looked straight ahead. "We're beating the bushes for anything, and I mean anything, that'll help."

"I'm working the problem too," Otto said.

"We know that you are. We couldn't do without you," Yemm said placatingly. "It's just that we don't completely understand what you're doing."

"I'm gathering data—"

"On Nikolayev. The one the Russians are looking for. He was an old Baranov man. We've got that much. But then we don't know where you're taking it." Yemm spread his hands. He was at his wit's end. "Do you think that he's the one gunning for the boss?"

"I don't know," Otto mumbled. They were skirting what to him was the main issue; the *only* issue. He was scared to death that Yemm would stumble on to it.

"But he does have something to do with it?"

Otto nodded.

"Okay, that makes sense," Yemm said. "At least we know why you went to France. Did you find him?"

Something flip-flopped inside Otto's gut. There was no way that he could let Yemm and his people get to Nikolayev first. There were too many questions that only the Russian had the answers for. Too much was at stake. "No. He might not even be in France."

"He's there all right. Or at least the Russians are telling anybody who'll listen that they think he's there."

"They're not so reliable anymore."

"Maybe."

"He could be anywhere by now."

Yemm seem to consider this for a bit. But then he looked up. "Why'd you go to France, then? I mean if you didn't think that he was there?"

"I wanted to make sure."

"Are you sure now, Otto?" Yemm asked. "I mean if you went there, and, as you say, you didn't find him, how can you be so sure that he's not there after all?" Yemm's eyes locked on Otto's.

Otto felt cornered. He was on the edge of panic. "It's just a feeling, ya know."

"No traces of the man? Not so much as a whiff?"

"*Nada.*"

A startled expression came across Yemm's features. "You're not giving up, are you? Just because you didn't find him the first time out, doesn't mean that you have to quit."

"I'm not so sure—"

Yemm shook his head. "We know that whoever is trying to kill Mac is working on the inside. Or with some serious help from someone on the inside. Someone who knows his movements. Knows about his family. So if there is a connection to Nikolayev, then it might be more than a simple case of revenge."

"How do you figure that?" Otto asked.

"They wouldn't have gone after the family, or you. They want Mac to step down, but it's not revenge. And I don't even think it's so simple as somebody not wanting Mac as DCI. I think there's more to it than that. Some plot, maybe political. I don't know. But if it was revenge, they'd just put a bullet in the back of his head. Or, since it's somebody inside the Company, maybe they have access to his complete file. If that got over to the Senate, they'd axe his nomination at the speed of light."

"The Senate is giving him a hard time, and he was almost killed in the islands."

"Hammond and Madden are just going through the motions because they don't have enough material to stop a presidential nomination, and they know it. And Hans Lollick was crude. Mrs. M. spotted it from the git-go because of the second bag."

"So I'll keep looking," Otto conceded. He wanted to be anyplace else except here.

"Nikolayev is the key for now," Yemm said. "We need to talk to him. You need to help us find him."

Otto nodded. "I'll do my best."

"I know you will," Yemm said. "We're all doing our best."

"Mac is my friend too," Otto flared. "I don't want any question about that, ya know."

"No question," Yemm said.

Otto stood up. "I never had a real family," he said.

"Is that why you called Mrs. M. to tell her about Elizabeth's accident?"

Yemm's accusatory tone put a knife into Rencke's heart. "I didn't want her to hear it from anyone else," he shot back defensively. "I knew that Liz was going to be okay."

"Did you know that she had lost the baby?"

Otto hung his head, suddenly ashamed, and even more frightened than when Yemm had shown up in his office. "Yes."

"Why'd you have to tell Mrs. M. about that?"

"She deserved the truth."

"Yes, I guess she did. We all do."

Yemm watched him leave. It was easy to tell when Otto was hiding something, but impossible to find out what it was. Or even in what direction he was heading. For all they knew Nikolayev and the trip to France could be totally unrelated to each other, and either or both could be smoke screens. False trails.

Back in his office Yemm phoned David Whittaker, who was the boss of Operations. Rencke had not requested authorization for the Aurora flight to France, nor had he checked in with the chief of Paris station when he'd arrived. In fact he'd slipped into France and got back out before anyone there had any idea something was happening.

"What was he doing over there?" Whittaker asked. "Did you get him to tell you?"

"He said he was looking for Anatoli Nikolayev, the one that the SVR has been looking for since August."

"Did he find him?"

"I'm not sure," Yemm said. "But I think that we should keep looking for him. Nikolayev just might have some answers."

"To what?" Whittaker asked, and Yemm had no reply.

ELEVEN

THE LORD IS MY SHEPHERD; I SHALL NOT WANT.
HE MAKETH ME TO LIE DOWN IN GREEN
PASTURES: HE LEADETH ME BESIDE THE STILL
WATERS.

HE RESTORETH MY SOUL: HE LEADETH ME IN
THE PATHS OF RIGHTEOUSNESS FOR HIS
NAME'S SAKE.

YEA, THOUGH I WALK THROUGH THE VALLEY OF
THE SHADOW OF DEATH, I WILL FEAR NO EVIL;
FOR THOU ART WITH ME; THY ROD AND THY
STAFF THEY COMFORT ME.

OLIVET

The message left for him at all ten trigger points was the same. *Found the novel by B. that you are looking for. 703-482-5555.* It was ten at night, and the weather had turned bitterly cold. Standing on the street corner making his calls to Paris he'd become thoroughly chilled. Hurrying back to his room at the Hôtel Le Rivage on the Loiret River, he didn't know if he'd ever be warm again.

He'd cocked the hammer and the gun had been fired. Not

just once, but at every one of his markers. And so soon the speed took his breath away.

But the response was nothing more than he'd asked for. It was a U.S. number, and the area code was for Langley, Virginia. Presumably the CIA.

Alone, as he had been for several years, Nikolayev tried to sort out his mixed emotions. With no one to go to for advice, making up his mind seemed more difficult than it used to be. He was a Libra. The scales of justice. Sympathetic to both sides of every issue. Indecisive, his wife would have said.

The fact of the matter was that he had worked for General Baranov. He had been a Department Viktor boy. *Mokrie dela.* Wet affairs. The spilling of blood. But even though they'd all mouthed the patriotic slogans: *Long Live the Worker*; *Down with the Bourgeoisie*; *The Workers' Paradise Is at Hand*, no one believed such nonsense in their heart of hearts. Look around at the dull, gray, drab cities, if you wanted the proof. Look at the cheerless *kollectivs*. Think about their dreary existence. But Baranov had offered them a chance to escape. A chance to make a difference in the world. A *Russian* difference.

Thirty years later they were still picking up the pieces of Baranov's obsessions. Once started down any path the general could never be turned away.

Over too many vodkas one night he'd told a few friends that he was like the American writer Steinbeck's motivational donkey. The jackass with the carrot dangling in front of his nose. No matter how hard the donkey tries to reach the carrot he will never succeed. But in the trying the donkey *will* move the cart forward.

All the names on the Martyrs list were Baranov's carrots; his obsessions. Now, even after his death, the carrots still dangled, and the donkeys still moved forward.

In this case it was a deadly insanity.

Collectively, Department Viktor had been guilty of horrendous crimes against humanity. But individually each First Chief Directorate employee was guilty of nothing more than doing his or her job to the best of his or her ability. Come to work at seven to have a good breakfast for kopecks on the ruble in the Lubyanka cafeteria; work at a desk until noon when it was time for the second meal of the day downstairs; then back to work until five, when it was home to vodka.

Nikolayev stopped in the deeper shadows across the rue de la Reine-Blanche from his hotel and studied the front entrance. The few cars that passed did not linger, nor did the two couples walking arm in arm entering the small hotel seem suspicious.

His messages had been found and responded to. But no one had come here. Yet.

Up in his small, but pleasantly furnished room he retrieved the first of the three CDs that he had prepared during the several months of his exile from Moscow. They, along with his laptop, a few items of clothing and his heart medicine, which was almost all gone, were all he'd taken from the farmhouse outside Montoire. After Paris it was too dangerous for him to stay there.

The concierge was off duty at this hour, but the night clerk phoned for a cab to take him to the nightclub L'Empereur, a few kilometers away down in Orleáns. On the ground floor was the bar, one dining room and the dance floor. Upstairs was another, smaller, more intimate dining room, and in front overlooking the street were eight or ten tables, each with its own computer and Internet connection. The charm of the place, for Nikolayev's purposes, was that L'Empereur's Internet connections went through an anonymous remailer in the Czech Republic. You could chat to anyone about anything online and no one could tell where you were actually located. It was very private, very discreet.

He paid the deposit for the computer time, which amounted to the cost of the two-drink minimum, and within a couple of minutes was seated at one of the machines waiting for it to boot up while he stared down at the busy street. France was truly one of the last egalitarian nations. You could be anybody, hold any belief—religious or political—be of any sexual persuasion and still be welcome in France providing you broke no French laws and paid French taxes if you had an income.

The international reverse directory listed the telephone number as an "Information Blocked," entry. It was about what Nikolayev expected if the number was a CIA listing.

He had the computer place the call. It was answered on the first ring by a machine-generated man's voice.

"You got my message and now you want to talk. First you need to verify your identity. You are in possession of data that is of interest to us. Send it now. You may follow up in twenty-four hours. If the information is not valid, this number will no longer be answered."

The logo of the Central Intelligence Agency came up on the screen briefly, followed by Nikolayev's old KGB identification number.

The screen went blank, and a computer connection tone warbled from the speakers.

The fact of the matter was that they were all guilty of Baranov's crimes. They were all willing participants in his grand schemes. Now, after all these years, he wasn't going to be allowed his peaceful retirement. His wife was gone, and soon so would his own life be forfeit unless he did something. He was just a frightened old man, but he didn't want to leave this kind of legacy.

There'd been enough killing in his lifetime. Rivers of blood had been spilled. Enough was finally enough.

Nikolayev brought up the CD drive and pressed the enter key. The computers connected, and within thirty seconds the contents of his disk had been transferred.

He broke the connection, retrieved his disk and headed back to his hotel to wait, not at all sure where he was headed or what the outcome would be.

CIA HEADQUARTERS

Hurrying down the aisle between the machines to his office, Otto felt like the French mime Marcel Marceau. He was caught in an invisible box. He could feel the walls and ceiling with his hands, even though he couldn't see them. And then the box began to shrink. At first he had room to move, but inexorably the collapsing walls began to restrict his movements, making it nearly impossible to do anything, even breathe. In the end he was pressed into a tight little ball of arms and legs, his wide eyes looking out at the world from a cage that was killing him.

Someone was in his office looking at the displays on his monitors. He was wearing a gray suit. His broad back was to the door.

"Now who the hell are you?" Otto demanded. "And what the fuck are you doing here?"

The man turned around. He wasn't anyone Otto knew. He was big, like a football player, but he was smiling pleasantly. "Sorry to barge in on you like this, Mr. Rencke. But we need just a few minutes of your time downstairs. If you don't mind."

"I do mind," Otto shot back. "Downstairs where? Who are you?"

"Roger Hartley, sir. Internal Affairs. It's about the Air Force. They're usually slow on the uptake, but they've sent us a bill. For the Aurora flight." Hartley shook his head in amazement.

"What's that got to do with me?"

"You authorized the flight, sir," Hartley said sternly.

"Have Finance pay it."

"How shall we log it? The flight has to be tagged to a current operation. And there was supposed to be a second signature—"

"Special Operation Spotlight," Otto practically shouted. These kinds of things were never handled this way. They went through channels. He wanted to turn and run away. His ability to control someone was inversely proportional to that person's IQ. He was frightened of the goons.

"We weren't given the heads-up. Nobody has heard of such an operation."

"Well, it's under the DCI's personal imprimatur, so if you want to know anything else, you'll have to take it up with him."

"If we could just have a file reference, it would help—"

"Get out of here," Otto shrieked. He hopped up and down

from one foot to the other. "Oh, man, get the fuck outta here now. I mean it."

Hartley stepped back in alarm. "Okay, take it easy, Mr. Rencke. We don't need that information right this instant."

Otto moved away from the door, keeping the big table between himself and the IA officer. "Just get out of here. I've got work to do, man. No shit, Sherlock. No happy crappy. I shit you not."

Hartley turned and walked out of the office, leaving Otto vibrating like an off-key tuning fork.

A telephone chirped somewhere, and someone slammed a file drawer or cabinet door. His eyes strayed to his search engine monitors. They were all varying shades of lavender, but on one of them locusts were jumping all over the place.

Nikolayev had found his message and had sent a reply. Already. Bingo.

BETHESDA

Alone with his thoughts, McGarvey stood at the tall windows at the end of the busy hospital corridor from Katy's room. She had drifted off to sleep again, which, according to Stenzel, was the best thing for her. It was her brain's way of protecting itself so that it could heal. Her subconscious was sorting out her conflicting emotions. Or at least the process was beginning. He wished that he could do the same; drop out, turn around and run away, bury himself in some remote European town, set himself up as an eccentric academic. It was a role that he had played to the hilt in Lausanne when the Swiss Federal Police had sent Marta Fredricks to fall in love with him.

Who watches the watchdog? It was a fundamental problem that every intelligence organization faced. And one that every intelligence officer had to grapple with at his own personal level. The business got to some good people—burned them out, ruined them, so that when they retired they were no longer fit to stay in the service; nor were they equipped to step so easily into civilian life.

"If you don't have someone you can trust, you have nothing," his father had advised him when he was having his troubles in high school. "Don't give in to the Philistines, but don't close your heart."

He'd mistaken his father's meaning for years, thinking that the old man had meant that he should find a woman to fall in love with and make a life. He'd tried in college and again in the military, but until Kathleen every woman he'd gotten close to finally repelled him. Either they were idiots, figuring that they could catch a man by playing dumb, or they made it their life's ambition to transform him into something he wasn't; into what their ideal man was supposed to act like, dress like, talk like. When he met Katy all that changed. The first time he saw her, his chest popped open, and his heart fell out onto the floor. She was good-looking, and she was smart. A bit arrogant, somewhat self-centered and opinionated, but so was he all those things, and she was all the more interesting for those traits. In the end, though, after Elizabeth was born, and after his first few years with the CIA and the unexplained long absences and finally Santiago, she had finally tried to change him, mold him to her own ideal image. She gave him the ultimatum: Quit the CIA or leave. He left. His father had been wrong.

Only his father hadn't been wrong. A few years later, when John Lyman Trotter called him back from an uneasy retirement to unravel a problem at the highest levels within the CIA, he found out the hard way that without trust, without honor, there was nothing. In the aftermath of those difficult times the best DCI ever to sit on the seventh floor was dead, the victim of a General Baranov Department Viktor plot; Kathleen's onetime lover, Darby Yarnell supposedly a former spy himself and a former U.S. senator, lay shot to death in front of the DCI's house, and ultimately, John Trotter, one of the few men McGarvey had ever trusted, was dead as well at McGarvey's hands. Trotter had been the ultimate spy within the CIA, the deeply placed mole that Jim Angleton had nearly brought down the Agency trying to catch.

His father had been right after all. If you have no one to trust, then you have nothing. That was his life for a lot of years until he came back. Until he and Kathleen remarried, until their daughter came back into his life, until he brought Otto in from the cold, until he surrounded himself with good people. Yemm, Adkins, Dave Whittaker, Carleton Paterson.

"Trust," he said to himself, unable finally to hold back his fears. He couldn't trust any of them. And yet for his own salvation he had no other choice.

He turned as a very large man in a dark suit and clerical collar emerged from the elevator and shambled like a bear up the corridor to the nurses' station. He wore old-fashioned galoshes, unbuckled, but no overcoat. There was something vaguely familiar about the man, though McGarvey was certain they'd never met. Peggy Vaccaro got to her feet, and McGarvey walked back to her.

"Are we expecting anyone?" he asked.

"Someone called from Mrs. M.'s church a couple of hours ago, asking about her."

A nurse came out of the station and brought the cleric back. "This is Father Vietski from Good Shepherd Church. He asked if I would verify who he was." She was grinning. "He's okay, as long as you don't let him get started telling jokes about the Lutherans and Baptists."

"Next time I have a story about evil nurses," Vietski said. His voice was rich and deep, with maybe a hint of a New York accent.

"I don't want to hear it," the nurse said laughing, and she left.

The priest gave Peggy a warm smile, then turned his gaze to McGarvey, a little sadness at the corners of his mouth. "I'm Kathleen's parish priest. You must be Kirk McGarvey."

"I don't think we've ever met," McGarvey said. "But you look familiar."

"I have one of those faces," he said. "And maybe you saw one of our church bulletins. Kathleen has been helping out in the office whenever she can." He glanced at the door. "Will she be all right?"

"We hope so," McGarvey said.

"The poor woman has been driving herself unmercifully lately. Trying to be all things for everyone. She can't go on."

"What do you mean?" McGarvey asked, careful to keep his tone neutral. This was something new, something he didn't know anything about.

"The church," Vietski replied. He shook his head. "Good Shepherd is falling apart. We need eleven million dollars to rebuild, and dear Kathleen has taken it upon herself to raise the money. All of it."

"I'm sorry, she hasn't said anything to me about it," McGarvey admitted. "We've had some family problems—"

Vietski reached out and touched McGarvey's arm. "No need to explain," he said. "All of us have our trials. And I think at times she might be a little ashamed of her faith, if you know what I mean."

It seemed to McGarvey that the priest was reaching out for his own assurances. It was as if he was trying to *draw* strength instead of give it. "I don't think that my wife would have remained with something she didn't believe in."

Vietski smiled and nodded. "May I go in for just a few minutes?"

"Maybe later, she's sleeping now."

"I won't wake her, I promise," Vietski said earnestly. "But just a few minutes. I'd like to sit with her and say a little prayer. I think it would mean something to her."

McGarvey glanced at Peggy, who raised her eyebrows. Then he nodded. "Okay."

Vietski went into Kathleen's room, closing the door softly behind him.

"He's a troubled man," McGarvey said.

"But he seems to care," Peggy Vaccaro replied. "That's something."

The blinds were shut and the room was dark. Kathleen was asleep. Vietski moved to her side and made a sign of the cross over her head and began to pray, his voice soft, but filled with emotion.

"The Lord is my shepherd; I shall not want. He maketh me to lie down in green pastures: He leadeth me beside the still waters. He restoreth my soul: he leadeth me in the paths of righteousness for his name's sake. Yea, though I walk through the valley of the shadow of death, I will fear no evil; for thou art with me; thy rod and thy staff they comfort me . . ."

THREE

BLOWBACK

And oftentimes, to win us to our harm,
The instruments of darkness tell us truths,
Win us with honest trifles, to betray's
In deepest consequences—
—Wm. Shakespeare

It's blowback, plain and simple. The policy was kept
from the American public all these years, and now
we're reaping the unintended consequences.
—CIA, anonymous

TUESDAY

ONE

"YOU DON'T BELIEVE IN GOD, BUT YOU *DO* HAVE SOME OF THE ANSWERS."

ANDREWS AFB

McGarvey was seated in the back of the DCI's limo headed east on I-495 across the river, lost in thought, as Dick Yemm expertly maneuvered the armored Cadillac through the lunch hour traffic. Otto Rencke sat in back with McGarvey. Yemm had snagged him at his apartment before coming out to Chevy Chase.

"Liz is going to want to see you," McGarvey had explained to Otto.

She'd sounded distant and frightened on the phone last night. He glanced over at Otto, who was staring out the other window, then at Yemm, who was watching in the rearview mirror. Everyone's imagination was working at full tilt. All of them were waiting for the next shoe to drop, for the next attack to come. And everyone was looking to him for support, for answers.

They passed Temple Hills as an air force transport took off from Andrews a couple of miles away. He felt a spasm of fear for his daughter, for what this latest attack was doing to her spirit. Losing the first baby had been almost more than she could endure. Only Todd had been able to bring her back, to make her laugh again. This time was worse. The loss wasn't a natural miscarriage. It was murder. He didn't know how Liz was bearing the pain and the fear. And he didn't know if Todd, who was suffering his own demons, would be able to be as strong this time as he had been the first.

"I'm here, baby," he mumbled to himself. "This time I won't leave." He wanted her to get the message loud and clear.

"Mac, oh wow, are you okay?" Otto intruded.

McGarvey came out of his thoughts. Otto's eyes were round, his hair went in every direction. He was frightened. "I'm okay. How about you?"

"I shouldn't have called Mrs. M., ya know. I'm sorry."

There. That had been on McGarvey's mind. Yemm said that Otto told him Katy deserved the truth. But that made no sense under the circumstances. Katy needed protection. There was something else. The scratching, nagging was still there. Coming on even stronger than before.

"No. You shouldn't have. I would have taken care of it," he said, and Otto quickly looked away. What to make of his behavior? Whom to trust? Larry Danielle would know. "What's going on, Otto? I have to know. Talk to me."

Otto refused to turn back. "I don't know what you mean."

"Yes, you do. It's why I brought you out here this morning. So we could have a chance to talk."

"*Nada*," Otto murmured. He laid his forehead on the window.

"*Nada*'s no longer an acceptable answer," McGarvey pressured.

"I don't know . . ."

"Lavender," McGarvey prompted. "Start there. You're searching for something, and it's coming up lavender." But Otto didn't answer.

They arrived at Andrews main gate, and the air policemen on duty saluted the car and passed them through. Yemm drove directly over to the VIP hangar, where the CIA's Gulfstream would come after landing. The flight was still at least twenty minutes out, and there was no activity in or around the hangar, though the big doors were open. Yemm parked on the apron in front of the doors.

"Take a walk, Dick," McGarvey told Yemm. "Find out when the flight lands."

Yemm turned and looked at Otto who stared out the window toward the control tower, then at McGarvey. He didn't think that it was such a good idea leaving the DCI here unprotected, even if he was with a friend. "I can call Operations."

"Get out of here, Dick."

Yemm looked at him questioningly. Under the CIA's Standard Operating Policies he would be within his rights, as the DCI's bodyguard, to refuse a direct order if he thought that the DCI's life would be jeopardized because of it. It was the same SOP that the Secret Service agents guarding the President of the United States followed. He knew that McGarvey could take care of himself. Nonetheless, he took his job seriously. But he nodded finally. "I'll be back in ten."

When Yemm was gone, McGarvey got out of the limo, walked around to the front and leaned against the hood. An old KC-135 tanker came lumbering in for a landing. The Boeing 707 was still majestic after nearly a half century of service. He remembered as a kid riding one out to Saigon on his first assignment.

"I don't know what holds it up, ya know," Otto said at his side.

"Physics?"

"Nah."

"Then it has to be trust," McGarvey said.

"Sometimes that's not so easy."

"Between friends."

"Yes, especially between friends. Real friends, ya know."

"I'd like to think that I have real friends."

Otto gave a little shuffle. He was becoming agitated. "You do, Mac. Honest injun."

"Special Operation Spotlight."

"What?"

"I want to know what it is. Why it's lavender. And what it has to do with Nikolayev and your trip to France." McGarvey gave Otto a penetrating stare. "I want to know what it has to do with me and my family."

"It's nothing more than a research project. I'm running

down a few loose ends that Elizabeth came up with in the archives."

McGarvey shook his head. "Somebody tried to kill you, me and my wife, and now our daughter. And you tell me that you're working on a research project? Bullshit, Otto. Pure, unadulterated bullshit."

"My machines are running the programs while I'm looking for bad guys."

"Okay. What have you come up with?"

"It's too early to say."

Otto was backing himself into a corner, and McGarvey was worried that he was losing it. He was hiding something. But he always told the truth no matter how painful or embarrassing it might be.

"Give me one thing, then," McGarvey said, keeping his patience. "For instance, tell me about Nikolayev. He worked for General Baranov in the old days. Does that have something to do with this?"

"Nothing . . ."

"That's not true, goddammit," McGarvey pressed. "You don't spend that kind of computer time on a research project when someone is trying to kill you and the people around you. And you don't come up with some bullshit operational title and go off commandeering a hypersonic spy plane to take you to France."

Otto was alarmed, he seemed to be vibrating. "That's not true . . ."

"Louise was waiting here to pick you up when the Aurora landed. Dick saw the whole thing. Makes her an accessory. Do you want us to bring her in for questioning?"

Otto put a hand to his mouth.

"It wouldn't do her Air Force career much good if the head-hunters investigated her for murder and treason. Even if she was cleared, she'd be tainted in the eyes of the promotions board. She might even lose her clearances."

"Why are you doing this?"

"Because I'm tried of screwing around. I want the truth."

"I don't have the answers, Mac. I swear to God," Otto cried in anguish.

"You don't believe in God, but you *do* have some of the answers."

Otto started to dance from one foot to the other. His sneakers were untied again, his shirt was stained with something, maybe mustard, and the welts and scabs on his head punctuated the massive bruising all over the left side of his face. He looked pitiful, even crazy.

But there was too much at stake to let him off the hook, friend or not. McGarvey had known that it would come to this with Otto. Just as he knew that he was the only one to confront him; he was the only person on the face of the earth other than Louise Horn to whom Otto would listen.

Stenzel had warned him that confronting Otto head-to-head might drive him over the edge. But then he might already be over the edge and looking for a way back. Sometimes behavior like Otto's signaled a desperate plea for help. "There's simply no way to know for sure until he falls apart and we can pick up the pieces."

"It's okay," McGarvey said. He wanted to put his arm around Otto's shoulder, friend-to-friend. But he didn't dare. Otto was simply too fragile now. "It's okay. Just tell me what you can. I need something to go on."

Otto stopped dancing as if he were a mechanical toy winding down. McGarvey glanced toward the active runway. Liz's plane would touch down soon. She was another fragile spirit he would have to find the strength to protect and comfort. But they still had a few minutes. Otto was staring at him.

"In August one of my search programs came up with a hit," Otto said softly, as if he were afraid of being overheard. "An old KGB general was found shot to death in his Moscow apartment. A suicide. But there were questions."

"What search program?" McGarvey asked.

"I got the idea last year when I was digging through your old operational files." Otto was hesitant. McGarvey nodded reassuringly for him to go on. "You crossed paths with some bad people. I thought that maybe someday one of them might come looking for you. Revenge, ya know. Settle old scores. You pissed off some serious dudes."

McGarvey watched him. Otto was choosing his words with

care. With too much care. There were things that he knew that he did not want to reveal. "Who was he?"

"Gennadi Zhuralev. Nobody important, except that he worked for Baranov, and that program was watching for Baranov connections."

"Was he murdered?"

Otto shrugged. "Probably. But what got me interested was that another old Baranov hand, Anatoli Nikolayev, went missing the very same day, and within twenty-four hours the SVR launched an all-out search for him. That was too coincidental for me."

"The Russians traced him to France, and so did you."

"That's right."

"But why, Otto?" McGarvey asked. "Why have you gone through all the trouble to find some old Russian?"

"Because the SVR wanted him big-time. So I figured he had to be worth something."

McGarvey shook his head. "I don't buy it. People disappear from Russia all the time, most of them smuggling something valuable out with them. They're draining the country, so the SVR wants them back. The FBI usually gets those requests for help, but Fred Rudolph has heard nothing."

"He was a Baranov man," Otto said lamely.

"Baranov is dead, and Nikolayev is very old. Where's the interest?"

"He didn't want to forget," Otto said with difficulty.

"Forget what? What do you mean?"

"He was reading the old files. Interviewing people."

"Baranov's files? Department Viktor people?"

Otto nodded.

"Including my involvement?" McGarvey asked.

Otto nodded again.

"So what?" McGarvey said, but then he stopped himself. "He found out something that somebody in Moscow doesn't want found out."

Otto watched him but said nothing.

"It has something to do with what's happening around here. Where's the connection, Otto? Where's the lavender?"

Rencke flinched as if he had been burned. "I'm not sure, Mac. Honest injun."

"It's some operation that lay dormant for all these years until Nikolayev stumbles on it. He hits a trip wire, and the thing starts." McGarvey focused on Otto. "What is it?"

Otto was vibrating again, a look of terror on his face.

"You found Nikolayev, and you must have made contact with him. Is that right?"

Otto shook his head.

"Goddammit, you didn't come back from France empty-handed. I know you didn't. What did you find out?"

Otto's lips worked as if he wanted to say something, but he didn't.

"Spotlight is your operation to find out what Nikolayev is up to. And you found out something. What?"

Yemm came around the corner of the building. McGarvey spotted him and angrily waved him back.

"Their plane is on final, boss," Yemm shouted. "You have about five minutes." He turned and went into the hangar.

McGarvey turned back to Rencke with a mixture of frustration, pity and anger. "Somebody is trying to kill me. Or at the very least stop me from becoming DCI. A number of our people have pegged you as the chief suspect. They think that you've gone around the bend."

Otto hung his head. "I know."

"You can't do this alone, Otto. You can't fight the war by yourself. Let me help. It's what I do for my friends. It's the least I can do."

"Network Martyrs," Otto mumbled.

McGarvey's eyes narrowed. Something in the sudden mood shift as Otto spoke the words was disturbing. "Was that a Baranov operation?"

"Like CESTA and Banco del Sur, but a lot more specific." Otto was desperately afraid of something. "Nikolayev found the file at Lefortovo."

"How do you know that?" McGarvey asked. It was a reasonable question under the circumstances. "Did you talk to him when you were in France?"

"No. He was in Paris, but I didn't see him. I couldn't. Somebody tried to kill him in front of the Louvre. They killed another man instead. The one Nikolayev had gone to see. Just like Zhuralev in Moscow."

"Was he another Baranov man?"

"Valdimir Trofimov. He was Baranov's special assistant for about ten years." Otto looked off in the distance as the CIA's Gulfstream approached the end of the field for a landing. "Nikolayev doesn't have all the answers either."

"How do you know?"

"He wouldn't be running for his life."

"What about Network Martyrs?"

"He was living in an apartment in Montmartre. I found a scrap of paper with the name."

"Now we're getting somewhere. We can give this to Tom Lynch. His people can search the apartment. They might find something we can use." Lynch was chief of the CIA's Paris station.

"The Russians have already been there. They were right on my heels."

"Did you get the scrap of paper?"

Otto looked down and shook his head. "No. But I hacked the SVR's mainframe in Moscow." He looked up. "Baranov planted a very deep cover agent here in the States almost twenty years ago. When the time was right the agent would be activated and would assassinate the target." Otto blinked furiously. "The target is you, Mac. Oh, wow, and the agent has been activated."

The hairs prickled on the back of McGarvey's neck. "Who is the assassin?"

"I don't know," Otto said, unable to meet McGarvey's eyes. He was lying again. He knew, or at the very least he suspected who it might be.

"It's someone close," McGarvey said. "We know that much. Do you have a list?"

"Not one that has any meaning. Nothing makes any sense." Otto started to dance from foot to foot again.

There it was again. The business about trust. If he couldn't trust his friends, who the hell was left?

"I have my own list," McGarvey admitted. "You're on it. So is Yemm."

Maybe he had suspected all along that Baranov would come back. The look in the general's eyes when he died wasn't one of defeat, but rather one of cunning and malevolence. Bravado, as he lay bleeding to death outside East Berlin, or some knowledge that he would get his revenge in the end?

McGarvey had never really understood Baranov's motivation for coming after him. If the Russians had wanted McGarvey dead, they'd had plenty of opportunities to put a bullet in the back of his head. No one could go through life without making a mistake.

Now he had to wonder again, if indeed this was a Baranov operation that had been put in place more than ten years ago.

Was the general's desire for revenge nothing more than insanity? Some international game of chess played for a grudge? A vengeance game? It was probably something they would never know for sure, because the only man who understood was dead.

Pride? Ego? Saving face?

The Gulfstream touched down with a puff of smoke from its tires. "I'll find Nikolayev, but we gotta keep Paris station out of it," Otto said. "If the Russians find out that we're after him, too, there's no telling what'll happen. If they get to him first, they'll kill him, just like they did Zhuralev and Trofimov. They want to bury the mess that Baranov made. We'd never know the whole truth until it was too late." Otto looked up, pleading. "Don't you see, Mac, you gotta let me work on it my way."

A towing vehicle came across the apron and pulled up where the Gulfstream would stop. The driver glanced over at McGarvey and Otto, then looked away. A gas truck came from the same direction and pulled up as Yemm came out of the hangar.

"I don't think we have a lot of time left," McGarvey said. "Don't screw around, I can't give you much more slack."

"I'm trying," Otto said quietly. "I'm trying real hard to keep it together."

McGarvey watched as the Gulfstream came toward them, not at all sure what he was going to say to his daughter. What he *could* say that would help, except that he loved her.

The tow vehicle driver brought the jet to a halt, then motioned for the pilot to cut the engines. They immediately began to spool down, and Yemm went over to help as the door came open and the stairs were lowered.

Otto stepped away from the car. "She'll be okay, Mac. Todd will take care of her." There was a note of something, desperation maybe, in his voice. But he was not lying.

"Isn't he on your list of suspects?" McGarvey asked, even though the question was cruel.

Otto looked sharply at him, surprise and a little doubt showing in his eyes. "You're kidding, right?" he said, but McGarvey didn't know if he was kidding. All he knew was that once you started down the slippery slope of mistrust there oftentimes was no way back. He was trying, but he was sliding again.

"Boss?"

The jet's stairs were down. Yemm stood by at the open door. He was waiting.

McGarvey fixed a smile on his face and boarded the plane. The pilot on the flight deck gave him a nod.

"We had a smooth flight, Mr. Director," he said.

McGarvey glanced at him. "Thanks," he said. His eyes slid past the copilot and the young woman who was the flight attendant, to his son-in-law, perched on the arm of Elizabeth's seat, looking like he would take the head off anyone who so much as twitched near his wife. Then he looked at Liz, and his smile almost died.

Elizabeth's face was puffed up and badly bruised. Her eyes were swollen half-shut and bloodshot. She wore one of Todd's flannel shirts, her left arm was in a sling. It was obvious from the way she held herself that she was in pain, especially in her lower back. She shivered in anticipation. Her mouth was screwed up in a grimace that made it impossible to tell if she was wincing in a sudden sharp pain, or she was trying to smile.

Her skin, where it wasn't black-and-blue, was pale, almost translucent. Even without the marks, she was obviously a sick woman. The medical report McGarvey had read said that she had lost a significant amount of blood. It would take time for her to recover.

"Hello, sweetheart," McGarvey said soothingly. He went to her and gently kissed her forehead.

She looked up at him just like she had when she was a little girl, before he and Katy had separated, waiting for him to tuck her in for the night and listen to her prayers.

"You're back home now, and everything's going to be fine." He glanced at Todd, who gave him a very determined look in return. "The doctors say that you'll come out of this just fine. How do you feel?"

Her eyes squinted, and a couple of tears rolled down the side of her face. She picked a small, brown stuffed bear off the seat beside her and hugged it close with one arm.

"They killed the baby, Daddy," she said, her voice impossibly young. McGarvey almost lost it. She looked over her father's shoulder. "Where's Mom? Why isn't she here?"

"She wasn't getting any rest, so the doctor put her in the hospital. Just for a couple of days. She'll be home tomorrow."

"Was it because of me?" Elizabeth demanded. She looked up at Todd for support. He didn't avoid her eyes.

"Partly," McGarvey admitted. "But whoever tried to get you, has tried to eliminate us, too. Which is why all of us are going to play it by the book and let Security do its job."

"Is she okay?" Elizabeth insisted.

"She'll be fine in a day or two. She just needs the rest, that's all."

"Are you sure?"

He nodded.

She looked over her father's shoulder again. Otto and Yemm had boarded the airplane and stood hunched over in the aisle.

"Oh, wow, Liz, are you really okay?" Otto asked.

"I'll live," Elizabeth replied. "Are you back at work?"

"Yeah."

She brushed at a tear and faced her father. "Okay, it's over.

Todd and I are back, and we're going to find the bastards who are doing this to us." Gone was the little girl. She had become the strong, determined young woman she prided herself on being. A McGarvey.

"You're not going anywhere except to the hospital," McGarvey told her.

"Yes, to see Mom—"

"And then the doctors. You're not going anywhere until they give you a clean bill of health."

"I'm not going to lie around a hospital while someone tries to kill you. I don't have a concussion, and I didn't break any bones. I lost some blood and I lost the . . . baby." Her breath caught in her throat. "It's happened to other women, and it's happened to me before. But I'm not an invalid."

"No. But you're my daughter," said McGarvey, "and before you do anything you're going to heal. They'll probably want to hold you overnight, and if that's what they want, that's what they'll get." McGarvey looked up. "Right, Todd?"

Elizabeth started to protest, but Todd shook his head. "Just listen for once, Liz. Please. The rest of us can't do our jobs if we have to ride herd on you."

"I'm okay," she shot back crossly. She started to rise, but she winced in pain and slumped back.

"Dick, call an ambulance," McGarvey said.

"No," Elizabeth protested. "I'll go to the hospital, and I'll stay there until they say I can go back to work." She looked up defiantly. "But no ambulance."

"Okay, sweetheart, no ambulance. But I'll hold you to your promise."

BETHESDA

Otto rode in the front with Yemm, the bulletproof divider up, while McGarvey rode with his battered daughter and son-in-law in the back. He wanted to get the story, the *whole* story, from her.

He wasn't going to bring up what Todd had told him before the weekend, that she and Otto had put their heads together and were working on something in secrecy. He wanted it to come from her without pressure. She was too brittle now; the right push could send her over the edge. All of them were on the brink, but especially Katy and Otto and now Liz.

She remembered skiing, but not the accident. "Todd was behind me. He was shouting for me to slow down." She still held the teddy bear. She smoothed its pink bow. "I have to thank Ms. Swanfeld."

"The bear came from everybody upstairs," McGarvey said.

She nodded. "Somebody was holding my hand and calling my name. It was Doris, my work name, but I knew that I was supposed to respond, say something, anything." She shook her head in vexation. "But it was like I was having a nightmare. I knew that I had to keep running, but it was impossible because I was up to my knees in glue." She looked up at her father. "I knew that you were going to be mad at me."

"I'm not mad at you, Liz. It wasn't your fault."

"If I hadn't gone skiing—"

"Then they would have tried something else. And maybe you wouldn't have been so lucky."

She shuddered and looked away. "Some luck," she muttered bitterly.

"Why you?" McGarvey asked. He glanced at Otto, who was looking straight ahead, giving no indication that he knew what was being discussed in the back.

"I don't know, Daddy," Elizabeth said. "I can't figure it out. If someone is trying to kill you, why come after me or Otto? And if they're just trying to get you to quit, then they've got to start realizing that they're going about it exactly the wrong way."

"Have you been working on anything that might make you a target?"

"Do you mean that the attack on me might have been co-incidental?" Liz shook her head. "It's not likely. The Semtex they used in my bindings came from the same batch they used on your helicopter."

Lips pursed, McGarvey counted to five before he responded. "How do you know that?"

"Jerry Kraus's people came up with a match."

"But how did you find out, sweetheart?"

"I don't know. I think maybe Todd mentioned it."

Todd shook his head, and Elizabeth caught it.

"Maybe Otto told me, then."

"When did you talk to him? Was it yesterday?"

"It must have been," she said, her anger rising. She hated to be put on the spot. "We left early this morning, so it was probably yesterday afternoon. I don't remember."

"I shouldn't think so," McGarvey said, sympathetically. "Not with all you've been through. But I'll talk to Otto when we get to the office and clear it up."

"Clear up what?" Liz demanded. "Where's the mystery?"

"It's a Russian thing. Something out of my past that we're trying to get a handle on," McGarvey told her with a measured nonchalance. "Could be that it's them gunning for me. Otto has probably come up with something, too, but you know how he is. Unless he's got it nailed down cold, he keeps whatever he's working on to himself." McGarvey shrugged. "I thought that if you had talked to him, he might have said something."

"Oh, that," she said. "It has something to do with General Baranov, you're right. And with a Department Viktor shrink who's supposed to be on the run from the SVR. But I don't know a lot more than that."

"Is that what you two have been working on so mysteriously?"

"I've been working on your bio," Elizabeth responded too quickly. "I would never have guessed one-tenth of what you did."

"Does Otto think that Nikolayev is gunning for me?"

"He's too old. But it might have something to do with whatever he took out of Moscow with him." She shook her head. "I just don't know, Daddy. Honestly. I wish—"

"You wish what, sweetheart?"

She looked a little embarrassed. "I wish sometimes that we could just all go away someplace and just be together."

"Maybe in a time machine?" McGarvey suggested.

She smiled and reached for her husband's hand. "Only if I could take Todd with me."

Peggy Vaccaro was sitting across from a sleeping Kathleen in the darkened hospital room when McGarvey and Elizabeth showed up. Otto and Yemm went to the waiting room. Todd went downstairs to speak with Dr. Mattice, who was on his way over on McGarvey's call to see about admitting Elizabeth at least overnight.

"Good heavens, Liz, we were all so worried about you," Peggy Vaccaro said in a soft voice, getting up. They hugged lightly. "How are you?"

"I've been better," Elizabeth said. "How's my mother?"

"A lot better." Vaccaro looked over at McGarvey. "Dr. Love was in again this morning, and they did another test downstairs. An EKG, I think, and something else. We didn't know exactly what time Liz was coming in, and the doctor wanted Mrs. M. to get some rest, so he gave her a light sedative."

"Did he say anything about her condition?" Elizabeth asked.

Peggy Vaccaro smiled. "That's the good news. She's going to be okay." Again she looked at McGarvey. "She can go home tomorrow morning at the latest, Mr. Director. That's really good news."

"Yes, it is," McGarvey agreed. He watched the play of emotions across his daughter's face. When he and Katy separated, Elizabeth had blamed herself for the divorce. She felt as if she hadn't been a good enough daughter to keep them together. It was because of her that her parents no longer wanted to live together. The same expression of guilt creased her face now with lines of worry and doubt. It was because of her that her mother was here like this.

Elizabeth brushed a wisp of her mother's hair off her forehead, then bent down and kissed her cheek.

"She's going to be really happy to see you," Peggy Vaccaro said.

"I'm not going anywhere, Peg," Elizabeth said. She turned to her father. "I'll stay here with Mom until she wakes up. Take Otto back to work."

"I'll leave Todd here," McGarvey said.

"Yeah," Elizabeth replied absently. She looked at her mother. "He and I have some things to work out."

McGarvey's heart went out to his daughter. He wanted to cradle her in his arms for the rest of her life, to protect her from the demons and gremlins. But he couldn't do it. Leastways not like that.

"It'll be okay, baby."

"I know it will, Daddy, because we'll make it so." She looked at him. She was crying again. "*You'll* make it so."

TWO

IT WAS AS IF HE WERE BEING TEASED BY SOME
TRUTH, SOME SUDDEN INSIGHT THAT WOULD
MAKE EVERYTHING CLEAR TO HIM.

CIA HEADQUARTERS

McGarvey rode alone in the backseat out to Langley, Otto once again up front with Yemm, content to be alone for a little while with his thoughts. Idly he watched the traffic. In a way Washington was like Los Angeles. People were on the go, moving, always in a hurry. Nothing stayed the same. Everything was in a constant state of change. Focusing on any one thing or person for very long was more difficult than ever. Cell phones and the Internet had not isolated people as many critics had predicted. The new technologies brought people together. But only superficially. These days you were far less likely to talk to a neighbor three houses away than you were to an anonymous chatroom personality halfway around the world. And now there was terrorism.

It was an issue of trust.

McGarvey understood the concept at the gut level. But it was a forgotten muscle in his body, a gene that somehow had not been switched on at birth. And the harder he tried to trust people, the more he wanted it, the more he wanted to rely on someone, to go back-to-back with them for protection against the world, the more difficult it became.

After Santiago he had run to Switzerland to lick his wounds. It was the most neutral place on earth that he could think of. The CIA had abandoned him, the Senate oversite committee, one of whose key members was Darby Yarnell, had thrown him to the wolves, and even Katy had given him an ultimatum: "Me or the CIA." So he had bailed out.

The Swiss Federal Police knew who he was, of course, and his presence in Lausanne made them nervous. Not enough to kick him out of the country, but enough to send three cops to watch over him. One was Dortmünd Füelm, who became his partner in a bookstore. The second was a young woman who passed herself off as Füelm's daughter. She kept trying to get McGarvey to sleep with her. And the third was Marta Fredricks, who shared his apartment, his bed and his life until the end, when he was recalled to Washington. She had fallen in love with him, and their parting had been difficult for both of them.

"But I love you, Kirk. Doesn't that mean something to you?"

McGarvey lowered his head. Marta said that to him the day he walked out on her in Lausanne. And she said it to him again in Paris, where she had come looking for him. He rejected her both times because he was not able to trust her, not even a little. The first time her heart had been broken, and the second time in Paris, when he had sent her away, she was killed in the crash of a Swissair flight. He could never forget her last words, or the look on her face.

They crossed the river and went down the Parkway to the CIA. The afternoon was clouding over. It looked like snow again. They were passed through the gate, and Yemm pulled up at the executive entrance. McGarvey let himself out and went inside. Otto and Yemm came right behind him.

"I've got work to do," Otto mumbled, and, head down, he hurried off to the computer center.

"Are you going to need me, boss?" Yemm asked.

"No."

Yemm hesitated just a moment. "Liz is going to be okay,

and so is Mrs. M. now that we know what's going on."

McGarvey looked at his bodyguard curiously. "What's going on?"

"Somebody's after you, and they're not above going after your family to get to you." Yemm shrugged pragmatically. "Except for the chopper pilot on Hans Lollick, nobody's been killed."

Scratching, nagging, worrying at the back of his head. He wanted to run. "Except for the baby," McGarvey said, and he took the elevator upstairs leaving Dick Yemm standing flatfooted in the corridor.

Ms. Swanfeld was waiting for him when he barged through the outer office and into his office. She took his coat, hung it up, then got him a cup of coffee, into which she poured a healthy measure of brandy.

"I thought that you could use this," she said, setting it down on the desk.

He smiled tiredly. "The boss isn't supposed to be a drunk."

She smiled faintly. "President Lincoln had the same problem with Grant."

"I wish it was that simple," he said. "What's on the schedule?"

"You're supposed to be on the Hill at two."

"Not today."

"Very well. Mr. Paterson thought that might be the case. He would like a few minutes of your time this afternoon."

"Whenever he's free."

"Barry Willis of the *New York Times* is coming at five-thirty for a backgrounder on the Havana incident. But I suspect that he will actually ask you questions about the Virgin Islands."

"Reschedule him for sometime next week."

"Yes, sir," she said. "In that case, except for Mr. Paterson, you are free for the remainder of the day."

"I want a staff meeting at five. I'd like to see the preliminary NIE and Watch Reports. I'd like to speak with Fred Rudolph at some point, and then the President." McGarvey glanced at the door to Adkins's office. "Is Dick here this afternoon?"

"Yes, sir. But he had a terrible night of it. Mrs. Adkins is back in the hospital."

McGarvey felt terrible for him. "I've tried to force him to take a leave of absence. But he won't do it."

"Neither would you, Mr. Director," Ms. Swanfeld countered sternly.

"But I'm—"

"Indispensable?" she asked.

He was going to say under fire, but he just shook his head. "Point well taken."

"How is Elizabeth?"

"She won't let go of the teddy bear. She says to tell everybody thanks."

Ms. Swanfeld smiled warmly.

"She's black-and-blue, and her back hurts, but she wanted to come back to work this afternoon."

"Good heavens. Pardon me, sir, but you are not going to allow that child to resume her duties this soon, are you?"

"No, they're keeping her overnight at the hospital, and she'll be out on sick leave for at least a week. Maybe longer. My wife will be returning home, probably tomorrow morning. I'll see if I can't convince Elizabeth to come home to help out. Her mother could use her."

"Indeed," Ms. Swanfeld said. Her manner brightened, as if a burden had been lifted. "I'll go make your calls."

"Give me a half hour."

"Yes, Mr. Director." Ms. Swanfeld went to the door. "I'm glad Elizabeth is back safe and sound."

"So am I."

McGarvey stared out the windows at the deepening gloom as he finished his coffee. Then he went next door to his DDCI's office. Adkins, in shirtsleeves, was just sitting down at his desk as the outer door from his office closed.

"Who was that?" McGarvey asked.

Adkins looked up, startled. "Oh, hello, Mac. Elizabeth got back okay?"

McGarvey nodded. "She's going to spend the night in the hospital. We'll see tomorrow. But it's good to have her back." He glanced at the door.

"That was Bob Johnson, he had a final report on Otto's accident. Somebody did tamper with the wheel bearing. Curious though, whoever did it wasn't a mechanic. They just jacked up the car, took the wheel off and dug around in the wheel bearing well with a screwdriver, or something."

"So it could have been Otto himself."

Adkins nodded glumly. "But whoever did it wasn't trying to fix anything. They were trying to sabotage the wheel so that it would come off."

"I was told that Ruth's back in the hospital. What happened, Dick?"

"She had another relapse," Adkins said, looking down at his hands. "This time she was puking up a lot of blood. But there are no bleeders. Nothing they can fix."

"Ulcers—"

"She's riddled with cancer. It's everywhere in her body. She's disintegrating from the inside out."

McGarvey was disturbed. "I can't believe that you came in today. Get the hell out of here. You need to be with your family."

"The girls arrived last night, they're with their mother." He shook his head again. "There's nothing I can do for her that makes any sense. She's in intensive care, and—"

"And nothing, Dick." McGarvey softened his tone. "I mean it, you have to get back to the hospital, if for no other reason than your daughters."

"They don't want me."

"Bullshit, and you know it. I'm placing you on sick leave right now. Dave Whittaker can help take up the slack for the time being."

Adkins's mood, which seemed terribly matter-of-fact, did not match the situation. It was denial. This wasn't happening to him. By throwing himself into work he could forget for a few hours what was really going on around him.

And yet there was something else. Another layer of meaning in Adkins's gestures and words. As if he were hiding something so terrible that he had to watch his every movement lest he give himself away.

"I'm ordering you out of here," McGarvey said. He gestured

to the pile of folders on the desk. "Are those the NIE and Watch Report?"

Adkins nodded.

"Give them to me, then put on your coat, tell your secretary that you'll be gone until further notice, get in your car and drive over to the hospital."

Adkins reluctantly handed the thick file folders to McGarvey. "There've been no substantive developments in the past five days."

"Call me when you can. Let me know what's happening," McGarvey said. "Tell Ruth that . . . we're thinking of her." McGarvey went to the door.

"I hate to leave like this, Mac."

"I know," McGarvey said, and he walked back into his own office.

He sat down at his desk and forced himself to flip through the reports. No matter what else happened to them individually, the business of the world and therefore the CIA, continued.

Adkins came to the door a few minutes later, his coat on. "I'm gone then," he said.

"If you need us, we're here for you, Dick," McGarvey said.

Adkins nodded. "I know," he said. "Good luck." He turned and walked out.

McGarvey was about to call after him, to tell him that no matter how long it took he would be welcomed back with open arms, when his secretary buzzed. "What is it?"

"It hasn't been a half hour, but Fred Rudolph is on one for you. Do you want to take it, or should I ask him to call back?"

"I'll take it," McGarvey said. He punched one. "Fred, what do you have for me?"

"We're having no luck tracking down Nikolayev in France, and now Dmitri Runkov has disappeared."

"What are you talking about, disappeared? Did he return to Moscow?"

"Not on any flight out of Washington or New York," the FBI supervisor said. "He's apparently not at home, and he's not available at the embassy."

"What about his family? Are they still in Washington?"

"His wife and kids are at the house, living like they normally have. Grocery store, the dry cleaners, the bank, gas station, liquor store, little league hockey. But no Dmitri."

"Has this happened before? Has he disappeared like this, I mean?"

"He's played games with us, but never like this. Never for so long. Hours usually, never days."

Mysteries within mysteries. Nothing was as it seemed to be. The one idea that would solidify everything danced at the edges of McGarvey's understanding. It was as if he were being teased by some truth, some sudden insight that would make everything clear to him.

"If he hasn't managed to slip out of the country under our noses, then it means he's gone to ground for some reason," Rudolph suggested.

"That doesn't make him guilty of anything," McGarvey countered, working it out. "Maybe he's just a cautious man."

"You might be right, Mac. But if that's the case, if he's just ducked into the nearest bunker, it means that he's expecting an explosion. Soon."

"It would seem so," McGarvey said. "Dmitri knows something that we don't."

"We'll keep trying to dig him out," Rudolph promised. "In the meantime, maybe you should take his example and keep your head down, too."

"The thought has occurred to me," McGarvey said. "Keep in touch."

"You too."

McGarvey had Ms. Swanfeld call the White House. They got Anthony Lang, the President's chief of staff.

"He's on an extremely tight schedule today, Mr. Director," Lang told McGarvey.

"I need a minute of his time," McGarvey insisted.

"He'll call you from Ottawa. His helicopter is here—" Lang was interrupted. "Just a minute."

The President came on. "You've certainly put a burr under Hammond's saddle. If he could arrange for a firing squad, you'd be against the wall before sundown."

"He has an inside source here at the Agency," McGarvey

told the President. "When we run him down, I'm going to nail Hammond publicly."

"Not such a good idea," the President disagreed. "You and I are in a tough spot right now. I have a vote on my armed forces modernization bill coming up that Hammond and Madden are going to pull out all the stops to oppose. And some nut with a grudge is out there gunning for you and your family.

"Now, I'm not willing to kiss Hammond's ass, just like you're not going to surround yourself with the National Guard. When you find your leak, you can hang him or her. They'll deserve it. But not publicly. We're going to give Hammond that round. In return he's going to give us your nomination, and he's going to roll over and play at least neutral if not dead on my bill. It's two for one. Not a bad return."

"Until the next time—"

"Tom Hammond is an elected representative of the people. He's not going away anytime soon, and I wouldn't want him to. He serves a very useful purpose. He's part of the system, and we'll live with him. In the meantime, give me what I want, and Hammond will give us what we want, which should clear the way for you to find out who's after you."

"No further hearings."

"Not until you're in the clear."

McGarvey could hear the deal maker in the President. Haynes was famous for it. Someone trying to harm the director of the Central Intelligence Agency was a big deal. But not as big a deal as arms limitation talks, or world trade agreements, or terrorist attacks in Washington and New York. Every event had its own perspective against the backdrop of the world's problems. One man, even one as important as a DCI, could not swing the balance of millions of lives in jeopardy. It was a fact of life. Reality.

"Have a good trip, Mr. President," McGarvey said.

"You'll find out what's happening. You always do," the President said. "But stay safe."

Lawrence Haynes was the most popular president since Reagan because he was an honorable man with a squeaky clean past and a picture-perfect wife and daughter whom the

American public had adopted from the beginning of his campaign in New Hampshire. But he had retained his popularity because he kept his administration simple.

Simplicity had become the White House watchword. The most complex and perplexing problems were broken into their constituent parts, each much simpler and easier to deal with than the whole. His staff found the new way of thinking a breeze. And so did the public.

McGarvey got up and went to the windows that looked over the Virginia countryside toward the Potomac River. Snow was falling in delicate, almost weightless flakes. The whispering nagging was there at the back of his head, but he was beginning to understand the why of someone coming after him, and he felt that Nikolayev might have the answers to the how. It was something psychological.

Keep it simple. Always simple. When he had the answers to the first two elements—the why and the how—he would have two legs of an isosceles triangle, and the third would be a fait accompli.

THREE

"MY HUSBAND KILLED HIM, YOU KNOW. SHOT
HIM RIGHT THROUGH THE OLD EYEBALL."

BETHESDA

Norman Stenzel tapped a Marlboro out of his pack
and lit it, tossing the match in the ashtray on the
long conference table. His neurologist friend, Dr.
Robert Love, sat across from him. They'd been going over
Kathleen McGarvey's medical file and the results of her
tests—or rather, the lack of results—for the past hour. As far
as Stenzel was concerned he was no closer to understanding
what was happening to the woman than he had been in the
beginning. The joke among psychiatrists when they didn't
know what was wrong with a patient was to simply say that
they were nuts.

"There's nothing wrong with her, Norm," Dr. Love said. He
and Stenzel were opposites. Love was a precise man, in his
manner, in his impeccable suits and hand-tailored shoes and
two-hundred-dollar haircuts, in the twelve-cylinder Mercedes
that he drove. Stenzel, on the other hand, was a dreamer, a
speculator. He looked and acted shoddy; his hair was too long,
his corduroy trousers were baggy and his eleven-year-old
Chevy Blazer was pockmarked by rust and dents as if it had

been in a war zone. But they respected each other's professional abilities, and they were friends.

"Except that she's nuts," Stenzel replied.

"There's nothing wrong inside her head. No lesions, normal EEG, nothing from the MRI, no tumors, no bleeders, no asymmetries. Nothing showed up from the lumbar tap, her sugar level was normal. Nothing obviously wrong with her blood chemistry. She has a slightly higher than optimal B/P, her cholesterol is at 190, her lipids and tryglicerides are just about what you'd expect for a woman of her age and lifestyle." Dr. Love spread his hands. "She's as healthy as you or I."

"Puts the ball back in my court," Stenzel said. Which was about what he figured would be the case. Though it would have been easier had they found a small lesion or even a benign tumor somewhere on her temporal lobe. It would have made understanding and then treating her symptoms a lot simpler.

"Schizophrenia?"

"That was my first thought, but I've gotten a lot of contradictory test results." Stenzel frowned. "Something else is happening. It's as if something's pushing at her. Something that she's terrified of."

Dr. Love closed the folders he'd been reading from. They'd met at the hospital rather than at their offices for convenience sake. "Well, from what you've told me about her situation, it's a wonder she's not a raving lunatic."

"That's precisely the problem, Bob. She isn't raving. At least she's only lost control the one time, so far as we know. But the life she's had, and especially what's been going on over the past week or so, should have forced her into nervous collapse."

"She's tough. She'd have to be, to be married to someone in her husband's position."

Stenzel shook his head. "That's the other part of the problem. Her position. She's carrying around a load of guilt issues, just like the rest of us. Most of them are crap. But she's taken on the problems of a half-dozen charities, including her church, as if they were her own. The things they're saying in her husband's Senate confirmation hearings are depressing her.

And she's gone through her daughter's pregnancy and miscarriage as if she had been carrying the baby herself."

"She sounds like the typical Beltway wife. But, look, I'll run the tests again. Maybe we missed something."

"No, I don't think so. If you thought it was necessary to redo the tests, you would go ahead and do it." Stenzel looked away for a moment, resigned. Dr. Love got up. "We'll see you and Marie Saturday night, then?"

Stenzel nodded. "Yeah. Thanks for your help, Bob."

When Dr. Love left, Stenzel remained seated at the table to finish his cigarette. He was down to a half a pack a day now. But it was hard.

He'd seen other cases like Kathleen's before. The CIA was tough on its employees and their families. The sometimes long absences, the constant pressure to "get it right," because lives were on the line, the almost constant harping and criticism of the CIA in the media. In polite company admitting that you worked for the CIA was worse than admitting that you worked for the *National Enquirer*. You got no respect. It took its toll.

And yet Kathleen McGarvey's case was different. One day she seemed fine, and the next her test scores were off the charts. Nothing made sense.

There was a deepening of all of her emotions. She was madly, almost maniacally, in love with her husband, wanting to lash out and crush whoever was trying to do him the slightest harm. Yet a few hours later, sometimes only a few minutes later, she talked with complete candor about why she had left him twenty years ago, and how the pressures of his position since his return were driving her to distraction again.

One day she talked about raising even more millions for the Red Cross and for Good Shepherd Church. Twist a few arms, dress the President down, if need be. Hell, pick pockets, if it came to that. She'd do it gladly. The next day she wondered aloud why anyone would give her so much as a dime. She was a nudge; pushy, brassy, always with her hand out. She claimed to have no friends except those who could help her causes.

Some of her tests, including the Rorschach, indicated a suicidal tendency one morning, but by that afternoon her reaction to the inkblots was completely normal. At times she was so irritable that the slightest noise in the corridor would set her off; she would scream obscenities and threats to "kill the next cocksucker" who walked through the door.

At times she was deeply paranoid, yet minutes later she was normal. But her mood swings did not seem to be getting worse, as if her disease were progressing. Instead, they were steady. They followed the beat of some metronome inside her brain.

There was an underlying hate there, too. One that was concealed much of the time. It was the pattern of guilt-hate that she was going through that Stenzel was having a tough time unraveling. The simple answer was that she hated the CIA for what it had done to her and her family. But there was something else going on inside her head; something deeper that she was not consciously aware of. Maybe something out of her past. Some guilty secret, just like the ones every one of us carried around in our heads. But it was a secret that bubbled to the surface whenever she was under extreme stress.

Stenzel bundled up his files and stopped off at Kathleen's room. He wanted to talk to her for a few minutes to see if it was feasible to release her in the morning as he had promised McGarvey. But she was sleeping, and he didn't want to wake her, so he headed down to the cafeteria, his stomach rumbling. He had forgotten to eat lunch.

Otto Rencke stood in the stairhall looking out the narrow window in the fire door as Dr. Stenzel disappeared down the corridor. Janis Westlake sat on a folding chair outside Mrs. M.'s door. She was dressed in a stylish dark suit, and she was armed. Her job was to protect Mrs. M. and limit visitors to those on the list. Otto had learned this afternoon that his name had been removed.

He used his cell phone to connect with one of his computer programs, which searched for and dialed the direct number to the nurses' station on this floor. It rang twice.

"Gale Moulton."

"This is Dick Yemm. I need to talk to Ms. Westlake on

guard duty at six-eleven. Something's wrong with her phone. Could you get her for me?"

"Does she know you, sir?"

"Yes, she does."

"Just a moment, please."

Otto watched from the stairhall as the nurse came down the hall. She said something to Janis Westlake, who got up and followed her back down the corridor. He broke the connection, pocketed his cell phone, stepped out into the corridor, and, keeping his eye on the backs of the retreating women, hurried down the corridor and slipped into Mrs. M.'s room.

She was sleeping, but the IV drip of sedatives had been removed from her arm. The room was in semidarkness. Otto jammed the chair under the door handle so that it could not be opened from the outside, then approached the head of the bed.

His eyes welled with tears, and it became difficult for him to catch his breath. His heart felt as if it were fibrillating in his chest, and his knees threatened to buckle at any second.

"Oh, wow," he muttered under his breath. God forgive him for what he was about to do. He knew no other way to get the information he needed to save their lives. But it was like raping your own mother.

He took out a mesh-covered ampule about the size of a cigarette filter, broke it in two, and held it under Kathleen's nose.

She reared back, as if she had received an electric shock, but then the combination of amyl nitrate and sodium pentothal hit her bloodstream, and she opened her eyes.

"Hello, Otto," she said sweetly. "What are you doing here?" She looked as if she had awakened from a very good dream.

"Hiya, Mrs. M. I thought I would stop by to see how you were doing."

"My mouth's a little dry." She smacked her lips. Otto got the glass of water from the tray and held it for her. When she had taken a drink he put it back. She smiled. Her eyes seemed a little wild. "Thanks, that was peachy."

"I have to ask you something," Otto started.

"Can I go home now?"

"Pretty soon. But I want to know if you remember Darby Yarnell?"

"Oh, sure. He was a peachy guy. My husband killed him, you know. Shot him right through the old eyeball." She made a pistol of her fingers and fired off a shot. "Bang, bang, el dedo. That's Spanish for verrrry dead."

Otto was sick at his stomach. "Did Darby ever mention the general to you?"

Kathleen's face darkened for a moment, but then she grinned. "Oh, sure. He said that Illen had gone too far this time."

"Was he talking about General Baranov?"

Kathleen held a finger to her lips. "Shhh. We're not supposed to mention that name. Never. Never."

"About Dr. Nikolayev? Did you ever hear that name?"

Her face screwed up in concentration. At any other time she would have looked comical. She shook her head. "Nope." She suddenly looked sly. "Darby and I had sex, you know. He was pretty good, but not as good as my husband."

Otto felt terrible. He didn't want to hear this. But it was important. "Did you ever go to Mexico with Darby?"

"Nope."

"How about Russia? Did you ever go to Moscow?"

"Nope."

"Did you ever leave Washington with him?"

"Nope. I'm practically a hometown girl. I've never been anywhere except with my husband." She glanced at the door. "I want to go home now. I'm fucking well tired of this shithole."

Otto closed his eyes for a second. When he opened them, Kathleen was staring at him. "Did you ever meet General Baranov?"

For several seconds it didn't seem as if she was going to answer the question. But she nodded. "He came to Darby's house one night."

"Did you talk to him?"

"He said that I was beautiful." Kathleen drifted off, her eyes losing their focus for a little bit.

"What else did he tell you?"

"I don't remember," she mumbled.

"Please, Mrs. M., I have to know."

She whimpered. "He told me to go away. I didn't belong there."

"What else?"

"He told me to stop playing games and go back to my husband. My husband needed me."

It wasn't what Otto had expected to hear. Yet coming into this he didn't think that he had a real idea what she would tell him. He was on a mission of exploration. "Did you stay the rest of the night anyway?"

"Nope. I went home, and Darby got shot in the eyeball. Poor, beautiful Darby." She closed her eyes. "He had everything. But it wasn't enough. Not nearly . . . enough."

Otto watched her face for a minute or two, his heart breaking. She'd had an indiscretion. She was human after all, not the flawless woman he'd imagined she was. In the end he'd been disappointed in, or at the very least angered by, every woman he'd ever known, especially his mother. But he wasn't angry with Mrs. M. He was sad for her, and he wished that he had the magical power to erase some of her past. She was sleeping now.

He turned away from the bed and removed the chair from the latch. Liz was cool. And he still had Louise.

He girded himself, then opened the door and stepped out into the corridor. A startled Janis Westlake jumped up.

"Where were you?" Otto demanded before she could say anything. "This room was left unguarded. Thank God nothing happened to Mrs. M. Where were you?"

"I was taking a phone call," she said. "Sir, you're not supposed to be here."

"Since when?" Otto demanded.

"Since this afternoon, on Mr. Yemm's orders, sir."

"We'll see about that. In the meantime, where is Dr. Stenzel?"

"He said that he was going downstairs to the cafeteria," Janis Westlake said.

"Don't leave your post again," Otto ordered, and he headed

for the elevators. At the corner he looked back. Janis Westlake was gone, and the door to Mrs. M.'s room was open.

Dr. Stenzel was seated alone in the nearly empty cafeteria, eating a cheeseburger and fries with a large Coke. Otto got a couple of cartons of milk and went over to him,

"Mind if I join you?"

Stenzel looked up and frowned. "As a matter of fact I do mind. I'd like to eat my lunch in peace."

Otto sat down anyway. "Listen, Doc, I'm sorry about being such an asshole the other day. It's just that I've got a lot of shit going on." He bobbed his head. "You know what's been happening. Sooner or later they're going to get really lucky, and it'll be more than Liz's baby that gets hurt."

Stenzel said nothing. He studied Rencke's eyes.

"Look, they're like family to me, ya know. The only family I ever had. I'd do anything to protect them." Otto shook his head. "Even if it means pissing you off." Otto flashed his most charming, sincere smile.

After a beat Stenzel's expression softened. "You *are* an asshole," he said. "But you're a fascinating asshole." He glanced at the cartons of milk. "Milk?"

"They didn't have any cream, and no Twinkies. This'll have to do."

"What are you doing here?" Stenzel asked. "Your name has been taken off the visitor's list, and Elizabeth already checked herself out and went home with her husband."

"Is she okay?" Otto asked, alarmed. "She was supposed to spend the night."

"She'll be fine."

Otto searched Stenzel's face for any sign that he was lying. But the psychiatrist was telling the truth. "I've got a question about Mrs. M.'s visitors."

"I don't know why your name was taken off. You'll have to talk to Security."

"No, I meant who's been here to see her, besides us, and Mac and Liz. Has there been anyone else?"

"Her doctors—"

"No, I mean someone else. Someone not connected with the hospital or with the Company."

Stenzel thought for a moment, then started to shake his head, but stopped. "The priest."

"What priest?"

"Vietski, or something like that. He's the parish priest at Good Shepherd, where Kathleen attends. Mr. McGarvey said that he stopped by."

"Is his name on the list?"

"According to the nurses he's practically one of the staff. A lot of military and government employees go to Good Shepherd."

"Mac knows that he was here?" Otto asked. He wanted to make sure.

Stenzel nodded.

"Who else has been to see her?" Otto pressed. "Friends? Someone from one of her charities? Maybe the Red Cross? One of their neighbors?"

"Nobody," Stenzel said. "Security is keeping a tight watch on her. Nobody who isn't supposed to be here has seen her."

Otto got up to leave, a sick feeling in the pit of his stomach. "You're wrong, Doc. I got in to see her."

Dick Yemm got off the elevator on the sixth floor and hurried past the nurses' station to Janis Westlake, who jumped to her feet when she spotted him.

"How is she?" he demanded.

"Fine."

"Okay, what the hell is going on?"

"One of the nurses said that there was a call from you. But there was nobody on the line."

"I didn't call—"

"No, sir. I think that it was Mr. Rencke. When I got back to my station he was coming out of Mrs. McGarvey's room. I think that he made the call to get me away from the door."

Yemm was angry. This shouldn't have happened. "You checked on her? Nothing's wrong?"

"She's fine," Janis Westlake assured him.

"Did he say where he was going?"

"He asked where Dr. Stenzel was, and I told him the cafeteria."

Dr. Stenzel came up the corridor, stopped in the nurses' station for a moment, and emerged with a patient clipboard and chart. He looked up, seeing Yemm and Janis Westlake with concerned expressions on their faces.

"Is something wrong?" he asked.

"Have you seen Otto Rencke?" Yemm demanded.

"In the cafeteria. He left just before I did."

"Did he tell you where he was going?"

Stenzel shook his head. "No, but he told me that he managed to see Mrs. McGarvey."

Yemm shot Janis Westlake a dark look, then turned back to the psychiatrist. "What'd he talk to you about?"

"He wanted to know who'd been here to see Mrs. McGarvey, other than us and the hospital staff. I told him that so far as I knew the only other person up here was the priest from her church."

"Yeah, he checks out, and there's been no one else," Yemm said. "What else did he want to know? Did he ask you why his name had been pulled from the list?"

"No, but like I said, he admitted that he was able to see her anyway."

"I'm doubling the guard," Yemm said.

"Might be a moot point. I'm going to be discharging her soon."

"I'm still doubling the guard, no matter where she is," Yemm insisted. "Is she ready to go home?"

"Probably not. But I can't keep her here against her will. It's just that going back to the house might not be the best thing for her so soon."

"We're trying to get them to go to a safe house where they'd be easier to watch. Her and Elizabeth. But they're stubborn."

Stenzel managed a faint smile. "Runs in the family," he said. He pushed open the door and went into Kathleen's room.

The television was on and tuned to an episode of *ER*. She was propped up in bed, smiling. She had fixed her hair and put on a little makeup. She looked up. "Dr. Stenzel," she said. "When can I go home?"

"How are you feeling, Kathleen?"

"Bored—" she said, and the door closed.

"I'm sorry about the screwup, sir," Janis Westlake said.

"Don't worry about it," Yemm told her. "Rencke is a lot smarter than the rest of us. That's why I'm calling for backup."

She was startled. "Sir, do you think that it's him?"

Yemm shrugged. "I don't know. Hell, I don't know anything now."

FOUR

BARANOV CHOSE TO BRING DOWN AS MANY
PEOPLE AS POSSIBLE WITH ONE STROKE; EVEN
BRING DOWN ENTIRE ORGANIZATIONS. NOT
ONLY KILL THE MAN, BUT KILL THE IDEA . . .

FORT A.P. HILL, VIRGINIA

Rencke crossed the river on I-495, but instead of taking the George Washington Memorial Parkway back to the CIA, he continued to I-95 and headed the fifty miles south to the Agency's records storage facility outside of Fredericksburg. He wasn't exactly a welcome figure at the underground installation, but his presence was tolerated because everyone there knew what he could do to the place with the proper computer virus. The records at A.P. Hill were old files, going all the way back to 1946, when the CIA was formed, and some even farther back to the WWII days of the OSS. They were paper documents, stored in file folders, classified by era, and cross-referenced by department, operation or finance track, and tucked away in bins stored on shelves stacked eighteen feet high, that ran row and tier for miles. All of it was eight hundred feet underground in what had been an old salt mine. Lighting had been installed, along with plumbing, tile floors, in some places walls and doors, and offices and conference rooms, along with a sophisticated air-handling system that kept the place at a dust-free constant temperature and humidity. But all of it was run by computer, using, almost exclusively, programs that Otto Rencke had designed and installed some years ago when he had done the freelance work of reorganizing the CIA's computer system. No one knew more about A.P. Hill than Otto did. So he was never turned away when he came knocking at the door.

He set up his laptop in one of the conference rooms, plugging into the system's mainframe. He was assigned an electric golf cart so that he could get around the stacks. But he was not offered any assistance. The file clerks and computer custodians knew better. If Rencke needed something, he would find them. But when he had the bit in his teeth he wanted to be left alone.

Rencke stopped in midstride and looked out the windows. They faced the broad main aisle that ran the entire length of the facility. The overhead lights disappeared in the distance. The last time he was here about two years ago he had looked down McGarvey's past because of another difficult operation. Those had been sad days when he'd seen the Kansas Highway Patrol's graphic accident scene photographs of Kirk's parents. They'd been killed by the Russians, maybe even at General Baranov's behest. Even then it was obvious in some circles what McGarvey would become. He'd shown his mettle in Vietnam. And he'd shown his nature at the CIA's training facility, acing all of his courses, and in every case showing up even his instructors.

Was that it after all? General Valentin Illen Baranov come back from the grave to carry out his revenge for not only what McGarvey had done, but for what he was about to become? Nikolayev's initial message from Paris had hinted at as much. But then he disappeared. He was not answering Rencke's queries. Maybe he had gotten frightened off. Or maybe the SVR had gotten to him and either taken him back to Moscow or killed him. But so far the death of a Russian man, other than Trofimov, in Paris or elsewhere in France, had not shown up on any of Rencke's search engines. But that didn't mean much. Maybe Nikolayev's body had been hidden.

Rencke focused on the aisle through the stacks. Nothing moved out there. But the answers, if they were anywhere on earth, were here. And he had a starting point; or rather he had two out of three legs of a triangle, with McGarvey at one point and Baranov at the second. The third was the assassin who had gone active under Network Martyrs. The three names were bound by the most intimate of relationships, that of the killer and their victim.

He went back to his laptop, pulled up a search engine, and found and printed out a surprisingly short list of Baranov references. When the computer was finished, he took the cart out into the stacks, stopped at the address for each of the Baranov files, retrieved them from their bins, and moved on to the next. He was finished in less than twenty minutes and he took the eight files back to the conference room, where he spread them in chronological order on the long table.

He began to read.

Valentin Illen Baranov was born in Tbilisi, Georgia, a true Cossack he was fond of telling his staff, during the Second World War, though his exact birth date and parents' names were not known.

He was not a particularly outstanding student, except that unlike the other boys he never fought or got into trouble. His talent had been to get the other boys to fight for him, even though they didn't want to.

Even then he was perfecting his leadership talent. The secret is easy, he confided to an intended victim whom McGarvey rescued, you simply have to believe in people. Make them believe in you. Make them believe in their heart of hearts that they can do absolutely anything so long as someone believes in them. In a way it was exactly like love, he said.

After four years at the University of Moscow, where he studied international law and four languages—English, Chinese, Japanese and Arabic—he enlisted in the Missile Service where he was assigned to the GRU, Military Intelligence unit. This was during the era when the missile defense ring around Moscow was being constructed. Security on the massive project was so tight that the CIA files (see cross ref CKBANNER through CKOTIS) contained very little information of any real strategic value.

Following four years in the service he was discharged as a major, when he went immediately to work for the NKGB, where his rise was even more spectacular than it had been in the military.

He had the Midas touch. Every operation he became involved with turned out to be a gold seam, providing the Soviet Union with a wealth of information. He was rewarded with limos and drivers. He was given a brand-new, one-thousand-square-meter luxury apartment on Kusnetzki Prospekt in leadership row. He was given a dacha on the Istra River outside the city. He was given not only a free rein over the KGB's Department Viktor, but he was awarded with a highly prized diplomatic passport. He had money and power and the freedom to travel anywhere in the world at any time he wanted to for any purpose that he desired. Presidents and prime ministers didn't have that kind of power.

Rencke tried to read between the lines. Had Baranov been seeking the ultimate challenge? A lot of men in his position couldn't be satisfied with routine assignments.

Had McGarvey become his Everest?

Darby Yarnell had probably been one of Baranov's unwitting pawns from the very beginning of Yarnell's CIA career in Moscow. Darby was a man who had an overabundance of belief and confidence in himself. And his attitude manifested itself in the way he dressed, in the gourmet style he preferred to dine in, in the Jaguars and Aston-Martins he drove, and in the way he treated people.

Yarnell had convinced himself that Staff Sergeant Barry Innes, a young crypto operator at the Moscow embassy was on the KGB's payroll. He never explained how he knew this, he just did. Rather than simply find the proof, arrest the kid and send him home for trial, Yarnell came up with Operation Hellgate.

The Russians had snatched one of our people, and Yarnell wanted to cause them as much grief as possible. He wanted to stick it to them. Quid pro quo. But it depended on pretending that we didn't know Sergeant Innes had been turned. Innes was promoted to technical sergeant, placed in charge of CIA encrypted communications and was practically force-fed information that was so fantastic that the Russians slavered at the bit for more.

But the most clever part of Hellgate was the specific information given to Innes. Most of it was false, but not all of it. Yarnell argued that the Russians would have to be given something legitimate, from time to time. Something that they could verify as true, so that they would swallow the lies. And that's exactly how headquarters approved it. In that way actual intelligence information was passed to the Russians.

It had been the most perfect of Baranov's schemes to that date. No one knew who was pulling the strings, not poor, dumb Sergeant Innes, who was spying for the money so that he could support his young wife and child living back home in San Diego. Not anyone from the embassy, or back in Langley. And most especially not Darby Yarnell himself, who in the very end was proven to be nothing but a dupe.

Sergeant Innes got himself shot to death by Yarnell's manipulations, the spy of ours whom the Russians had snatched was given back, and Hellgate was deemed a success. Yarnell was a rising star.

McGarvey was not a part of that Moscow operation, but Darby Yarnell became the bridge that linked him to Baranov.

After Moscow, and after a brief stint in Langley, first on the Russian desk and then, at Yarnell's own request, on the Latin America desk, Yarnell was assigned to the U.S. embassy in Mexico City. He was the logical man for the job. He had taught himself Spanish in eight months flat, he had worked the CIA's Latin America desk, and with his Moscow background he could counter what was the largest KGB operations center out of Moscow, in the Soviet's Mexico City embassy.

Baranov was the star there as he had been in Moscow, running a pair of intelligence networks called CESTA and Banco del Sur, which collected information throughout Latin and South America.

The game in those days, before the Bay of Pigs, was to infiltrate as many governments and government agencies as possible. The Soviets, and the Americans, did this by befriending various government employees in a variety of ways. The seductions very often involved honey traps, with beautiful young women imported from Moscow or Siberia, or from Atlanta or California. Exotic women to Latin Americans. Most

often the schemes involved a lot of money: nice houses, luxury
cars, televisions and stereos; anything that the average low-
paid government employee could scarcely dream of, let alone
possess.

The Russians were winning the game because they were
more ruthless than the Americans, until Darby Yarnell showed
up. Within a couple of months he was throwing his own lavish
parties all over Mexico City, and at a CIA-run house on the
Pacific Coast. His target was Evita Perez, twenty and beautiful.
Her mother was the third daughter of the governor of the state
of Hidaglo, and her father was the assistant secretary of finance for the federal government. They were an old, presti-
gious Mexican family, with important contacts throughout the
country.

After their wedding and honeymoon, Yarnell surrounded
himself with a crowd at their palatial home outside Mexico
City and at other times at their mountain home, or at the sea-
side CIA house.

Darby's mob, as he called them, were mostly Mexican and
Latin American high government officials, and the product he
was sending back to Langley was nothing short of stellar.

But Baranov's, and therefore Yarnell's, chief target (an operation that ruined the poor young Evita) was another rising
star within the CIA. Donald Suthland Powers, who would later
become the Director of Central Intelligence.

Yarnell, under Baranov's expert direction, set up a series of
sophisticated honey traps for Powers, in which Powers would
appear to be in Yarnell's debt. The operation was a lengthy
one, and extremely delicate. Powers, who trusted Yarnell until
the very end, never suspected that he was being manipulated.
But step by step he was placed in incriminating circumstances—showing up at a nightclub known to be a communist
hangout; driving through a communist neighborhood at the
young hours of the day, and too often, being photographed
time and again in the vicinity of known KGB agents. All of
it was staged, of course, and to Powers's discredit, he never
once bothered to take a good look around him.

That operation did not come to fruition until years later,
well after Yarnell quit the CIA, and even after he'd given up

his Senate seat to become a lobbyist for a number of powerful multinational corporations and adviser to the President of the United States.

The other shoe fell when Powers was appointed to run the CIA by a president who, like everyone else, had been dazzled by Yarnell.

McGarvey was called out of retirement in Lausanne, Switzerland by a fantastic tale of betrayal supposedly leaked by Artime Basulto, a Cuban who had supported Batista until the revolution. Basulto, by then living in the States as a drug dealer, was, like everyone in the charade, being manipulated indirectly by Baranov. The target was Powers, of course, as well as the credibility of the entire Central Intelligence Agency. An incompetent president and an out-of-control Congress had hired Powers, supposedly a traitor to run the CIA. The weapons were Powers's indiscretions in Mexico City and the dogged determination that McGarvey had shown in Vietnam and later in Chile and Germany.

McGarvey was sent to investigate Yarnell, and in so doing unwittingly forced Yarnell into killing Powers, which in turned forced McGarvey to put a bullet into Yarnell's brain.

Neat and tidy. Except that in the end, Donald Powers, who was an innocent man and an outstanding DCI, was dead. Poor Evita, who had learned to believe in Baranov, shot herself to death. And as a bit of insurance, as a backstop against future events, Baranov arranged to make McGarvey witness Darby Yarnell's seduction of McGarvey's ex-wife.

Was it happening again, Rencke wondered, sitting back and closing his eyes. Baranov had guessed that someday Powers would rise to head the CIA, so he had sown the seeds of the man's destruction years earlier. Had he also seen McGarvey's rise and sown the seeds of *his* destruction?

All the clues were there. Everything that he needed to know in order to unravel the problem was in front of him, and yet he was blind.

He got up and began hopping from foot to foot, the rhythmic motion keeping time with his thoughts.

Putting a bullet into Powers's head in Mexico City in the early days would not have been the Baranov style. The Russian had never been interested in merely bringing down a single individual, because he understood that when one man fell there was usually another to take his place. Instead, Baranov chose to bring down as many people as possible with one stroke, even bring down entire organizations. Not only kill the man, but kill the idea, kill the confidence in the institution.

That would help explain all the targets this time: Kathleen and Yemm in the USVI, Elizabeth in Vail, and even himself on the Parkway.

But he couldn't see it. He could not see the whole picture.

Something was missing. Something vastly important. Something that he should know.

Otto stopped. Christ. Goddamn hell. Most of the people Baranov manipulated did not know that they were being managed. They had no idea. They were never *allowed* to see the whole picture.

Network Martyrs was at least twenty years old. Its trigger point was probably the same kind of trigger that had led to Donald Powers's downfall. McGarvey had been appointed to head the CIA, that was the opening bell. It was something that Baranov could not allow, and he would stop, even from the grave.

Still, that was only a part of the structure. Who was the Darby Yarnell this time? Who was the catalyst? Who would actually hold the gun to McGarvey's head and fire the shot?

Nikolayev? An old Russian Department Viktor psychiatrist? Possibly.

He went back to his laptop and restarted his search, this time widening the base to include all of Baranov's Department Viktor personnel and activities.

FIVE

HE KEPT COMING BACK TO THE SAME
CONUNDRUM: WHO CAN A SPY TRUST?
WHO CAN HE BELIEVE IN?

CIA HEADQUARTERS

McGarvey walked back to his office after the five o'clock staff meeting, the tall, ascetic DDO David Whittaker beside him. Since Adkins's forced leave of absence, Whittaker had agreed to temporarily fill in as acting Deputy DCI. He had shown his abilities at the meeting. His was a steady hand, and being number two wasn't such a huge leap from being boss of Operations, which was the CIA's largest directorate.

But he wasn't happy with the promotion. Adkins was a friend. "I didn't know that Ruth was that sick. It's got to be hitting him pretty hard."

"He didn't call you?" McGarvey asked, walking into his office. Ms. Swanfeld handed him several phone messages.

"No. When did he leave?"

"Earlier this afternoon. I had to practically call Security to drag him out of his office." McGarvey took a critical look at Whittaker. "His wife's in the hospital, but he didn't want to be with her. Does that make any sense to you, Dave?"

"The girls are here."

"That's what he said."

They went into McGarvey's private office and Whittaker closed the door. He seemed sheepish. "You probably don't know Dick's situation. At home. He loves Ruth, there's no doubt about that. And she loves him. But they're not really friends, like Sandy and me. Since the girls were old enough to go shopping it was Ruth and them in one camp, and Dick in the other. They treat him like gold when he's home. But to them he's more like a . . . guest in his own house."

"I see," McGarvey said. It explained Adkins's reluctance to leave. He had more friends here than at home. And his wife would find more comfort with her daughters than with her husband. "Sometimes the world's a bitch."

"The arrangement worked for him," Whittaker said. "Until now."

McGarvey felt sorry for Adkins. It was one more bit of bleak news. "Does Security know about his home life?"

"No, and it's none of their business."

"Bullshit," McGarvey shot back. "Does he have a girlfriend, David? An outside interest? If his home life is so cold, who could blame him? You know the drill. It happens all the time."

"It's not like that, Mr. Director."

McGarvey studied his new DDCI for a beat. "It's not like that because you don't want it to be, or because you don't know?"

"Dick is an honorable man."

McGarvey had heard that term before. He was no closer now to believing that such a noble passion existed than he had been as a young man before Vietnam. "I'm sure he is," he said. "But he's out."

"What do you mean?"

"I mean he's not coming back until Security and the FBI can run another full background check on him."

"You can't do that to him, not now," Whittaker argued.

"Yes, now," McGarvey replied. "For the good of the CIA."

"You sonofabitch," Whittaker blurted.

McGarvey nodded. "I am indeed," he replied mildly. "But we have a job to do, and as long as I'm sitting behind this desk I won't allow anyone to get in my way." Who to trust? He had asked that question all of his adult life without a satisfactory answer. But Adkins was out there alone, on an emotional limb. It made him vulnerable. And vulnerable men were almost always the first to fall.

Rick Ames was a drunk, and he liked to spend more money than he earned. On top of that he had a raging ego that allowed him to believe that he was truly smarter than everyone else. So he had sold out to the Russians.

He was no different than most other spies, including Robert Hanssen, who traded his secrets for money. He, too, had had a huge ego, thinking that he was better than everyone else. And he, too, had had his point of weakness in the stripper whom he had befriended and supported.

Of course for every spy who turned out to have his vulnerabilities, there were ten thousand really vulnerable men who were not spies.

McGarvey simply could not be certain about Adkins. Not now, not with so much going on around him. Even if it meant pushing away the very people who could help him the most, he had to have people he could trust.

Whittaker saw the struggle in McGarvey's face. "Sorry, Mac. I shouldn't have run off at the mouth like that."

"Yeah, I know the feeling," McGarvey said. "Are you still interested in the job? Because I need somebody up here who knows the drill."

Whittaker nodded. "Am I going to have to move into Dick's office?"

"It'd make life easier."

Whittaker nodded again. "I have a few things to square away with my people first, but I'll be in place by noon tomorrow."

"Fair enough. You'll be briefed then."

"Right," Whittaker said. He headed for the door, but McGarvey stopped him.

"One thing, Dave. I don't want you talking to Dick until he's cleared."

Whittaker wanted to object, but he realized the necessity of keeping his distance. "Okay," he said.

When Whittaker was gone, McGarvey flipped through the phone messages his secretary had handed him. Fred Rudolph had called a couple of minutes after five, followed by his son-in-law Todd, and then Stenzel.

It was after six, so he told Ms. Swanfeld that she could leave for the day, and gave Yemm the heads-up that there would be no swim today, and that they were going over to the hospital as soon as he cleared up a few things on his desk.

Rudolph was still at his desk in the J. Edgar Hoover Building when McGarvey's call went through.

"Whoever says government servants don't earn their pay is nuts," McGarvey said.

"What else would I be doing if I wasn't here? Having a drink in front of the fireplace at home while my wife made dinner and my adoring children brought me my slippers and pipe?"

"You don't smoke. And anyway you'd be shoveling off your driveway. Have you looked outside lately?"

"No, and I don't want to. That's where all the bad guys are lurking," Rudolph said. "The Russians are hunkering down. Not just Runkov, but *all* the Russians."

"What about the ambassador?"

"Except for Korolev. He's skiing with his family in Aspen. All that's left at the embassy is a skeleton staff. And it's the same in New York. The entire Russian delegation to the UN went on recess."

"When?"

"Over the past few days," the FBI's Special Investigative Division director said. "But not one of them has returned to Moscow."

"Have you found Runkov yet?"

"Yeah, he's been home all along. Just keeping his head down like all the others. We got a good picture of him through an upstairs bedroom window. But he hasn't been outside even to pick up his newspaper."

"Korolev is skiing, and everyone else is hiding."

"Whatever is going to happen will go down soon," Rudolph said. "Maybe it's time that you duck for cover yourself."

"I'm considering it."

"I think you should do more than that."

"Right, Fred. Keep me posted, would you?" McGarvey said.

"Okay. But let me know what you decide."

"Will do," McGarvey promised, and he hung up. Rudolph was wrong. The Russians had been lying low for more than the past few days. Runkov's absence last week at the hearings had sent a clear enough message. Something that they did not want to get blamed for was about to happen.

In the meantime, he would have Internal Affairs start Adkins's background investigation before they got the FBI involved.

He got an outside line. The number Todd had left was for his cell phone. His son-in-law answered on the second ring.

"Hello."

"Where are you?"

"Hi, Mac. We're home. But you better get over to the hospital before it's too late. Mrs. M. was agitating to get out of there."

That was what Stenzel's call was probably about. "I'll head over there right now. But what's going on, Todd? Why'd you take Liz home? She was supposed to stay the night."

"I couldn't stop her. She and her mother had a long talk, and when Liz came out she was pissed. She insisted that we were going home."

"What'd they talk about?"

"I can't get a thing out of her, except that she wants to get back to work."

"It's out of the question."

"That's what I told her. But she thinks that something's going to happen any minute now."

"So do I," McGarvey said, making his decision. "I'm taking Liz and her mother out to the safe house first thing in the morning."

"That's a good idea. I can get back to work and help stop this guy, whoever the hell he is."

"Do you have a security detail out there with you?" McGarvey asked. He was having strong premonitions of disaster now. Especially because Todd and Rudolph were telling him practically the same things.

"Parked out front."

"Okay, stay tight for tonight, and I'll see you in the morning."

"All right," Todd said. "But I meant what I said before. When we get this guy he will not stand trial."

McGarvey closed his eyes for a second. That was the old way. *His* old way. "I hear you," he said, and he hung up.

He called for Yemm, but the night officer of Security said that Yemm was on his way up.

Next he called Stenzel, catching him in his car about a mile from the hospital. He was on his way back to the CIA. He sounded out of breath, as if he was sprinting down the highway and not driving.

"Your wife checked herself out of the hospital about fifteen minutes ago, Mr. Director."

A cold fist clutched at McGarvey's heart. "Why didn't you stop her?"

"I'm her doctor, not her jailer," Stenzel shot back angrily. "Besides, I was going to release her in the morning anyway. She's not cured. She's a long way from that. But she is much better."

"Are her security people with her?" McGarvey demanded at the same moment Yemm walked into his office. His bodyguard nodded that they were.

"They weren't very happy, but there wasn't much that they could do except go along with her."

"Okay, I'm heading for home now. Is there anything else I need to know? Anything that I can do to help?"

"Get her out of town, Mr. Director," Stenzel offered. "I don't give a damn where you take her, just make sure that it's someplace safe."

"First thing in the morning."

"About time. Let me know where you wind up, because I want to keep seeing her. I think that I might be able to get a handle on her problem if I have just a little more time. I'm almost there."

"I know the feeling," McGarvey said for the second time in less than ten minutes.

Yemm got McGarvey's coat from the closet. He was agitated. "I just found out about it myself a few minutes ago," he said. "Janis called me and said that they were headed back to the house."

"Who else is with her?" McGarvey asked, as they headed out of his office and down the corridor to the executive elevator.

"Peggy Vaccaro is with them. They got one of the surveillance vans that Tony Parker and John Hernandez were using. They all went together."

"Did you call for backup?"

"We'll get to your house first," Yemm said. "And at this point there's nothing wrong, boss. Mrs. M. checked herself out of the hospital, and she agreed to do what her security team told her to do."

"Where are they right now?"

"When I talked to Tony they were just leaving the hospital parking lot. It'll take them fifteen minutes to get to your house. It'll take us thirty."

Downstairs they got into the DCI's limo. As soon as they cleared the building, McGarvey tried his home phone number. On the second ring it rolled over to his own cell phone. Katy wasn't home yet.

He lowered the bulletproof partition to the front seat. "There's no answer at the house. Try the security detail."

Yemm had the car phone in his hand. "They're coming up on the Connecticut Avenue exit. Do you want me to call the MHP for backup? They might have a unit in the vicinity."

"Do you think it's necessary?"

"We'd have to give them an explanation," Yemm said. "Do you want to talk to your wife?"

McGarvey looked out the window as they merged onto the George Washington Memorial Parkway. There was a lot of traffic tonight, slowed by a heavy, wind-whipped snow that was already piling into drifts. "No," he said. "Just get me home as quickly as you can, Dick. It's a bad night."

"That it is," Yemm replied.

Who to trust? Who to trust? He kept coming back to the same conundrum: Who can a spy trust? Who can he believe in? His circle of friends and close acquaintances, people he surrounded himself with, people who meant the most to him, was very small. And it was dwindling even more every day.

Otto had gone off the deep end again. Yemm was acting strangely. Adkins was under extreme pressure. And even Todd wasn't himself. Everybody had gone crazy all of a sudden.

McGarvey sat back in his seat and unconsciously reached inside his coat for a cigarette, remembering that he had quit. Dr. Anatoli Nikolayev had apparently stirred up a hornet's nest in Moscow six months ago. The SVR was looking for him, but either they weren't looking very hard, or he was better than they were. Knowing Baranov and the people who worked for him in the old Department Viktor days, he had a pretty fair idea that it was Nikolayev leading the SVR investigators around in circles.

This whole bizarre situation had a Baranov stench to it. But the general was dead. Long dead. McGarvey could feel the recoil of his pistol when he put a bullet in the Russian's brain.

But if it was Baranov after all, if it was some long-range scheme that he had placed on automatic before his death, there would have to be people around with strong ties to that past.

Someone like poor Evita Perez and Darby Yarnell and that crowd. All of them were dead, too. But there were undoubtedly others. Sleepers, the Russians used to call them. Deep-penetration agents who worked in ordinary jobs in their host countries. Barbers, engineers, doctors, lawyers, even intelligence officers. People who lay low, sometimes for years, until one day they were called into action. People whose loyalty was assured because they were paid well, and because of the promise that when their missions fully developed they would hit the jackpot—a big payoff.

They crossed the river on I-495 and a few miles later merged with I-270, which formed the northern curve of the Beltway around Washington.

McGarvey looked up. Yemm was speaking on the phone. He had sped up considerably despite the heavy traffic and the increasingly slippery road. Something was wrong.

"What's going on, Dick?"

"Parker's not answering. Neither is Janis. I'm trying Peggy's cell phone now." Yemm's replied were curt.

McGarvey speed dialed his home number. Kathleen answered on the first ring. "Hello?"

McGarvey forced himself to calm down, to keep an upbeat tone in his voice. "Hi, sweetheart. I'm on the way home. What're the girls fixing for dinner?"

"Don't be mad, Kirk. I just couldn't stay another night in that hospital. The place was driving me crazy."

"I'm glad you're home. I missed you," McGarvey assured her. "You must have just got there. Anyway let me talk to Peggy for just a minute, would you?"

"They're still out talking to the guys in the van and the chase car," Kathleen said lightly.

"What chase car's that?" McGarvey asked. All the gravity suddenly leaked out of the limo. It felt as if the elevator cables had snapped.

"It's a Mercedes. Dark blue."

"Are you sure?"

"I'm standing at the front window looking at it."

"Listen to me, Kathleen. I want you to lock the front door, then go upstairs to our bedroom. There's a pistol in my nightstand. I've shown you how to operate the safety."

"Kirk?" Kathleen's voice was small.

"Do it right now, Katy."

"What's wrong?"

"Maybe nothing, but just in case there is, I want you to do that for me right now. Lock the door, then go upstairs and get the gun."

"All right, if you say so," Kathleen said.

McGarvey held his hand over the phone. "My wife's alone in the house. She says that Janis and Peggy are talking to the guys in the van and in a chase car. Dark blue Mercedes."

"No chase car, boss," Yemm said grimly. "I'm alerting Maryland Highway Patrol and our people. Tell her to sit tight, we'll be there in a flash."

"Okay, Kirk, the front door is locked," Kathleen said.

"Are the girls still out by the van?"

"Just a minute," she said. "Yes, they're still there."

"Can you see inside the car? How many people there are? Maybe just the driver?"

"I can't see a thing. I think the windows are tinted or something."

"Go upstairs now and get the gun. I don't want you to let anybody in the house. Nobody, do you have that?"

"Nobody except for you, Kirk?" she asked in a tiny voice.

McGarvey wanted to reach through the phone and hold her. "Just me, Katy. I'm coming to you as fast as I can."

"Please hurry, darling."

"Go upstairs, but stay on the phone with me," McGarvey said.

They came to the Connecticut Avenue exit, and the limo's rear started to drift out as Yemm took the ramp too fast. But he was an expert driver, and after the car fishtailed twice he had it back under control, blasting through an orange light and heading south, through traffic.

"MHP has a unit about ten minutes out," Yemm said.

"Are you upstairs yet, Katy?" McGarvey asked. He cradled the phone between his cheek and shoulder.

"Yes."

McGarvey took out his pistol and checked to make sure that it was ready to fire, then laid it on his lap. "Get the gun."

"I'm getting it."

"I want you to switch the safety off," McGarvey said, as Yemm raced through a red light. Several cars slid off the side of the street into parked cars.

"It's off."

"Now I want you to turn off the bedroom lights, and sit down in the corner so you can see the bedroom door."

"I don't understand—"

"Just do it, Kathleen," McGarvey ordered. "Then stay there until I get home. If anyone comes through the door, I don't care who, besides me, I want you to point the gun at them and pull the trigger. And keep pulling the trigger."

"Hurry," she said. "I'm frightened."

"We're only a few blocks away," McGarvey said.

Yemm took the Mac 10 submachine gun from its holder on the transmission hump, took his left hand off the steering wheel long enough to yank back the cocking handle on top of the receiver, then powered down the passenger-side window. "I'll make one quick pass," he said.

"Concentrate on the Mercedes, I'll watch the van," McGarvey said, powering down his window.

"Kirk, are you talking to me?" Kathleen asked.

"No, sweetheart, I'm talking to Dick. Hang on."

Yemm slowed down as they passed the golf course, and he turned down Country Club Drive. The house was at the end of a cul-de-sac. The van was parked in front, but there was no sign of the Mercedes. Nor was there any sign of the girls or of Parker or Hernandez.

"We must have just missed them," Yemm said.

"Katy, are you okay? No one has tried to come into the house?"

"I'm okay, Kirk. All the doors are locked."

"Sit tight, we're right outside."

Yemm raised the Mac 10 as he drove slowly past the van. There was no movement. The van's windows were all closed, and they couldn't see anyone inside. It simply looked like a vehicle parked on the side of the street.

They drove around the circle and stopped in the middle of the street just behind and to the left of the van. Nothing seemed out of the ordinary in the neighborhood. The snowfall was heavier than it had been at Langley, and already whatever tire marks or footprints there might have been had completely filled in.

"Stay here, Mr. Director," Yemm said, getting out of the car.

"Yeah, right," McGarvey replied. He climbed out of the limo on the opposite side from the van, behind Yemm.

"Goddammit—"

"I'll cover your back, Dick," McGarvey said. "But take it nice and easy."

Yemm decided not to argue. He moved around the front of the limo. McGarvey slid into place behind him so that he had a clear sight line over the long hood.

Keeping the Mac 10 trained on the driver's side window, Yemm gingerly approached the van. He bent down and looked under the vehicle, then studied the area around it before he cautiously looked through the window.

For several long seconds he just stood there, but then he lowered his gun and looked over his shoulder. "They're all in the back."

The hairs prickled on McGarvey's neck. He knew what Yemm was going to say next.

"There's a lot of blood. I think they're all dead."

"Christ." McGarvey turned and looked at the house. "Wait for the backup," he shouted, and he sprinted across the street and up the driveway to his house.

On the porch he fumbled his keys out of his pocket, hurriedly unlocked the front door and shoved it open with his foot. He slid left, out of the firing line from anyone in the stairhall.

There was nothing. No movement. No sound. Not even the alarm. Kathleen had forgotten to turn it back on.

"Katy?" he shouted. He'd left his phone in the car.

"Kirk?" she called from upstairs.

"It's me. Are you okay?"

"Oh, Kirk, thank God," Kathleen cried. She appeared at the head of the stairs, the pistol still in her hand, pointed toward the open front door.

"Put the gun down, Katy. Everything's fine now—"

A tremendous explosion shattered the night air, flashing like a strobe light off the thickly blowing snow, the noise hammering off the fronts of the houses in the cul-de-sac.

McGarvey fell through the doorway and turned in time to see a huge fireball, blown ragged by the wind, rising into the sky from where the van and Yemm had been.

SIX

MAC HAD GIVEN HIM THE LEGITIMACY THAT HE
HAD SEARCHED FOR ALL OF HIS LIFE. RENCKE
HAD A PLACE.

FORT A.P. HILL, VIRGINIA

Arkady Aleksandrovich Kurshin was the only man
ever to have nearly bested McGarvey.

Looking up from the covering file for Operation
Countdown, Rencke wondered how he could have forgotten
the Russian assassin's name. Baranov had been the manipu-
lator behind Kurshin's delicate, even balletic, but deadly
moves. And yet it was Kurshin who had stolen a nuclear missile from a U.S. storage bunker in what was then West Germany. It was Kurshin who had managed to hijack a U.S. Los
Angeles class nuclear submarine and kill its entire crew. It
was Kurshin who had nearly embroiled the entire Middle East,
including most of the oil-producing nations, in a nuclear confrontation with Israel. And it had been Kurshin who had finally
led McGarvey to his face-to-face confrontation with Baranov.

McGarvey had been maneuvered to the meeting with the
KGB spymaster in a Soviet safe house outside of East Berlin.
But the purpose of the meeting was never made clear. It was
possible that Baranov simply wanted to kill McGarvey. It was
equally possible, maybe even likely, that Baranov thought he
could somehow turn McGarvey as he had turned Yarnell and

Evita Perez and Artime Basulto and even John Lyman Trotter, Jr., McGarvey's friend in the CIA.

It would have been a coup. A triumph of epic proportions. Like turning Luke Skywalker to the dark side in the *Star Wars* movies.

It didn't happen, of course. In fact, Baranov's wild gamble had turned against him. McGarvey assassinated him, and then back in West Berlin, where Trotter had been waiting for word from Baranov, McGarvey killed his old friend. Trotter had been a Baranov man. Seduced by the Georgian's delicate touch; by the sheer brilliance of his personality.

Rencke closed his eyes. Baranov's had been a siren song to just about every one of his targets. Those he could not convert, like Powers and McGarvey, he marked for elimination; Powers when he had become DCI, and McGarvey once in East Germany and again now.

On a separate level, McGarvey's confrontation with Arkady Kurshin came about a year after East Berlin, in the tunnels beneath the ruins of a castle in Portugal. Rencke had read that chilling report. The two assassins, McGarvey and Kurshin, each at the height of their powers, had come head-to-head in a tunnel filled with Nazi gold and the bodies of some dead Jews. There was an explosion, darkness, the tunnel filling with water.

Rencke shook his head. He felt claustrophobic each time he thought about it. That had been a close call; one that by McGarvey's own admission, could have gone either way. He'd been lucky.

There had been other operations. Baranov was at least fifteen years older than McGarvey. He'd had fifteen years more experience. Fifteen more years to develop his tradecraft.

But it should have been all over in the East Berlin safe house. And in the tunnel in Portugal.

Rencke got up and went out to the central corridor. There were forty men and women working here, and yet the vast cavern seemed to be deserted.

The answers, if there were any after all these years, were here somewhere. But he still could not make sense of what he knew.

There were common threads. Points of similarity and even contact between all of Baranov's players. Between Yarnell and Powers. Between Kurshin and McGarvey. Even between Evita and Basulto. Bridges that linked them together, with Baranov as their center span.

Someone was trying to assassinate McGarvey because he had become boss of the CIA. It was a Baranov operation that had been put in place as long as twenty years ago. One that had recently been triggered.

Nikolayev was one of the keys. One of Baranov's players. Who else? Where were the bridges?

Someone came out of the main office by the elevators and headed toward him. He caught the motion out of the corner of his eye, and he turned his head.

He knew. It came to him all at once. Suddenly he saw everything. Or at least most of it. All the clues had been in front of him since August, but he had never looked directly at them like he was looking now directly at the clerk. Delicate. Simple. Even beautiful.

And frightening beyond anything that Rencke had ever imagined.

A young Air Force staff sergeant whose name tag read FED-ERMAN, came down the corridor in a rush. He was agitated. "Mr. Rencke, the operations officer is trying to reach you, sir. It's urgent."

Rencke looked at the young man, still amazed at what had been hidden in plain sight in front of him all this time.

"Sir, this has to do with the director."

Rencke slowly focused. "What did you say?"

"The OD said that there's been another attempt."

"Shit. Shit." Rencke turned and hurried back into the conference room, where he phoned Langley.

"Operations."

"This is Rencke. What's going on?"

"There's been an explosion in front of Mr. McGarvey's home in Chevy Chase. Security is on the way, and the Maryland Highway Patrol is already there."

"Was anyone hurt?" Rencke tried with everything he possessed to stay on track. Not to go crazy. But it wasn't easy.

"We don't have all the details yet, sir. The director was not hurt, but the security detail might have been involved."

"That'd be Dick Yemm."

"Yes, sir. He does not respond to his pages. Mr. Whittaker has been informed, and he's issued the recall for all his officers."

"Send a chopper down here for me. I'll be waiting by the main parking lot."

"Sir, that won't be necessary—"

"Do it now," Rencke said menacingly. "Right now." He hung up, but sat in front of the phone for a full minute as he came to grips with his emotions, which were jumping all over the place.

He knew the why, he had a fair idea of the how and a very short list of the who. But he needed the proof, because nobody, not even Mac, would believe him without it.

First, he had to make sure that Mac and Mrs. M. were okay. And Liz. He couldn't forget about Liz.

Rencke bundled up his computer, not bothering to shut it down or log off the repository's mainframe, and took the elevator to the surface.

He was stopped at the security checkpoint in the arrivals hall, and his bag was quickly searched before he was allowed to pass through.

The snow had tapered off somewhat, but there were halos around the lights. Rencke ran across the driveway, past the flagpole and the bronze Civil War cannon on the median, and stopped at the edge of the nearly empty parking lot.

He started to hop from one foot to the other. The helicopter wasn't here yet. He cocked an ear, but he could not hear it approaching.

"Goddammit." If his ride wasn't here in five minutes, they'd pay. Someone would pay with their balls.

He took out his cell phone and speed dialed McGarvey's number. It rang four times, then rolled over to the locator at Langley. Rencke broke the connection. Mac had his hands full right now dealing with the mess.

He telephoned the hospital and asked for Kathleen McGarvey's room.

"I'm sorry, sir, Mrs. McGarvey was discharged from the hospital this afternoon," the operator informed him.

"On whose orders?"

"I don't have that information, sir. You have to talk with the patient's doctor."

"Okay. Okay. Connect me with Elizabeth Van Buren's room, please."

"One moment, sir," the operator said. She came back. "I'm sorry, Mrs. Van Buren was also discharged this afternoon."

Rencke cut the connection and speed dialed Liz and Todd's home phone. Todd answered on the first ring.

"Hello."

"Is Elizabeth with you?" Rencke blurted. "She checked out of the hospital."

"She's here, in the tub," Todd replied. "Is something wrong, Otto?"

Rencke closed his eyes, the cold air suddenly felt good on his hot face. He was relieved. At least Elizabeth was safe for the moment. "They made another attempt on Mac. There was an explosion in front of his house. But the OD said he was okay."

"What about Mrs. M.?"

"She checked out of the hospital, and now I can't reach her." He heard the helicopter in the distance. It was another cause for relief. "I'm heading over to their house now. Whittaker might recall you, but don't do it, Todd. Stay there with Liz until we can figure out what we're going to do next."

"Mac told me that he was opening the safe house in the morning. Told me to stick it out here until then."

"Good idea."

"Okay, there's a call on my other line. It's the Company."

"Take care of Liz."

"Hey, I love her, too, remember?"

Rencke speed dialed his own apartment, but there was no answer. He and Louise had agreed that she should return to work at the NRO. She was doing nobody any good by staying home. She wanted to be with him 24/7, but that wasn't possible.

But he had hoped that she might have come home a little

early today. He desperately wanted to talk to her. To hear her voice. He needed comforting.

A navy Seasprite Lamps-I, three-man, multipurpose helicopter came in low from the northeast and touched down in the parking lot in a flurry of blowing snow.

The copilot helped Rencke into the empty crew seat, and handed him a crash helmet, which he donned and plugged into the ship's communications system.

"I need to get to the director of Central Intelligence's house," Rencke spoke into the mic. "It's up in Chevy Chase. If you don't know the way, your operations officer can get it from Langley."

"We know the way, sir," the pilot said, and the machine lifted into the air with a sickening lurch.

Rencke hated all helicopters. In fact he didn't care much for any kind of transportation except the World Wide Web.

He hunched down in his seat and pulled his seat harness a little tighter. His shoulder was hurting him, and for the first time today he realized that he was hungry. It was time to go home, where Louise would have something good waiting for him. She claimed that she was a horrible cook, but he knew better.

The view out the cockpit windows was nothing but swirling snow, with a kaleidoscope of meaningless lights somewhere below. Air pockets caused the helicopter to jump all over the place. But the pilot and copilot seemed unconcerned.

Washington was like a powerful magnet from which Rencke could not escape. He'd been lonely as hell in Rio, but happy as a clam in France. Until Mac came calling with his problems. He told himself that he had no choice. Mac was his friend. Mrs. M. and Liz were like family. He had to help them. He had to be here in Washington near them, to keep them out of trouble, to keep them safe from harm.

But the truth of the matter was that he'd searched for legitimacy all of his life. When he was fourteen his father started beating him and calling him a queer boy. And that same year his mother, in a drunken rage, told him that she wished that she'd had an abortion rather than giving birth to him.

In college he'd been treated with some respect because he

was bright, but he'd been kicked out when they found him screwing the dean's secretary on the dean's desk. That was at a Jesuit university. They didn't even ask him to leave. He just packed up that afternoon and got out.

And in the Air Force he'd been treated okay, that is after he'd made it through basic training, because he had a handle on mathematics. But that job had lasted only a couple of years, when he was caught having sex with a supply sergeant. A male supply sergeant.

In the CIA, after he'd doctored his records, he thought that he'd found a home. Though he didn't have a lot of friends in those days, at least he had some respect, even though he knew that they called him names behind his back.

Then Mac came along. Right off the bat Rencke knew that McGarvey was his kind of a person. Just standing in the same room with him gave you a confidence you never had before. And when Mac patted you on the shoulder and told you that you did good, it was like a frosty pitcher of cream and a plate of Twinkies. It didn't get any better.

But Mac was drawn again and again back to Washington. So Washington had become Rencke's magnet because Mac was a friend and because Mac believed in him.

Mac had given him the legitimacy that he had searched for all of his life. Rencke had a place.

CHEVY CHASE

The helicopter touched down at the far end of the cul-de-sac just long enough to drop Rencke off. He turned away as it rose into the blowing snow and peeled off to the south.

There were police cars, fire rescue units, two ambulances and a dozen civilian vehicles choking the street. All of them had their red or blue lights flashing. The effect was surreal in the snow. Police tactical radios were blaring, and there had to be at least fifty uniformed cops along with FBI agents in blue-stenciled parkas and a lot of civilians, most of whom were CIA security officers.

Rencke made his way over to the remains of the van and

the burned-out shell of the DCI's limo. The Bureau's forensics people were sifting through the wreckage, finding and removing bodies and body parts. Flash cameras were going off all over the place.

A Montgomery County sheriff's deputy intercepted Rencke. "Let me see some ID."

Rencke held up his CIA card, and the cop shined a flashlight on it, comparing Rencke's face to the photograph.

"Mr. McGarvey's over in his driveway," the cop said.

Rencke mumbled his thanks and skirted the people and equipment gathered around the remains of the van. It was probably one of the on-station vehicles they'd used to stand watches in front of the house. The explosive device that had destroyed it had been very powerful. There was debris all across the cul-de-sac and up in people's front yards. The force of the blast had been enough to partially destroy the limo parked several yards away.

Looking at the wreckage of the scene reminded him of what the aftermath pictures of the chopper explosion in the Virgin Islands looked like.

McGarvey stood at the end of his driveway with a group of CIA security people, a MHP captain and the FBI's Fred Rudolph. They looked up as Rencke approached.

"Where's Mrs. M.?" Otto asked, unable to contain himself any longer.

McGarvey smiled tiredly and laid a comforting hand on Rencke's arm. "She's okay. She's inside, and there's somebody with her."

"Oh, wow, I was really scared, ya know." Rencke glanced over his shoulder at the technicians and security people working around the van. "Where's Dick?"

"He didn't make it. He's dead," McGarvey said. "He got caught in the explosion."

"Who else?" Rencke asked. His throat was constricting.

"Janis and Peggy, and a couple of guys from Security. Looks like they had been shot to death before we arrived. Then the van was booby-trapped. Whoever it was drove a dark blue Mercedes."

Rencke closed his eyes. He was sick at his stomach. He felt

like a traitor. Dick Yemm had been on his short list of suspects. He and his Beltway computer friend, who was ex-KGB."

"We're heading to the safe house in the morning," McGarvey said.

"Why not now?" Rudolph interjected.

"Not in the dark," McGarvey told him. "And not until we can get everybody calmed down."

"We'll set a trap," Rencke said. "You and I, Mac, wherever it leads. We'll set a trap. Cause I know . . ."

"You know what?" McGarvey asked sharply. He was concerned, troubled, even a little apprehensive. Rencke had never seen that kind of a look on Mac's face before. It frightened him badly.

He stumbled back a pace, confused now by all the lights and movement. He felt like a moth that was fatally caught in the light of a very powerful flame. A seductive flame. He was being drawn to his destruction.

"We'll do it, Mac," he cried in anguish. Tears streamed down his cheeks, his long, frizzy red hair whipped wildly in the wind, and his jacket was open, revealing his dirty MIT sweatshirt.

He began hopping from one foot to the other The cops and security people watched him in open amazement. He was a spectacle.

He looked up and spotted a pale, round face in an upstairs window for just a moment before it disappeared.

"Jesus, Mary and Joseph," he muttered.

FOUR

THE 23RD PSALM

The hour of departure has arrived, and we go our ways—I to die and you to live. Which is better God only knows.

—Plato's *Apology*

Man is a prisoner who has no right to open the door of his prison and run away . . . A man should wait, and not take his own life until God summons him.

—Plato's *Phaedo*

WEDNESDAY

ONE

"VASHA WAS FAMOUS FOR SPREADING LIES
AND DISUNITY LIKE ROSE PETALS ON FRESH
GRAVES. HE ALWAYS MANAGED TO INCLUDE
THE THORNS."

OVER THE ATLANTIC

Six miles above the unforgiving winter ocean, Otto
Rencke tried to put a cap on his fear.

The cabin aboard the Company's VIP Gulfstream
was luxurious compared to the cramped cockpit of the Aurora.
But the jet was slow, and Rencke was impatient. The only
light came from the open cockpit door. It was four in the
morning, and the crew thought that he was sleeping. They left
him alone, which is what he wanted, what he needed, so that
he could put his thoughts in order.

Nikolayev was the key to the puzzle. Otto had known it
almost from the very beginning, in August, when the KGB
psychiatrist had walked away from Moscow. Some premoni-
tion, some inner voice, something inside of his gut started
telling him that there was an operation brewing. Sometimes
they started that way. A spy drops out of sight. Classified
records turn up missing. The authorities in the host country
pick up their heads and the hunt begins.

But he hadn't been one hundred percent sure, so he brought
Elizabeth into his confidence. She was in the middle of re-
searching her father's old files for his CIA biography, so she

had become something of an expert on the subject. Nikolayev was an old man, a name out of the Baranov past. He had been a Department Viktor man, which meant that he knew about ruthlessness. And he was suddenly a loose cannon.

But he had not dropped out of sight inside Russia, something that was apparently quite easy to do these days. He had come to the West, first to establish a safe haven for himself, then to make contact with the CIA. He had used a supposedly anonymous remailer to send a sample of his information to the address that Rencke had provided. But it was just a sample. Tantalizing. A glimpse into Baranov's mind, a mad genius from the past. But useless in terms of finding out who was gunning for McGarvey.

Rencke looked at his hands, which were shaking. He had gone without sleep for a couple of days now, living mostly on Cokes and on black beauties. Another day or so, and he would crash. It was inevitable.

Baranov, according to Nikolayev, had set up Network Martyrs, which was a group of sleeper agents in the States. That had been more than twenty years ago. When the time was right for a particular unit of the network to accomplish its task, he would be awakened.

One of Network Martyrs sleepers had been reactivated. The target was McGarvey.

But after that brief message, Nikolayev no longer responded. He didn't answer his e-mails. Nor did he reply to Rencke's queries at the letter drops in Paris that he had established to initiate the first contact.

It could be something so simple as Nikolayev's own death. Perhaps the SVR had found him after all and put a bullet in his brain. Or perhaps he had died of a heart attack; he was an old man.

The real mystery were the misdirections, if that's what they were. If McGarvey was the target of Network Martyrs, and if the sleeper assassin had been awakened, by whatever means, then why hadn't a simple, straightforward attempt been made on the DCI's life? Why target Otto? Why sabotage Elizabeth's skis in Colorado? And, if the sleeper was a Baranov-trained assassin, why the clumsy attempts on Mac's life in the Virgin

Islands and again just hours ago in front of his house?

Were they the missteps of an amateur, Rencke wondered. Or signals that something else was happening. Something that was just outside of his understanding.

Rencke laid his head back. Their ETA was 6:00 A.M., which was 11:00 A.M. in France. Two hours from now. He had time to catch a little sleep. He needed it to keep his head on straight. He was starting to lose track of his logic. Nikolayev's anonymous remailer hadn't been so anonymous after all. The service providers in the Czech Republic were not on the cutting edge. Cracking them had been easy. But not now. He couldn't think straight.

When Otto woke up, the Gulfstream was coming in for a landing at Pontoise Air Force Base outside of Paris. They were far enough north that the winter sun, even at eleven in the morning, was low in the hard blue sky. But unlike Washington there was little or no snow on the ground. France had had a mild winter. Tough on the skiiers, but easy on everyone else.

He popped a black beauty and looked out the window, bleary-eyed, as a dark gray Citröen sedan came across the tarmac and pulled up in front of base operations. When the Gulfstream rolled to a stop and the door was opened, Rencke pulled on his jacket and got his laptop. His head was already beginning to clear, though he felt a little disjointed.

"Get some sleep," he told the cockpit crew. "We're heading home in a couple of hours."

"What do we tell the French?" Captain John Brunner asked. He'd been called away from what was supposed to have been an early night. But this was part of his job.

"They won't ask," Rencke said. "But they'll probably offer you something to eat and a bed at the BOQ. Don't get too comfortable."

The Citröen's driver came over and took Rencke back to the car. Like all the officers in the *Service de Documentation Extérieure et de Contre-Espionage*, Action Service, the young man was built like a Chicago Bears linebacker.

He politely held the door for Rencke to get in. A man in civilian clothes was waiting in the backseat.

Action Service major Jean Serrou, the man Rencke had contacted yesterday, was not much older than his driver and just as competent-looking.

"M. Rencke, I presume. You had a good flight?"

They shook hands. "Yes, but it was a little long."

Major Serrou smiled and nodded. "The Aurora is much faster."

"But not very roomy. I'll be taking him back with me," Rencke said. "If you've found him."

"We have," Serrou said. He motioned for the driver to head out. "He is staying at a small hotel in Olivet, just outside of Orleáns. It is less than one hundred kilometers from here. We can be there within the hour."

"That is very good work, Major," Rencke said. He was starting to fly a little.

"It was simple once you told us from where he was sending his computer messages." This was a back channels request, not an official one, from a high-ranking officer of the American intelligence establishment to the SDECE's Service 5. Not too many questions would be asked. But Serrou did have his people to think about. "Is this the same man the Russians are looking for?"

Rencke nodded. "But they mustn't know that we have found him. Not just yet."

"He is a very old man then, not very dangerous?"

"Don't underestimate him," Rencke warned. "I hope that you told this to your operators?"

Serrou smiled knowingly. "They are quite well prepared." The French Action Service was somewhat like a combination of the British SAS and the American SEALs, with a bit of the FBI thrown in. They were well trained and bright. "But tell me, do you expect any trouble?"

Rencke had thought about that on the flight over. He shook his head. "No. He might even be expecting me. In any event I'll go in alone. On my own responsibility."

Serrou shrugged. "As you wish."

OLIVET

They parked at the end of the block one hundred meters from the small five-story Hôtel Rivage. It was right on the river, and next door, diners were seated at a very small sidewalk café. The sun was high enough now so that it provided a little warmth.

Rencke was homesick for his life here. He had been lonely, but content and even happy at times in France. Yet he didn't want to be doing anything else, except what he was doing; helping his friends. He had a family now.

"I have two people posted in a third-floor apartment across the street," Serrou said. "In addition there are three teams of two operators each circulating on the street. On foot, pushing a baby carriage, driving a delivery van. And I have one team on the river aboard a barge."

Rencke looked sharply at the Frenchman. "That's a bit much for one old man."

Serrou shrugged. "So was calling us." He held up a hand before Rencke could comment. "In the old days when you were fighting with the Russians, we French didn't mean much to you. So, correctly, DeGaulle kicked your military asses out of our country. He allowed the CIA to remain, but not the military. He was a practical president. And now that the Russians threaten only themselves, you still don't think much of us."

"I have lived here."

"Yes, and for the most part we had no objections. As long as you did not conduct business on French soil, and as long as you did not endanger French citizens, we were content with your presence. Yours and Kirk McGarvey's." He held Rencke's gaze. "Now we only wish for the truth sometimes. Even perhaps just a little truth."

Rencke glanced out the window at the hotel. A young couple was just coming out. The woman pushed a baby carriage. "Someone tried to assassinate our Director of Central Intelligence," he said. "Once in the Caribbean and once again in front of his own house."

"This is fantastic." Serrou pursed his lips. "The Russians searching for Dr. Nikolayev, your bringing the Aurora here, and then your telephone call yesterday all begin to make perfect sense." He looked down the street. The young couple had disappeared around the corner. "Is he an important man?"

"I think he came to warn us," Rencke admitted.

"The SVR wants to stop him from telling his story and thus embarrassing Moscow."

"Something like that."

"*Oui*," Serrou said. "So that is why we took this job so seriously. In the end perhaps we will protect him from the Russians."

"Have there been any signs that they're on to him?" Rencke asked.

"No. But we have our eyes open." Serrou was assessing Rencke. "Do you still mean to see him alone?"

"I think it's what he wants," Rencke said. "Has he been out of the hotel?"

"Three times since yesterday. Once for his newspapers this morning—Paris, Washington, and New York—and twice for his meals."

"He hasn't used the phone, or tried to return to L'Empereur to send another e-mail?"

"*Non*," Serrou said. "He is in three-eleven. At the end of the corridor in front."

Rencke watched the street for a few seconds. "If he agrees to come with me, we'll need to get back to Pontoise as quickly as possible."

"We want him out of France. Good luck."

"Thanks," Rencke mumbled. He got out of the car, crossed the narrow street and walked past the sidewalk café to the hotel. He could smell the river mingled with odors from the restaurant. It was very French.

The concierge and deskman looked up but said nothing as Rencke crossed the lobby and took the stairs up to the third floor. He had not brought a pistol, but he had brought his laptop. If Nikolayev did not want to come back to Washington, shooting him would do no good. But perhaps he had something else to download from his computer. It is what he had promised at in his first message. There was more.

The third-floor corridor was empty and quiet. Not even the occasional street noise penetrated this far. The air smelled neutral, or perhaps a little musty. Age. The building was probably more than two hundred years old.

Rencke went down the corridor to three-eleven and listened at the door. If there was anyone inside, they were being very quiet. No movement. No sounds whatsoever.

He shifted his laptop to his left hand and knocked. Someone stirred inside, and a moment later the dead bolt was withdrawn and the door opened. A tall man, very old and thin, the skin on his cheeks and around his eyes shiny and papery, like blue-tinged parchment, stood there. He wore gray trousers and an old fisherman's sweater. His thin white hair was mussed, but he did not look surprised.

"Well, you're not a Russian or a Frenchman, which means that you must be Otto Rencke," Nikolayev said in English. His accent was British, and his voice was whisper-soft, yet Rencke could hear the Russian in him.

"I got your message, Dr. Nikolayev."

"And you want more. But you wonder why I stopped sending." Nikolayev turned away from the door and went to a writing table, where his laptop was open and running.

Rencke entered the small room and closed the door, but did not bother locking it. With luck he wouldn't be here long. "Your remailer is not very secure."

"I discovered that for myself after the fact," Nikolayev said. He stood with his back to Rencke, looking out the window, watching the comings and goings down on the street. "Once I sent you the first batch of material I got nervous. I sent myself an e-mail, then traced it to where it originated. It was not easy for me, but I did it. So I assumed others could." He turned around. "I figured that I had a fifty-fifty chance that it would be either you or my own people coming for me. There are still friends in the Czech Republic who cooperate with the SVR."

"Why didn't you disappear?"

"I was on the verge of it when the French Action Service

showed up and threw a cordon around me." He had a warm smile. "Marvelous young boys. I actually felt safe for the first time since August."

"Okay. You sent us a message about General Baranov's Network Martyrs. Someone has tried to assassinate McGarvey, so here I am. We need your help."

A hint of amusement came into Nikolayev's eyes. "It's refreshing for a Russian to hear an American ask for help—"

"Don't jerk me around, Anatoli Nikolaevich," Rencke said harshly. He tossed his laptop on the bed and brushed the Russian aside so that he could get at his computer. But Nikolayev reached out and touched the escape key, and the screen went blank.

"First we will establish some ground rules, as you call them," Nikolayev said.

"It'll take me sixty seconds longer without your help than with it to get inside your computer," Rencke told him. "I've followed you for six months because a very good friend of mine has been put in a dangerous position. I know what you were, who you worked for and why. So don't try to bullshit me. You're shaking in your slippers. First it was Zhuralev in Moscow, then Trofimov in Paris. You're next."

"You're right, of course," Nikolayev said softly. He was struggling with himself. Trying to make a decision that made sense. Yet he was a Russian. And that died hard. He took two CDs from the writing table's drawer and gave them to Rencke. "That's everything I found. Where are you at now?"

"I'll look at these on the way back," Rencke said. "Somebody is trying to kill Kirk McGarvey, and they're not going to quit until they succeed. But a lot of what I've come up with doesn't make any sense yet. It doesn't fit a pattern."

"Tell me."

"Okay, so Baranov realized twenty years ago that McGarvey was going to be a somebody if he survived long enough. Baranov was a vain sonofabitch, maybe even nuts, so he put a sleeper in the States, and when the time was right the sleeper would be activated and set up the kill. Well, the time is apparently right, so why hasn't Baranov's sleeper done the job?"

"You said they already tried."

"But it was crude. Everything I've learned about General Baranov tells me that he was anything but a crude operator. And there have been attempts on my life, and on the lives of McGarvey's wife and daughter and his personal bodyguard."

"And what conclusions are you drawing?" Nikolayev asked. He was an instructor filled with patience for a student. Rencke didn't mind.

"Everybody suspects everybody else."

"That isn't so crude," Nikolayev observed. "It's what Baranov planned to happen. Are you familiar with the Donald Powers operation and the Darby Yarnell files?"

"I've read them."

"Vasha was famous for spreading lies and disunity like rose petals on fresh graves. He always managed to include the thorns." Nikolayev studied Rencke for a few moments. "You are close to McGarvey, yet you yourself are a suspect. Isn't that true?"

"Yes."

"Anyone in his inner circle could be the killer."

"Yes."

"Perhaps even his son-in-law."

It was a bridge that Rencke had not wanted to cross. And now that he had he felt no better than he had before. He shook his head. "Todd's too young."

"Then it's someone else. Maybe the SVR in Washington. Perhaps someone from his past. Someone who twenty years ago might have been a nobody and is now a power in Washington. Or perhaps someone who was a nothing then, and still is a nothing, someone completely out of sight. A janitor, a former lover, a cop with the FBI, an officer inside the CIA."

"It has to be someone on the inside who knows Mac's movements."

Nikolayev dismissed the objection. "That kind of information is easy to acquire. The CIA, just like our KGB, is filled with holes like Swiss cheese through which the mice scurry."

"I wanted to set a trap," Rencke said bleakly. "But now—"

"But now you're not sure of your information," Nikolayev said. He glanced out the window again. "Do you know what I did in Department Viktor?"

"You were a psychologist."

Nikolayev nodded. "I worked on a number of projects in those days with LSD and a dozen other mind-altering drugs. We were trying to perfect the brainwashing techniques that the Chinese had used during the fighting on the Korean peninsula. Deprogramming and reprogramming, mostly. Autohypnosis. Reinforcement. Guilt. Hate. Anger. Gullibility. All the strong human emotions."

"The CIA tried the same thing, but we dropped it. Supposedly your guys dropped it, too."

"Everyone except for Vasha. It was to be his ultimate weapon."

"Did it work?"

Nikolayev cocked his head as if he was listening for something. Perhaps an inner voice. "It worked," he said. "With drugs we needed only a few days, a week at most, for the conversions. Some religious organizations have come to use almost the same techniques. We found people who were convinced that something was wrong with them. People who were facing what were, to them, troubling and complex problems. We gave them the simple answers they were looking for. We gave them a sense of belonging, of self-worth, of well-being. In return they gave us their free will."

"Did you have to bring them to Moscow to do it?"

Nikolayev shook his head. "It could be done anywhere. Moscow. Paris. London. Washington." He looked down. "It took eight steps with drugs. First, seclusion. No one else was with the subject except for their handlers. Second, was instant intimacy. The subject was given a strong sense of hierarchy. Who's the boss. Who's the leader. Who is the one with all the answers. Third, was giving them the instant sense of community. They belonged. Fourth, they were made to feel guilty for everything around them. Fifth, was sensory overload: lights, noise, hot-and cold-water baths, sleep deprivation, hunger, pain. That was the hardest step to accomplish because we were erasing what amounted to the surface manifestations of their personalities. We could never achieve a complete blank slate, we couldn't go that deep. But we could wipe the surface slate clean. Of course that set up a lot of serious problems in the subjects. But it didn't matter to Baranov that we were driving people to the edge of insanity, so long as we accomplished his missions.

"When that was accomplished, the subjects were indoctrinated to our way of thinking, which we tested in steps seven and eight. First they had to appeal to their control officer for something, anything, it didn't matter what. The right to use the toilet, maybe. Then for graduation the subjects would recite their personal testimonies. Who they had become, what their mission was."

Rencke understood that as smart as he thought he was, he had no answers now. No suggestions. He knew machines, not people. The killers could be anyone. Finding them could be impossible. "That's horrible," he murmured.

"It's worse than that," Nikolayev said, his voice whisper-soft. "Monstrously worse, because the subject is never aware that they had been brainwashed."

"It could be me," Rencke blurted. He tried to examine what was in his own mind. He'd been going crazy lately. His head throbbed, his legs were weak. Stenzel had looked into his brain and seen . . . what? He'd seen whatever Rencke wanted the psychiatrist to see. He'd been playing games with Stenzel; or had they not been games. Maybe they were something else. Preplanned. Implanted in his thoughts.

But Louise knew him, and loved him, as Mac did. Wouldn't they have seen something?

"Yes, I considered that it could be the assassin coming here to kill me," Nikolayev said. He partially withdrew a pistol from his trousers pocket. He'd purchased it a few days ago from a French mafiosa in Marseilles. "But you would already have tried to kill me, and I was ready." He put the gun back in his pocket.

"Did you find names in the files? Do you know who it is?"

"All I got was the name of one target. Kirk McGarvey. There are others, but their names died with the general."

"How can we stop them, then?" Rencke asked, still examining his own inner feelings.

"We'll set a trap, just as you suggested," Nikolayev said. "There is a weakness built into the process. There has to be a permanent pairing; an operative and the control officer. The effects of our brainwashing technique lasts only one week, maybe a few days longer, before it begins to fade. It has to be reinforced. If we can see them together, we might have a chance. We might recognize something."

"They'll come to Mac. The killer and his control. We'll arrange it," Rencke said.

"Nikolayev rubbed his chest. He looked a little pale. "Yes, we will. You and I, before it's too late. And when they arrive, we'll be there. If we're careful, they'll never know that it's a trap."

"You'll come back to Washington with me?"

"Of course," Nikolayev said. "It's why I left Moscow in the first place. To see an end to this." He pursed his lips. "You were right about something else, too. I am shaking in my boots. I would like to live out the remainder of my life in peace and some comfort."

"That's all any of us want," Rencke said, thinking about his father, and especially his mother. It's all he ever wanted. Something else occurred to him. "Martyrs suddenly went active. Something triggered it. What?"

"Money," Nikolayev said. "All these years after Vasha's death, payments were automatically made from Swiss banks directly to the control officers. They were the ones who had to reinforce the brainwashing every week." Nikolayev shrugged. "It was steady money with the promise of even more money when the mission was accomplished."

"So what set it off?" Otto asked.

"A team in the SVR has been looking down the old operation tracks for just those kinds of accounts. When they find them, they close the accounts and take the money. Somehow this control officer was warned or found out on his own that his funds were going to be cut off, so he went active, hoping for the big payoff anyway."

"Money," Rencke said disparagingly.

"Don't underestimate its power," Nikolayev said. "Money has always meant even more to a communist than it ever has to a capitalist."

TWO

(McGARVEY) FELT IMPOTENT TO STOP THE
THREAT TO HIS FAMILY, AND WHAT IT WAS
DOING TO THEM ALL. YET HE COULD NOT BACK
AWAY. HE COULDN'T RUN. NOT THIS TIME.

CHEVY CHASE

McGarvey stood at a bulletproof window in a front bedroom looking down at the cul-de-sac as a somber gray dawn arrived. He smoked a cigarette he'd bummed from one of his security people. Kathleen slept in the master bedroom, two female security officers in the room with her.

She was up now. He could hear the shower running. One of the security officers came to the door with a cup of coffee for McGarvey.

"Thought you could use this, Mr. Director," she said.

McGarvey took it. "Thanks. How's my wife doing?"

"She had a pretty good night, sir," the young woman said. Her name was Gloria Sanchez. She was dressed in blue jeans and a sweater, and she looked like a high school sweetheart. Actually she was married with two children and was an expert on the firing and hand-to-hand combat ranges. She was an ex–navy SEAL.

"How soon do we get out of here?"

"About an hour to finish getting it organized, sir," Gloria said. "Will you be wanting breakfast?"

"No thanks." McGarvey gave the street a last glance just as an older gray Chevy Suburban stopped at the checkpoint. The remnants of the van and limo had been removed, and a pair of Montgomery County sheriff's cruisers blocked the entrance to the cul-de-sac. They were checking everyone. The Chevy probably belonged to one of the neighbors or their kids, though he didn't recognize the car.

He walked back to the master bedroom, and Chris Bartholomew, the other security officer, left. The shower had stopped. He knocked on the bathroom door. "It's me."

"You can come in," Kathleen said.

She was drying herself. Her hair was wet and hung in strings. Her skin was red from the hot water. And she had no makeup on.

"You look good this morning," he told her, and he meant it. She was beautiful.

She glanced at herself in a full-length mirror and smiled wryly. "You're prejudiced."

"Yup," McGarvey said. He took her in his arms and held her close. She relaxed into him.

"I want this to be over with now, Kirk," she said in a small voice.

"Soon."

"I want our life back."

"Me too," McGarvey said, and they kissed deeply. When they parted Kathleen shivered.

"Tell me that it's Sunday, we're all alone in the house, and we've got the rest of the day together," she said.

He draped the towel around her shoulders and held her close again for a long time. "We're going out to the safe house in Cropley this morning. The girls have packed up most of the things you'll need. You'll have to figure out what else you want to take."

She looked up and gave her husband a hard expression, her left eyebrow arched. She did not like people handling her things. "Nobody said anything to me."

"Last night was difficult, Katy."

Her attitude softened. She glanced away. "I'm sorry, I'm being selfish. Those poor people. Dick was a friend." She looked back. "It has to end sometime, Kirk. We can't go on like this indefinitely. I can't breathe half the time. First the helicopter, then the hospital and now this. And Elizabeth and the baby." She closed her eyes tightly. "Why? What do they want?"

"They don't want me to take the job."

"Then quit," she shot back.

"Not now, Katy. I can't. Not like this."

"Men," she said. She started to hum, as if she had been plugged into an electric circuit. Her muscles bunched up.

McGarvey held her tighter. "Easy, Katy," he soothed. "Security," he called over his shoulder.

"Here," Gloria Sanchez said a couple of seconds later at the door.

"Get Stenzel up here on the double."

He heard her talking into her lapel mic, but he couldn't make out the words.

Kathleen's strength was increasing. She seemed to be on the verge of an epileptic seizure. Her face was that of a stranger. Her eyes were dilated. Unfocused. Foamy spittle flecked the corners of her mouth.

"Stick with me, sweetheart," McGarvey told her. "Come on, it's okay. You're safe. No one is going to hurt you."

"Kirk . . . what's happening to me?"

"You're having a reaction," McGarvey said. "Honest to God, Katy, it'll be okay. I promise you. Please. Come on, Katy, stay with me."

"Help me, for God's sake, help me," she shrieked. Her eyes rolled back in their sockets, her entire body went rigid, and her grip on McGarvey's arms was as strong as a weight lifter's.

Suddenly she went limp and urinated down her legs in a soft stream that puddled on the tile floor. The mask of agony and terror melted from her face, and she blinked as if she were coming out of a daze.

McGarvey picked her up and took her into the shower. He turned on the warm water with one hand, and gently soaped her body, cleaning her. She could only hold on to his arm for support, almost completely incapable of helping herself.

When he was finished, Gloria was there with a towel. Together they got Kathleen dried off. McGarvey picked her up and carried her into the bedroom, where Gloria threw back the covers. He got her into the bed and pulled the covers up. Kathleen was shivering again, but she wasn't convulsing.

Stenzel appeared in the doorway, took one look, then came over and brushed them aside. He checked Kathleen's pupils and took her pulse.

"What the hell is happening to her?" McGarvey demanded.

"It's a delayed reaction from last night," the psychiatrist said. "She's gone into overload." He prepared a syringe with twenty-five milligrams of Librium, swabbed Kathleen's right arm, and administered the drug. She watched everything he did, but she didn't fight him.

"We can't take her back to Bethesda," McGarvey said.

"No, but I'm going with her," Stenzel replied. He checked her pupils and pulse again, and grunted in satisfaction. "How are you doing, Kathleen?"

She smiled wanly. "Better now," she answered. She looked over at her husband and at Gloria Sanchez, and gave them a smile. "Sorry. I'm not as strong yet as I thought I was."

"You'll be okay now," Stenzel told her. He tucked her bare arm under the covers. "I want you to relax for a little while."

"But I'm not tired," she objected.

"I know. But I want you to take it easy. Just for a half hour or so. Will you do that for me?"

She nodded. "Sure." She closed her eyes. She was asleep almost immediately.

"I don't know how much longer I can keep her on track," Stenzel told McGarvey out in the hall. "She needs to be hospitalized. In a clinic somewhere where she can get some proper rest."

Chris Bartholomew got a towel from the guest bathroom down the hall and gave it to McGarvey. "Thanks," he told her.

She nodded and went into the bedroom to help with Kathleen and help clean up.

"We have to get past this first," McGarvey said. He felt impotent to stop the threat to his family and what it was doing to them all. Yet he could not back away. He couldn't run. Not this time.

"I know. But the sooner that's done, the sooner I can start to help your wife."

"What's wrong with her, Doc?"

A troubled, pensive expression came over the psychiatrist's face. "She's—" He shook his head. "I don't know. She has the classic symptoms of a half-dozen psychoses, but not all the symptoms of any one of them. Deepened emotions, grandiosity, depression, bouts of violence and abnormal muscle strength, irritability, hallucinations, seizures, paranoid suspicions, loss of libido followed by hypersexuality." Stenzel spread his hands. "I don't know."

"Will she be able to travel in an hour?"

"She'll be sedated. Not out of it, but calmed down. The move shouldn't disturb her."

Gloria Sanchez came out of the bedroom. Kathleen was already up. She had put on a robe and stood in the middle of the room looking at them. She was smiling timidly.

"Tony has a priest at the front door, says he would like to see Mrs. McGarvey. His name is Janis Vietski of Good Shepherd Church here in Chevy Chase. He checks out."

"I know him," McGarvey said. "Tell him that we appreciate his coming over, but not now."

"Yes, Kirk," Kathleen said. "Please. It would mean a lot to me before we leave."

McGarvey looked to Stenzel for an opinion. The doctor shrugged. "Can't hurt," he replied in a soft voice that wouldn't carry. "Might even help calm her down."

"Would you like to get dressed first?" McGarvey asked his wife.

"No. I'd like to talk to Father for just a minute, then I'll get ready, and we can leave." She seemed to be brittle and withdrawn. But that was to be expected.

McGarvey gave Gloria the nod. "Have him come up."

The security officer said something into her lapel mic. A minute later Father Vietski, looking something like a shaggy bear with longish dark hair and beard, a stained black jacket and clerical collar, and unbuckled winter boots appeared at the head of the stairs.

He laid his topcoat and hat on a chair and shambled over, a look of sympathy on his pleasantly broad Slavic peasant's face. He didn't appear to notice that McGarvey was wet.

"Mr. Director, I came right over the moment I heard the terrible news," the priest said, shaking McGarvey's hand. His voice was rich and warm, concerned. "God bless us all that you and Mrs. McGarvey were not injured."

"Thank you," McGarvey said. He'd never really examined his faith, although he knew that he sided with Voltaire in his distrust of organized religion. But Katy got comfort from the Church. At this point that meant a lot to him. And Vietski seemed to have a genuine regard for her.

The priest noticed Kathleen standing in her robe in the bedroom. "My dear sweet Kathleen, what has happened to you?" he said warmly. With eyes for no one else but her, he entered the bedroom, waited until the security officer got out, then closed the door.

"Five minutes, then I want him out of here," McGarvey told the security people.

"Yes, sir."

"When he's gone, I'd like you to help her get ready to travel," McGarvey said.

"I'm staying with her," Stenzel said.

"Good," McGarvey replied. "Now, where's Jim?" Jim Grassinger had taken over as head of McGarvey's security detail.

"He's in the dining room. You need to get out of those wet clothes, sir," Gloria Sanchez said.

"I will," McGarvey said. He gave her a smile. "Thanks for your help."

"Yes, sir."

McGarvey changed clothes, then went downstairs. He stopped in the front hall. Everything was unraveling around him. Katy's disintegration and seizure. Liz and the baby. And last night Dick Yemm's death. That part should not have happened. The security team in the van was too good to let someone in an unknown car get that close to them. And Yemm should have known better than to barge into the van the way

he had without backup. The Bureau had found no trace of the
blue Mercedes that Kathleen had seen from the window. But
when they did finally run it down it would help clear up some
of the mystery.

Grassinger was in the dining room with three other security
officers. Detailed maps of the Washington area, including the
small town of Cropley a few miles up the Potomac from the
capital, were spread out on the table. Grassinger, a tall, square-
shouldered, serious man was on the encrypted phone to Operations at Langley. "I'll get back to you," he said. He broke
the connection.

"Gloria tells me that we can get out of here within the hour,"
McGarvey said. "What's the drill?"

"We're driving you and Mrs. McGarvey out to Cropley in
the spare limo. The long way."

"Norm Stenzel will be riding with us."

"Okay, Dr. Stenzel, too, plus two security people and your
driver," Grassinger agreed. "We'll do a number of switchbacks
and feints, which will give our chase cars room to make sure
that we get out clean. We'll have two helicopters in the air,
at a distance, to help cover our tail as well. But everything is
going to be discreet. Nothing will appear to be out of the
ordinary."

"What if there's trouble?"

"We call for backup and head to whichever is closer at that
moment, Langley or Cropley."

"How about Todd and Elizabeth?"

"Nearly the same drill, Mr. Director, except that Van Buren
will drive his own SUV out to Cropley, using a number of
switchbacks. There won't be any security in the car with him
and your daughter, but there will be chase cars and a helicopter
aloft to make sure they run into no trouble. They'll arrive at
Cropley thirty minutes ahead of us."

"Any reason for that?"

"Sir, Todd wants to make a quick sweep of the property
himself before you and Mrs. McGarvey get out there."

"That's fine," McGarvey said. "I want your people to remain out of sight. This is going to be as low-key a move as
we can make it."

"Yes, sir, that's what we figured. There's no use advertising what we're doing."

McGarvey had always taken a hand in his own safety. But now in his position he had to rely on others to make sure the job got done right. He didn't like it.

One of the security officers was on the phone. He touched the mute button. "Mr. Director, the President would like to speak to you."

"Do you want us to get out of here?" Grassinger asked.

"No," McGarvey said. He took the phone and touched the MUTE button. "This is McGarvey."

"Please hold for the President, sir," Haynes's secretary said.

The President came on. "Good morning, Kirk. How are you doing?"

"Good morning, Mr. President. We're hanging on. But I'm going to be gone from Washington for a few days. I'm taking my family to a safe house."

"After last night, that's a good idea," the President said. "I want you to consider something while you're gone. I want you to think about withdrawing your nomination. Linda and I know what you and Kathleen are going through, and we would not blame you if you stepped away. Hell, having Hammond and Madden on the warpath is bad enough, but this now, attacks not only on you but on your family, is beyond the bounds."

"Thanks for the offer, Mr. President. But when I quit it won't be like this."

"I understand. What can I do to help?"

"Keep Senator Hammond off my back until we get this settled," McGarvey said. He'd given the problem some thought. "He's still got a pipeline into the CIA. He's coming up with information that's only discussed between me and my directorate chiefs and their immediate staff. We're trying to plug the leak now. But if you could invite him over to the Oval Office and have a chat with him about the facts of life, it might help. I don't want him to know where I've taken my family. If he inadvertently lets something slip, it could get to the wrong people."

"Consider it done, Kirk," the President said. "How long do you think that you'll be out of action?"

"Not long."

The President was silent for a moment. "I'm not going to ask how you know that. So I'm just going to wish you good luck. If there's anything else, anything at all, that I can do for you, let me know. It'll be done."

"Thank you, Mr. President. I appreciate that." This was one president who was as good as his word, McGarvey thought.

David Whittaker was in his limo on the way to CIA headquarters when the locator caught up with him. When he answered the car phone he sounded cranky. Like the rest of them he had been up all night dealing with the aftermath of the latest attack.

"How's traffic on the Parkway this morning?" McGarvey asked.

"Shitty as usual," the acting DDCI replied. "How's it going out there?"

"We're getting set to head out to Cropley," McGarvey said. The green light was on, indicating their call was encrypted. "Have you heard from Adkins?"

"He's back home with the girls," Whittaker said wearily. "Ruth passed away last night."

McGarvey lowered his head and closed his eyes. "I'm sorry, David. I didn't know that she was that bad. How's he holding up?"

"He's taking it hard, Mac. And he's going to want to come back fairly soon. Work's the best antidote for some people."

Life was sometimes not very fair. And just now there were a lot of problems piling up all around them. "One thing at a time," McGarvey said. What he did not need was a grieving Deputy DCI on the seventh floor. Especially not one who might be a suspect himself.

"What do I tell him?"

"I'll take care of it," McGarvey said.

"He's a friend—"

"He's my friend, too," McGarvey flared. "But we have a job to do. All of us, especially you. The world hasn't been put on hold just because somebody is gunning for me. And neither is the Agency going to be put on hold." McGarvey glanced at Grassinger and the others, who were studiously poring over the maps. "Have I made myself clear?"

"Perfectly, Mr. Director," Whittaker replied. His tone was frosty.

"Good," McGarvey said. "I want you to talk to Otto this morning. He was shook up, but he said that he had an idea for a trap."

"He took the Gulfstream back to France last night. Lynch said he's already in-country."

McGarvey wasn't surprised. "I think that he's trying to make contact with Nikolayev. Have Paris station keep an eye on him, but tell Lynch not to interfere."

"All right."

"Let me know as soon as he gets back to Washington. And in the meantime I'll want regular staff reports. We can tele-conference over the secure TV link. I'll let you set up the times. Anything above the line occurs, I want to hear about it immediately. I'm going to Cropley, not Mars."

"Yes, sir," Whittaker said. He hesitated. "Mac, I understand about Dick. It's a tough call, but you're the one in the hot seat. We're all with you. One hundred percent. And not just until this situation is resolved. I mean for the long haul."

"Thanks, David. It's good to hear that."

CROPLEY, MARYLAND

Kathleen refused to be bundled up in a blanket, or in any other way pampered. "I'm worn-out, I'm not a cripple," she said crossly.

She and McGarvey sat in the backseat of the limo. Stenzel and Gloria Sanchez sat in the facing seats, and Grassinger drove with Chris Bartholomew riding shotgun.

Media trucks and vans were parked along the side of the street almost all the way back to Connecticut Avenue. Chevy Chase police and Montgomery County sheriff's units held the reporters at bay and kept them from taking up the chase. The limo's windows were tinted so that no one could see inside, anyway. And fifteen minutes earlier, one of Grassinger's people had delivered a one-page news release promising that the DCI would hold a news conference at Langley sometime later today.

"It's a feeding frenzy," Stenzel observed, as they were passed through the checkpoint. They headed north on Connecticut Avenue toward the Beltway and sped up.

The news media had finally gotten onto the story that at least two attempts had been made on the life of the director of the CIA, the latest attack in front of his house.

"It's been a slow season," Gloria said.

"One good thing with all this attention, no one in their right mind would try to do anything," Stenzel said.

Gloria shook her head. "I hate to disagree, Doc, but this sort of confusion can work as a very good cover."

It had begun to snow again. When they reached the Capital Beltway and turned west, Kathleen turned and watched out the window. The trees and the hills were being covered with a fresh blanket of snow that made the world look clean and pretty, like a Currier and Ives Christmas lithograph. She was smiling, but she said nothing, and McGarvey was content just to look at her.

One other time in their marriage he had been as frightened of her fragility as he was now. It was a couple of days after Elizabeth was born, when they brought her home to their small apartment in the city. Kathleen's pregnancy had been a normal one, no emergencies, no terrible cravings or debilitating morning sickness. But it had been long, and they were both glad the night her labor pains began and her water broke.

McGarvey had done her breathing exercises with her so earnestly that night, that he had hyperventilated and almost passed out waiting for her to get ready to go to the hospital.

In those days, in a lot of hospitals, prospective fathers were not allowed into the delivery rooms. They had to remain in the waiting rooms, pacing the floor, having no idea what was happening until a nurse came out to tell them.

When they got home with Elizabeth, MacGarvey and Kathleen were determined to be the perfect parents, despite McGarvey's job with the CIA that was starting to take him away from home for long periods. Kathleen did not breastfeed, so McGarvey was able to help with the bottles and formulas. He had also practiced changing diapers on a doll that Kathleen had bought for him.

The first time that it was his turn, Kathleen was in the kitchen doing the formula. He went into the baby's room and stopped in the doorway. The shades were drawn and the room was in semidarkness. Liz was awake and mewling softly, but not really crying yet.

He could clearly remember her baby smell, how tiny beads of perspiration formed on her rosebud lips. She scrunched up her face and looked at him as if she knew who he was and exactly why he had come to her crib.

She was bundled up in a pink blanket. He laid out the tiny diaper and baby powder, undid the blanket and started to undo the bottom of her nightshirt when he felt something on her stomach. He reared back in a sudden, absolute panic.

His and Katy's biggest concern throughout her pregnancy was that she would lose the baby, miscarry. But another concern for McGarvey, one that he never shared with Katy, and one that kept him awake nights during the nine months, was that the baby would be born malformed. With a club foot, or a harelip, or blind, or with too many fingers or toes or arms.

He gently felt the front of Liz's nightshirt, and it was still there. A tiny lump in the middle of her belly. Sticking straight up. His worst fears were true. Somehow Katy hadn't seen it, and the doctor and nurses hadn't said anything. Or maybe they all knew and were afraid to tell him.

Liz had something growing out of her belly. It was a third arm. He was convinced of it. Some tiny, but horribly grotesque growth out of her body.

He looked over his shoulder at the open door. Katy was just down the hall. How in God's name could he tell her about this? He was the father. This was his fault. He was one hundred percent convinced of it. The shame was almost more than he could bear.

His heart hammered as he carefully untied Liz's nightshirt and pulled it back. He had to see. He had to know so that he could figure out how to break it to Katy.

For several seconds he stared at his daughter's rounded belly. A small bandage had been placed on the end of the tied-off umbilical cord. He looked at it, and he knew exactly what he had felt, and the mistake he had stupidly made, and yet he had a very hard time coming down. His heart pounded all the way through the diapering.

When Katy came back with the bottle she stopped in the doorway, a smile on her face, just like her smile right now looking out at the fresh snow.

McGarvey looked up at her. "She's perfect," he said.

"So are you," Kathleen had told him.

He had never told her about that incident. And, he figured that if he searched his memory he could probably come up with other things that he hadn't told her. When this situation was resolved, he promised himself that he and Katy would start over. Really start over this time.

Grassinger took the Beltway Bridge across the river back into Virginia and immediately turned south on the George Washington Memorial Parkway to the CIA. Chris Bartholomew was in constant encrypted radio contact with Operations, who kept up a running report on the traffic behind and in front of them.

There were a number of news media vans and trucks at the front gate as the DCI's limo was passed through. Grassinger drove directly across the Agency's grounds to the south exit, on Pike Road, which led back to the Beltway. They recrossed the river, still clear according to their chase units.

Grassinger drove north to River Road, which was Highway 190, and turned west toward the town of Potomac. He was making a big circle around Cropley. He was taking no chances with the DCI's safety.

Chris Bartholomew turned around. She was from Wisconsin and tiny, just making the Agency's minimums for height and weight. Her husband argued that good things came in the smallest of packages. Everyone in the Office of Security agreed.

"Mr. Van Buren and your daughter are at the safe house, Mr. Director," she said. "They had no trouble."

"Good," McGarvey replied. "What's our ETA?"

"We'll be there in about twenty minutes," Grassinger told him.

"I'll let Mr. Van Buren know—"

"No," McGarvey said. "You may tell security on the grounds. But no one else."

Grassinger gave him an odd look in the rearview mirror. Chris Bartholomew didn't miss a beat. "Yes, sir," she said. She turned back to the radio.

Kathleen ignored the exchange. It was the Librium that Stenzel had given her. The drug made her docile.

"Is there something we should know about, Mr. Director?" Gloria Sanchez asked.

"There might be bugs in the house," McGarvey said lamely. "Besides, there's staff out there."

"The house was swept about an hour ago, and we sent the staff away four days ago, sir," she said. "The only people with Todd and your daughter now are John Blatnik's team. Four inside and six outside. They're rotated by pairs every two hours."

"It'll be a moot point in twenty minutes," McGarvey said, closing the conversation. Gloria nodded, and Stenzel's attention remained fixed on Kathleen.

McGarvey turned back to his thoughts. He'd made an automatic decision that he refused to examine. The problem he'd faced all of his life was when you don't trust your friends and the people nearest to you, who can you trust? Who *should* you trust when you have to place your personal safety into the hands of relative strangers?

This was an odd and troubling time. For the first time in his life he was coming face-to-face with himself, with what made him tick. He hadn't come up with any of the answers to the dozens of questions he was asking himself, or at least he wasn't coming up with any answers that made much sense. He could not reconcile his first instinct to run with his extremely strong sense of responsibility for the people he loved and for the weaker people around him.

Had Senator Madden pressed him on the incident in high school with the football bullies, he would not have been able to tell her the real reason he'd stepped in. It had been something automatic. Despite the opinion of the people in the Agency and in several White House administrations he'd served under, he was not a hero. He was a pragmatist, a realist, probably an egoist—someone who was self-centered, arrogant, conceited, even selfish. Maybe all that, but he could not think of himself as a hero to anyone, for the simple reason he had no earthly idea what heroism was.

Voltaire, among others, had hinted that egoism, which McGarvey figured was his driving trait, was the idea that morality, in the end, always rested on self-interest.

McGarvey wasn't a hero; he was simply a man who did not know how to follow orders, a man who valued his opinion above the opinions of almost everyone else, but a man who did not know how to give up. When he ran, it was always to find a new ground on which to fight his battles.

Not much of a prize for Katy and Liz, he thought. But it was all he had to give them, and he did love them with everything in his soul.

Grassinger came to the snow-covered gravel road that led away from the federal parkland along the river, one mile to the house around 9:00 A.M. The forest was thick with tangled underbrush that even in winter provided a lot of cover.

The house looked as if it had been plucked from a Kentucky horse farm and transported here. It was complete with expansive lawns, white wooden fences, paddocks, horse barns and an indoor riding arena, as well as other outbuildings. A couple of years after the Aldrich Ames case had broken, another criminal in the CIA had been discovered. This one didn't make the news because he hadn't sold out to the Russians. Instead, he had ripped off the Agency for something over four million dollars by tapping into several of the CIA's offshore operating funds accounts.

The Cropley house nestled on one hundred acres of forested hills, had been his. Now it belonged to the CIA. Anonymous and therefore safe.

There were fresh tire tracks in the still-falling snow, and some footprints leading from the house back into the woods, but no activity that they could see driving up. It wasn't until McGarvey got out of the car that he smelled the woodsmoke coming from a fire on the living room hearth. Smoke began to come out of the broad chimney. Somebody had just laid the fire.

John Blatnik, the chief of on-site security, came around the east corner of the house, speaking into his lapel mic. He had a Colt Commando slung over his shoulder. He looked very serious in his white parka and snow boots.

"Welcome to Cropley, Mr. Director," Blatnik said. Like a lot of men in the Office of Security, he looked like a linebacker. "Mr. Van Buren and your daughter are inside."

Stenzel and Gloria Sanchez helped Kathleen out of the limo. She was almost asleep on her feet. "I'm putting her to bed right now," Stenzel said.

"Put her in the master bedroom," McGarvey told them. "Upstairs, in the back."

Kathleen gave him a flaccid smile, and Stenzel and Gloria took her inside.

Todd came out of the house. "Hello, Mac. Any trouble on the way out?"

"No. How's Liz?"

"She didn't get any rest last night. But she promised to get some sleep as soon as she saw her mother and talked to you."

Grassinger stepped away to speak to Blatnik, but Chris Bartholomew remained a few feet away from McGarvey. She'd unbuttoned her jacket.

"What's the situation here?" McGarvey asked. He wasn't ready to go into the house yet.

"Tony's got some good people working for him. The house is secure. They have the infrared and motion detectors up and running around the perimeter, as well as the built-in stop sticks and explosive charges on the driveway. And they're adding two lines of claymores on either side of the driveway to give us another layer of defense. We've mounted infrared sensors on the roof as well as a remotely operated portable radar unit behind the barn. It's not very big, but I'm told it'll give us a good warning of anything incoming."

"That depends on how badly they want to hit us," McGarvey countered.

Van Buren nodded. "But they have to find us first." He looked toward the tree line. "Short of stationing the National Guard out here, we're about as safe here as we'd be anywhere else."

They went into the house, where McGarvey was introduced

to four of Blatnik's security people. They were all young, and were friends of Todd and Liz, so they were taking this situation personally. Someone brought the bags in from the car and took them upstairs.

Elizabeth came down before McGarvey could go upstairs to see how Kathleen was doing. His daughter looked battered. Her face was puffy and terribly bruised. She walked hunched over and stiff because of the pain. But when she saw her father she managed to smile.

"Hi, Daddy," she said.

He took her in his arms and gently held her for a few moments, a lump in his throat. The bastards had hurt his baby girl. They had killed his granddaughter. They would pay. God, how they would pay.

"You should be in bed," McGarvey told her.

"Later," she said. "Has Otto found Nikolayev, yet?"

"He went back to France to look for him. How long have you two suspected that something was going to happen?"

"Since early September, but we weren't sure of anything." She looked inward and shook her head. "I wish we *had* said something. Maybe none of this would have happened. But we just didn't know."

"They would have found another way," McGarvey said. "But, yes, you and Otto *should* have given us the heads-up. We could have put some more resources on it."

"I'm sorry, Daddy," Elizabeth said, her eyes brimming. She was angry with herself for being so weak. Her internal struggle was plain on her face. "I left a disk for you in the front study. It has everything that we managed to come up with."

"I saw Otto's copy," McGarvey said. He glanced at his son-in-law, who looked as if he was ready to rip the arms off someone. Anyone. "I'm sending Todd back to Langley to wait for Otto."

"I want to go, too," Elizabeth said.

"Don't be a dumbbell," Todd told her.

She flared, but backed down. "He's a friend of the family, so don't go playing macho man."

"He's my friend, too," Todd told her.

Grassinger had come in with Blatnik. "Right," he said. "I'd

like to hold a security briefing now, then I suggest that we all settle down for a few hours. It's been a long night, and it could get even longer."

McGarvey was tired, but Grassinger's security briefing had been short and to the point. Anything within a mile or two of the house was in detectable range. That included vehicles passing on the highway and anything in the sky. The first lines of defense were the perimeter sensors and alarms. The second line were the stop sticks that would shred tires and the explosives that would shred bodies. The final line was the house itself, which had bulletproof polycarbonate windows, steel-reinforced doors and a bombproof safe room in the basement. The phone and electrical lines were encased in flexible steel sheaths and buried deeply. In addition there were wireless links to the outside world from every room in the house. And there were silent alarms connecting to the CIA, FBI, Maryland Highway Patrol, and Montgomery County Sheriff's offices.

Terrorists had breached the house a couple of years ago, but the security measures had been considerably beefed up since then. Such an attack could not succeed this time.

Yet everyone felt gloomy. It was a bunker mentality that was almost as bad as it had been for some people in the aftermath of the World Trade Center attacks. McGarvey had seen the mood in the eyes of his staff during the afternoon's teleconference. And he could hear it in their voices as he spoke to them at various times during the interminably long day.

Fred Rudolph from the FBI was having no luck tracking the blue Mercedes, at least not in the immediate area of Washington, D.C., so the search had gone nationwide.

Nor were there any signs that the Russian intelligence operation in Washington and New York was getting back to normal.

"Runkov and everyone else are hunkered down and staying there," Rudolph said. "It's unprecedented. They know something that we don't, but they're not talking to us."

McGarvey looked in on Kathleen after lunch but she was

still sound asleep. Stenzel said that she might sleep the rest of the day and through the night.

"It would be the best thing for her," the psychiatrist said. He came down to the kitchen with McGarvey to get something to eat. The refrigerator, freezer and pantry were well stocked, but no one had developed an appetite for much of anything other than coffee and sandwiches.

Elizabeth came in from the study. "I just talked to Todd. Otto is on his way back. Nikolayev is with him."

"When do they get here?"

"Late tonight," Elizabeth said. "I talked to Tom Lynch, too, and he said everything went well. The French were cooperative, and there was no trouble whatsoever."

"That's good to hear. Can we talk to Otto in the air?"

"I tried. He's probably turned off his phone for some reason, so unless you want to call the crew on an unsecured channel, we'll have to wait until they get here."

"We'll wait," McGarvey told his daughter. "I want Todd to call me the minute they land. Nikolayev can be put up in the VIP quarters at Andrews until we find out what he knows."

"It has to be something, Dad. Otherwise, he wouldn't have bugged out of Moscow the way he did, and the SVR wouldn't be so hot to find him."

"We'll see soon enough," McGarvey said. "In the meantime, did you get any sleep this afternoon?"

"A couple of hours," she said. "I'm too keyed up."

"Nightmares?" Stenzel asked gently.

She shot him a defiant look. But then nodded. "I'm holding my baby and someone is coming to take her away from me." She lowered her eyes.

McGarvey almost lost it. Like Todd, he wanted to lash out, to rip off somebody's arms. But he didn't have a target. Yet.

"I can give you something," Stenzel suggested, but Elizabeth shook her head.

"No drugs," she said. "At least I know the nightmares are my own."

"How do you feel, sweetheart?" McGarvey asked her. "Physically, I mean."

"A lot better than I think I should." She gave Stenzel another defiant look. "How about going for a walk?"

Grassinger came to the kitchen door. He gave McGarvey a nod. "Now, but not after dark, Mr. Director."

"A short walk," McGarvey told his daughter.

They got their coats and boots, and when they were dressed, McGarvey transferred his Walther PPK into an outer pocket. Elizabeth also carried the compact German police pistol, and she put hers in an outside pocket, too.

The snow had stopped for the moment, and it had turned sharply colder, so they could see their breath. They started off behind the house toward the riding arena that was housed in a long, corrugated metal building that was even bigger than the barn. The only footprints in the snow along the path were their own. The sky was dark and low, casting a gloomy pall over the dark woods and gray fields.

"I was starting to get claustrophobic in there," Elizabeth said.

"I know how you feel," McGarvey replied absently. He couldn't stop thinking about her nightmare.

"What's wrong with Mother?" she asked.

"She's overloaded with everything that's been happening—"

"That's not true," Elizabeth cut him off. "Not Mother. She's stronger than that. A lot stronger."

"I don't know what's wrong with her," McGarvey admitted tiredly. "Hell, even Stenzel doesn't know for sure. She's had every test in the world, and they've all come up negative. There's nothing physical that they can find."

"She acts like a zombie one minute, and completely normal the next. I'm telling you that being around her is like being in the Twilight Zone. She's my mother, and yet she's not. She's like a stranger."

They stopped. "Part of it is because of what happened to you in Vail. It tipped her over the edge."

Elizabeth looked inward. "Todd said that she called the hospital a bunch of times. He said she was like a crazy woman."

"I know, sweetheart. All we can do is get over this hump, then we'll get her some help."

Elizabeth touched her father's sleeve. "Is this almost over?"

He looked into her eyes, which were older than her years. He gave her a reassuring smile. "Soon, Liz. Real soon. I promise."

THURSDAY

THREE

"WHO IS MY ASSASSIN?" McGARVEY ASKED.

ANDREWS AIR FORCE BASE

On the bridge across the Potomac south of the city the sodium vapor lights were a harsh violet, interfering with McGarvey's view of the White House, the Capitol Building and the Washington Monument. He rode shotgun beside an unhappy Grassinger in an Office of Security Ford Explorer. It was after two-thirty in the morning, and Nikolayev was ready to talk. Despite Security's sharp warnings to stay put, McGarvey felt that he had no other choice but to go see the man. Find out what they were facing. Whatever was going to happen would go down within the next twenty-four hours or so. McGarvey was certain of it. They would lay out the bait, set the trap and sit back to wait. Nikolayev was the key, as he had been since he'd gone walkabout in August.

The Capital Beltway was all but deserted. The weather system that had dumped eleven inches of snow on the Washington area in the last week was gone, leaving behind near-zero temperatures and a crystal-clear sky. It was as if the entire city was holding its collective breath, waiting for the next shoe to drop. This was ancient Rome, with her granite buildings, senators and monuments. And the barbarians were massing at the gates.

"Pardon me, Mr. Director, but wouldn't it have been easier to bring this Russian to Cropley," Grassinger asked. He drove with his eyes constantly scanning his mirrors. A Mac 10 was ready in the rack in front of him, and another was lying on the seat between him and McGarvey.

"Someone might be watching," McGarvey said. "I don't want him spotted, and I definitely don't want to lead anybody back to the safe house yet."

"That's what I'm afraid of," Grassinger said. "The 'yet.'"

"This won't be easy," McGarvey said.

They took the Beltway exit to Andrews main gate.

"Bad police work," Grassinger murmured.

"Maybe. But we'll do it my way."

The air force cops at the gate stiffened to attention and passed them through when they realized who McGarvey was. The base was as quiet as the highway. The CIA's Gulfstream had been the last flight of the night, and nothing was leaving until after dawn.

Grassinger drove them directly across the base to the VIP quarters housed on the top floor of a three-story building next to base headquarters. The Charge of Quarters was expecting them, and he passed them directly up.

Todd met them in the dayroom that looked off toward the runways and rotating beacon atop the control tower. He'd been going for forty-eight hours straight without rest, and he looked haggard, but determined.

"He won't talk to me," Todd said. "He keeps repeating that he'll wait until he sees you."

"Where's Otto?" McGarvey asked.

"In there with him. They've been drinking vodka and talking about old times."

"Which old times are those?" McGarvey asked.

"I don't know. That's what Otto says every time he comes out to ask for more vodka." Todd turned to Grassinger. "You guys shouldn't have left Mac off the reservation. We could have brought Nikolayev out to the house."

"My call," McGarvey said. "Wait out here with Jim, I shouldn't be too long."

"I want to sit in—" Todd started.

"No." McGarvey went down the hall to the west suite, knocked once and went inside.

Otto and Nikolayev sat across from each other, a coffee table laden with vodka, glasses and trays of crackers and cheeses and caviar, between them. A stack of file folders was piled up on the floor next to where Nikolayev sat. They looked up, Otto with a startled expression, like a deer caught in headlights, and Nikolayev with an expectant, interested smile, like a scholar ready for a student's question.

"Oh, wow, Mac, I got him," Otto gushed. He jumped up. "This is Dr. Nikolayev. He promised to help us."

"Good job, Otto," McGarvey said. His eyes never left Nikolayev's. "Why don't you give us a few minutes alone to get acquainted?"

Otto hopped hesitantly from one foot to the other, but then he nodded. "Sure." He glanced at the Russian. "Anyway, we're almost there." He went out the door, closing it softly behind him.

"*Dawbra Ootra, Guspadyna* Nikolayev," McGarvey said. Good morning, Mr. Nikolayev.

"Actually it's Dr. Nikolayev, Mr. Director. But please, you may call me Anatoli Nikolaevich." Nikolayev motioned for McGarvey to have a seat. "Please."

"Why did you leave Moscow?" McGarvey asked. He went to the door and checked the corridor to make sure that no one was there, listening.

"Because of something I found out," Nikolayev said, watching McGarvey's movements.

"What was that, exactly?" McGarvey checked the windows and drew the blinds. He stopped and directed his gaze toward the Russian.

"I was doing research for a book, about the KGB during the Cold War years, when I stumbled across references to a General Baranov operation that I thought had been discussed but never implemented. Network Martyrs."

"What next?" McGarvey prompted. He checked the telephone, but the line was dead. Nevertheless, he unplugged it from the wall.

"When I began to realize that the operation might be closing down, I made an appointment to see an old Department Viktor chief of staff. Gennadi Zhuralev. But they got to him before we could talk."

McGarvey took out what appeared to be a penlight from a pocket and used it to scan the lights, wall sockets, switches and pictures hanging on the walls. If there was a bug, the penlight's bulb would flash. But nothing happened. The room was clean.

"Who are the *they*?"

"I didn't know at the time. But now I think they were probably mafiosa hired by someone inside the SVR, or maybe in the Kremlin. Someone possibly in Putin's office, or very close, who wants to sweep everything under the rug." Nikolayev shrugged. "It's happening all over Russia, but especially Moscow. America's cooperation is too valuable to jeopardize."

McGarvey motioned Nikolayev to his feet. The old man stiffly complied, and McGarvey quickly frisked him for weapons. But Nikolayev came up clean. He sat back down.

"Why'd you run? Did you think that they would come after you for disturbing the files?"

"That's exactly what I thought," Nikolayev said. "So I pulled the file I needed and took the first train to Leningrad and from there Helsinki and then a flight to Paris."

"How about Vladimir Trofimov?"

"He was General Baranov's chief of staff in the early days. The sixties and seventies. I thought that he might have some of the answers."

"That was going too far back, wasn't it?"

"No. Actually it was the beginning of the project. Baranov's dream."

McGarvey stood across from the old Russian, but he said nothing. He waited for Nikolayev to continue.

"Like your people, we were working on behavior modification techniques using a combination of psychological means, and of hallucinogenic drugs such as LSD and derivatives from peyote and some other plants that Banco del Sur supplied us with from Mexico. It was brainwashing. An extension of what the North Koreans and Chinese were doing in the fifties."

The realization of the full measure of Baranov's scheme began to dawn on McGarvey. "You're saying that the sleeper agents Baranov sent over here, the assassins, were brainwashed?"

"That's exactly what I'm saying. Gennadi Zhuralev had made a copy of the list of assassins and their targets for insurance. He left a marginal note, apparently by mistake, in one of the files. He was the director of resources, so he certainly had the means." Nikolayev shook his head. "But they got to him first."

"What about Trofimov?"

"He was chief of staff, as I said, so I thought that he would have seen the list and maybe he would remember some of the names. But he only told me one. It was you. Baranov had placed you at the head of the list."

"How many others were there?"

Nikolayev spread his hands. "Maybe as many as a dozen. But it's highly unlikely that all of those people are still alive."

"Who is my assassin?" McGarvey asked.

"I never saw that list. But from what Otto tells me, it has to be someone very close to you. Or at least someone with reliable intelligence about your movements." Nikolayev picked up the stack of file folders and offered it to McGarvey. "These are his suspects."

McGarvey hesitated a moment before he took the files. There were seven of them. He was almost afraid to look at the names. "Did you recognize any of these?"

"Not beyond the obvious," Nikolayev said. "But Otto told me that there might be one more name to add to the list. He wasn't completely sure yet, but when he was, he would name the person."

The first of the folders was Dick Yemm's. McGarvey looked up. "This man is dead."

"I know. But Otto said that Mr. Yemm remained a suspect, which in effect would mean that the threat was over." Nikolayev seemed suddenly very tired. He idly rubbed his chest.

"Remember that if the SVR had these names, they would all be targets for assassination themselves."

The second file folder was a dossier on Dmitri Runkov, the Russian SVR *rezident* at the Washington embassy. He was hiding out in his house, but Fred Rudolph had admitted that if the Russian intelligence officer wanted to get out of there without being seen, it was possible.

"I don't think it would be Runkov himself," Nikolayev said. "But rather someone who Runkov knows here in the States. A sleeper resource. An agent buried so deep that he's beyond detection by U.S. authorities, but who could be accessed by a handful of people in an emergency. The Washington *rezident* being one of them."

The third file folder was marked UNKNOWN. In it, Otto had laid out the parameters for the assassin. A bulletproof identity, good intelligence, nearness to McGarvey, knowledge of explosives and a dozen other traits.

The fourth file folder contained the dossier of Bob Johnson, Jared Kraus's number two in Technical Services. According to Otto's notes he was Senator Hammond's source within the CIA. Otto had learned that from various computer and telephone taps he had conducted of his own accord. He had not blown the whistle on Johnson's talking to the senator because the man was one of the suspects as McGarvey's would-be assassin.

The fifth folder contained Otto's own dossier, without notes other than Stenzel's psychological profiles on him.

"Unique, wouldn't you say, for a chief investigator to name himself as a suspect," Nikolayev said.

McGarvey made no comment. How much control or self-awareness would a brainwashed person have? Maybe none.

The sixth and seventh file folders contained dossiers on Dick Adkins and on Todd Van Buren. Adkins was old enough to have come under Baranov's influence while the general was still alive, but Todd had been a young man then. Still in grade school or junior high. Otto's notes listed him as a "secondary," but a suspect nonetheless.

"A recruit trained by the original agent's handler," Nikolayev explained. "But you need to know something else, Mr.

Director. In fact if there is a possibility of identifying and catching the killer, it will be because of the existence of a second group. One even more important than the list of suspects themselves."

"What are you talking about? What group?"

"Their control officers." Nikolayev became introspective. He looked away momentarily. "When we were doing this work we succeeded brilliantly. The conditioning could be done in a week's time. But there was always a problem that we could not overcome. The conversions last only seven days, sometimes as long as eight or nine days, but that's it. After that the subjects slowly began to return to normal, or at least to a near-normal psychological state. In fact within twenty-four hours of the deadline, the subjects became useless for our purposes."

Something else dawned on McGarvey. "You were in on it from the beginning. That's why you came out to try to stop Martyrs. Your conscience was killing you."

Nikolayev nodded heavily. "I directed the project."

"Knowing what Baranov was going to use it for?"

Again Nikolayev nodded. But he looked up. "I won't make excuses, except to say that you were our enemy. Americans might have feared that our nuclear weapons would rain down on their heads, and rightly so. But Russians were just as frightened. We wouldn't have spent billions of rubles building our subway system as bomb shelters."

"Point taken," McGarvey conceded. "If we find out who has a control officer, and keep them apart long enough, we'll have our sleeper. How?"

"You must offer yourself as bait. It will mean shutting down your security measures at the safe house Otto has told me about. Sending away your security team. And then inviting each person on the list to come out for a chat. One-on-one."

McGarvey put the folders aside. "Did Otto give you any hints who the eighth suspect might be?"

"No."

They were his friends, most of them. Even family. It was monstrous. Worse than he had feared. But despite himself he could see the logic in Otto's list of suspects. They were the people who, in the deepest recesses of his heart, he himself had suspected. "What about Runkov and the dossier Otto designated as unknown? How do we get word to them?"

"Otto has access to your law enforcement computer systems in the Washington area. He can place your present whereabouts on those Web pages. *En claire*. The right people will see it soon enough."

"The assassin won't come."

"Yes he will, and you know it. Most of those people are your friends. But so will the assassin's control officer have to make an appearance. To reinforce the conditioning."

"You'll be waiting."

Nikolayev nodded. "With help. Someone from the FBI or from your Office of Security. Once the principals show up, whoever comes next will be our link to the assassin."

"I'll have Jim Grassinger assign someone to you. In the meantime, you'll remain here."

"I suggest that we get this over with as soon as possible, Mr. Director."

"Tonight," McGarvey said. "It gives us the entire day to get ready." At the door he turned back. "But what did the sonofabitch hope to accomplish by killing me? I'm just one man."

"He's already done more than that if you stop to think about it," Nikolayev said. "Nobody in the intelligence community in Washington completely trusts anyone else. You don't trust your own friends. I'm sure that the mistrust at Langley is hampering operations. From what I read in the newspapers you and the President are at odds with Congress. You're so distracted, in fact, by the attacks on your family, that your job is suffering. And were Baranov alive now, I have no doubt that he would have planned for some spectacular event to happen in the midst of all the confusion."

"But he's not," McGarvey said, once again seeing Baranov pitch forward dead.

Nikolayev nodded. "Good luck, Mr. Director."

McGarvey returned to the dayroom, where he took Todd aside. "I want you to stick around here and keep an eye on him for the rest of the night. We'll send out your relief. Then

I want you to go home, get something to eat, grab a shower and get some sleep."

"Did he tell you anything that'll help?"

"Not much. I want you to come out to Cropley tonight. At eight."

"I'll be there as soon as I'm relieved here—"

"Eight," McGarvey said.

Todd wanted to argue, but he nodded. "How's Liz?"

"She was finally sleeping when I left."

"Good."

McGarvey took Otto downstairs, Grassinger right behind them.

"I want you to go home and get some sleep now, and that's an order," McGarvey told him.

"Okay, Mac, whatever you say. But did Nikolayev give us anything?"

"He said that you have an eighth suspect."

Otto's head bobbed up and down as if it were on springs. "But I'm not sure yet. Honest injun."

"Give me a name."

"No," Otto said. He was acutely distressed.

"I'll need to know pretty soon," McGarvey said. "I can't do this in the dark."

Otto held his silence. He looked guilty of something.

"Okay, get some sleep, and then you can work on it this afternoon. I want you to come out to Cropley tonight around eight. Alone."

"The trap?"

"We'll talk about it then," McGarvey promised. "And have Louise fix you something decent to eat. You look like hell, Otto."

FOUR

AN ALMOST INFALLIBLE MEANS OF SAVING
YOURSELF FROM THE DESIRE OF SELF-
DESTRUCTION, IS ALWAYS TO HAVE SOMETHING
TO DO, VOLTAIRE WROTE A COUPLE HUNDRED
YEARS AGO. IT WAS JUST AS TRUE NOW AS IT
WAS THEN.

CROPLEY

McGarvey stood at the front door in the stairhall, looking out the narrow window. Clouds had moved in again, lending the distant woods a forbidding feeling. Creatures were gathering up there in the darkness. Watching, plotting, waiting for the correct moment to strike.

Nothing moved that he could see. Blatnik's people were well hidden in the trees and brush flanking the long driveway. The rear of the house was covered by motion detectors and infrared sensors. If anything stirred up there, alarms would sound in the house.

It was after lunch. Everyone had gotten at least a few hours' rest, and over a large lunch of fried chicken and potato salad that Elizabeth made, the mood was light. Even Jim Grassinger, who refused to have a beer but instead drank warm Coke straight from the can, had eased up and cracked a joke or two.

Liz and her mother were outside behind the house making a snowman or something under the watchful eyes of Gloria Sanchez and one of Blatnik's people.

McGarvey was unsettled. Running away to choose the time

and place for his battles had always minimized the risk to his family but did nothing to protect them from harm. Bringing them out here did the opposite: It actually maximized the risk to them. But he would be here at their side when the bad guys came calling.

There was no mistake in his or anyone else's mind that he wasn't the only target. Kathleen and Elizabeth were targets, too. Their deaths at the hands of an assassin would almost as effectively destroy his usefulness as a DCI as would his own death. No one talked about it, but he'd heard the apprehension in Whittaker's voice, and seen it on the faces of his staff this morning during the teleconference.

Stenzel came down the hall from somewhere in the back, and McGarvey turned away from the window. Now it would begin, he thought.

"They said that you wanted to see me, Mr. Director," Stenzel said.

"I'm sending you back to Langley this afternoon," McGarvey told the psychiatrist.

Stenzel was startled. "What's up? Is something wrong? I mean it'd be a lot better if I stuck around to monitor your wife's condition."

"It's just for overnight," McGarvey explained. Grassinger appeared in the doorway from the dining room, which they continued to use as their operations center. "Dr. Stenzel is leaving. Get somebody to take him back to Langley, would you?"

"Sure thing. When?"

"Now," McGarvey said.

"Well, let me have a word with her first—"

"No. I want you to leave right now."

Stenzel glanced up the stairs. "What about my things?"

"You can come back out first thing in the morning," McGarvey said. "This is only for tonight."

Grassinger was surprised, but he said nothing. He stepped back into the dining room, issued an order into his lapel mic, then returned with Stenzel's coat. A minute later one of Blatnik's people drove up.

"Are you going to tell me what's going on?" Stenzel asked.

He was vexed. "Your wife could have another breakdown at any moment."

"It's a risk we have to take," McGarvey said. "Until morning."

Stenzel appealed mutely to Grassinger, who didn't blink. He pulled on his coat, gave McGarvey another look, then left without a word.

"What's going on tonight, Mr. Director?" Grassinger asked. "Does it have something to do with the Russian?"

"I have a couple of phone calls to make, and then we'll talk. I'm going to force the issue, and I'll need your cooperation, your full cooperation. Do you understand?"

"No, sir. But we'll do whatever it takes. We can't go on like this forever."

"No we can't," McGarvey agreed.

He crossed the living room and went into the study in the opposite wing of the house from the dining room and kitchen. He kept the door open so that he could see anyone coming, and telephoned the Agency locator at Langley, who rang through to Bob Johnson in Technical Services.

"Good afternoon, Bob, this is Kirk McGarvey, I need a favor sometime tonight, if you guys aren't too busy."

"No, sir. Let me get Jared—"

"No, I don't want to bother him. He's got his hands full with the VI and Vail investigations, and I just need someone who understands alarm systems. But I don't want just anyone. I need someone I can trust."

"Yes, sir," Johnson replied cautiously. "What can I do for you?"

"Something's not right with the system here. Could be that someone's tampered with it. I just don't know. Can you come out here tonight. Say around eight to take a look?"

"I could come right now."

"No, later. I don't want to make a production out of this, in case someone has sabotaged the system. Do you understand?"

"Yes, sir. Perfectly. I'll be there at eight."

"Good man. See you then."

"Let your security people know that I'm coming."

"Oh, don't worry about them. That's why I want the alarm system checked."

Next he called Fred Rudolph at his office in FBI headquarters. "I need a favor, no questions asked."

"Why doesn't that surprise me?" Rudolph said. He was straitlaced. He did everything by the book. Or at least he tried to do it that way. He and McGarvey were opposites, but they respected each other. "What can I do for you, Mac?"

"Put me on your medium security website," McGarvey told him. "I want it to look as if someone released a confidential memo by mistake."

"What memo?"

"You're concerned that the DCI is out here with little or no security because he's pigheaded. The Bureau needs some direction."

"Who am I supposedly sending this memo to?"

"Senator Hammond. But you're not really going to send it. It's a draft memo. But I want it on the website."

"So the Russians can see it," Rudolph said. "If it's them, they'll come out guns blazing. Shootout at the OK Corral. That's your style."

"Post it a few minutes after six tonight. It'll look like a shift change error."

"Tell me that you're not really sending your security away," Rudolph said.

"No questions, Fred, remember?"

"All right. I can do that for you. Against my better judgment. But in the meantime, I'm going to double the surveillance on the Russians, and on Senator Hammond's office because there's a good chance he'll see it, too."

"Your call. But if someone heads out this way I don't want your people to interfere with them."

"Can we at least give you a heads-up?"

"I'd appreciate it."

Rudolph was silent for a moment. "Do you think it'll go down tonight?"

"I hope so."

"Did your people find Nikolayev?"

"He's here in Washington."

"Okay then, good luck," Rudolph said. "Just watch your ass, will you?"

"Sure thing," McGarvey promised.

He went down the hall through the garden room so that he could look out a back window. Katy and Liz had built five small snowmen and were working on a sixth. The figures' heads were larger than their bodies, and they seemed to be leaning backward, looking up at the sky. They all faced the same direction, toward the east, McGarvey realized, and the scene was somehow disturbing. Gloria Sanchez and one of the outside security people stood by watching.

McGarvey returned to the study, where he telephoned Adkins's house. A young woman answered. Her voice was soft. Barely a whisper.

"Hello."

"This is Kirk McGarvey. I'd like to speak with Dick Adkins."

"Yes," she said. Her voice was inflectionless, like a zombie's. "Father," she called away from the phone. "It's Mr. McGarvey."

Adkins came on almost immediately. "Hi, Mac." He had already talked to Whittaker twice about coming back to work. McGarvey could only imagine what was going on at his house with his daughters.

"I'm sorry that I didn't call sooner," McGarvey said. "I couldn't believe the news when David told me. I'm really sorry, Dick."

"She hid it the whole time. She was driving up to a cancer clinic in Baltimore for the past year. Sometimes the girls took her. I never knew."

McGarvey didn't know what to say that was appropriate. Katy would know, but he hadn't told her. "Ruth was a strong woman."

"That she was."

"Will there be a memorial service?"

"On Saturday at Grace Lutheran. But of course we don't expect you or Kathleen to be there, under the circumstances."

"We'll be there, Dick. This other business will be settled by then."

"Oh?"

"I hate to ask this, but can you come out here tonight?"

"Cropley? Sure. What time?"

"Eight," McGarvey said. Adkins had practically jumped at the invitation. Whatever was going on at the house could not be pleasant for him.

"Let security know I'm coming."

"That won't be a problem. Just drive up to the house. I'll see you then."

Adkins wanted to say something else. McGarvey could hear it in his hesitation. "Okay," he said at last. "See you then."

When McGarvey came into the dining room Grassinger was looking out the bow windows toward the horse barn and riding arena. His hands were clasped behind his back and he rocked on his heels as if he was thinking about something in time with a beat. He was alone.

"I've been asking myself what does it mean by 'forcing the issue.' I can think of a dozen different possibilities, not one of them with a shred of common sense to it. And needing my cooperation, my 'full cooperation,' is something even more worrisome to me. I'm saying to myself that since we can't go back to business as usual until the operator or operators are bagged we need to do something really creative to get the job done. Offer them bait. I think that's what the director is suggesting. The bait being himself, of course. Now, that's not acceptable, not within my charter. So what to do? Maybe reason and logic?"

"They have all the time in the world, Jim," McGarvey said. "But that's a luxury we don't have. As long as I stay in the bunker they'll bide their time."

Grassinger turned around. He wasn't a happy man. "So we just open the doors to the keep for them, Mr. Director? Is that what you're asking me to do?"

"Something like that."

"Then they'll waltz in here and kill you and your family. They will have won."

McGarvey smiled faintly. "It might not be all that easy for them."

"No offense intended, sir," Grassinger apologized.

"None taken. I'm not suggesting that we lower our guards and turn our backs. But it has to look that way, and it has to be convincing."

Grassinger was somewhat mollified. He nodded. "Well, sir, what do you have in mind?"

"Who's with Nikolayev at Andrews?"

"I sent young Chris Bartholomew. She knows what she's doing."

"I want him brought out here tonight around seven. Find a place along the highway so that he can see someone coming from the city. He'll have to be hidden, but near enough so that he can identify whoever is in the car coming down the driveway."

Grassinger nodded. "I know a couple of spots that might work. Is Chris to stay with him?"

"No, I want you there. You might have to move your people in a big hurry."

"Who are you expecting, sir?" Grassinger asked. He had a sour look on his broad face, as if he knew that he was going to hear something disagreeable.

"Dick Adkins, Otto Rencke, my son-in-law and Bob Johnson from Technical Services."

"I know them all."

"They'll be the ones coming in the open, but there might be someone else in the first batch who won't want to be seen."

"Russians, maybe? That's why we have our own Russian watchdog?"

"That, but there's more," McGarvey said. This wasn't easy.

Grassinger nodded, tight-lipped. "There always is, isn't there."

"All of those people are suspects," McGarvey said.

It took a moment for the implications to set in and Grassinger reared back, but he recovered. "Dear Lord," he said. "Does Nikolayev know who it is? Will he recognize this person?"

"The assassin has been brainwashed. Sometime in the past. By the Russians. Nikolayev was one of the designers of the program, and according to him the conditioning doesn't last very long. So the killer needs a control officer. Someone to reinforce the training on a regular basis. He thinks that the assassin's control officer will try to come out here tonight, too."

Grassinger worked to grasp the enormity of what McGarvey was telling him. "Why would they expose themselves like that?"

"I don't know," McGarvey said. But he had his guess. If the killer was one of his friends, they would need to be reinforced in order to pull off such an act.

"Whoever comes out in the end will be the control officer," Grassinger said. "All we have to do is match that person with one of the people in the house."

"You can deploy your officers along the highway, out of sight."

"But they're your friends, Mr. Director. Your own son-in-law."

"I know," McGarvey said. "I'm going to shut down the alarm system and forward defensive measures. But I'll leave the detectors in the woods behind the house active in case someone tries to sneak through the back door."

"I'll put a couple of people up there."

"Okay. But nobody moves until Nikolayev or I give the word. We're going to do this once, and only once."

An almost infallible means of saving yourself from the desire of self-destruction, is always to have something to do, Voltaire wrote a couple of hundred years ago. It was just as true now as it was then.

Grassinger got on the radio to summon Blatnik as McGarvey walked back to the garden room and stepped outside.

On the snow-covered back patio McGarvey watched Kathleen and Elizabeth together. It was like the early days, before the split, mother and daughter together and happy. They were close again after years of distance: For Katy because she saw so much of her estranged husband in her daughter's actions and mannerisims. And for Liz because her mother refused to consider allowing Kirk back into her life, even though it was clear that she'd never stopped loving him.

But that was the disagreeable then. This was the hopeful now, because even though they had this trouble hanging over them, they were together. That's all that really mattered.

"Very impressive, but what's it supposed to mean?" McGarvey asked, starting across the backyard to them.

They had finished with the sixth figure. Kathleen spun around so fast at the sound of his voice that she slipped and fell on her rear.

For a moment no one moved, but then Elizabeth shrieked with laughter and helped her mother up.

"Why it's Aku-Aku, dear," Kathleen said, taking a sideways glance at their handiwork. She and Elizabeth exchanged a knowing look.

"Easter Island, Daddy," Elizabeth explained. "You know, the statues."

Gloria Sanchez shook her head. She had no idea what it meant.

"Okay, so you're tired of the cold and snow and you're pining for a South Seas cruise? Is that it?" McGarvey asked. Something was odd here. Something off. But he felt as if he were the only one sensing it.

"It's Mom's idea," Elizabeth said.

"They're waiting for the dawn, Kirk," Kathleen told him. "You know, it comes up in the east. Morning. The new day and all that." She got the pensive look that had been so common lately. "Todd and Elizabeth are going to adopt, so we'll be grandparents after all. Ruth is no longer suffering, the poor dear. And tonight you're going to catch the killer. I just know it." She glanced again at the snow figures. "So all we have to do is survive until morning."

There was nothing McGarvey could say.

Kathleen smiled. "Close your mouth, dear," she told him.

FIVE

SHE MAKES US BLINDLY PLAY HER TERRIBLE
GAME, AND WE NEVER SEE BENEATH THE
CARDS. FATE. LUCK. CHANCE. DESTINY.
VOLTAIRE HAD BELIEVED IN ALL OF THAT, BUT
McGARVEY WASN'T SURE THAT HE DID.

CROPLEY

From the windows in several upstairs rooms McGarvey checked the front and back areas around the house. It was 7:30 P.M. and already dark. Lights from the downstairs windows spilled yellow patches on the snow. Blatnik's and Grassinger's people had withdrawn to the highway and behind the house in the woods. The only ones left in the house besides McGarvey were his wife and daughter. A radio played downstairs in the kitchen, but the silence in the house was oppressive.

Nothing he could see moved out there, so he went downstairs. At the keypad in the front stairhall he switched off the house alarms. The sensors in the woods behind the house would remain on, but the defensive measures between the house and the highway had been disabled. If Nikolayev was right, the assassin would arrive in the first batch, the assassin's control officer later. They couldn't be sure until then.

McGarvey took out his pistol, checked the action and returned it to the holster at the small of his back.

The question that had been pressing him all day intruded again. If it came to it, could he pull the trigger on a friend?

Presumably the assassin had been brainwashed. He was sick. Shooting him would be like killing a cancer patient when the cure was readily available. Yet the assassin would be dangerous.

Elizabeth came down the hall from the kitchen, rolling down her sweater sleeves. "Almost time?" she asked. Her face was badly bruised.

McGarvey nodded. "You're supposed to be taking it easy, remember?"

She shrugged. "I'll live, Dad. Honestly." She smiled wanly. "Anyway, I'm becoming quite the domestic. But I was raised by a neat freak, remember?" She glanced up the stairs. "Where's Mom?"

"She's taking a hot bath. Stenzel left her something to help her get to sleep afterward."

"Good idea," Elizabeth agreed. Unsaid between them, but understood nevertheless, was that it would be better if Kathleen remained upstairs, out of the way until the issue was resolved. She would be safe.

"Are you armed?" McGarvey asked.

Elizabeth nodded. "But I don't know if I could shoot Dick Adkins, or, God forbid, Otto." She was deeply troubled. "How couldn't we have known, being around them all the time?"

"They might not even know themselves," McGarvey told her. She hadn't mentioned her own husband's name, though when McGarvey had told her that he was coming out here tonight with the others she had reacted as if stung.

"The ice bucket in the living room is full, I laid out some snacks, and there's beer and wine in the fridge." She grinned despite herself. "I even brought some Twinkies for Otto."

"Did you get some cream for him, too?"

"Two percent milk. Somebody's got to start slowing him down. Louise won't."

"Jim, are you set up there?" McGarvey spoke into his lapel mic. There was no answer. "Jim?"

Elizabeth watched him. He shook his head, so she tried. "Jim, do you copy?" After a moment she shook her head. "Nothing."

McGarvey called Grassinger's cell phone. The security chief answered on the first ring.

"Yes."

"Is your earpiece working?" McGarvey asked.

"I just talked to Tony," Grassinger said. "Are you having trouble?"

"Liz and I can't get through."

"It's the base unit at the house, Mr. Director. I'll send someone down to look at it."

"Are you and Nikolayev in position?"

"Yes."

"Then sit tight. We'll use the phone."

"Yes, sir."

"Your people know what to do," McGarvey said as a statement not a question.

"Yes, sir," Grassinger replied, and McGarvey could hear an edge of impatience in the man's voice. He'd been insulted. But it couldn't be helped. McGarvey needed his people to be sharp.

Nikolayev and Grassinger waited in an Agency SUV parked off the highway. The vehicle's lights were off, and they were well hidden in the trees and brush. From their position they could see a couple of hundred feet of highway and the first fifty feet of the driveway. But sitting in the car was uncomfortable because it rested at an uneven angle to the left. Nikolayev didn't complain. His life had taught him to endure.

"Will it be somebody you know?" Grassinger asked. He was behind the wheel. Nikolayev was in the passenger seat at an angle above him.

"Everyone I know is too old for this sort of thing," the Russian replied mildly. He had night-vision binoculars, which he raised to his eyes. "Rencke gave me a list of names and photographs, but there are blanks, you know."

"What good is waiting out here, then? What are we supposed to do?"

Nikolayev lowered the binoculars and gave Grassinger a hard stare. "You can only hope to protect them in hiding for so long. So we do this tonight to end the waiting." He glanced toward the highway. "In the first arrivals, anyone who shows up who has not been invited will probably be our man," he explained. "After that, after everyone is here, we wait. Whoever comes next will be the control officer. We will have to match that person to someone already in the house and warn McGarvey."

"Whoever comes in from the woods behind the house will be our man," Grassinger suggested. "Let's not forget that avenue."

"They won't come that way," Nikolayev disagreed. He raised the binoculars again as headlights flashed on the highway. Moments later a dark-colored Ford Taurus station wagon slowed and turned onto the driveway. "Adkins," he said. "Number one."

Grassinger called McGarvey. "Adkins is coming your way."

"Right," McGarvey replied, and broke the connection.

McGarvey met Adkins at the front door as his DDCI came across the broad porch with a look that was a study in contrasts between despair and eagerness.

"Thanks for coming out tonight," McGarvey said. "The timing couldn't have been worse for you. I'm sorry."

"Duty calls," Adkins offered. "I couldn't stay there. At the house. It's crazy with all the relatives in from out of town. Not what Ruth would have wanted."

Elizabeth had put a fresh log on the fire in the living room. As McGarvey helped Adkins off with his coat she came out.

"Hello, Dick," she said. She offered her cheek for a kiss. "You have Todd's and my condolences for Ruth. It was terrible. I couldn't believe it when my dad told me."

"Thanks, Elizabeth. I appreciate your concern. I really do. Especially right now when you're recovering from your own accident." Adkins's lips compressed. "Ruth would have said that better than I did."

She touched his arm. "It doesn't matter how it's said."

"Are you armed?" McGarvey asked.

Adkins's mouth opened. He looked from McGarvey to Elizabeth and back. He nodded. "Considering what's been going on, yes, I'm carrying a weapon."

"You'd better give it to me. I'll put it in the closet with your coat."

Adkins complied, handing his 9mm Beretta to McGarvey. "I don't usually carry a gun, you know," he apologized.

McGarvey put it in the closet, and they moved into the living room, where Elizabeth poured Adkins and her father a brandy. She got herself a Perrier with a twist.

Adkins stood with his back to the fireplace as if he was trying to get warm. But a thin sheen of perspiration covered his forehead. He wore an old burgundy sweater and jeans. His eyes darted from McGarvey to Elizabeth. He was waiting for something. Expecting to be told something. And he was nervous about it. His attitude and dress made him appear boyish.

"What's this all about, anyway, Mac?" he asked. He glanced toward the hall. "And where's Kathleen tonight? She's okay now, isn't she?"

"She's fine, Dick. She's upstairs. I've called a few people to come out tonight because I have something to tell everybody."

"Any hints for your number two? Maybe I could offer a suggestion or two."

"We'll wait for the others," McGarvey said. The cell phone rang out on the hall table, where he'd left it. "Excuse me."

"Do you want some ice, Dick?" Elizabeth asked.

The call was from Grassinger. "Your son-in-law is on his way."

"Thank you."

"Wait," Grassinger said. "Wait a second. Another car is coming."

McGarvey looked out the hall window, but he couldn't see any headlights in the woods yet. The highway was almost a mile away.

"It's Bob Johnson. He's on his way to you."

"Okay. The last one should be Otto."

"In this batch," Grassinger said.

Laying the phone down, McGarvey went back into the living room, where Elizabeth was refreshing Adkins's drink.

"That was Todd. He's coming down the driveway," he told them.

Elizabeth smiled with pleasure. "Oh good."

Headlights flashed in the living room windows and moved out to the stairhall. McGarvey went to get the door at the same time a second pair of headlights appeared up on the driveway in the woods.

Todd got out of his car and looked back. "Someone is right behind me," he said.

"Did you get a look at who it was?" McGarvey asked from the doorway. He wanted to maintain as much of the fiction for as long as he could. At least until they were all in place. But he hated it; the lying. His stomach was sour.

"No," Todd said. His right hand was in his jacket pocket. Presumably he had his gun there. It was one of the things McGarvey needed to know.

A light-colored car came down the long, circular driveway, past the frozen fountain and horse paddock, its headlights illuminating the front of the house.

"It's Bob Johnson," McGarvey said. Todd had no reaction.

Johnson parked his car behind Todd's and Adkins's cars and got out. He hesitated for just a moment, then came around to where Todd waited. He carried a small leather case. They shook hands. "Hello, Todd. How're you doing tonight?"

"I've been better. You?"

Johnson shrugged. He looked at McGarvey in the doorway. "Good evening, Mr. Director. I brought my tool kit."

"That won't be necessary," McGarvey told him. "There's nothing wrong with the alarm system."

"Sir?"

"Come on in, and I'll explain everything," McGarvey told him. "Leave your tool kit in the car."

The Technical Services deputy did as he was told, and he followed Todd onto the porch and into the house.

"Is Dick here?" Todd asked.

"He's in the living room. Otto should be showing up at any minute." McGarvey had them hang their coats in the hall closet. "Are you carrying a weapon?" he asked Johnson.

Johnson shook his head. He was a few years older than

Todd, but his hair was cut short in a butch and his narrow face, with its freckled red cast, made him look like a kid. He was startled by the question. "We carry multitesters in my shop. Not guns."

"Would you mind?" McGarvey asked. He made an even more startled Johnson spread his legs and stick out his arms. McGarvey quickly frisked him.

"Can you tell me what's going on, sir?"

"Aside from the fact that you've been pumping classified information to someone on Senator Hammond's staff, I don't know," McGarvey said coolly. "But that's what we'll find out tonight."

Johnson was taken aback, but he didn't protest; nor did he seem defiant. He was a kid caught with his hand in the cookie jar.

"Leave your gun in the closet, would you, Todd?" McGarvey asked his son-in-law.

Todd's left eyebrow rose, but he did as he was asked without a word, and they all went into the living room. He gave his wife a kiss. "Hi, sweetheart, how're you doing?"

"Just peachy," she said. She gave Johnson, who wasn't sure what to do, a nod.

"Why don't we all just have a seat," McGarvey told them. "Otto is on his way out. He said that he would give me a call from the highway so we can shut down the security system for him."

"Who else is coming?" Todd asked. He knew that something was going down, but not exactly what.

"Just Otto for now," McGarvey told him. The phone rang in the hall. "That's him." McGarvey went to answer it. "Who is it?" he asked softly.

"Otto Rencke," Grassinger replied.

"Okay, keep your eyes open. I don't know who else might show up, or how long it might take, but just keep your eyes open."

"Will do, sir," Grassinger said. "Watch yourself down there. Give a whistle, and we'll come running."

"There's been no movement behind the house yet?" McGarvey asked.

"Nothing. Not even a deer or a rabbit."

McGarvey put the phone down on the hall table and stood stock-still for a long moment. He could hear the murmur of low conversation in the living room, but he couldn't make out what was being said.

Headlights flashed in the woods, and McGarvey went to the door as Otto came down the hill in an Agency Ford Bronco. He parked behind the line of cars in the driveway. He jumped out and rushed up the walk, slipping and sliding in the snow. His frizzy hair flew in every direction, his coat was unbuttoned, his sweatshirt was dirty and his jeans hung loosely on his hips. In the glare of the porch light his face was sallow.

"Oh, wow, Mac, am I late?" he gushed, scuttling across the covered porch.

"You're just in time," McGarvey told him. "I'm glad to see you." He gave Otto a warm embrace. "Did you bring a gun with you tonight?" he whispered into Otto's ear.

"I don't have a gun, Mac. Honest injun." He swallowed hard. "I wouldn't know what to do with one if I had it. Probably shoot myself in the foot or something, ya know?"

"Okay," McGarvey said, and he brought Otto into the house, where they hung his coat in the closet and joined the others in the living room.

Otto stopped in his tracks. "Oh, wow," he murmured. He hopped from one foot to the other a couple of times, looking at each of them, his mouth opening and closing as if he were a fish out of water.

These people were on his list; all of them except for Runkov, the one unknown, and the eighth name, which he wouldn't tell anybody. And Yemm, of course, who was dead.

McGarvey watched the play of emotions on Otto's face, trying to judge what it was his old friend was thinking. But with Otto that was almost always impossible. Sometimes Otto admitted *he* didn't know what he was thinking.

No one knew what to say or do. McGarvey motioned for Otto to have a seat in front of the fireplace, but no one else moved. They were waiting, like lovers just before the climax: breathless, unfocused, thinking only of themselves at this exact moment, wondering how it was they were here, and exactly what would happen next.

McGarvey walked over to the sideboard. He poured a small brandy and drank it. These were friends. Longtime friends, some of them. Loves. Acquaintances. But McGarvey had no questions about how he had gotten here. He'd built this prison for himself brick by painful brick over a twenty-five-year career with the CIA. Overzealousness. Not staying within the strict letter of the law. Taking matters into his own hands. Straying from the fold. Running with the wolves in the night; or rather *not* running with the wolves. His entire career he had been guilty of the sin of individualism. Working under his own charter. Operating by his own set of rules. His own personal code of honor, if an assassin could be said to have such a code.

He'd been called an anachronism, finally, by a deputy director of Operations in the Company a few years ago. The West had won the Cold War. The bad guys had all packed up and gone home. McGarvey's brand of justice was no longer required. Thanks, but now it's time for you to go.

But that was before Osama bin Laden and his ilk.

Besides that he could not go. Because he'd never found the answers to the questions that were at the core of his existence. He had a sense of honor, but it never seemed to square with the real world. He thought he knew what a hero was, but the older he got the less certain he became of that.

Duty. Responsibility. Passion. The nineteen men who died striking the World Trade Center towers, the Pentagon and those heading for the Capitol Building who crashed in a field in Pennsylvania all felt that they had duties. They certainly had passion. And they accepted a warped sense of honor and responsibility. For a time they'd even been heroes to some people; to a lot of people actually. And not just Afghanis or Islamic fundamentalists, but some Americans and French and Germans. People who believed that the U.S. was evil and needed to be struck down.

Did he understand any of that yet? McGarvey didn't think he did. In fact he felt that he had never been further away from understanding anything than he was at this moment.

He turned to face them. "Somebody is trying to kill me. And one of you may know who it is."

"It could be somebody else," Otto cried. "Honest to God, I've tried to find out. I've done everything I could." He lowered his head. "Honest injun, kimo sabe. Honest, honest." He began to cry, his shoulders shaking. But no one reached out to him.

She makes us blindly play her terrible game, and we never see beneath the cards. Fate. Luck. Chance. Destiny. Voltaire had believed in all of that, but McGarvey wasn't sure that he did.

In the SUV beside the highway, Grassinger's fingers drummed on the steering wheel. If all the principals were already in the house, and the only one they were waiting for now was the assassin's control officer, then didn't it make sense to reactivate the defenses along the driveway? He had a mind to call McGarvey and suggest just that. But the director would be having a busy time of it right now, sorting out the who's whos.

He had wanted to station a couple of Blatnik's people in the house, or at the very least outside nearby, but McGarvey had been very specific on that point.

It was dead cold in the car with the engine off. He glanced at Nikolayev, who was hunched down in his overcoat and appeared to be dozing. Not as cold as Moscow gets. Or Siberia.

"There's a car coming your way," Tony Blatnik radioed.

"Stand by." Grassinger spoke into his lapel mic. He reached over and nudged the Russian, whose eyes opened. "Someone's coming."

Nikolayev sat up and brought the binoculars to his eyes as there was a flash of headlights up on the highway.

Grassinger entered all but the last number of McGarvey's cell phone.

The headlights briefly illuminated the trees as the car slowed and turned down the driveway. It was an RAV4 sport utility vehicle. Grassinger recognized it immediately.

"A woman," Nikolayev said.

Grassinger raised his binoculars to make sure, although he knew who it was. Louise Horn's profile showed up clearly for a moment until her car disappeared into the woods. Of all the suspects down at the house, Otto Rencke, in Grassinger's mind, was the worst-case scenario.

"It's Louise Horn. Otto Rencke's friend," Grassinger said. He didn't know how McGarvey was going to take the news.

He hit the last number of McGarvey's cell phone, then started his car and eased it out of the ditch and up toward the highway.

McGarvey's phone rang once, and then a recorded voice came on. "The number you are trying to reach is busy. If you wish to leave a message please touch star and wait for the tone."

Grassinger broke the connection and tossed the phone aside. "Tony, we have a problem," he said into his lapel mic.

"We're moving now," Blatnik's voice came back. "Who is it?"

"Rencke."

Two Agency SUVs with Blatnik and three of his people made it to the driveway by the time Grassinger and Nikolayev reached the paved surface.

"Tell them to be careful," Nikolayev cautioned. "Rencke could have contingencies."

Grassinger immediately understood what the Russian meant. If it was Rencke, he might suspect that someone was up here. Once Louise Horn was safely down the driveway he might switch the defensive measures back on. There were stop sticks out to one hundred yards from the clearing above the house. Inside that line were contact mines that would explode if a vehicle passed over their pressure pads. Antipersonnel claymore mines were set up in the woods on either side of the road.

"Tony, I want you to pull up before Point Alpha," Grassinger radioed. He hauled the big SUV off the highway and careened down the driveway as fast as he could keep the car on the snow-covered dirt road.

"We're just about there."

"The PDS might be rearmed," Grassinger shouted. It was the Perimeter Defense System.

"Okay, we're stopping," Blatnik radioed back.

Grassinger raced around a long curve and saw the taillights of the two SUVs stopped up ahead. They had run without headlights. He shut his off as he swept down into a hollow and back up the other side to stop right behind them. They weren't far from the house here.

Blatnik and his people were gathered on the road. They had drawn their guns. Grassinger and Nikolayev hurried to join them.

"We'll have to go on foot from here," he told them. "But stay out of the woods. The claymores might be hot."

"They could have the driveway covered from below," Blatnik cautioned. "We'd be sitting ducks as soon as we got out in the open."

"It's a chance we'll have to take," Grassinger replied. "Have your people move in from the back."

Blatnik radioed the orders.

Grassinger and Nikolayev started down the driveway, Blatnik and the others behind them.

"What exactly is it that we're waiting for?" Adkins asked. No one wanted to look at the others. But each of them understood McGarvey's logic in bringing them here like this. At one time or another they had all suggested the same thing; that whoever was gunning for McGarvey had to be someone very close. Like someone in this room.

"For someone to blink," McGarvey answered absently. He thought he'd seen a light up on the hill.

"Is someone coming?" Elizabeth asked.

Headlights emerged from the woods and started down the hill. "Yes," McGarvey said. He went out into the stairhall, shut off the lights and withdrew his pistol.

He watched from the hall window as the car came toward the fountain and paddock, but he couldn't tell what kind of a car it was. Why hadn't Grassinger called?

Elizabeth came from the living room. "Who is it?" she asked.

"I don't know yet. Call Jim and find out what's going on."

The car moved fast, fishtailing as it came around the curve on the west side of the paddock.

"The phone isn't here. Do you have it?" Elizabeth asked.

"Never mind," McGarvey said. He must have put it in the living room.

Then the car came around the sweep of the curve and he could see that it was Louise Horn's bright yellow RAV4 with an American flag on the radio antenna.

Elizabeth was at his side. She recognized the car, too. "Hell," she said softly.

"Keep everyone where they are," McGarvey told her. He locked the closet door and slipped the Walther's safety catch off and stepped outside. He stood in the deeper shadows between the front door and the lights spilling from the living room windows.

He was angry that they had gotten to Otto. Mad at Louise Horn for taking advantage of his vulnerabilities. Otto had never had any sort of a real life. From what McGarvey knew of his background, Otto's childhood had been a living hell—a mother who didn't want him and a drunken stepfather who belittled and beat him, mentally as well as physically.

He was upset with himself that he hadn't seen and recognized the signs in Otto in time to help. McGarvey wanted to lash out at someone, at anyone for what had been done to his friend. Otto *was* his friend; in actuality his only friend, and McGarvey had let him down. There was no clear path out of this dark morass. Not for any of them. There was no solution that would make it all better. There was no going back.

McGarvey wanted to think that he had suspected Otto all along. Because Otto as the assassin could do the CIA the most harm. But even in the last few days when the circle of suspects had diminished to a handful, McGarvey had refused to believe in his heart that it could be his old friend. Anyone but Otto.

The RAV4 slid to a stop behind the line of cars. Not bothering to switch off the engine or the headlights, Louise Horn scrambled out of the car and headed up the driveway in a dead run, her civilian jacket open. As she came up the walk, McGarvey saw that she carried something small and black in her right hand.

"That's far enough, Louise," McGarvey said from the darkness.

Louise reacted as if she had been shot. She stopped dead in her tracks. "The killer is here," she whispered breathlessly. "They used your cell phone, Mr. Director."

"I used my cell phone—"

"I'm not talking about the calls that you made to your security people. Someone called a blind number in Chevy Chase just a few minutes ago. I was waiting on the highway monitoring the calls. Otto gave me the intercept equipment." She held up the special cell phone she carried in her right hand. She talked in a rush, words tumbling on top of each other.

"What was the number?" It was a trick, though he didn't want it to be.

"I don't know, Mr. M., it was blocked from the intercept program, and it was encrypted," Louise said. "Did you call someone in town?"

"No—" McGarvey said, when all the lights in the house went out.

Grassinger and the others ran as fast as they could, finally reaching the spot where the driveway emerged from the woods. He stopped and raised his binoculars in time to see McGarvey and Louise Horn facing each other on the porch when the lights in the house went out.

"Rencke's spotted her and shut off the lights," he said.

Nikolayev stepped off to the side and held on to a tree for support, while he massaged his chest with his other hand. Even in the darkness they could see that he was in trouble.

"Go," he croaked. "No time. Go."

Grassinger looked again at the porch. McGarvey and Louise Horn were gone. The front door was open.

He and the others headed down the driveway at a dead run, leaving the Russian to look after himself. If McGarvey had allowed them to station a couple of their people near the house, they wouldn't be in this situation right now. When they wrote the after ops reports, Grassinger would make sure that that part got included.

McGarvey stood in the darkness of the stairhall listening with all of his senses for something; anything. Louise Horn stood behind him and to his right. The house was deathly still except for the crackling of the fire on the hearth.

"Liz?" he called softly.

"Here." Her voice drifted out from the living room. The flickering light from the fireplace cast shadows on the ceilings and walls.

"Where's Otto?"

"He's here," Elizabeth said.

"Who's missing?"

"No one."

That made no sense. Unless someone had gotten through Blatnik's people in back, no one was here to cut the power. It could have been done from the highway, but Grassinger and his people were on the lookout up there. They would have spotted something.

"Someone is coming down the driveway," Louise said softly. "Four . . . no, five of them on foot. Running."

McGarvey heard the noise. Soft, like a small animal mewling in pain.

It came from the darkness at the end of the corridor that led back to the kitchen. "Somebody find a flashlight," he said. He transferred his pistol to his left hand and moved past the entry to the living room. Liz and Todd and the others were silhouetted by the flames in the fireplace. The whimpering was louder now. It wasn't coming from the kitchen. It was coming from the basement door under the stairs. Someone or something was just on the other side; perhaps crouched at the head of the stairs; frightened, in pain. The main breaker panel, where the electricity could have been turned off, was downstairs. But everyone was still in the living room, Louise had just arrived and no one could have come from the back. They wouldn't have gotten past Blatnik's people let alone defeat the sensors strung along the property line.

Just as he knew in his heart that the assassin was not Otto, he finally accepted who it was. Accepted the fact that he had known, or at least felt at some visceral level, who it was. Baranov's creation. The brainwashing had occurred over fifteen years ago. So long a time ago that it seemed to be in a completely different era; a time when we were naive as compared to now; a time in which the battles were simple: It was us or them. Each side had its generals, and each side had its handmaidens.

The crying increased in intensity to a low growl; an animal warning its prey that it was on the verge of striking.

McGarvey knew exactly when and where the psychological conditioning had taken place. He knew why. And he knew the assassin's control officer. The call had been made to him on the cell phone in the stairhall. All the other phones in the house had been switched off.

An intense, deep sickness spread through his body. All of his life he had been afraid to trust anyone for fear of what their betrayal would do to him. He had blocked almost everyone he'd ever come in contact with from knowing who he really was. In time he'd even forgotten how to trust himself so that like everyone else he didn't know who he was. A part of him held itself aloof from his own inner thoughts and feelings. He had been living two separate existences. One in which he functioned on a day-to-day level; with friends and acquaintances, with lovers and family. And another in which he existed like a bear holed up in its den for the winter. Run. Run. Run. Hide. Don't let anyone get too close.

Despite all of that, people admired him. Respected him. Trusted his judgment. Trusted him to take care of them. They even loved him, some of them. Or at least they loved as much of him as they were allowed to access.

He couldn't say why he was that way; perhaps it was because his parents were too old to have children when they did. His sister in Utah was cold and aloof. There'd been love in the family, growing up, but no closeness. He knew that his father loved him, but his father never once told him so. And neither had his mother. It had left an empty spot in his soul, one that for most people was filled with the emotion of belonging.

That's what he had missed all of his life. A feeling that people could love him for *who* he was, not for *what* he was.

McGarvey flattened himself against the wall next to the basement door and reached over with his free hand to turn the knob. The flickering reflection of the firelight was surreal.

The growling stopped.

McGarvey closed his eyes for a moment, trying to blot out the horror of this, then pulled the door open and stepped back.

Kathleen, her narrow, pretty face screwed up in a mask of rage and hate and venom, her lips curled back from her teeth in a feral snarl, her eyes wide and insane burst through the doorway. She raised a big Glock 17 nine millimeter pistol and fired four shots as fast as she could pull the trigger, straight ahead into the wall, blasting big chunks of plaster everywhere.

"Mother!" Elizabeth screamed from the living room entry.

Kathleen swiveled toward Elizabeth's voice, bringing the pistol around in a tight arc, the muzzle ending up a few feet from her husband's face.

"Hello, Katy," McGarvey said. His gun hand was at his side, the pistol pointed toward the floor.

Kathleen started to shake the way she had at the house when she'd gone into convulsions. She tried to speak, but it came out as a low-throated growl. She was obviously going through an internal struggle that threatened to blow her into a million jagged pieces.

McGarvey could sense that there were people behind him, but he didn't take his eyes off Kathleen's. He raised his free hand to her. "Give me your gun, sweetheart. Please."

Kathleen flinched. She took a half step forward, the pistol never wavering from the middle of her husband's face.

"No one's going to hurt you, Katy," McGarvey said gently. "We're all here. All of your friends. Liz and Todd, too. We've come to help you, darling."

He tried to smile, but he could see Darby Yarnell using her. Baranov arranging for her training; holding her hand, telling her that she should go back to her husband, that she didn't belong with them. All the while they were battering down her defenses; tearing apart the very attributes that made her human, that made her who she was.

Once again he wanted to lash out at them. But they were both dead. And that they had died at his hands, even though the events had occurred more than a decade ago, gave him just the tiniest amount of satisfaction at this moment. They had gotten to his wife and damaged her, for no other reason than some insane plot to arrange for the murder of someone at some distant time and place. Now they were dead.

Kathleen had been programmed to kill her husband if and when he was ever put up for Director of Central Intelligence. All these years her control officer had been Father Vietski; every week he had reinforced her training; built upon the artificial hate and fear and blind passion that they had mercilessly conditioned into her. He'd done it for nothing more than money.

It must have been difficult, McGarvey thought, because by nature she was not a violent woman. Anything but. Stenzel would say that she fell apart mentally because she had an impossible time dealing with the contradictions that were tearing apart her soul. On the one hand she was programmed to assassinate her husband. And on the other, she loved her husband, and killing him was unthinkable. It's why she had sabotaged Otto's car, to force her husband into stepping down from the appointment. She'd also talked Otto into wearing his seat belt so that he wouldn't be seriously injured.

She couldn't have sabotaged Liz's skis. McGarvey was pretty sure that they would find out it was Father Vietski on one of his trips to the house. Vietski had supplied the Semtex and the fuses. The fact that her daughter had been so terribly hurt that she had lost the baby had sent Kathleen into an even deeper spiral toward insanity. It was exactly what Vietski wanted because it made her more pliable.

He'd also supplied the Semtex and extra beach bag for the helicopter. The bomb was supposed to kill them. End it once and for all. But Kathleen had subconsciously worked it out so that she could warn them away at the last minute.

All of the misdirections, even the symptoms of her illness

were an effort by her subconscious to remove the reason for her programming. If her husband stepped down she would not have to kill him.

It had come down to that simple choice in her mind.

But McGarvey loved her as much as she loved him. He would give her another choice.

"You don't have to kill me, Katy," he said.

She flinched again. Her gun hand shook. At this distance it would be impossible for her to miss if she pulled the trigger. "Yes," she said, the single word strangled in her throat.

"No, Kathleen," McGarvey said. He raised his pistol to his temple. "I won't let you do this. You don't have to kill me. I'll do it."

"No!" Elizabeth screamed in anguish.

Kathleen's eyes were wild. A tic developed in her right cheek. Spittle drooled from a corner of her mouth. She had been given a new, terrible choice. She didn't know what to do. She was overloading.

McGarvey cocked the pistol. "It's okay, Katy," he said. He began to pull the trigger.

"Kirk!" Kathleen screamed. "My God, what have I done?" She lowered her hand and let the big gun drop to the carpet runner. "No," she said softly. "No."

She stepped foward, tentatively, and then as McGarvey uncocked his pistol and lowered it, she came into his arms and began to cry.

"Hello, Katy," McGarvey said. "Welcome home."

EPILOGUE
AFTERMATH

Tell me not here, it needs not saying,
What tune the enchantress plays
In aftermaths of soft September
Or under blanching Mays,
For she and I were long acquainted
And I knew all her ways.
—Alfred Edward Housman

Surely goodness and mercy shall follow me all the
days of my life: and I will dwell in the house of the
LORD for ever.
—23rd Psalm

BE CAREFUL WHAT YOU WISH FOR,
YOU MIGHT GET IT.

WASHINGTON

The cherry blossoms along West Basin Drive were in time for Easter. Kathleen watched from the backseat as the DCI's limousine swept grandly toward the Ellipse and the White House beyond. She smiled with pleasure, her eyes clear, no longer troubled. It was as if she had finally awakened from a very long nightmare. The bright morning perfectly matched her light mood.

"I've never seen them so pretty," she said to her husband, seated beside her. He squeezed her hand, and she looked out the window again. "Kinda makes you feel like a Roman general off to his reward from Caesar after the war, doesn't it?"

"Sorta," McGarvey told her.

All of them had awakened from a long nightmare. The past three months had been all the more difficult because they had to pick up a lot of pieces; tie up a lot of loose ends; heal a lot of wounds. And for him personally, he'd had to deal with the apologies for suspecting his friends and treating them the way he had. They understood. Or at least they said that they understood. But he'd seen the odd glance from Dick Adkins, felt the momentary distances from Otto, and even saw the occasional hesitation in his own son-in-law's eyes.

Kathleen's initial recovery had come quickly once she was free from the weekly reinforcement by her control officer. She didn't remember a lot of what happened, though she had dreams that when she awoke she could not remember.

An Internal Affairs investigation codirected by Whittaker and Stenzel with representation from the FBI and Secret Service Office of White House Security, cleared Kathleen of any responsibility for the deaths of the helicopter pilot in the USVI, and of Dick Yemm and the four security officers in front of the house.

It had been she, of course. But the investigators concluded that her mind and therefore her actions had been controlled by outside forces. The deaths were listed as: by person or persons unknown. Unoffically it was given to understand that the murders were directed and carried out by the Russian mafia for as yet unknown reasons.

But the real healing would be a long time in coming, McGarvey thought. It was one of the reasons he'd decided to stay on at the CIA—to make everything right, so far as that was possible. And, because Kathleen would not let him simply walk away from a job that was, in her words, "tailor-made" for him.

He would give the Agency three more years, then he would pull the pin for good. It was a time period both he and Katy could live with, and it corresponded with what remained of the President's term of office.

Adkins had agreed to stay on as McGarvey's deputy director, as did the others on his staff: David Whittaker, Jared Kraus, Tommy Doyle and Otto.

Especially Otto. McGarvey did not want to lose his old friend, who had gone through his own terrors of the damned over the past few months. The eighth name on Otto's list; the one that he had trouble admitting even to himself, was Kathleen's. Otto had put it together before anyone else had: the business with Baranov and Darby Yarnell; even the possibility that Janis Vietski was her control officer. That night he'd stationed Louise Horn on the road with a telephone intercept device to listen for a call to Vietski. If the priest couldn't come to the house, then he and Kathleen would talk on the phone.

Which is exactly what happened. And which was why Otto had placed his own name on the list so that when the trap was sprung he and Louise would be there to give whatever help they could give.

They passed the John Paul Jones Memorial and headed north on Seventeenth, the Washington Monument rose grandly on their right.

McGarvey did feel like a Roman general, he supposed, heading to the palace for his reward. He just wasn't so sure that swearing him in as DCI was such a reward after all.

Be careful what you wish for, you might get it.

Kathleen turned. She straightened his tie and brushed a loose strand of hair from his forehead. "Otto and Louise are riding over with Todd and Elizabeth." She smiled. "I'm proud of you, Kirk. We all are."

"It'll be a busy three years, but I'll keep a lid on it, I promise you, Katy. Not too much traveling. I can promise you at least that much. I might work late, but I'll stay in town most of the time."

She laughed out loud. The sound was musical. "Tell me another story, sailor."

Grassinger was driving. He'd taken over Dick Yemm's position. He glanced in the rearview mirror and grinned. He had pitched his bitch in the post ops debriefings, but the director had not shot him down. He had agreed with his security people. And that made McGarvey not only the boss, in Grassinger's mind, but a sharp operator to boot.

"I won't bullshit the troops," McGarvey told his people. "Nor do I expect you to bullshit me. I want to hear it like it is. Do you read me?"

Loud and clear, Grassinger thought. Loud and clear. It was getting to be a real pleasure getting up and going to work in the mornings. That was something new.

"It won't be like before," McGarvey told his wife. He was apologizing too much, but his family had paid a horrible price for what he was. Over the past months Katy would stop in the middle of something and look up at him, a sudden terror in her eyes. She had been brainwashed into killing her husband. She didn't want to do it, of course. Such an act ran counter to everything she stood for. At the very end McGarvey had come to that understanding, so he had given her another choice. An impossible choice, actually. She did not have to kill him because he was going to commit suicide. But she could not let him destroy himself. That was *not* a part of her brainwashing. She no longer had to carry out her prime instruction, and therefore she was able to act on her own to save her husband's life.

Kathleen smiled patiently, as if she had waited for him to work all that out in his head. "Don't you know, darling, that nothing stays the same." She shook her head. "We can never go back, thank goodness, even if we wanted to."

Constitution Avenue was busy this morning. Life was back to normal in the capital city. The terrorism here and in New York City last year, and the terrorism within the CIA over the winter, was behind them. McGarvey had done some thinking about the next three years, but he had given even more thought to what would come after.

Kathleen, Liz and Todd and the children they planned to adopt, and finally the book about Voltaire that he'd been working on for ten years. Maybe he'd even smoke a pipe and wear tweed jackets with elbow patches.

Nikolayev was dead. They'd found his body slumped next to a tree beside the driveway above the safe house that night. He'd had a long-term heart condition. All the excitement and the physical exertion had finally killed him.

Father Vietski disappeared that night from Good Shepherd and no one had heard from him since. Otto's best guess was that the Russian mafia, which had apparently been contracted by the Kremlin to clean up the mess that Baranov left, had killed him and buried his body somewhere. They had killed Zhuralev in Moscow and Trofimov in Paris. They were thorough. Vietski's body would probably never be found.

As the President had promised, Senators Hammond and Madden had come around, finally seeing the merits of hiring an intelligence professional to run the CIA. Bob Johnson had cooperated with Internal Affairs, admitting that he had supplied information to Senator Hammond's staff almost from the day that he had started working for the Company. What wasn't clear was why; except that both Hammond and Johnson were from Minnesota.

Johnson was allowed to resign with the understanding that he would never work in any sensitive government job. Ironically, even Senator Hammond refused to hire him.

"A penny," Kathleen said. "You were a million miles away just then."

McGarvey came back. "Roland and Peggy had their boat moved to the Bahamas. They want us to take a week off and go sailing with them. What do you think, Kathleen?"

They came to the west entrance to the White House grounds on New York Avenue. Grassinger pulled up at the guard house.

"Katy," she corrected. She nodded. "I'll be happy to go anywhere, as long as it's with you."